Praise for Debbie Mason

"I'm hoping *Summer on Sunshine* the Rosetti women...I'm nowhere near ready to say farewell to this family!" —TheRomanceDish.com

"I've never met a Debbie Mason story that I didn't enjoy." —KeeperBookshelf.com

"I'm telling you right now, if you haven't yet read a book by Debbie Mason, you don't know what you're missing." —RomancingtheReaders.blogspot.com

"Mason always makes me smile and touches my heart in the most unexpected and wonderful ways." —HerdingCats-BurningSoup.com

"Wow, do these books bring the feels. Deep emotion, heart-tugging romance, and a touch of suspense make them hard to put down." —TheRomanceDish.com

"I always count the days until the next book!" —TheManyFacesofRomance.blogspot.com

"Debbie Mason writes in a thrilling and entertaining way. Her stories are captivating and filled with controlled chaos, true love, mysteries, amazing characters, eccentricities, plotting and friendship." —WithLoveForBooks.com

Three Little Wishes

Three Little Wishes

DEBBIE MASON

FOREVER

New York Boston

Forever
Hachette Book Group
1290 Avenue of the Americas, New York, NY 10104
read-forever.com
@readforeverpub

First Edition: May 2024

Forever is an imprint of Grand Central Publishing. The Forever name and logo are registered trademarks of Hachette Book Group, Inc.

The publisher is not responsible for websites (or their content)
that are not owned by the publisher.

The Hachette Speakers Bureau provides a wide range of authors for speaking events. To find out more, go to hachettespeakersbureau.com or email HachetteSpeakers@hbgusa.com.

Forever books may be purchased in bulk for business, educational, or promotional use. For information, please contact your local bookseller or the Hachette Book Group Special Markets Department at special.markets@hbgusa.com.

Library of Congress Cataloging-in-Publication Data

Names: Mason, Debbie (Novelist) author.
Title: Three little wishes / Debbie Mason.
Other titles: 3 little wishes
Description: First edition. | New York : Forever, 2024. | Series: Sunshine Bay ; 2
Identifiers: LCCN 2023054972 | ISBN 9781538725337 (trade paperback) |
    ISBN 9781538725351 (e-book)
Subjects: LCSH: Meteorologists—Fiction. | Aunts—Fiction. | Actresses—Fiction. |
    Family secrets—Fiction. | Television stations—Fiction. | LCGFT: Novels.
Classification: LCC PR9199.4.M3696 T47 2024 | DDC 813/.6—dc23/eng/20231204
LC record available at https://lccn.loc.gov/2023054972

ISBNs: 978-1-5387-2533-7 (trade paperback), 978-1-5387-2535-1 (ebook)

Printed in the United States of America

LSC-C

Printing 1, 2024

For our adorable grandson, August Wilder.
You're our wish come true.

Chapter One

"What was it you said last night on the evening news, *Lucy*? A thirty percent chance of light rain, was it?" Amos, the seventysomething fisherman in the yellow raincoat and hat shouted at Willow as she battled the gale-force winds and lashing rain on her way back to the TV station, goading her as he always did whenever her weather forecast was the least bit off.

He'd no doubt been standing in the window of Brew Bros hoping to catch a glimpse of her. The coffee shop was half a block from the station. She cupped one claw-covered hand to the side of her mouth while clamping her other claw-covered hand on the head of her lobster costume to keep the wind from ripping it off.

"The rain *is* light, Amos!" At least it had been when it started twenty minutes before. "It's just that the winds are a little stronger than the satellite images indicated. Blame it on climate change," she yelled, forcing a wide smile so he wouldn't think she was shouting at him because he'd embarrassed her.

She was a Rosetti. She didn't embarrass easily.

But besides Amos and the over-seventy crowd, no one in

her seaside hometown took her forecasts seriously. How could they when she delivered the weather in costume? Which was one of the reasons she hadn't complained—much—a few months earlier when her boss at Channel 5 had informed her she'd be reporting the weather as Lucy the Lobster. The Lobster Pot on Main Street must be raking it in if it could afford to advertise on Channel 5 from May through September.

She looked down at the costume clinging to her like a second skin. It was an improvement over the itsy-bitsy yellow polka-dot bikini that Don, her boss, had made her wear the previous summer.

"A little rain? It'll take me at least three hours to bail out my boat. If I hadn't listened to you, I would've put the cover on!" Amos yelled, throwing up his arms and nearly upending his to-go cup of coffee.

The violent flapping of the awning above Brew Bros' front window drowned out Willow's sigh. Amos had a point, and she felt a smidgen of guilt for missing the band of storms currently in a holding pattern over Sunshine Bay. She'd had a lot on her mind the night before so it was possible her calculations had been off and this wasn't a fluke weather event.

"Tomorrow's going to be a gorgeous, sunshiny seventy-three degrees, and I'll come give you a hand after I wrap up the morning weather report. We'll have your boat mopped up in no time." Her heartfelt offer earned her a derisive lip curl. Honestly, there was no pleasing the man.

"You know, Amos, not all storms come to disrupt your life. Some come to clear your path," she said, quoting Paulo Coelho while walking backward into the wind on the sidewalk. "Maybe the universe is trying to tell you something."

Like that it was time for him to sell his boat. Last month, a search party had gone out at two in the morning looking for him. He'd fallen asleep on board his boat and was headed for Canada.

"Stop spouting claptrap and watch where you're..." He trailed off, his eyes going wide.

She was about to glance over her shoulder to see what had caught his attention when her back slammed into the pole holding up the Bookworm's awning, the action emptying a gallon of water onto her head.

Sputtering, she jumped out of the way to avoid another bucketful, only to get hit by a surf-size wave when a black Mercedes sped through a puddle on the road. Muddy water dripping off her face and her costume, she roundly cursed the entitled jerk as he whizzed by. Of course it was a man, and a tourist. Those definitely weren't cape plates.

As she wiped her face with her forearm while the driver continued blithely along Main Street, all smug and warm and dry, a gust of wind pushed her around as if she were a blow-up punching bag.

Willow wondered what else life had in store for her. The wind picking her up and hurling her onto the roof of a car? The poles holding up the awning coming loose and stabbing her in the heart?

All right, so she was being dramatic. But in her defense, if she had any luck at all these days, it was bad luck. Case in point, two weeks earlier, her landlord had informed her his son was moving back to town and Willow had a month to find somewhere else to live. Right, because finding a place to rent mid-July in a beach town was so easy. Don't even get her started on affordability.

Everything in and around Sunshine Bay was rented until

at least September. Everything except her aunt Eva's place, which was located within spitting distance of her mother's and grandmother's apartments. It was also within spitting distance of La Dolce Vita, her family's restaurant, where Willow was currently waitressing part-time in order to cover her monthly expenses. She was as close to broke as she'd ever been, and that wasn't going to change if the rumor at work was true.

After the death of the founding family's matriarch and company CEO fifteen months earlier, Bennett Broadcasting Group had begun divesting its assets, of which Channel 5 was one. Except that according to gossip, Bennett Broadcasting wasn't selling the TV station in Sunshine Bay, they were closing it.

Willow stomped along the sidewalk, cursing Bennett Broadcasting Group's acting CEO, Noah Elliot, entitled tourists with no respect for pedestrians, and the gale-force winds and teeming rain.

"You've got the face of an angel and the mouth of a fisherman, Lucy!" Amos shouted after her with what sounded like an admiring chuckle.

She waved goodbye as the wind buffeted her from one side of the sidewalk to the other. Amos was right. She had been spouting a pile of crap. Storms weren't a good thing. They didn't clear a path. They wreaked havoc wherever they went, and she had a feeling a storm of epic proportions was coming her way if actress Camilla Monroe, her estranged aunt, agreed to appear on *Good Morning, Sunshine!* They needed star power to launch the inaugural episode of their new and improved morning show, and people would definitely tune in to see her aunt.

The objective was to convince Bennett's acting CEO that they had a viable business plan to increase Channel 5's viewership exponentially as well as its advertising dollars, and Willow's idea for *Good Morning, Sunshine!* was how they'd do it. Surely then Noah Elliot would see the value of selling the station instead of closing it.

But Willow was getting ahead of herself. Her aunt might not even agree to appear on the morning show. After all, she hadn't spoken to Camilla directly. Her aunt's agent had finally gotten back to her with a number, and she'd spoken to Camilla's assistant earlier that morning, explaining that she had something urgent to discuss with her aunt.

If Willow thought her life had sucked these past few weeks, it was nothing compared to how badly it would suck when her family found out she was inviting Camilla to Sunshine Bay. In Willow's twenty-eight trips around the sun, it was the most disloyal thing she'd ever done. She was selling out her family for a chance at making her dreams come true.

But it wasn't just about her and her dreams. It was about everyone she worked with at Channel 5. They were her family too, and they needed the inaugural episode of *Good Morning, Sunshine!* to wow Noah Elliot when he met with Don in two weeks' time.

Willow's aunt wasn't exactly an A-list celebrity but she'd had the dubious honor of spending the better part of the year on the front pages of the tabloids. She was also a hometown girl, even if she hadn't set foot in Sunshine Bay for the past two decades, which would make her appearance on the morning show even more of a draw.

Willow's boss had agreed. It was just a happy coincidence that hosting a show like *Good Morning, Sunshine!* was

Willow's dream job and Don had promised her a seat at the table. *If* they could change Noah Elliot's mind about closing the station. They had to change his mind.

She waited for her internal defense of why she'd had no choice but to call her aunt to relieve the guilt she felt at betraying her family. Instead, the mistress of guilt, her grandmother, Carmen Rosetti, popped into her head, listing everything the family had ever done for Willow while demanding to know what they'd done to deserve her betrayal.

Willow sighed. No one did guilt like an Italian grandma, even if she was only in Willow's imagination.

But all thoughts about the eventual showdown with her family vanished the moment she spotted a familiar black Mercedes idling in the parking lot next to the station.

Her antennae bobbing in front of her face, Willow ran into the lot, unable to avoid a pond-size puddle. Water seeped into her clawed feet, and she looked longingly at the station. Right about now, she'd kill for dry clothes, a cup of hot coffee, and the doughnut her friend and camerawoman had promised her. *Ha!* It was going to take a lot more than a coffee and a doughnut for her to forgive Naomi for making her walk back to the station.

Willow marched to the Mercedes, ignoring the thought that her anger at the inconsiderate driver might be a tad over the top. The occupants of the luxury vehicle needed to know the speed limit on Main Street was not fifty miles per hour before they once again ventured onto the roads, putting innocent pedestrians' lives at risk.

The town council had lowered the speed limit on Main Street to twenty-five miles an hour in early June. Motorists going over the new limit wouldn't start being ticketed until the end of summer. Something that Willow had no intention of sharing with this particular speed demon.

She spied the Mercedes's license plate and rolled her eyes. A New Yorker, figured. She couldn't make out much more than a shadowy torso through the fogged-up windows but she heard a deep, muffled voice that seemed to confirm her initial impression that the driver was a man. Since she couldn't make out another occupant, she assumed he was on the phone.

She rapped lightly on the fogged glass. The shadow moved, and her gaze narrowed. Did he just turn his back on her? If he thought she'd let his dangerous driving go unchecked, he had another thing coming. He was a menace on the road. He had to be stopped, or at the very least schooled on proper driving etiquette. She also expected an apology—a genuine, heartfelt apology. Some groveling wouldn't be out of place.

As she lifted her hand to knock on the window again, a gust of wind shoved her into the car, causing her lobster claw to slam onto the glass. The shadow jerked away as though she'd terrified him. Then, just as quickly, he went back to carrying on his conversation on the phone as if she weren't there. Of all the nerve.

"I can see you in there, and I'm not going anywhere so you might as well lower the window."

It went down a few inches. Dark, long-lashed eyes under inky brows stared at her. "Yes?" he drawled, his voice smooth and deep. It was the kind of drawl that insinuated she was wasting his precious time.

Well, too bad for him. "Are you aware that you were going fifty in a twenty-five?"

"I'm sorry, are you a crosswalk monitor? Traffic control?"

"Do I look like a crosswalk monitor or traffic control?" She gave her head a disbelieving shake at his condescending tone, the water flying off her antennae unintentionally hitting him in the eyes. She pressed her lips together. It took a moment before she was able to say, without a gurgle of laughter in her voice, "Sorry. I have no control over my antennae."

He raised an arrogant eyebrow, holding her gaze as he brought a starched white handkerchief to his face. Wiping the water droplets away, he ignored her apology, responding instead to the question she'd asked in a tone as superior as the look in his eyes.

"No. You don't look like a crosswalk monitor or traffic control, which is why I asked. Because unless you are, I have no idea why it's any concern of yours. But I assure you, I wasn't driving over the fifty-mile-an-hour speed limit." His voice was as dry as the desert.

"Ha!" She pointed her lobster claw at him, and he jerked back. "The speed limit is twenty-five miles an hour."

"No, it's—" His window went up.

"Seriously?" She rapped on the glass.

He held up a finger while typing on his phone.

She had no idea who this guy thought he was and raised her hand to knock on the window again, only he suddenly lowered it and her lobster claw clunked him on the forehead instead of the glass.

She winced. "I'm sorry. I didn't mean to smack you."

Rubbing his now-damp forehead with his handkerchief, he drawled, "You'll forgive me if I don't believe you."

He was as bad as Amos. Her apology had been heartfelt.

"No. But if you apologize for nearly drowning me when you drove through the puddle like you were an extra in *Fast & Furious*, I'll *consider* forgiving you."

She wasn't sure, but she thought there might be a hint of amusement lurking behind his dark eyes. Then he angled his head and, in his smooth, superior voice, said, "I didn't think it was possible to drown a lobster."

Huh. She hadn't expected him to have a sense of humor. Unwilling to give him the satisfaction of seeing her smile or hearing her laugh, she once again cleared the amusement from her voice. "Don't give up your day job."

"What makes you think I'm not a stand-up comedian?"

"You're not funny."

"Or perhaps you don't have a sense of humor." He reached for his ringing phone. "Except the fact you don't mind walking around in public dressed as a giant lobster suggests that you do. Now, if you don't mind, I need to take this call." The window began going up as he greeted the person on the other end.

"I most certainly do mind," she said, sticking her lobster claw through the window to keep it from closing. She winced. She'd unintentionally punched him again, this time in his ear.

"Sorry. I didn't mean to do that. But you owe me an apology, and I'm not leaving until I get one."

His shoulders—which she couldn't help but notice filled out his navy suit jacket very nicely—rose, and he blew out what could only be described as a thoroughly ticked-off breath.

"I'll be with you in a moment," he said to whoever was on

the other end, and then he looked at her and, in that patronizing tone that made her grit her teeth, said, "I'm sorry that my car sprayed you while you were standing too close to the curb in a torrential downpour."

She stared at him. "You can't seriously be putting the blame on me."

He lifted a broad shoulder. "If the claw fits."

"You aren't funny."

"I believe we've already established that." He lifted his hand, shooing her away as if she were the hired help. "Now, if you don't mind, I have to take this call." He didn't give her a chance to respond, pressing the window's lever instead.

"Wait! My claw's caught." She ripped her hand from inside the costume before it got squashed between the glass and the frame, staring at the claw dangling from the now-closed window. Even if she hadn't seen the corners of his lips curve, it was obvious he was inwardly laughing. He couldn't hide the amusement in his eyes when he looked from the claw to her.

She tugged it free and slapped the glass, cursing Mercedes Man all the way to Channel 5.

When she opened the front door and stomped through the station's lobby, Naomi, her six-foot-tall, stunning Black camerawoman, who'd recently shaved her head, was talking to her girlfriend, Veronica, at the reception desk. Petite with curly black hair and an effervescent personality, Veronica was the yin to Naomi's yang.

Naomi turned, grimacing as she took in the state of Willow's costume. "I'm sorry. If you hadn't rolled around on the wharf, I would've driven you back to the station. But my truck's new, and I'd never get the smell of dead fish out of it."

Retrieving a mug and a chocolate doughnut with pink

sprinkles from Veronica's desk, Naomi held them out as if they were a peace offering.

Willow considered refusing the doughnut and coffee to make a point that her forgiveness couldn't be bought, but who was she kidding? She could totally be bought. Besides needing a hot cup of coffee and a sugar infusion the way she needed her next breath, she could never hold a grudge, no matter how hard she tried.

She freed her hands from the claws and accepted the mug and doughnut from Naomi, taking several sips of coffee before biting into the doughnut. She hummed her appreciation and thanks as she savored the sweet, chocolatey goodness.

"You're forgiven," Willow said, wiping her mouth and then setting the half-eaten doughnut on Veronica's desk. "But if I smell like dead fish"—she totally did—"it's your fault. Yours and Don's." They were the ones who'd insisted that she do the broadcast live on the pier in gale-force winds.

According to Naomi and their boss, ratings were highest when Willow reported out and about in Sunshine Bay. "You're just lucky the wind knocked me down on the wharf and didn't send me flying off the pier. Otherwise, you would've had to call water rescue." She didn't add *again*.

As if on cue, footage from that morning's weather broadcast at the pier appeared on every screen in the station, including the one hanging on the whitewashed brick wall behind Veronica. And there was Lucy the Lobster (aka Willow) lying stretched out on the wharf, hanging on to a lamppost for dear life. Guffaws of laughter filled the station when she began shouting her weather report while her body twisted in the wind. Needless to say, bleeps were interspersed throughout the broadcast.

"I'd like to see you guys walk in my claws for a day," she shouted to be heard above the laughter, groaning when footage of a seal chasing her across the rocks at Hidden Cove began playing on the screens. "You made a blooper reel of me?"

"Don't blame me," Naomi said, pointing at the other camera operators, who were roaring with laughter as the bow of the boat Willow was standing on hit a wave and tossed her into the ocean.

She might not find her blooper reel as funny as some of her coworkers but she knew they weren't laughing at her... All right, so they were totally laughing at her, but not in a mean way. Every single person here would have her back, and she'd have theirs. Except maybe Don. She moved to the left and saw him leaning against the door of his glass-enclosed office, looking at the screen nearest him. He glanced at her and raised his coffee mug, shaking his head with a grin.

She smiled, raising her mug in turn. Their working relationship had improved once she'd realized he made the decisions he did not because he had an ax to grind with her or because he wanted to exploit her. He'd been trying to save the station. She just hadn't known it needed saving until a few weeks ago.

A sniff drew her attention to a teary-eyed Veronica, plucking tissues from the box on her desk.

Willow groaned. "Please tell me those are tears of laughter."

"How can anyone laugh at a time like this, Will? I don't know what I'm going to do without you guys, without this job," Veronica said, her voice clogged with tears.

"Oh, come on. You're acting like we don't have a chance of

changing Noah Elliot's mind." Willow glanced at Naomi and lowered her voice. "No calls?"

She'd only shared their celebrity guest's identity with her boss, Naomi, and Veronica. As much as she loved the rest of her colleagues, she didn't trust them to keep their guest star's identity a secret until she had time to break the news to her family.

Naomi glumly shook her head, reaching into the pocket of her jacket. She handed Willow her phone, and Willow entered her passcode. No calls, no texts, and no emails from her aunt. "It's still early. Her assistant said she'd call before the end of the day."

"But that's just it." Veronica blew her nose. "Noah Elliot moved up his meeting with Don. It's today."

Willow's heart jumped into her throat. *"Today* today?"

Veronica nodded, offering the box of tissues to several of their colleagues who'd congregated around the reception desk, noses red and eyes watery.

If Willow didn't turn this around, everyone in the station would be crying, including her. They might as well give up then. Tears wouldn't save the station, and they really, really needed to save the station, she thought, looking at the familiar faces of the friends she'd worked with since she'd begun volunteering at Channel 5 as a teenager. They needed a pep talk.

Willow put down her coffee mug, cleared a claw-size space on Veronica's desk, and then climbed on top of it. She ignored Don, who was on the phone, motioning for her to get off the desk.

She stuck two fingers in her mouth, whistling for everyone's attention. "Come on, people. This is a hiccup. We've got this. We'll pitch the idea to Elliot as if our guest celebrity has already confirmed. We know she will, right?" Willow put a hand behind her ear. "Right?" She got a few lackluster responses and said it again, louder this time.

She smiled encouragingly when several of the guys yelled, "Right!"

"That's more like it!" She pumped her fist and then continued. "I got Don on board with my presentation for *Good Morning, Sunshine!* And if I can convince Don, I sure as heck can convince Noah Elliot. Right?" She got several subdued "Right"s.

"Oh, come on. I'm wounded," she said to the downcast faces gathered around her. She lifted her gaze to the guys standing around the cameras on the set. "When have any of you known a man who can resist a Rosetti when she has her mind set on something?"

"Never!" the cameramen shouted while several of her female colleagues snickered.

"You know it. I've got this," she said in a singsong voice, adding a little shimmy-shake. "All I have to do is get my hook into Noah Elliot and reel him in." She cast an imaginary fishing line and reeled it in, earning herself some laughter and, even better, smiling faces. She could do this. *They* could do this.

Veronica tapped her claw-foot, and Willow looked down. Widening her eyes, Veronica lifted her chin at something behind Willow.

She turned to see a man standing in the lobby. She'd know those inky, arrogant eyebrows and sardonic dark eyes anywhere. It was Mercedes Man. He was way taller and way broader than he'd looked sitting behind the wheel, and even more intimidating.

She fisted her hands on her hips. "What are you doing here? Did you follow me?"

Before he could answer, Don hurried past the desk, throwing her an exasperated look while extending his hand to Mercedes Man. "Mr. Elliot, welcome to Channel 5!"

Chapter Two

Camilla Monroe read the last line of dialogue and lowered the script onto her lap. She glanced at Hugh, the director, from under her fake lashes, trying to gauge his reaction to her audition.

Although she wouldn't exactly call it an audition, more of a formality than anything. Hugh knew her work. He'd directed her in the movie for which she'd received her first and only Oscar nomination, for Best Supporting Actress. She also considered him a friend. They'd known each other for fifteen years.

His auburn head was bent, nodding at something his pink-haired, twentysomething assistant was showing him on her phone. The young woman had annoyed Camilla from the moment she'd ushered her into the room. She was direct to the point of rudeness, barely looking up from her iPad. No respect, no warmth whatsoever. Camilla didn't know what was wrong with these Gen Zers. She much preferred Brenda, Hugh's previous PA. She'd loved Camilla.

This woman clearly did not, and it was just as clear to Camilla from the PA's sidelong glances while she whispered in Hugh's ear that she was critiquing her reading. Camilla had to get ahead of this. She needed this role too badly to let this...this pink-haired teenager sway Hugh.

Camilla's career was in desperate need of a reboot. Her image could use one too.

She looked at the script, praying that wasn't the reason for Pinky's whispers. People in the industry didn't read tabloids anymore, did they? Besides, even if Hugh's assistant did, what was the old adage? No publicity is bad publicity, right?

She briefly closed her eyes before pasting on a wide, confident smile. "I love everything Liane Morrison writes, and I can't tell you how much it means to me that you considered me for the role, Hugh," she gushed. *Too much?* she wondered.

She meant it, though. She'd read and loved every single one of Liane Morrison's novels, and the movie adaptations to date had been fabulous. Camilla had known from the moment she'd read the script that this one would be the same. The perfect vehicle to relaunch her career. It had *award winner* stamped all over it.

Hugh lifted his head and smiled. He was a lovely man with fabulous hair, a handsome face, and warm eyes. He reminded her a little of Sam Heughan, the actor from *Outlander*. Hugh's assistant caught Camilla studying him and raised a microbladed eyebrow, a proprietary look in her eyes.

Really, Hugh? Camilla wanted to say. He was forty-seven, the same age as her. What could he possibly see in a woman young enough to be his daughter? Camilla lost a little respect for him, and she'd respected him immensely. She'd thought he was different but she should've known better. All men were the same. Always on the lookout for an upgrade, trading you in as soon as a bright, shiny younger model came along.

Camilla swept her hair over her shoulder, glad she'd

listened to her assistant. Sometimes she thought Gail knew her better than she knew herself. Her new look had given Camilla the confidence boost she needed for today. The colorist had done an amazing job weaving honey and caramel lowlights throughout her creamy-blond hair. The warm colors complemented her tanned skin tone to perfection. The stylist had completed her makeover with soft bangs and layers that made her look more than a decade younger. According to Gail, she could pass for thirty-two.

While on the one hand, the compliment was just what Camilla needed to hear, it was also slightly concerning. She didn't want to look *too* young. The role she was reading for was that of a forty-year-old mother of two, Rachel West.

Camilla glanced at Hugh. His head was once again bent over his assistant's iPad. It sounded as if they were reviewing Camilla's reading. Fine, let them. It had been one of her best auditions in years. She'd nailed it. Except Hugh seemed unusually distracted and that worried her. It was his assistant's fault. Every time he'd opened his mouth to say something to Camilla, she'd shown him something on her screen.

Camilla cleared her throat and subtly arched her back, ensuring her boobs were shown off to their best advantage in the cream-silk wraparound dress. Her implants were fabulous and worth every penny she'd scrimped and saved when she'd first started out. They were the best investment she'd ever made. Her toothpaste-commercial-worthy smile came a close second. She flashed it at Hugh as soon as he lifted his head. He could date whomever he wanted. She didn't care. All she cared about was getting this damn part.

"This role was made for me, Hugh," she said, crossing her legs, letting the red Jimmy Choo dangle flirtatiously from her toes. His assistant rolled her eyes. Camilla didn't care if Pinky thought she was a sellout to womankind as long as she drew Hugh's attention to her long, toned legs, which were the result of daily two-hour sessions with her trainer. She'd use any means at her disposal to get this job—apart from sleeping with anyone, of course. If she didn't get this role, she was terrified her career would be over.

"I *am* Rachel West." Camilla wasn't blowing smoke. She'd identified almost immediately with Rachel. Like Camilla's, Rachel's life had imploded upon her discovering her husband was having an affair with a woman two decades her junior. Something else Camilla could sadly identify with: the young woman Rachel had taken under her wing at work was gunning for her job. The last two roles Camilla had auditioned for had been won by the much younger woman she'd mentored and considered a friend. She should've known better. It was a cutthroat industry. Everyone was out for themselves.

Hugh drew his eyes from her legs, clearing his throat before offering her what looked like a self-conscious smile. "Your read-through was great, Cami." His assistant said something under her breath. He glanced at her, nodded, and then returned his attention to Camilla while refusing to meet her gaze. Camilla wanted to howl.

"We're wrapping up auditions for Rachel today, and we hope to have a decision by the end of the week."

Camilla worked to keep the smile on her face and the panic from her voice. "I see. I didn't realize you were auditioning other actresses for the role." *Chin up, tits out*, she told herself as she rose from the chair. When her nose itched and her throat clogged, she silently repeated the advice her mother had given her decades before. *Don't ever let them see you cry.*

Hugh rubbed the back of his neck as he came to his feet. "Look, Cami. I—"

Once again, his assistant rolled her eyes, and Camilla clenched the script in her hand. She wanted to throw it at the condescending little twit.

"You passed them on your way in," Pinky said with a smirk.

"I couldn't have. The actresses waiting in the hall are all auditioning for Rachel's daughter." They had to be. None of them looked a day over nineteen, and Camilla didn't recognize any of them. Were they beautiful? Yes. Actresses of her caliber and experience? Definitely not.

Camilla walked to Hugh with sensuous grace, ensuring that she had his undivided attention.

His assistant snorted. Hugh shot her a look that had her bending her head over her screen.

"We've already filled the role of Rachel's daughter," Hugh said. "We gave the part to Lilianna Rose."

"Lilianna Rose? Hugh, she's a tween."

"I know, but she nailed the audition, Cami. The kid's a natural."

"So the actresses in the hall, they really are auditioning for the role of Rachel?"

He nodded, pulling his phone from his pocket. He glanced at it as he said, "They are."

There was so much wrong with that that she wanted to spit. She'd been coming up against ageism more and more as each year passed. Just like every other actress, she knew the score. Once a woman hit forty, the roles began drying up. Of course it wasn't the same for their male counterparts. At least fifty percent of the leading male roles in the movies went to actors in their forties.

Hugh's gaze met hers, and a muscle in his chiseled jaw bunched. He knew exactly what she was thinking. How could he not? They'd had this conversation before.

He rubbed his hand over his wavy auburn hair. "Are you going to be in town for a few days?"

"I can be. Why?"

"I'd like you to do a read-through with Clive."

She didn't have to ask *Clive who?* Hugh had directed the majority of Clive's movies, earning them both shelffuls of awards.

"Oh, so Clive's playing Rachel's husband?" she asked, holding his gaze to make her point. Clive was fifty-seven while Rachel's husband in the movie adaptation was forty.

Camilla had every right to be upset but it wouldn't get her the job. Instead of calling Hugh out on the double standard, she smiled winningly. "I'd love to do a read-through with Clive. It'll be great to catch up. We've always had amazing chemistry on camera." They had when they'd worked together in the past but she'd been much younger then.

Hugh's broad shoulders relaxed as if he'd been expecting her to call him out for the hypocrisy. "Great. Emily will be in touch with a day and a time once she's spoken to Clive."

The name didn't suit the young woman with the perpetual sneer. Her parents should've named her Wednesday. Other than her hair color, she had the same look and demeanor as Wednesday Addams in the Netflix series. And no way was Camilla leaving her future in Pinky's hands. She didn't put it past her to give her the wrong day and time.

Trying to come up with a work-around, she leaned in to kiss Hugh's cheek, lingering longer than was necessary. Long enough to discover that he smelled as delicious as she remembered. "Perfect," she said, her voice husky and low.

He leaned around her to open the door, looking a little flushed. "It was good seeing you, Cami." His low baritone was even deeper, huskier too.

She dipped her head, hiding her grin. They didn't call her a heartbreaker for nothing. At least in Sunshine Bay they had. She briefly closed her eyes. What was up with her? That was the second time today she'd thought about her hometown and her family. She locked thoughts of both away. Nothing good ever came of thinking about Sunshine Bay and her family.

She needed to focus. Smoothing her hands over her hips as if straightening her dress instead of highlighting her curves, she said, "It was great seeing you, Hugh. It's been too long."

Then she rested a finger on her chin, bringing his attention to her pouty, kissable lips. *Thank you, Dr. Vaughan.* "You know, since I'm going to be in town, why don't we go out and have a drink together?"

It was the perfect solution to the Pinky problem. Hugh could confirm the day and time of her reading with Clive, and Camilla would have the opportunity to point out that the lead actresses in the previous movie adaptations of Liane's books had all been in their forties.

She'd also remind him how well they'd done and what the entertainment industry seemed to forget: it was people over fifty who controlled seventy percent of the disposable income.

At the sound of whispering coming from her right, she cringed. What had she been thinking, asking him out as she stepped into the hall? She prayed the other actresses hadn't heard her or, if they had, that Hugh agreed to meet for drinks.

He looked as if he was about to nod when they were interrupted by a familiar male voice. "Camilla, what are you doing here?"

No. It couldn't be. She widened her eyes at Hugh.

He raised his hands. "I had no idea, Cami."

Pinky leaned past Hugh. "Giselle, we're ready for you now." Her black-slicked lips twisted in a smirk that she directed at Camilla before her face transformed, welcoming Giselle with a warm smile as if the two were BFFs.

For all Camilla knew, they could be. They were Gen Zers and were obviously into older men. Last year, Giselle had stolen Camilla's husband, Jeff, from her. Now her ex-husband, she reminded herself.

Hugh put a hand on Camilla's shoulder and gave it a comforting squeeze. Although if Pinky had shown him the tabloids' front pages from a few months earlier, it was possibly a warning squeeze and not a supportive one.

"I'm here until at least ten tonight. But I'll give you a call, and we'll grab lunch tomorrow. Okay?" He ducked his head to meet her gaze.

She nodded. "I'd like that, thanks." He had no idea how grateful she was. He'd saved her from looking like an idiot in front of her ex.

She took some measure of pleasure in knowing that Jeff would be furious that her friendship with Hugh might give her a leg up over his girlfriend. The fact that both Jeff and Hugh's assistant thought the gorgeous model had a chance to beat out Camilla made her stomach turn. The woman might be beautiful but she couldn't act her way out of a paper bag.

"Sorry. I need to get by," Giselle whispered, her shoulders hunched around her ears as if she expected Camilla to make a scene. Camilla rolled her eyes. She could only imagine the lies Jeff had told her. He'd had a field day with the press.

Or maybe Giselle felt guilty for breaking up their happy

marriage. Camilla snorted at the idea that her marriage had been a happy one as she stepped aside to let Giselle by. Camilla hadn't realized how unhappy she'd been until a week after catching Jeff and Giselle in her bed.

She turned to leave, which brought her face-to-face with Jeff, his eyes narrowed as he looked from her to Hugh. She wanted to smack his too-pretty face. She wasn't a violent person but her ex brought out the worst in her, which had unfortunately been enshrined on the front pages of the tabloids forever.

"You got this, Cami?" Hugh asked.

She nodded, wondering where Gail was. "I do, thanks."

For the past few months, her assistant had been running interference with Jeff to avoid more bad press. But Camilla wasn't about to let him get a reaction from her today. She wouldn't put it past him to have the paparazzi on standby.

He used to be a publicist and had taken over her PR when they started dating. She should've listened to Gail. She'd advised her not to hire him and then not to marry him.

Gail hadn't liked any of her previous husbands either, but she really, really hadn't liked Jeff. Sadly, Camilla had been head over heels in love with him.

She looked over her ex-husband's shoulder, waving and smiling as if someone were there. The second he turned to look, she hurried past him.

He grabbed her arm. "Don't think I'll let you get away with this, Camilla."

She stopped, looked down at his hand and then pointedly at the actresses sitting in the chairs in the hall.

He let his hand fall from Camilla's arm before leaning into her and whispering fiercely, "If you mess this up for Giselle, you'll be sorry."

"The only way your girlfriend has a chance at this part is if you called in some favors. And despite what you like to think, you don't have that much pull, Jeff."

Sadly, these days, she had less pull than he did. She wasn't worried as much about Hugh as she was about the producers. She didn't know who they were, and they held the purse strings.

She hooked the strap of her Coach straw tote over her shoulder. "You might want to think twice about sabotaging my chances of getting this role, Jeff. If I don't get it, I won't be able to afford your alimony payments." At least at their current amount.

That would be the one and only positive of not getting the role. She'd been angrier about having to pay Jeff alimony for the next two years than she had been when she'd discovered him in her bed with Giselle.

"I don't think that will be a problem. All you have to do is sell the house," he said with a smug smile. "In fact, with the rate of inflation, I'm thinking of asking for an increase." He waited for that to sink in before adding, "Now, if you were to put in a good word for Giselle with Hugh, I might—"

He didn't finish, and not because Camilla had punched him in the nose, rendering him speechless, but because Gail had appeared at her side and looped her arm through Camilla's, whisking her away.

"Don't say a word," Gail warned, her gaze moving from left to right. "You don't know who's listening, and the last thing you need is more bad publicity."

By the time they reached the lobby, Camilla was practically shaking with suppressed anger. "Did you hear him? Did you hear what he said to me?" she asked, unable to stay quiet any longer.

She pushed open the glass doors, yelping when a gust of wind and rain whipped open her dress. She fisted the fabric in her hand to keep it closed while joining Gail under the umbrella she held over her head. "Please tell me I didn't flash anyone who had their phones out."

She was extra careful these days never to put a wrong foot forward in public, which was why she ranted quietly to Gail about Hugh's PA, Jeff, Giselle, and the unfairness of it all while standing on the edge of the sidewalk, flagging down a cab.

Gail grimaced at her phone.

"What's wrong?" Camilla asked, worried that Jeff had already done something.

"Nothing. At least, I don't think it's anything to worry about." Gail offered her a closed-lipped smile. "We can talk about it when we get back to the hotel."

"No. Tell me now."

"Willow called. She says it's urgent. I told her you'd call her back before the end of the day." She held up her phone. "She texted to see if I had given you her message."

No, no, no. This couldn't be happening. The last thing Camilla needed was for her secret to come out. It would ruin her. She wouldn't stand a chance of getting the role. She—

"Cami!"

As she stepped off the sidewalk, Camilla glanced over her shoulder at Gail, and everything went black.

Chapter Three

Willow stood on her pink electric scooter, whizzing past the B and Bs and their rainbow-colored summer gardens and the eclectic mix of bakeries, bars, cafés, and shops that lined Main Street. It was just her luck that the sun had come out in time for the dinner crowd to fill up the patios.

Everyone from year-rounders to out-of-towners to waitstaff had an opinion of her five o'clock weather report, and they were only too happy to share them with her.

"What happened to Lucy?" "Why did you report the weather from inside the station?" "It was boring!" "So boring! Boo!" "We want Lucy!"

The questions and comments being shouted at her from both sides of Main Street affirmed Willow's belief that, other than Amos and the over-seventy crowd, no one really cared about her weather reports. All they cared about was Lucy the Lobster giving them a few laughs.

Everyone needed a laugh now and again and she was happy to provide them with one if it made their day a little brighter. But the last thing she could afford was for Bennett Broadcasting's acting CEO, Noah Elliot, to see her as a joke.

Despite the increasingly urgent to-do list on her phone, which included finding a place to live within the next two weeks as well as packing up her apartment, she'd wasted the entire day hanging out at the station in the hopes that Don would call her into his office to pitch the idea for *Good Morning, Sunshine!* while at the same time trying to figure out a way to prove she was up to the job.

It wasn't easy with her interactions with Noah playing in her head. In the end, she'd hoped that by presenting herself as a professional weatherperson, she might make him forget that she'd accidentally accosted him with her claw—three times—and then basically accused him of stalking her. In her mind, she'd erased the part about reeling him in with her imaginary fishing rod, convinced, or at the very least positively hopeful, that he'd missed that part.

She'd scraped her hair into a serious bun for her dinner-hour broadcast, put on a pair of thick black glasses she didn't need but that made her look bookishly smart—based on her coworkers' reactions, she'd nailed the hot librarian look instead—wiggled into a black pencil skirt, tucked in a white shirt, and then thrown on the black blazer she wore to funerals.

According to Veronica, Willow's efforts had been for naught. Noah Elliot had left the building while she was on the air and while Veronica had been fielding calls from unhappy viewers demanding that Lucy deliver the weather forecast instead of Willow.

Before leaving the station five minutes ago, Willow had poked her head into Don's office in hopes of learning what had transpired in his meeting with Bennett's acting CEO, but her boss had also been fielding calls from unhappy viewers, and he'd shooed her away with a disheartened look on his face. She would've preferred his usual scowl.

Since Willow couldn't stick around or she'd be late for her shift at La Dolce Vita, she'd tasked Naomi and Veronica with finding out when Don had scheduled the *Good Morning, Sunshine!* presentation for.

"Okay, thanks for sharing," Willow yelled, waving at Lucy's fans on the patios while forcing what she hoped resembled her usual bright and cheery smile.

Up until a few weeks ago, she'd never had to force a smile. She had ridden around town with a perpetual grin on her face. She'd loved life and felt blessed to live close to family and friends. It was easy to forget about the debt piling up and her not-so-fabulous part-time *career* when she was surrounded by so much love and natural beauty.

As she turned off Main Street and took a shortcut through an alley, her phone buzzed. Steering around some broken glass, she removed the phone from her pocket and glanced at the screen. It wasn't her aunt or her assistant. It was Veronica.

Willow returned her phone to her pocket, stuck in an earbud, and connected the call. Without preamble, she asked, "When's the presentation scheduled for?" Her question was greeted by muffled sniffing. "I can't understand what you're saying, Veronica."

A second later, Naomi's voice came over the line. "Because she's not saying anything. She's crying into a wad of soggy tissues."

Willow briefly closed her eyes and groaned. Not the smartest thing to do while riding a scooter, she decided, when she hit a pothole and nearly fell off. She regained her balance and asked, "What happened?"

"A better question would be, What's not happening? And if you haven't already guessed by the fact Veronica is crying—again—that would be *Good Morning, Sunshine!*"

Naomi didn't handle emotional people well so it had surprised Willow when her friends had started dating the previous year. Commercials, puppies, and sunsets made Veronica cry. She was a sensitive person. But just because she cried easily didn't make her weak. She was actually one of the strongest, kindest, most empathetic women Willow knew, which was why Naomi put up with her crying jags even though they got on her last nerve.

"It's because of me, isn't it?" After what had taken place earlier that day, she couldn't really blame Bennett's acting CEO but she had been hoping he'd give her another chance. After all, he'd nearly drowned her. "But Naomi, you and Don can do the presentation."

Over the past few months, Willow had been pushing Naomi to step out from behind the camera and take a more active role in production. She had great ideas and had helped Willow put the *Good Morning, Sunshine!* presentation together.

"From what Don said, it didn't have anything to do with you, Will. Elliot's mind was made up before he got here."

"So Don didn't even bring up *Good Morning, Sunshine!* to him?"

"Nope. He said Elliot wasn't interested in anything other than shutting down Channel 5 as quickly as possible. He's supposedly meeting with a real estate agent to sell the building and contents as well as the Bennett family's vacation home. He's leaving Sunshine Bay tomorrow morning."

Willow turned off the motor and hopped off her scooter,

wheeling it toward the familiar weathered gray building up the road. "Okay. This is good. We can work with this."

Naomi made an annoyed sound in her throat, and Willow pictured her throwing up her hands in disgust. There was nothing Naomi hated more than Willow's ability to find the positive in any situation. As far as Willow was concerned, it was her superpower. A superpower that seemed to be running a little low these days, she had to admit.

"Ugh, you are *positively* annoying, Willow Rosetti."

Willow laughed, surprised that she could given Naomi's news. "Good one. But I'm serious. I'll call Megan. If Noah's looking for a real estate agent on the cape, he'll go with her, and then we'll..." Willow sighed at Naomi's muttered aside. "I heard you, Naomi. This isn't me and my magical thinking at work. Megan's the best real estate agent on the cape, and Noah Elliot strikes me as a man who wouldn't settle for anything but the best."

He struck her as a jerk too but she wasn't about to share that with Naomi. If she did, she'd have to share about their disastrous first meeting. "Megan's been the top-selling real estate agent on the cape for two years running, and she lives in Sunshine Bay, so of course he'll go with her."

Willow crossed her fingers. Something had to go her way today, and her best friend taking on Noah Elliot as a client was the best possible outcome. Megan could stall him by convincing him he had to stay in town for at least another day to view and discuss the properties with her, especially the vacation home. Surely it needed some work before they put it on the market.

"Let's say you're right and Elliot hires Megan. How does that help us?"

Buoyed by Naomi's question—if Negative Naomi was willing to concede that Noah would contact Megan, then Willow had to be right—she did a happy dance before opening the door to the restaurant. Midtwerk, she noticed a black Mercedes pulling into the parking lot.

She groaned. *Seriously?*

"What's wrong?"

"I was celebrating you agreeing with me for a change, and Noah Elliot just pulled into the restaurant's parking lot. I'm pretty sure he saw me."

"That's great," Naomi said, sounding disconcertingly cheerful.

"No, it's not great. I was doing my happy dance. Don't laugh," she said when Naomi snorted. "He'll never believe I'm anything other than a flake now."

"Don't worry about it. He probably didn't see you. Besides, you've never worried if anyone saw you acting like an idiot before. Why worry about it now?"

"I said a flake, not an idiot," she grumbled, wheeling her scooter inside the restaurant.

Her previous scooter had been stolen from the bike rack in the parking lot a year before, and she'd been parking her current—delicately used—scooter inside the restaurant ever since. She couldn't afford to replace it.

"And Noah Elliot's not just anyone. He holds our futures in his hands," Willow reminded Naomi.

"Whatever. It can't be any worse than him seeing you reeling him in on your imaginary fishing rod or you accusing him of stalking you. Which, by the way, you never did explain to us."

All Willow could think about was Naomi confirming that Noah had seen her and her imaginary fishing rod in action. She swore. Obviously not under her breath as she'd meant to because she'd drawn the attention of the handsome bald man standing at the hostess stand in his white shirt and black pants.

Bruno raised a bushy silver eyebrow at her. He was her grandmother's fiancé and one of Willow's favorite people on the planet. She mouthed, *Sorry,* and he gave her an indulgent smile before confirming a couple's reservation and ushering them to a table.

"I'll tell you about it tomorrow," she promised Naomi. Then, feeling as if she could use her friends' emotional support, Willow added, "Unless you and Veronica want to stop by for a drink? On me." Well, on her family, she supposed.

A muffled conversation between the two women ensued before Naomi came back on the line. "We're going to pass, Will. No pressure, but I think we need to start looking at what's out there jobwise." She sighed. "Come on, Veronica, it's not the end of the world if we have to move."

"Don't you guys dare give up," Willow said, a touch of panic in her voice as she wedged her scooter behind the fountain with the gurgling statue of Venus at its center. "There's a reason Noah's coming to dinner here and my best friend is bound to be his real estate agent."

"Yeah, he's wants Italian food, and Megan is pretty much the only real estate agent in town."

"Thanks, Negative Naomi. I expect a coffee and a doughnut when I see you in the morning and share my positively fabulous good news."

"You'd better pray your forecast for tomorrow is right because we're heading to the sand dunes for your morning weather report. I'll bring Lucy," she said with an evil chuckle.

"Remind me again why we're friends?" When Naomi began listing all the reasons, Willow sighed. "I was being sarcastic."

As she disconnected and pocketed her phone, Willow glanced at the coins glinting at the bottom of the fountain. She wondered if any of them had once belonged to her or her sister or her cousin. Their mothers and grandmother had drilled into their heads that they were responsible for making their own wishes come true, but that hadn't stopped them from hedging their bets and making wishes every time they found coins while cleaning the restaurant.

They used to think La Dolce Vita's customers must all be rich to be so careless with their loose change until one night they'd caught Bruno placing coins under the tables and chairs.

Willow smiled at the memory as she reached in her pocket and pulled out a lint-covered quarter. Thinking she could use all the help she could get, she tossed it into the fountain. The quarter bounced off Venus's knee and rolled onto the floor.

"You have got to be kidding me," she muttered, bending to pick it up. This time, when she made her wish, she pushed up the sleeve of her blazer, stuck her hand in the water, and placed the quarter on the bottom of the fountain, snug between a nickel and a dime.

"Mommy, the lady is stealing money from the fountain!"

"No. No, I wasn't. Honest. See." She turned to the little boy, showing him her empty hands. "I just wanted to make sure my quarter stayed in the fountain this time." She lifted her head to offer his parents a convincing smile, only to meet the dark, sardonic gaze of the man standing behind them.

Really? Willow yelled silently at Venus. She'd wished for an answer to her problem, and what did she get? Her problem standing five feet in front of her, looking at her with an arrogant eyebrow raised.

"You know what? Save your money. Venus is falling down on the job and no longer granting wishes," Willow told the little boy while once again shoving up the sleeve of her blazer.

She stuck her hand in the fountain and pulled out the quarter, showing it to her audience. "It's mine." She put it in her pocket. The way things were going, she'd need it.

She turned and walked into her mother.

"Honey?" Gia Rosetti frowned, searching Willow's face before leaning around her to offer their audience a sweet smile.

Noah Elliot, Willow noticed, wasn't among them. She caught sight of his broad back, dark head bent, phone pressed to his ear as he walked out of the restaurant. A part of her wanted to chase after him and drag him back inside while the other part of her wanted to slam and lock the door behind him.

"Bruno will be with you in a moment," her mother said to the family of three and an elderly couple whom Noah had held the door open for. Maybe he wasn't a complete ogre.

Putting an arm around Willow's shoulders, her mother steered her toward the back of the restaurant. "Is everything okay?"

Willow wanted nothing more than to share her worries with her mother but she couldn't bear to tell her that in two weeks, she'd be homeless, most likely jobless—unless she counted working part-time at La Dolce Vita, which she didn't—with little more than a quarter to her name.

But she couldn't bring herself to do it, and the reason she couldn't had nothing to do with feeling guilty about Camilla. Neither was she worried her mother would be anything other than fully supportive if Willow found herself homeless and jobless.

The problem was that over the past year, Willow had come to the uncomfortable realization that she was the only Rosetti who hadn't made something of herself. If there were a photo under "Failure to launch" on Wikipedia, she swore it would have her face on it. As much as she doubted her family members were surprised—after all, when their mothers used to ask them what they wanted to be when they grew up, Willow had said "A beach bum"—it was important to her that she prove to them as much as to herself that she was a contributing, responsible, independent member of society. In other words, that she could adult with the best of them.

"I'm fine, Mom." She smiled and put an arm around her mother's waist, giving her a side hug.

Her mother, who was routinely mistaken for actress Eva Mendes, arched an eyebrow. "You were stealing money from the fountain."

"A quarter, and it was mine." She fished it out of her pocket and held it up. "I realized at the last minute it was my lucky quarter."

"You can't fool me, honey. We've heard the rumors that the station might be closing, and I understand how worried you must be. But it might not be the worst thing that could happen."

"How can you say that, Mom? I won't have a job, and I've been working at Channel 5 since I was in high school. It feels more like home than a job."

"I know, and I know how much you hate change and how much you love your friends at the station, but you're only getting part-time hours. At least if you were working for one of the big networks, they could offer you full time. Your first year at college, all you talked about was becoming the host of a morning show. It's not like you'd get the opportunity at Channel 5, even if someone else buys the station. And think of it: if you got a job in Boston, you could live with Sage. You two would have so much fun together."

Willow adored her sister, who was a high-powered divorce attorney. But as much as she loved Sage, Willow hated the idea of living anywhere other than Sunshine Bay. She hated it so much that the thought of moving from her beloved hometown made her heart race, and not in a good way. She felt faint, swamped by a wave of panic and sorrow.

And those feelings only intensified when her grandmother, who could pass for her daughters' older sister, walked over and shoved a bowl of gnocchi at Willow. As much as she'd hate to leave Sunshine Bay, the station, and her friends, it was Willow's love for her family that anchored her to this place.

"*Mangia.* You're fading away." Her grandmother's eyes narrowed behind her stylish red-framed glasses as she looked Willow up and down. "Who died, and why weren't we invited to the funeral?"

"No one died, Nonna. I decided to deliver the weather as my professional self instead of a lobster for a change." She kissed her grandmother's cheek and took a seat at the long table, the window on the back wall providing a spectacular view of the golden-sand beach and whitecapped waves in the turquoise bay.

The table was reserved for the family, their initials carved into the honey-colored wood. Each and every one of them, from Willow's mother and aunts to Willow and her sister and her cousin, had grown up at this table. They'd eaten their meals here, done their homework here, played restaurant and Barbies and done crafts here, talked about friends and boyfriends at the table. Some of the most meaningful moments of her family's lives had happened here, in a restaurant that had been owned by the Rosettis for generations.

She got a little emotional thinking about all the good times they'd shared and what her family meant to her. It didn't matter how desperate she'd been to save the station; she never should've reached out to her aunt. She should've found another way.

And as she sat at the table, lifting a forkful of gnocchi to her mouth, inhaling the fragrant basil scent, she promised herself she'd find one. As soon as she finished eating, she'd call her aunt's assistant, asking her to let Camilla know the matter had been resolved and thanking her for her time.

Then would come the hard part, convincing Noah Elliot to give them until the end of summer to find another buyer for the station. Willow pulled her phone from her pocket to call Megan, unable to resist taking another bite before she did. She moaned her appreciation. "This is so good, Nonna. What's the sauce?"

"How do you not know this? Pistachio pesto." Her grandmother pointed at the grainy olive-green sauce drizzled over the gnocchi and creamy white rounds of ricotta cheese.

"I don't need to know because I have a nonna, mom, and zia who are magnificent cooks and who love to feed me." She smiled at both her grandmother and her mother.

Ignoring their silent exchange—they were always on her case about learning to cook—Willow pointed at her phone and pressed an icon. "I just have to make a quick call." It went straight to voicemail. "Megan, get back to me as soon as you get this. It's an emergency." Willow disconnected and wolfed down the rest of the gnocchi. "So good. I wish I had time for seconds, but I don't." She pushed back from the table and stood up.

Her mother and grandmother said, "Sit."

Willow's knees went weak. Praying Camilla hadn't called them and ratted her out, she slowly lowered herself onto the chair. "What's wrong?"

Gia and Carmen took a seat on either side of her. "We're worried about you," her mother said, taking Willow's hand in hers. "Mr. Lowell called. He said he asked you to move out two weeks ago and that you haven't been looking for another place to live. He's concerned you won't leave."

Willow couldn't deny that the thought had crossed her mind. Channel 5 had done a story on a couple who wouldn't move out of their rental, and they were still there a year later. "I can't believe he told you guys. And how does he know I haven't already found a place?"

"Why wouldn't he tell us? We're your family," her grandmother said.

"I know, Nonna. But come on, I'm twenty-eight."

Her grandmother muttered something in Italian. Other than a few swear words and the restaurant's menu, Willow didn't speak or understand the language but she had a feeling

Carmen might've said something along the lines of *Twenty-eight going on twelve.*

Her mother sent Carmen a quelling look, which seemed to support Willow's suspicion. "He felt bad he had to ask you to leave. He knows July is a terrible time to find something to rent. Which is why your nonna and I wanted to suggest you take over your zia Eva's apartment."

Carmen nodded. "*Sì*, and you don't have to pay rent."

"I can't take advantage of you like that. As much as I appreciate the offer, and I really do, I can't take handouts anymore."

"So no more free food and drinks then?" Carmen asked, a hint of sarcasm in her voice.

"Ma, they need you in the kitchen," Willow's mother said, clearly exasperated with Carmen.

"Nonna's right." Willow traced her initials on the table as her grandmother walked off, yelling, "What do you want?" at the kitchen staff.

"Don't listen to her. There's nothing Ma likes better than feeding you girls. She's just upset you didn't come to us as soon as Mr. Lowell gave you notice. You know how much she hates being the last to know when it comes to her family. She didn't talk to your zia for a week when she found out from Bruno that they were spending the month in England."

Willow's aunt and uncle were in England for his daughter's wedding. Willow's cousin and her family were there too.

"Thanks, Mom. But Nonna has a point. I've got to get my act together. And I promise, I'll set some time aside this week to find an apartment."

Her mother leaned in and gave her a hug. "The apartment is yours if you need it. But look, there's Megan. Maybe she has something for you." She waved at Willow's best friend, who'd walked into the restaurant with none other than Noah Elliot at her side.

"Wish me luck." She kissed her mother's cheek before hurrying to where Megan and Noah waited by the hostess stand. "Megs!" Willow nodded at Noah and grabbed her best friend's hand. "I need to talk to you for a minute."

Megan gave her an *are you kidding me?* look while pulling her hand free and placing it on Noah's arm. "Maybe later. Bruno's holding a table for Noah and me. Have you two met?"

Willow held back an eye roll. Megan got all coolly professional when she was in the company of a potential client, especially one with money. And Noah looked and smelled like money.

Willow forced a smile, at the same time praying Noah didn't say anything about their disastrous first meeting to Megan, and held out her hand. "Not formally. Willow Rosetti, Mr. Elliot. I was hoping to have a chance to talk to you earlier but you'd already left the station."

His dark gaze roamed her face as he took her hand in his. Frowning, he said, "I thought your name was Lucy."

Megan laughed. "Everyone calls her Lucy because she reports the weather as the Lobster Pot's mascot. You have to see her in costume. It's hilarious."

"I have seen her in costume," he said, and Willow braced herself, waiting for him to out her to Megan. But instead, his gaze came back to her, and there was something about the way he was looking at her that made her feel as if she'd gulped down a glass of prosecco, all warm and fizzy inside.

"Are you the Willow from Hidden Cove? The summer of 2011?" he added when she simply stared at him, trying to process what he seemed to be suggesting.

Could it really be him? The Noah she'd hung out with at Hidden Cove for three weeks during the summer of 2011? The boy who'd worn glasses and had a mouthful of metal? The boy she'd thought was her best friend until he left Sunshine Bay and she'd never heard from him again?

She stared at him. "Noah?"

His dark eyes, which she'd thought were black but were really a deep indigo, crinkled at the corners, and a warm smile curved his lips. "Yeah. It's me."

Chapter Four

When Willow uttered a delighted cry and threw her arms around Noah's neck, she wasn't thinking about their earlier interactions or how his decision to shut down Channel 5 would shatter her hopes and dreams. She was remembering how he'd once turned the crappiest summer of her life into a happy, unforgettable one.

He uttered a low *oof*, rocking back on his shoes before his arms closed around her. He hugged her with much less enthusiasm than that with which she hugged him. This was nothing new. She'd been the spontaneous, affectionate, and yes, it must be said, loud and wild one in their friendship. Noah had been the standoffish, quiet bookworm who'd wanted nothing to do with her at first, which of course had been all the motivation Willow had needed to try to win him over. She hadn't met anyone she couldn't be friends with, and she'd needed a friend that summer. She'd sensed that Noah had needed one too. She'd never discovered why he gave off that vibe, but what she had discovered was that he had a surprising sense of adventure, a great sense of humor, and the best laugh ever.

She released him, stepping back and lightly swatting his rock-hard abs as he stared at her with a slightly dazed expression on his gorgeous face. She was about to give him crap for not showing up at Hidden Cove the last day of his vacation as he'd promised, but before she could, Megan, with her arms crossed and looking as if she'd sucked back a whiskey sour, said, "What am I missing? How could you two possibly not know that you knew each other?"

"We were fifteen and only knew each other's first names. And it's not like we look the same as we did back then," Willow said, still finding it hard to believe Bennett's acting CEO and her Noah were one and the same.

"Why wouldn't you share your last names? That's just weird," Megan said.

"No, it's not. When you were fifteen, you didn't go around introducing yourself as Megan Pecker," Willow pointed out, hoping Megan would let it go at that. Because while it was mostly true, Willow had another reason she hadn't shared her last name with Noah that summer. She might not be embarrassed by her family's exploits now, but she had been back then.

At Megan's ticked-off stare, Willow realized her best friend wasn't pleased she'd shared her former surname. Willow supposed she shouldn't be surprised. Even though Megan hated her cheating ex, she'd kept his last name, which went to show just how much she hated her own. Willow mouthed, *Sorry*.

She knew her apology wasn't accepted when Megan said, "I guess I wouldn't have wanted to share I was a Rosetti that summer either." Leaning into Noah, she lowered her voice. "The mayor had a heart attack in Willow's grandmother's bed. He was married, and it wasn't as if they could keep it on the down-low when the first responders arrived, lights flashing and sirens blaring." She snickered. "There wasn't much going on that night and half the town showed up, including the mayor's wife."

Willow's cheeks heated at the memory. After the news broke, her friends' parents had ensured that their daughters were too busy to hang out with her. Her sister and cousin hadn't been around for support either. Her cousin had spent her summers in England with her dad, and Willow's sister had accepted a summer internship with a local lawyer.

"The mayor's wife had left him the week before, Megan. They were separated." Willow glared at her friend, furious she'd bring that up here of all places, especially after how supportive Carmen had been throughout the breakup of Megan's marriage.

If Carmen had been standing close by, Willow would've done more than glare at Megan. Not that glaring at her was doing any good. Megan was focused on Noah, completely ignoring her.

"I bet you knew she was a Rosetti, didn't you?" Megan nudged Noah, giving him an encouraging wink. "With the amount of coverage Willow's grandmother and family were getting on Channel 5 that summer, they had to be the topic of conversation around the Bennett family's dinner table."

"I wouldn't know. I didn't spend a lot of time with my family that summer." He drew his gaze from Megan to her. "All I knew about Willow was that she wouldn't take no for an answer and seemed to be on a mission to push me out of my comfort zone and make me laugh." He smiled. "Some of my best memories of Sunshine Bay involved her."

Willow pressed a palm to her chest, touched as well as taken aback. It was surreal hearing those words out of Mercedes Man's mouth. "That's so sweet of you to say, Noah. I felt the same about you."

He raised his eyebrows, and she laughed. "Not that you pushed me out of my comfort zone or wouldn't take no for an answer." She was about to say she too had wonderful memories of their summer together but then recalled what Megan had said. "Um, are you related to the Bennetts?"

"My mother was Elizabeth Bennett."

Megan rolled her eyes. "Honestly, how could you not know this, Willow?"

"How was I supposed to know? I didn't know Noah's last name, and even if I did, it's Elliot!" She briefly closed her eyes while absorbing the news. Elizabeth Bennett had inherited Bennett Broadcasting Group when her father passed away in the fall of 2011 and had run the company until her death the year before. "I had no idea, Noah." She touched his arm. "I'm so sorry for your loss."

His nod was curt, a warning the subject was closed. "Thank you."

"This has all been very enlightening, but if you don't mind, we'd appreciate being seated *sometime* tonight," Megan said, looping her arm through Noah's while smiling up at him.

Willow grabbed a couple of menus from the hostess stand, fighting the urge to smack Megan with them. She was acting like a... Willow trailed off from the not-so-nice thought about her best friend's not-so-nice behavior when a life-changing realization came to mind. Noah Elliot was *her* Noah. He had fond memories of Sunshine Bay and of her. A smile turned up the corners of her lips. He couldn't say no to her. He'd said so himself.

On the promise of that thought, she was practically beside herself with joy and ran to the fountain. She reached in her pocket, tossed her quarter in, and whispered, "I'll never doubt you again, Venus. Thanks for making my wish come true."

She looked up to see Megan and Noah staring at her and tamped down the urge to do a happy dance. She smiled. "I'll take you to your table."

Noah walked beside her, his gaze roaming her face. "I should've known it was you. The name and costume must've thrown me. You haven't changed."

"I have so changed," she said, slightly offended, as she ushered them to a table near the back of the restaurant.

She had boobs now, a nice rack as a matter of fact. Her butt wasn't bad either. At fifteen, she hadn't had any curves to speak of. She'd been a late bloomer. Besides that, her hair no longer resembled a clown's wig. The humidity had turned it into a frizz ball until she'd learned the value of good hair product that ensured she always had long, beachy blond waves.

"You've changed too," she said as she stopped at a table for two in a private corner.

It was true. He no longer had a mouthful of metal. His teeth were toothpaste-commercial white and straight. Thick black-framed glasses no longer detracted from the beauty of his indigo eyes or slid down his strong, straight nose. A sexy five o'clock shadow darkened his chiseled jaw instead of the peach fuzz she remembered.

But she didn't feel comfortable bringing up those particular changes so instead she said, "You have to be at least six inches taller than me now."

She'd been five-nine since seventh grade. Noah had been shorter than her by at least an inch when they met. Now they were standing close enough that she had to tip her head to meet his gaze—close enough that she smelled his cologne or maybe it was his aftershave. She didn't know which, but from hugging him, she knew he smelled irresistible. She wanted to bury her nose in the warm curve of his corded neck and inhale the woodsy fragrance.

"At least," he said, his voice deep and velvet smooth but without the sardonic edge she'd heard in it earlier. He sounded amused.

She smiled, and his eyes warmed, crinkling at the corners. She liked this Noah so much better than Mercedes Man Noah. She even thought she might like him better than Summer of 2011 Noah, and she'd liked that Noah a lot.

Megan made as much noise as possible pulling out her chair, ensuring she had both of their attention. Willow loved her best friend, but ever since Megan had announced she was on the hunt for husband number two, she hadn't been acting like herself. She seemed a little desperate, and her desperation was putting a strain on their friendship. Willow didn't understand why Megan would want another man after the number her ex had done on her, but that was probably because Willow broke out in hives at the mere idea of a long-term relationship.

But it wasn't only their friendship feeling the strain. Several members of the Beaches, their squad, had commented that Girls' Night Out and Beaches Book Club were no longer as fun as they used to be, putting the blame squarely on Megan's obsession with finding husband number two.

Megan took the menus from Willow's hand, raising an eyebrow in a manner that suggested Willow was falling down on her waitressing duties and confirming that when she sighed and said in a haughty voice, "I'll have a mojito." Then, without so much as a glance at Willow, she smiled at her dinner companion, her voice low and sultry when she asked, "What will you have, Noah?"

Willow would've laughed if she weren't hurt by how Megan was treating her. Then again, maybe she was overreacting. These past months, she'd been overly sensitive when anyone seemed to suggest she didn't have her act together. Except Noah's brow was furrowed, his gaze moving from her to Megan and back again, suggesting that he'd noticed too.

He smiled at her. "Whiskey on the rocks, thanks."

She returned his smile and then headed for the bar, thinking of the best way to broach the subject of the sale with Noah as she filled their drinks order. With the fate of the station hanging in the balance, she was sure her mom and grandmother would understand if she took a break and joined Noah and Megan for a few minutes, perhaps while they were enjoying dessert.

But when Willow returned with a basket of warm homemade bread and a bowl of herbed olive oil for dipping, along with their drinks, Megan was already discussing the sale with Noah.

"I don't foresee a problem meeting your timeline. I've already made a list of developers to approach for the building on Main Street, and I can take care of selling the office furniture and equipment—"

"Here you go," Willow interrupted Megan, setting the drinks, bread, and dip on the table, surprised she managed to sound cheerful when she was dying inside.

"Thanks, Willow. The bread smells amazing," Noah said.

"Wait until you taste it. My grandmother makes the best—"

"Willow, do you mind? Noah and I are in the middle of

a conversation," Megan interrupted her with a pointed look. "We'll let you know when we're ready to order." She dismissed Willow. "Now, where were we?"

Willow stared at Megan. She'd brushed off Willow's request for a quick word while knowing exactly what she wanted to talk to her about. There was no way she didn't. And now it sounded as if she was seconds away from sealing the deal and Channel 5's fate, with no thought for the impact that it would have on Willow's and her colleagues' lives.

"Noah, if you don't mind, I need to talk to Megan for a minute," Willow said, reaching for her best friend's hand before she could object.

"Sure. No problem. I have a call to return anyway," Noah said.

If Noah hadn't mentioned the call, Willow had a feeling Megan wouldn't have acquiesced to her request. As it was, Megan muttered, "I don't know what your problem is, but you better make this quick" as Willow led her to the back door of the restaurant.

Willow opened her mouth to tell Megan exactly what was wrong when they stepped outside, only to discover all the tables on the deck were occupied. Willow smiled, nodding at the diners, asking each table if they were enjoying their meal while nudging Megan toward the stairs leading to the beach.

Once they were standing in the sand and out of hearing range of the diners on the deck, Willow said, "You know exactly what the problem is, Megan. If Noah closes the station instead of selling it—"

Megan rolled her eyes. "All you talk about anymore is the station. You're obsessed, and frankly, it's annoying."

"I'm sorry if you find it annoying, Megan. But my friends'

jobs and mine are on the line so I think it's understandable that all I've been thinking about is a way to convince Noah to sell Channel 5 instead of shutting us down. Honestly, as my friend, I'd think you'd be more sympathetic and supportive." She didn't remind Megan of the two years Willow had spent supporting her through her divorce. "I'd been planning to ask you to have my back and help me convince Noah to give us more time, which I know you knew."

Megan lifted a shoulder. "So what if I did? You might be my best friend but there's no way I'd mess up this deal by stalling the sale, even for you. Noah wants everything done like yesterday, and I'll do my best to make that happen. The way things have been going, I didn't think I'd make Real Estate Agent of the Year the third year running. But with the sale of the building on Main Street and the beach house, I actually have a chance now."

Willow studied her best friend and didn't like what she saw. She wondered how she'd missed the signs because, thinking back over the past year, Megan had given her plenty of signs. Her voice was subdued when she said, "I guess it's a good thing I don't need you after all."

Megan's eyes narrowed. "What do you mean?"

"I mean that I didn't stand a chance of changing Acting CEO Noah Elliot's mind, but this is *my* Noah we're talking about. You heard him. He never could say no to me." She allowed herself a small smile.

By the time Noah had paid the check, it was Megan who was wearing a smile. And it wasn't a small smile, it was big and smug.

Chapter Five

Y_{ou} made us change locations at the last minute, Will, and Noah's not even here," Naomi grumbled as she pulled her truck into the lot, her gaze moving from a man fishing off the large granite rocks that jutted into the bay to a windsurfer pulling her board into the sheltered cove.

"He'll be here," Willow said with a confidence she didn't feel. She glanced at her phone, wondering if she'd seem desperate if she texted Noah again.

They'd exchanged numbers the night before. Right after he'd squashed her hopes and dreams and made Megan's come true. No matter how convincing Willow had thought her arguments were, Noah hadn't been swayed. She'd seen a hint of Mercedes Man when he refused to even consider selling the station instead of closing it, laying out the reasons why that wasn't going to happen in a brisk, taciturn manner. Even though his reasons made sense and were based on facts, it had been disappointing to say the least.

He must've sensed her distress, reaching out and touching her hand, his gaze apologetic. It was nothing personal. Business was business. Of course Megan assured him he had nothing to apologize for. She was beyond thrilled when he signed the paperwork for the listings at the table while Willow looked on.

But Megan's smile had disappeared when they were getting up to leave and Noah had asked Willow for her number. He had business in Boston in a couple of weeks and suggested they catch up over drinks. Willow jumped on the opportunity but she didn't have a couple of weeks.

So she'd invited him to meet her at Hidden Cove this morning in hopes the memories inspired by their special place would succeed where she had failed. Or, at the very least, convince him to give her another day of his time to make her case. She'd used the excuse that he had to drive past Hidden Cove on his way out of town anyway. He hadn't said yes but he also hadn't said no. He'd told her he'd touch base with her that morning.

She'd woken Naomi up at the crack of dawn to tell her about the location change, and then she'd texted Noah a couple of hours later, hoping her offer to pick up their favorite s'more doughnuts from O Holey Glazed would be enough of an enticement. He hadn't responded yet.

Naomi reached into the back seat of her truck, grabbing her camera case and a bag. "And since he isn't here, you can wear your costume so Veronica and Don aren't fielding complaints the entire day." She tossed the bag to Willow.

"He'll be here. I'm sure of it. But on the off chance he doesn't come, I bet he'll watch my weather report now that he knows it's me. And since he will, I'll be reporting it as professional weatherperson me, not Lucy." She tossed the bag and costume into the back seat.

"Did you not hear one thing he said to you last night? Because unless you repeated an entirely different conversation to me and Veronica at the butt crack of dawn, there is nothing you can do or say that will change his mind. Even if he gave you a week to do it."

"I guess you missed the part where he told me I could convince him to do *anything*."

"When you were fifteen!"

"So? I haven't changed. I'm still me."

"You're right. You haven't changed. But I can guarantee with his pedigree and position at Bennett Broadcasting, Noah Elliot is nothing like the boy you used to know, Will." Naomi reached into the back seat, grabbed the bag, and tossed it to Willow before opening the driver-side door.

Willow's shoulders slumped as she reluctantly got out of the truck and dumped the costume onto the passenger seat. Naomi was probably right. She'd always been a good judge of character.

They'd been friends since grade school but she hadn't been part of Willow's high school crew. She hadn't wanted to be, and no matter how often Willow tried to include her, she wouldn't give in. She'd hadn't been a fan of Willow's friends, especially Megan.

If Naomi hadn't been at her grandmother's, Willow wouldn't have been friendless that summer. She probably wouldn't have met Noah. But maybe that would've been a good thing. She wouldn't have gotten her hopes up that he'd show this morning and that she'd have a chance of changing his mind. It didn't matter that the odds were stacked against her. All she'd ever needed was a smidgen of hope to believe anything was possible.

Willow took one last look at her phone. Noah still hadn't responded, and there was no sign of his car on the road to

Hidden Cove. With a dejected sigh, she stepped into the costume, pulling it over the cute pink sundress she'd worn in hopes of winning Noah over.

The bag of s'more doughnuts sitting on the console made her feel like a fool, and she quickly closed the door, stomping around the hood to Naomi's side. "You're as big a downer as you were at fifteen."

Naomi beeped the lock on her key fob and slung an arm over Willow's shoulders. "I prefer to think of myself as a realist, and face it, babe. Sometimes you need someone to pull your head out of the clouds."

"You weren't there. You didn't see him when he asked for my number or mentioned getting drinks," Willow said as they walked down to the rocks where they were filming her weather report.

"You always do this, Will. You think everyone's like you, sweet, kind, and loyal, but they're not. People suck."

Naomi had her reasons for having felt that way in the past. Her family had disowned her when she'd come out during senior year of high school. But there was something in her voice that made Willow look at her more closely. "Are you okay?"

She shrugged. "I applied for a position at WNBC in New York. If I get the job, Veronica told me she won't be coming with me."

This was exactly what Willow had been afraid of. Nothing would be the same for any of them if the station closed. She reached for Naomi's hand and gave it a squeeze. "Don't give up yet. Not on the station or Veronica."

At the low purr of an engine, Willow whipped her head around, barely restraining herself from jumping up and down as a familiar black Mercedes pulled into the parking lot. "I told you he'd come!"

Naomi shook her head. "Seriously, babe. When will you ever learn to play it cool?"

"Never." She grinned and was about to run over and greet Noah when her cell phone rang.

Naomi held her back. "Today you're going to. Now stop smiling and waving at him like you've been stranded in the desert for a week and he's a cool drink of water and answer your phone."

"I'm not waving and smiling at him like that. I'm being warm and welcoming," she said, despite having a feeling Naomi was right. Willow dialed down her smile to friendly and went to answer her phone. At the name on the screen, her body froze. "It's my aunt."

"Huh, so maybe I was wrong. Maybe there is something to this positivity thing."

"What do you mean?"

Naomi lifted her hand to the man getting out of his car. Willow hadn't thought Noah could look any more handsome than he had the night before in his navy suit but seeing him now in black pants and a white dress shirt with the sleeves rolled up, his dark hair messy, aviators shielding his eyes, and stubble shadowing his chiseled jaw, she knew she'd been wrong. Seriously wrong. Noah Elliot was off-the-charts gorgeous.

"Elliot's here, and your aunt's actually calling you back," Naomi said.

Despite being in hot-guy heaven, Willow didn't miss the uncharacteristically hopeful note in her friend's voice. "Right," she said, and answered her phone.

Naomi, Veronica, and everyone else at the station needed her to make this play. Somehow, someway, she'd make it up to her family. "Hi, Zia Camilla," she said as Noah walked toward them with a long, loose-limbed stride, an amused smile tugging on his lips. Everything about him screamed cool and confident. A far cry from the nerdy boy she remembered.

She returned her attention to her phone when a woman said, "Willow, it's Gail. Your aunt's assistant."

"Hi, Gail. Since you're the one calling, I take it my aunt isn't interested in talking to me." Willow didn't know whether to be disappointed or relieved.

"No. It's not that. I'd just told her you'd called when she was hit by an e-bike."

Willow gasped. "Oh no, is she okay?"

"She's in the hospital. She has a concussion, a pretty serious one, and her arm is broken."

Willow briefly closed her eyes before asking the question she was pretty sure she knew the answer to. "It's my fault, isn't it? She was upset when you told her I'd called and walked in front of the e-bike."

"No. If it was anyone's fault, it was mine. I should've waited to tell her. It surprised her. She was distracted by the news, not paying attention to what was going on around her."

It was kind of Gail to take the blame but they both knew it was Willow's fault. If she hadn't called her aunt out of the blue, she wouldn't be in the hospital.

Gail continued, her voice almost a whisper. "I realize Cami and your family are estranged but one of you has to come to New York. Your aunt has amnesia, Willow. She doesn't know me. She's asking for her mother and her sisters."

In the background, Willow heard a woman shouting for a phone. "That's her asking for the phone, isn't it?"

"More like demanding. Just a sec. Cami, I told you to give me a minute. I just need to finish this call, and then I'll give you your phone."

"No! Please, don't give her the phone and don't call my family. I'll handle it. I'll, um, I'll come to New York."

She didn't have a car or money for a plane ticket or probably even enough to cover bus fare, but she'd find a way. She had to. This was on her. "I'll call you when I'm on my way."

"Thank goodness," Gail said, sounding as if Willow couldn't get there fast enough for her.

After they said their goodbyes, Willow disconnected and stared at her phone.

"Willow, is everything all right?" Noah asked at the same time Naomi did.

There was nothing good about what had happened to her aunt, but something good might come out of it, Willow thought, lifting her gaze to Noah. He was heading back to New York this morning, and she needed a ride. It was a five-hour drive. Five hours in which he'd be stuck with her in a car and unable to escape. There was the added bonus of not having to call her sister to ask for a ride. She just hoped Gail didn't expect her to pay Camilla's hospital bill because then she'd have no choice but to call Sage and tell her what she'd done.

Willow explained what had happened to her aunt, leaving out that it was because of Willow that she'd wound up in the hospital. She'd tell Naomi later but it wasn't something Noah needed to know. "So it looks like I'm going to New York."

She held her breath, hoping Noah would offer instead of her having to ask.

"How? On your scooter?" Naomi asked since she knew the state of Willow's finances. Unlike Megan and the Beaches, neither Naomi nor Veronica encouraged her to live beyond her means. They were happy to do stuff that didn't cost anything. In fact, they encouraged it.

No doubt cluing in to the opportunity this presented, Naomi looked at Noah and said, "You're going back to New York this morning, aren't you? You could give our girl a ride, couldn't you?"

"You don't have a car?" he asked, a familiar sardonic edge in his voice.

Willow hid her disappointment by forcing a smile. "Don't worry about it. I'm sure I can figure something out."

Noah dragged his hand through his hair. "It's fine. I'll give you a ride but I'd like to be on the road within the hour."

They didn't get on the road in an hour. If they were lucky, they'd be on the road by two that afternoon.

The filming at the rocks hadn't exactly gone according to plan. Or, as Naomi explained to Noah after Willow's up-close-and-personal encounter with the deep blue sea, it had gone as it usually did whenever Willow was involved.

It had started off okay. In fact, better than okay. Willow had been beyond happy with how well it had gone. She was seconds from wrapping up and warning herself not to do a happy dance as soon as she signed off when the fisherman, who they later learned had never fished before but had agreed to be interviewed by Willow and then remain in the background, caught a fish.

He could barely contain his excitement, and Willow had clapped and cheered along with him. She hadn't cared if she looked unprofessional jumping up and down on the rocks, she was thrilled for him and got caught up in his happiness.

He'd had reason to be happy. He'd caught a blue fish, a big one, as in two feet long. Willow also knew it had to weigh at least fifteen pounds because, while reeling it in, the novice fisherman tried to swing it onto the rocks and hit Willow in the face with the fish instead, causing her to stumble and fall backward into the water.

The only positive thing to come out of it was that she'd gotten to hear Noah laugh again. The same deep, rumbly laugh she remembered from that long-ago summer. Except that when it came from the tall and exceptionally gorgeous man that Noah had become, she'd had an entirely different reaction.

She hadn't laughed herself silly as she had when she was fifteen. Nope, she'd gotten all hot and bothered. And when Noah had pulled her from the water, her body ending up pressed against his, she'd wondered if he knew. If her face hadn't given her away, she had a feeling her breathy "Thank you" had.

So that had been part of the delay. Noah went back to the hotel, showered, and changed, and Willow did the same at her place. Only she took longer because she had to help Naomi dry off the truck's seat and floor and listen to her complain about it smelling like fish.

When Noah met Willow back at the station an hour later, Don got hold of him, locking him in his office for another two hours while Willow convinced Veronica to cover for her when she was in New York. Convincing Veronica took less than a minute. She'd been dying for the opportunity to get on camera.

The rest of Willow's time was spent fielding suggestions about what to do with the five uninterrupted hours she had with Noah in the car. The longer she sat there waiting for him, the more outrageous the suggestions became. The one thing everyone agreed on was that this was the perfect opportunity to change Noah's mind, and they were counting on her to do it.

Which brought them to now.

"I promise, it'll take me two minutes at most," Willow said as Noah pulled alongside the curb in front of her rental. She'd gotten distracted helping Naomi clean her truck and had forgotten to pack a bag. She'd be in New York for at least two days.

Noah gave her a look that made her grin, and before she could remind herself that they weren't fifteen and best friends anymore, she launched herself across the console and kissed his cheek.

"Promise." She then launched herself out of the car before she did anything stupid. Or more stupid than kissing his cheek.

She ran up the steps, opened her door, smiled, waved at Noah, and then hurried into the two-bedroom house. She took the stairs two at a time and raced into her bedroom, wincing at her unmade bed, the clothes on the floor, and the empty boxes scattered around the room.

Grabbing a duffel bag from her closet, she walked to the dresser and pulled out drawers, pawing through the meager contents. Apparently, most of her underwear and nightwear were residing on the floor instead of in the drawer. She looked at the piles and, feeling overwhelmed, headed for the bathroom instead.

It was as messy as her bedroom but at least what she needed was sitting on the counter and the ledge of the bathtub. She swept her makeup into the cosmetic bag and tossed it into the duffel. As she turned to grab her shampoo, body wash, and hair products, she realized she needed to put them in a ziplock bag or the clothes she eventually packed would get wet. By the time she'd hunted down ziplock bags in her kitchen that was filled with half-packed boxes, she'd not only made a bigger mess, she'd gone over her promised two minutes by at least eighteen.

And she knew this because while kneeling on the floor in her bedroom, separating clean clothes from dirty ones in an effort to tidy up in case her landlord dropped by while she was away, she heard Noah yell into her house, "Willow, it's been twenty minutes. What are you...?" His voice trailed off before he finished his question.

She tossed the clothes from the clean pile on the floor into the duffel bag. "I'm coming!" she yelled, jumping up from the floor and running out of her bedroom.

She was attempting to zip the overstuffed duffel bag as she reached the stairs to see Noah standing in the entrance, staring into the living room.

"I'm moving," she said in an effort to excuse the disaster he'd walked into.

He didn't acknowledge her, and she wondered what had captured his attention. Following his gaze, she looked at the painting on the wall and smiled. Her mom had gifted her the painting on Willow's twenty-first birthday.

Willow hadn't been in the mood for celebrating. She'd had

a messy breakup with a man she'd thought was her one true love. In a family of cynics, she'd been a romantic. But he'd crushed her heart, destroyed her confidence, and made her feel like crap about herself and her life choices.

The painting was her mother's way of showing Willow how she saw her and how she wanted Willow to see herself. She'd titled it *The Heart of You*. In the painting, Willow lay on her stomach in the sand, her naked body gleaming golden in the sunlight, a pink floral scarf draped over her behind.

She looked as if she'd been caught midlaugh, her head thrown back in abandon, her blue eyes the same color as the ocean in the background, dancing with delight, her face lit up with happiness. The painting had become Willow's touchstone, a way back to herself.

"My mom painted it," she said as she walked down the stairs. "She's an incredible artist."

His eyes came to her. "She had an incredible subject."

Her cheeks warmed at not just his compliment but also how he looked at her when he gave it. Flustered by the intensity of his gaze and her reaction to it, she murmured, "Thank you" and then lifted her chin at the door. "We should probably get going."

He nodded, his gaze moving over the living room and kitchen. He shuddered.

"Hey, it's not that bad," she said, nudging him with her duffel bag. "I have a lot to pack, and I'm working."

He lifted an eyebrow at the clothes escaping from her bag. "It took you twenty minutes to pack an overnight bag."

"Sorry." She winced, shoving the leg of her jeans and the sleeve of her blouse into the duffel. "I had to sort through my clothes, and then I got worried my landlord would come in to check on things while I was away, and I tried tidying up a bit." She closed the door behind them and locked it.

"Unless there's an emergency, your landlord can't enter your home without your consent, Willow."

"Are you sure?" she asked, following him across the lawn to the car.

He held the car door open for her. "Positive. Did you not read your lease agreement?"

"Uh, no." She thought better of telling him she didn't have one.

Noah's gaze roamed her face, and whatever he saw made him shake his head. "You don't have a lease agreement."

"It's a small town. I've known my landlord since I was in grade school," she said instead of lying outright or telling him he'd surmised correctly.

"So what, you shook hands on it?" He sighed. "Of course you did." He closed her door and rounded the hood of the car.

Since he looked as if he planned on continuing the conversation when he got behind the wheel, she was relieved when his cell phone rang.

He looked at the screen, frowned, then connected the call. "Mrs. D, what's the—no, I'm not driving. Mrs. D, just spit it out." His face went blank as he listened to the woman on the other end.

From his blank expression, Willow wasn't sure whether he was bored or angry, but he cleared it up when he said in a voice coated in ice, "No, I do not want to talk to her. I'll deal with her when I get home."

He ended the call, started the car, and pulled onto the road. Eyes straight ahead, he said, "You're staying with me tonight. I'll bring you to the hospital in the morning."

If not for his ice-cold voice, Willow might've shouted, "Yippee!" She hadn't been looking forward to spending the night sleeping on a chair at the hospital anyway.

"Okay," she said slowly, afraid to anger him further. "And why am I staying with you?"

"To keep me from strangling my sister."

Chapter Six

Riley Bennett sat on a leather couch in her brother Noah's penthouse apartment in New York City, contemplating her summer wish list. Nowhere on her list did it say "Get picked up at the bus station by the cops."

She should've known Noah would've canceled their mom's credit card but she'd been hoping that, with all he'd had going on since their mom died, it would've slipped his mind.

Nothing slipped his mind. Nothing except her.

She'd heard from him ten times since she'd moved across the country to live with Billy, her father, in LA. She hadn't wanted to move or to live with Billy, who'd been even worse than Noah about staying in touch. So she'd barely known the guy, and what she'd known she hadn't really liked. And now that she'd been living with him and his new wife and their one-year-old twins for fifteen months, she pretty much hated him. If Billy's reaction to her fake news last month that she was attending the six-week GSTEM camp at NYU was anything to go by, he felt the same way about her.

He couldn't get rid of her fast enough. All he'd cared about was who was going to foot the bill for the camp. She'd lied and told him Noah was but that he'd have to pay for her flight. She'd planned on using her mother's credit card to buy a bus ticket from New York to Sunshine Bay. She'd been confident her father wouldn't call her brother. They didn't get along, like at all.

Billy had married their mother when Noah was thirteen. Billy blamed him for their divorce. Riley figured he was probably right to. Noah was smart, crazy smart. She bet that Noah had seen through Billy right away and done everything he could to get rid of him.

If her father had bothered to check, he would've discovered Noah didn't have a clue about the camp or that, with her grades, she wouldn't have been eligible anyway. With the move and everything, she'd missed a semester of school. She was starting tenth grade at a new school in the fall, something she didn't want to think about. She hadn't told anyone how nervous she was. Who would she tell anyway? It wasn't as if she had friends in LA, and all her father and his new wife cared about was the twins. Whatever. She didn't want to be stuck with them for the summer anyway.

She glanced at the wish list on her iPad. She'd made it after her father told her he wasn't going to put up with her moping around all summer with her nose stuck in a book and that she had to pull her weight around the house and help out with the twins. She missed her mom every day but she'd missed her even more when he'd said that to her. She needed to feel close to her mom again, and there was only one place she could think of where she would.

It wasn't the brownstone in New York where she'd lived her entire life. Her brother had sold it in January. Nearly everything that meant something to Riley and her mom had been sold in the estate sale. She'd been so mad at Noah when she'd found out what he'd done that she'd yelled at him, and no one yelled at her brother, even her mom. It was the first time she remembered Noah ever being angry, like really angry.

But he hadn't been angry at her. He'd been angry at Billy. Her father had told Noah that he didn't want her mom's stuff cluttering up his house and that Riley didn't want to be reminded of her mom and to go ahead and sell everything. He'd wanted the money from the sale, though.

It always came down to the money with him. As her legal guardian, Billy got an allowance—a generous one—from her trust fund to raise her. She didn't know what her mother had been thinking leaving her with him. Then again, it wasn't as if Riley could live on her own no matter how much she would've liked to. And it wasn't as if her single, workaholic brother had wanted her.

She glanced around Noah's apartment. It looked pretty much the same as his office—a lot of dark wood and heavy leather furniture—only with more rooms. There weren't any of her mom's things or any family photos or mementos that she could see. Then again, she hadn't snooped. Maybe he had some in his bedroom or his study. Except she kind of doubted it. He wasn't a sentimental guy. She had a few memories of being at his penthouse but Noah had mostly come to the brownstone for holiday dinners and such.

The only place left where she'd feel close to her mom was the beach house on Sunshine Bay. They'd gone a few times when Riley was younger but her mom had spent all her summers there as a kid. Staying at the beach house on Sunshine Bay was the first item on Riley's wish list. Now she just had to convince Noah not to send her back to LA and to let her spend the rest of the summer at the beach house . . . with him.

That was the second item on her list. Her brother was the only real family she had left.

She reached for the plate of cookies Mrs. D had left on the coffee table for her. She loved her brother's housekeeper and wished she could've stuck around so Riley would have support when Noah came home but it was getting late, and Mrs. D's husband had called three times, wondering when she'd be home.

At the sound of the penthouse door opening, Riley's hand froze over the plate of cookies. She scrambled back onto the couch, tucking herself into the corner. The excuses—lies—she'd come up with emptied out of her head now that Noah was here. She thought about pretending she was sleeping to put off facing her no-doubt-angry brother.

She heard a woman's voice and cringed. She'd met plenty of the women her brother had dated in the past. He had a type—models and socialites. Beautiful women who had no interest in getting to know his little sister. As super smart as her brother was, he didn't make very good choices when it came to the women he dated. Then again, they'd never lasted longer than a few weeks so maybe he didn't care, as long as they looked good on his arm. Except she didn't think Noah cared about that either. But what did she know?

A woman rounded the corner and blinked. Then her lips lifted in a smile, a wide, dazzling smile that made Riley feel like crying. She blinked to ward off the tears gathering in her eyes—how weird was that?—and tried offering one of her own. Her smile wobbled when her brother came into view.

The woman must've noticed because she turned on Noah and lightly swatted his chest. Riley's eyes went wide. She didn't know anyone who would dare swat her brother when he was angry, and he very obviously was. Most of the time people would run in the opposite direction.

"Noah, stop looking at her like that. You're scaring her."

Her brother looked down his nose at the lady—she was tall but Noah was way taller—and raised an eyebrow.

The woman rolled her eyes and laughed. Laughed!

Riley held her breath, waiting for her brother to explode. He didn't. Instead, he did something as shocking as Riley's urge to cry. He smiled. It wasn't a big smile, more like a twitch of his lips. Still, Riley gawked at him with her mouth hanging open.

His gaze moved to her, and he rolled his eyes. She might've laughed if he didn't follow up his eye roll with a raised finger, pointing it at her. "I have a call to make, and when I'm done, you have some explaining to do, Riley."

She gave a jerky nod. "Noah," she called when he turned to walk away.

He glanced over his shoulder.

"Please don't call Billy."

The woman stared at Noah's retreating back and shook her head. "All that man does is work," she said as she walked toward Riley.

She was beautiful, like way more beautiful than any of the women her brother had dated in the past. She had long, wavy blond hair and blue eyes that sparkled. She didn't dress anything like her brother's previous girlfriends. She wore pink sneakers with faded jeans and a sheer, flowy, floral top over a camisole instead of a tight, revealing dress and sky-high heels.

"Hi, Riley. I'm Willow," she said, extending her hand.

Riley shook it, thinking her name was cool, just like her. "Hi," she said. Then she asked, even though it was probably rude, but she couldn't help it because she was curious, "Are you my brother's girlfriend?"

Willow grinned, taking a seat beside Riley on the couch. "No." Then she added, maybe because Riley's disappointment showed on her face, "But we were friends a long time ago, when we were fifteen. We met at Hidden Cove on Sunshine Bay. We were pretty much inseparable for three weeks that summer."

Riley gasped. They'd known each other when they were the same age as her! "Do you live in Sunshine Bay or just vacation there?"

"I live there." She waved a hand in the direction of the study. "I actually work at Channel 5. I'm a weathergirl, or I should say weatherperson."

"That's so cool!"

Willow wrinkled her nose. "Between you and me, I'm not a very good weatherperson."

"I don't believe you. I bet you're really good at it." She couldn't imagine Willow being bad at anything she did.

"Aw, thanks, honey." She gave Riley a hug.

Riley froze. She couldn't remember the last time someone had hugged her. Her throat began to tickle and the backs of her eyes burned.

Willow pulled away. "I'm sorry. I can't seem to help myself. I'm affectionate but I need to remember that not everyone is."

"It's okay. I didn't mind."

Willow's gaze roamed her face, and her smile faltered. Riley didn't think she believed her and was going to explain her reaction. But she kind of didn't want to because she was afraid she might cry if she told Willow no one had hugged her since her mom's funeral.

Willow reached in her back pocket and pulled out her phone, entering a passcode. "Trust me. You'll believe me after you see this. Here, watch." She pressed Start.

It was a video of Willow delivering the weather in a lobster costume. Not once, but several times, and in each one, something hysterical happened to her.

By the time the video ended, Riley was laughing so hard that she could barely speak. Once she'd stopped laughing, she said, "You have to put that on TikTok."

"No way. It's bad enough everyone in Sunshine Bay thinks I'm an idiot," she said, then groaned. "If my coworkers think there's a chance it'll go viral, and they can figure out a way to monetize the video, they'll totally do it, especially now that we're all going to lose our jobs." She squeezed her eyes shut and gave her head a small shake. "Ignore me. I shouldn't have said that."

"It's okay. I know my brother is selling off Bennett Broadcasting. Our mom would want him to. I want him to." She bit her lip at how that must sound to Willow and tried to explain. "It's a lot, running the company. Noah's a lawyer and the head of the legal department and mostly doesn't have a life outside of work. It's worse now that he's taken over from our mom." She clenched her teeth before continuing, her voice barely a whisper. "Our mom worked all the time too. Running the company killed her. She wouldn't want Noah to have a heart attack and die like she did."

"Oh, Riley, I'm so sorry about your mom."

Riley didn't know why, maybe it was the compassion in Willow's eyes or maybe it was because she'd kept everything bottled up inside since her mom died, but she threw herself sobbing into Willow's arms and told her everything, even about her wish list. And while she did, Willow murmured words of comfort and stroked her hair, and then she muttered what she'd do to Billy if she ever saw him, and that made Riley snort-laugh.

When Riley finally stopped crying and snort-laughing, she pulled away from Willow, embarrassed. "I'm sorry. I—"

Willow cut her off by putting her hands on Riley's shoulders and looking her in the eyes. It was then she realized Willow had been crying too. "You don't have a single thing to apologize for. I'm honored that you felt comfortable sharing with me." She swiped a finger under her lashes, gave a firm nod as if she'd convinced herself of something, and smiled. "Now we just have to figure out a way for you to accomplish your goals, starting with spending the summer in Sunshine Bay."

Riley stared at her in awe. "You're going to help me?"

"Of course I am. Just think of me as your fairy godmother."

Riley giggled. Giggled! "You look more like a fairy princess than a fairy godmother."

"You're sweet," Willow murmured as she glanced down the hall, looking preoccupied. Then she returned her gaze to Riley. "The first thing we have to do is convince your brother to go along with my plan."

Riley's shoulders slumped, and she shook her head. "He won't."

"He has to," Willow said with a determined expression on her face. "There's nothing more important than family. And Riley, I think, as much as you need him, your brother needs you. We just have to make him see that."

Riley wasn't as confident as Willow. Her brother didn't seem to need anyone. "He doesn't really like to be told what to do."

Willow laughed. "You're not telling me something I don't know." Her laughter faded, and she took both of Riley's hands in hers. "I need to be honest with you. If we can convince Noah to let you stay at the beach house for the summer, it works for me too. I'm trying to convince him to sell Channel 5 instead of closing the station, and I need time to do that."

"He's not selling it?" Riley asked, surprised. Her mom had always told her that the TV station on Sunshine Bay had a special place in Riley's grandfather's heart. It was where Bennett Broadcasting Group had gotten its start.

"No, he supposedly tried and got no interest. I think part of the problem was that he doesn't feel Channel 5 is a viable investment and didn't try very hard. But my coworkers and I have some really good ideas to increase revenue and viewership. We just need time to implement them." She smiled and gave Riley's hands a little shake. "But even if I didn't personally benefit from you, and hopefully Noah, staying in Sunshine Bay this summer, I'd still want to help you."

"Why?"

"Because I remember what it's like being fifteen. It can suck, and even having a loving and supportive family like I did, and still do, it took a fifteen-year-old nerd with dark hair, glasses, and braces, who at first didn't want anything to do with me—"

Riley's eyes went wide. "How could he not want anything to do with *you*?"

Willow laughed. "You'll have to ask your brother."

"Noah was the nerd?"

"He was, and he also turned one of the worst summers of my life into one of the happiest. And I want to do that for you."

"So Noah was like your fairy godmother?" Riley's voice

gurgled with laughter as she pictured her tall and handsome big brother wearing a dress and waving a wand.

Willow grinned. "More like my Prince Charming," she said, then wrinkled her nose. "It would be easier to convince him if he was still my Prince Charming instead of Mercedes Man and CEO Noah."

Riley frowned. She was about to ask Willow what she meant when she heard a sound. She glanced over Willow's shoulder, letting out a small *eek* to warn her that Noah was walking into the living room.

Willow must've mistaken her warning *eek* for a distressed *eek* because she didn't look around or stop talking. "Don't worry, honey. You leave everything to me. I'll convince Noah—"

Her brother fisted his hands on his hips and said, "No."

Willow whirled around. "What do you mean no? You don't even know what I was going to say."

"All I needed to hear was 'I'll convince Noah' to know what my answer will be, and I'll repeat, the answer is no. Absolutely not."

Willow gasped and shot to her feet. "You can't say no!"

"I just did."

Willow closed the short distance between them and leaned into him. "Well, you can't. I'm not one of your employees who you can simply boss around or ignore."

Noah crossed his arms and raised an eyebrow. "Does your paycheck come from Bennett Broadcasting Group?"

"Fine. Maybe I am, but this has nothing to do with that. It has to do with your sister."

"Yes, *my* sister." He raised his gaze to Riley. "The study, now," he said before returning his gaze to Willow. "My housekeeper has no doubt prepared a meal for me. Feel free to eat it. The kitchen is that way." He lifted a hand, pointing in the direction of the kitchen.

"Riley, stay right where you are," Willow ordered without looking at her. Then she rose up on her toes and got way into the space of Riley's now seriously ticked-off brother. "You will lecture her over my dead body."

"Don't tempt me," Noah said, his voice low and flat.

"You have no idea, absolutely no idea, what she's suffered. And do you know why that is, Noah? Because you don't call her every day, you don't even call her once a week or once a month!" And then Willow told him everything Riley had told her. Riley didn't know whether to laugh or cry, but she was leaning toward laughing at the dazed expression on her brother's face as he watched Willow, who was kind of dramatic, and the way she talked about Billy was all kinds of funny.

But when Willow stopped talking and let out a shuddered sob, Noah's face softened, and he lifted a hand to the back of Willow's head and brought it gently to his chest, gathering her into his arms.

Then he looked at Riley with the same soft expression on his face and held out his arm. "Come here, Tink. You can stay at the beach house," he said, and Riley started crying. Not because he'd made her wish come true but because he'd used her nickname. The one her mom had called her.

Chapter Seven

Cami woke up in the hospital bed for the second day in a row. The previous day was a blur. She'd slept through most of it but there were a couple of things that stood out. She lifted the sheet. She hadn't been dreaming. She had boobs. Big boobs! She remembered thinking they didn't feel like normal boobs. She'd touched them to make sure. She thought about touching them again, just to make sure they were still there and it wasn't just that the sheet had bunched up.

She peeked over the sheet to make sure she was alone, groaning when she spotted the dark-haired woman sitting in the chair across from her hospital bed. She was on her . . . Cami searched her brain for what she'd called it. Then it came to her, an iPad. Whatever the heck an iPad was. All Cami knew was that it was in Gail's hands. All. The. Time.

That was the woman's name, and she'd been there since Cami had first woken up in the hospital. She'd told Cami she was her PA. Cami hadn't known what a PA was, but she'd figured out later it must be a short form for *pain in the ass*. She felt sort of bad for thinking about Gail as a pain in the ass. She was mostly nice, and she seemed upset Cami didn't have a freaking clue who she was, but she wouldn't let Cami call her family. Who did that? A PA, that was who.

Cami's mother and sisters would be worried sick about her. Angry too. At least her mother would be when she got a load of the cast on Cami's right arm. Cami wouldn't be waiting tables for a while. Her sisters would have her back, though. They always did. They were the best. She loved her sisters more than anything. She loved her mother too, but she could be a PA. Even more of a PA than Gail.

Cami's mother was strict, way stricter with her than she'd been with her sisters. Her sisters said it was because Cami pushed their mother's buttons and no one knew what she'd get up to next. According to them, she'd been precocious as a child and was wild as a teenager. Cami conceded that she'd been a little out of control in her early teens but that had changed when she started dating Flynn.

She glanced at her cast, imagining her mother's reaction when she found out what had happened. Cami never should've taken a running leap off the dunes on a dare, especially in the dark. She wouldn't have if she hadn't been drinking with her friends. If her mother found out she'd been drinking, she'd probably ground her for the rest of her life.

It was Flynn's fault. Not the drinking too much or the jumping off the dunes in the dark, but why she'd been in the mood to drink. He'd been her boyfriend for two years, and now she didn't know what he was to her. Things hadn't been the same between them since he'd gone away to college, and the other night, she'd made them worse. He'd been mad at her for flirting and drinking, but what had he expected? She'd missed him like crazy when he was away, and she'd thought she'd have him home for the whole summer.

But on their way to the party at the dunes, he'd told her he'd decided to take a summer class and was going back in two days. So of course she'd acted out and flirted. Who wouldn't when her boyfriend decided he'd rather take a course at his fancy new school with his fancy new friends than spend the summer with her?

He'd be gone by now. He might not even know she'd been hurt. He'd left the party early. It was the guy she'd been flirting with who had taken care of her while they waited for the ambulance.

A dull ache spread behind her eyes as she tried to remember his name. He was hot, as hot as Flynn, but his good looks were more in your face. He knew it too. He was cocky and a little wild. She rubbed her fingers between her eyes as she searched her brain for his name. The dull ache morphed into a sharp, blinding pain, and she whimpered.

"Cami, are you all right?"

As the pain subsided, Cami opened her eyes to see Gail looking concerned and rising from the chair. "I'm okay. I just want to go home."

"The doctor will be in shortly. If he okays your release, you can go home today," Gail said, walking toward the bed. The door to Cami's hospital room opened before Gail reached her, and she turned.

A woman walked in. She hesitated and then gave Cami and Gail a nervous smile while leaning back and motioning for someone they couldn't see beyond the door. Cami didn't recognize the woman but she looked a little like Cami herself, only a lot older. She wondered if they were related somehow, and the thought made her chest tighten. Was her mother so mad at her that she'd sent a relative Cami didn't know to come get her?

Cami wouldn't be surprised if she had. A few months earlier, her mother had disowned Cami's oldest sister just because she'd gotten married. It had been awful, and Flynn being away at school had made it worse. The backs of Cami's eyes began stinging. She hated that her mother and sister weren't talking. She hated that her sister had moved away, just like Flynn. Nothing was the same anymore. She wanted Flynn back, and she wanted her family back the way it used to be.

As Cami was thinking this, struggling not to cry, a man walked up behind the woman. Cami's mouth dropped open. What the heck were they giving her for pain medication? The man looked like the guy she'd been flirting with at the dunes, only he was way older, and his hair was dark, not fair.

The ache behind Cami's eyes came back, and she rubbed her fingers up and down the bridge of her nose in an attempt to take the pain away.

Gail didn't notice. She was too busy smiling and walking toward the man and woman with her hand extended. "Willow. I'm so glad you could come. They're releasing Cami today. She wants to go home."

What a weird name, Cami thought, wondering what would possess someone to name their kid Willow.

"That's great," Willow said, giving Cami a tentative smile as she gestured to the man behind her. "This is Noah, and this . . ."—she reached around the man and drew a girl from behind him—"is Riley. Noah's sister."

Cami's chest loosened when she saw someone close to her age. Riley had shoulder-length dark hair, big hazel eyes, and freckles sprinkled on her nose and cheeks. She looked nice, and Cami decided to test this theory by smiling at Riley and giving her a finger wave.

Riley returned her smile and waved.

Cami opened her mouth to tell Riley she could come sit on the bed with her if she wanted but got distracted when Gail said, "She wants to go home to *Sunshine Bay*, Willow."

Gail made it sound as if she were giving away state secrets. Cami supposed she shouldn't be surprised. Gail had been saying weird things in weird ways since Cami opened her eyes the day before.

"Oh," Willow said, looking as if Gail had told her Cami wanted to walk on the moon. "I thought she'd want to go to LA."

Of course Cami wanted to go to LA. Who didn't? She wanted to be an actress. Maybe her mother had shared that with this Willow person. "I can't go to LA. I'm only seventeen," she said in case her mother had forgotten to mention her age.

They stared at her, and Willow looked as if she was about to hurl. The man dipped his head to Willow's ear and said something. She closed her eyes and nodded, murmuring, "I'm okay."

Why was he worried about her? She wasn't the one lying in a hospital bed with a broken arm and a headache. A doctor came into the room, followed by Cami's nurse from the previous day. Cami wasn't a fan of the nurse. Every time Cami asked to call her mother or her sisters, she deferred to PA Gail, and every time Cami asked for a mirror, she ignored her. She wouldn't even let Cami get up to go to the bathroom. She had to use a freaking bedpan. Cami couldn't wait to get out of there, which was why, when the doctor smiled and asked how she was feeling, Cami said, "Great!"

"No headaches or dizziness?"

"Nope," Cami said, shaking her head. She immediately stopped shaking it. She felt as if she were on a ride at the fair, and now she probably looked as if *she* wanted to hurl.

"Good. Now, I just have a few questions for you," the doctor said, pulling a stool to the bed. He had one of those iPad things too. "Cami, do you know who the president is?"

This again? Seriously? "Bill Clinton." She sighed, sharing a *duh* look with Riley, who was standing beside her brother. Riley pressed her lips together as if she was trying not to laugh. "And before you ask, it's July 12, 1994. I'm seventeen. My mother is Carmen Rosetti, and my sisters are Gia and Eva. Our family owns La Dolce Vita, an Italian restaurant on Sunshine Bay." She smiled at the doctor. "Now can I go home?"

He patted her hand and then turned to Willow, who'd come to stand at the foot of the bed. "You're Ms. Monroe's niece?"

Who the heck was Ms. Monroe? And what did she have to do with Cami?

Willow glanced at Cami, bit her bottom lip, and nodded. "I am."

"I'll be releasing your aunt into your care, but I'll need to go over a few things with you before she's discharged," the doctor said, and stood up.

Willow didn't look as if she was going to hurl anymore. She looked as if she was having a panic attack. "Can you, uh, give me a second, please?" She whirled around before the doctor answered and grabbed the Noah guy's hand, dragging him out the door.

"While Willow's talking to Noah, we should get you dressed, Cami," Gail said. She walked to the chair, picked up a suitcase Cami hadn't noticed, and then returned to her side. Setting the suitcase on the foot of the bed, Gail opened it.

Cami stared at the underwear, dress, and high heels Gail held out to her. How old did she think she was, forty? "Whose clothes are those?"

Gail glanced at the nurse, who nodded. "They're yours."

Cami made big eyes at Riley and then said to Gail, "Ah, no they're not. Look at them. Do I look like I'd wear something like that? Maybe you got Willow's aunt's suitcase."

"You are Willow's aunt, Cami," Gail said carefully.

"No, I'm not. She's old! Besides, her aunt's name is Ms. Monroe."

"You're Ms. Monroe," the nurse said in a calm, soothing voice. "You were hit by an e-bike and—"

Cami's heart raced, and she strained to get the words out of her mouth. Her brain felt fuzzy. "No. I jumped off the sand dunes and broke my arm."

The nurse nodded. "You're right, you did. In July 1994." She reached for Cami's hand and gave it a reassuring squeeze. "It's 2024, and you didn't jump off a sand dune. You were hit by an e-bike."

Cami's gaze shot to Riley, seeking support from the only person in the room she trusted. She didn't know why she trusted her to tell her the truth but she did.

Riley glanced at Gail and the nurse as she walked to the side of the bed. "It's true. It's 2024, and Joe Biden is president, not Bill Clinton."

"But it can't be true. That would mean I'm ... I'd be ..." Her eyes felt as if they were going to pop out of her head.

"Forty-seven. Look at me. I can't be forty-seven." Frantic, she reached for Riley's hand but half of Cami's was in a cast. "Do I look like I'm forty-seven?"

Riley's hand gently closed around the fingers that poked from Cami's cast. "No."

Cami let out the breath she'd been holding but sucked it back in when Riley continued. "You look like you're in your early thirties. You're really pretty," Riley rushed on as if her heart was racing as fast as Cami's. "I've seen one of your movies, and you're a really good actress too."

"I'm an actress?"

Riley nodded. "You were nominated for an Oscar."

This time Cami's heart raced from excitement, not panic. Of course she was still panicked but the news that her dream of winning an Oscar might've come true overrode the bad news that she'd slept through more than half her life. At least in that second it did. "Really? Did I win?"

The nurse chimed in before Riley could answer. "You suffered a blow to your head and have amnesia, Cami. It might take some time but the doctor is confident your memories will return." She smiled. "I know this is difficult. But you're lucky. Your injuries could've been much worse."

"I need to go to the bathroom." She needed to see for herself that she wasn't seventeen. And this time they couldn't stop her.

The nurse nodded and glanced at Gail. "Do you have a mirror?"

"Now you're going to let me look at myself?"

"We were hoping your memory would've returned this morning, and we didn't want to upset you if it wasn't necessary," Gail said, getting a bag out of the suitcase. She unzipped it, took out a compact, and handed it to Cami. "You aren't wearing makeup, and you haven't done your hair, but you'll look more like yourself once—"

Cami opened the compact, held it up to her face, and screamed. The face in the mirror blurred in front of her eyes and then everything went black.

Chapter Eight

You don't think she fainted again, do you?" Willow whispered to Noah as she glanced in the back seat of the Mercedes. Riley had on headphones, listening to an audiobook, while Willow's aunt listed to the side, her head lolling on her shoulder.

It would be an understatement to say Noah had been unhappy with Willow's suggestion that Cami stay at the beach house with Riley until Willow had broken the news to her family that her estranged aunt was in town.

Even the doctor, who'd stopped to speak to Willow after leaving her aunt's hospital room, had taken one look at Noah and told Willow he'd leave the paperwork, instructions for her aunt's care, and his number should she have any concerns at the nurse's station. Willow had just shared her aunt-staying-at-the-beach-house idea with Noah.

Her aunt's bloodcurdling scream had interrupted Noah telling Willow just how unhappy he was.

He raised his aviator-covered eyes to the rearview mirror. "No. The doctor told you what to expect. She's sleeping. Feel free to do the same."

After her aunt's fainting episode, the doctor had ordered

a precautionary CT scan and some other tests, which hadn't raised any further concerns, and that was when he'd shared with Willow the instructions for her aunt's care, verbally and on paper. Noah hadn't been in the room when the doctor spoke to her. He'd taken a call and had been in the hall, but he'd read the paperwork while they waited for her aunt to be released.

"I'm not taking a nap while you're driving, Noah. That would be rude. Besides, you didn't get much sleep last night."

As soon as Riley and Willow had stopped sobbing in his arms and then celebrating Riley coming to Sunshine Bay for the summer, Noah had ordered them to eat and retired to his study. He'd been on the phone when Willow peeked in to say good night after midnight. He'd nodded and continued with his conversation.

"You don't have to worry I'll fall asleep at the wheel, Willow. I can function on very little sleep."

"I don't like to argue with you but we covered a story—"

"We've clearly established that you do. You've argued with me more than anyone in my entire life, and I've been in your company for less than forty-eight hours."

"Are you talking about friends or employees or friends who are employees? Because if you're talking about employees or friends who are employees, they don't count. They wouldn't argue with you because you're their boss."

He turned his head and raised an eyebrow.

She grinned. "Your scary-angry face doesn't work on me. I was around when you were perfecting it at fifteen." She didn't share that rather than finding the look that came over his face intimidating, she found it devastatingly attractive.

"Scary-angry face?"

Before she could respond, his phone rang. She sighed. Of course it did. His phone never stopped ringing. It had been the same when they'd driven to New York the day before.

"Robyn, I'm in the car. You're on speaker."

"It's just me, Robyn," Willow said, waving her fingers even though Noah's assistant obviously couldn't see her. She'd gotten to know Robyn on the drive to New York and liked her a lot.

Noah angled his head, looking at her through his sunglasses. If she could see his eyes, she imagined they'd be giving her a *seriously?* look.

"Hi, Willow. How did it go with your aunt?"

Willow smiled. Robyn was so nice. "It—"

"Robyn, I imagine you were calling me for a reason. A reason that has nothing to do with Willow and her aunt."

"Noah!" Willow gasped, then, noting the firm set of his jaw, decided not to push her luck. She didn't want him taking out his frustration with her on Robyn. It had become obvious over the course of the past twenty-four hours that Willow frustrated him a lot. "I'll get your number from Noah, and we can chat later, Robyn."

"I'd love that!"

"Do you mind if I talk to Robyn now?"

"Be my guest," she said, pressing her lips together to keep from laughing. Noah had no idea how easy he was to tease or how much she enjoyed getting a reaction from him.

Robyn's voice came through the speaker, sounding professional and competent, which Willow knew, from listening to what had felt like hours of their conversations, she was. Then again, Noah wouldn't put up with anyone who wasn't excellent at their job.

"I got in touch with the real estate agent first thing this

morning as you requested, Noah, and asked her to pause the beach house listing. She had an interested party and wasn't pleased. I have a feeling you'll be hearing from her."

"I don't know why I would, but I trust your read on the situation, Robyn. Thanks for the heads-up."

In the past twenty-four hours, Willow had discovered several things she liked about CEO Noah. As much as he was driven and demanding and didn't suffer incompetence lightly, his employees clearly liked and respected him. In all the conversations she'd been privy to, and there had been many, he had been polite, respectful, and appreciative.

She'd suspected he was a micromanager and had been surprised to discover he wasn't. He was confident in his staff's ability to deal with difficult negotiations and routinely delegated assignments, even if his staff believed they required his expertise. And it had to be said that Noah was extremely good at his job. But if his employees weren't as confident in their abilities as Noah was, he patiently coached them until they were, and when those same negotiations went smoothly, he refused to take credit.

"No problem," Robyn said. "I've heard back from the IT specialist that I had check on your home office at the beach house. There are issues that may take him some time to resolve so I'm afraid working remotely will be difficult. The network is patchy."

"That's fine. I'll come back to New York and work in the office until—"

"You don't have to, Noah." Willow jumped into the conversation, unwilling to let the opportunity pass. "I'm sorry for interrupting but there are no network issues at the station, and I'm sure Don would be happy to give up his office for you."

"Willow's right, Noah. It's a good option."

She wanted to kiss Robyn. It wasn't a good option. It was perfect. Willow would have Noah right where she wanted him. He'd get to know her coworkers and realize what Channel 5 meant to them, and what it meant to the people of Sunshine Bay.

"I suppose that would work. At least until I get Riley settled. If you could let Don know—"

"It's okay. I can take care of it, Robyn," Willow said, holding up her phone.

"No worries, Willow. I've got it. Thanks, though."

"She's waving her phone and bouncing in her seat, Robyn, so it's safe to say Willow would like to handle it."

Robyn chuckled. "Works for me."

"Yay! I'll get on it right now."

She couldn't help herself and did another little dance in her seat. She felt Noah's eyes on her, so she smiled at him and shrugged. He shook his head and returned to his conversation with Robyn, setting up what sounded like a hundred meetings to take place over the next few days.

Seconds after she'd shared the awesome news with Don, Naomi, and Veronica and gotten things sorted on their end, she bit the bullet and called her sister. Her call went to voicemail, and she left a message for Sage to call her back. As soon as she disconnected, her cell phone rang. She glanced at the screen. It wasn't Sage, it was Megan.

Willow took a deep breath and brought the phone to her ear. "Hey. What's up?"

"Where are you? And don't try and tell me you're at work. I called the station and the restaurant."

Willow swore under her breath, murmuring, "Sorry"

when Noah glanced her way. Flipping Megan was going to ruin everything. Willow hadn't been scheduled to work at the restaurant the night before, so she hadn't needed to come up with an excuse as to why she needed the night off. Her mom and grandmother didn't have time to watch Willow's dinner-hour weather reports, and it wasn't as if anyone who did would say anything. Lucy the Lobster was delivering the weather, and that was all anyone cared about.

"Who did you say sorry to? Are you with someone?"

"I am, so if you don't mind, I'll talk to you when I get home." Willow heard Megan breathing over the line.

Noah interrupted Robyn, who was relaying an issue with one of the lawyers of a company in negotiations to buy a block of Bennett Broadcasting's holdings, with a "He what?" that was one decimal shy of a bellow.

Willow stared at him, stunned, and then realized she hadn't disconnected from Megan. "Okay. Gotta go. Bye."

She wasn't fast enough, and she knew this because Megan screeched in her ear. "I knew it! You're with Noah."

"So what if I am?"

"Really? You ruin my sale, and that's all you have to say?" Megan blew a gusty breath over the line. "Honestly, I don't know why I'm friends with you. You can't take it that I'm successful, can you?"

"Please tell me you're not actually accusing me of sabotaging the sale of the beach house because I'm jealous of you?" Willow whispered, partly because she was stunned by the accusation and partly because she didn't want Noah to hear her.

"Robyn, I need to take care of something. I'll call you back."

Willow closed her eyes, praying he wasn't disconnecting from Robyn because he'd heard her. She knew her prayers had gone unanswered when Noah said, "Willow, put Megan on speaker."

Willow waved her hand, mouthing, *It's fine* only for Megan to continue ranting in her ear. "That's exactly what I'm accusing you of. I've made top real estate agent of the year for two years running, and you're a part-time weather girl who runs around in a lobster costume. Of course you're jealous of me."

"You do it or I will," Noah said.

Willow's shoulders rose and fell on a sigh, and then she reluctantly did what he asked. "Megan, you're on—"

"Don't try and deny it, Willow. I should've dumped your sorry ass after the fiasco with the house flip. Everyone warned me not to go into business with you, but did I listen? No. I did not."

Noah raised an eyebrow as if asking Willow if she wanted to respond but she was so shocked she didn't know what to say.

Obviously taking her stunned silence as permission to intervene, he said, "Megan, this is Noah Elliot. I heard one side of your conversation with Willow, and you seem to be under the mistaken impression that she was the reason I paused the sale of the beach house."

"Ah, hi, Noah. No. I . . ." Megan blew out another of her put-upon breaths before saying, "I'm sorry, Willow, but I can't cover for you any longer. Noah deserves to know the truth."

Willow frowned. "The truth?"

"Yes. He deserves to know that there's *nothing* you wouldn't do to keep him from closing the station. She wanted me to stall the sale of the beach house and of the building on Main

Street to give her time to change your mind about closing Channel 5, Noah."

"You're not telling me anything I don't know, Megan. And to be honest with you, I find Willow's loyalty to her coworkers and to Channel 5 admirable."

"You do?" Willow blurted.

He smiled. "I do."

"Another man falls to the Rosetti charms," Megan muttered before adding, "Well, good luck with that, Noah. Willow is known as one of the Heartbreakers of Sunshine Bay for a reason. None of her relationships, and let me tell you, she's had many, last more than a few weeks. But hey, I'm sure you'll enjoy it while it lasts. I hear she's good in bed."

Without looking at Noah—she didn't want to see his reaction—Willow took the phone off speaker and brought it to her ear. "What the hell was that?"

"The truth."

"No. It wasn't the truth, Megan. It was you behaving true to form when something doesn't go your way. You owe me an apology, a big one, a humongous one, and until I get it, I don't want to talk to you." She disconnected, barely restraining herself from throwing the phone at the windshield.

She glanced at Noah. "I'm sorry you—"

He held up a finger, and she realized he was waiting for a call to connect. His jaw was tight, his expression blank, and when a woman answered, "Cape Cod Realty," his voice was as cold as ice. "This is Noah Elliot. Put me through to your boss."

"Yes, sir. Right away, Mr. Elliot."

"Thank you."

Willow groaned. There was only one reason Noah would

put in a call to Megan's boss. He was going to demand his listings be given to someone else. She might be furious with Megan but she'd been her best friend forever, and Willow didn't want her to suffer the consequences of what Noah was about to do. "Can we talk about this, please? I know Megan was—"

"Don't defend her."

Willow didn't get a chance. Megan's boss came on the line. And from the simper in her voice, if Noah asked her to fire Megan and strip her of her real estate license, Willow had little doubt the woman would make it happen. She made it clear she'd do anything to make Noah happy and not lose him as a client. Willow wondered what it must be like to have everyone groveling at your feet, willing to do whatever you asked.

Unable to stand any more of Megan's boss kissing up to Noah, Willow glanced in the back seat, thinking she'd chat with Riley. But Riley, like Willow's aunt, was asleep. At least Riley was asleep. Willow was a little worried Cami was comatose and reached between the seats to gently shake her leg, relieved when her aunt muttered, "Leave me alone."

She would've been more relieved if her aunt hadn't muttered her demand in the voice of a surly teenager. When Cami had come to after fainting, she'd refused to hear anything about her life as a forty-seven-year-old, and she had done this by acting like a four-year-old and covering her ears.

The doctor had advised Willow not to challenge Cami or put any undue pressure on her to remember. Instead, he'd recommended that she slowly reintroduce her aunt to people and places that would trigger her memory. Willow knew three people who'd be triggered by seeing Cami in Sunshine

Bay—her mother and grandmother, and her other aunt, when she returned from England.

With Cami staying at the beach house, Willow had bought herself some time. She'd told Cami that the family had taken a much-deserved vacation and would be away for a week. But unless her aunt's memory returned within a few days, she doubted she could keep her under wraps for that long. Sunshine Bay wasn't exactly New York City. She had no choice. She needed backup.

She faced forward, about to try calling her sister again, when she heard Noah say, "Correct. I want the sale of the building and equipment paused as well. I'll be running the company from the station in the interim."

"So you want both sales paused until the end of August?" Megan's boss asked.

"No, slate the building and equipment in for the first week of August, possibly sooner. It all depends on the contractor. I'll be in touch if anything changes."

Yay! She had more than two weeks to change his mind. Willow celebrated in her head, refraining from doing another happy dance in her seat.

Noah said goodbye and disconnected. "Willow, nothing's changed," he said, his voice firm.

"Why would you say that? I know you won't change your mind."

"Really? So why do you look like you were caught mid-dance?"

She looked down at herself. He was right. "I was just exercising my fingers." She glanced at him. "Megan was telling you the truth, you know. I did ask her to stall the sales to give me more time to change your mind."

"She doesn't deserve your loyalty, Willow. But I appreciate

your honesty, even if it's unnecessary. As I told her, you're not telling me anything I didn't already know."

"So you won't be surprised when I tell you I'm not giving up?"

He sighed. "No. I'd be more surprised if you did. But Willow, the outcome will be the same. No matter what you do."

She briefly closed her eyes. Megan owed her way more than an apology. "Okay, it was obvious what Megan was implying, but I hope you know me better than that, Noah. I wouldn't try and manipulate you or seduce you to get you to change your mind."

"You could try," he said with a wolfish grin. "But even with your considerable *charms*, I should warn you that I'm immune to seduction and manipulation when it comes to business."

She stared at him. "Did you just say you wanted me to try and seduce you?"

Before he could answer, a petulant voice from the back seat asked, "Are we there yet?"

Chapter Nine

We'll be there soon," Willow told her aunt, casting a distracted smile over her shoulder before turning on Noah. "I can't believe you're suggesting that I try and seduce you," she whispered, ignoring the butterflies dancing in her stomach.

"I was teasing you, Willow. I thought it was time for a little payback. Or are you going to deny you've spent the better part of today teasing me?"

"I didn't tease you like that! And in case you've forgotten, we have an impressionable teenager in the car."

"Two."

"Two what?"

"Two impressionable teenagers."

She groaned. "Don't remind me."

"Ah, Noah, I kind of have to go to the bathroom," Riley said.

Willow swatted Noah's arm, sending a pointed look from the back seat to him.

"She didn't hear me," he said under his breath before meeting Riley's gaze in the rearview mirror. "We'll be at Willow's place in about five minutes."

Willow's gaze shot to the familiar scenery rushing past the passenger-side window. She hadn't been paying attention. She looked back at her aunt. "Cami, you should catch a few more z's. The doctor said you need lots of sleep, remember? And it'll take me a while to pack up some things for you."

Her aunt had refused to wear her own clothes and was wearing a pair of pull-on palazzo pants Willow had brought with her and the top Willow had worn the day before, albeit with a pair of Jimmy Choos that probably cost more than Willow made in a month. Apparently seventeen-year-old Cami didn't have a problem wearing designer heels.

"And a bag for yourself," Noah reminded Willow.

"I don't think that's a good idea."

And she knew this because, even before he'd teased her about seducing him, she'd fantasized about kissing him. She blamed being trapped in a car with him for five hours, ten if she included today, for those hot, seductive images that were burned into her brain. Then again, he was the most beautiful man she'd ever seen. He even smelled great, and his deep, velvet-smooth voice...Yeah, totally fantasy inducing.

After Noah had held her in his arms at his apartment the night before, her fantasies had progressed from kissing to making out, and she was afraid the temptation of being under the same roof with him for a week would be too much to withstand. She wasn't exactly known for her self-discipline. It didn't help that she hadn't had sex in almost a year. In an effort to become a contributing, responsible adult who would make her family proud, she'd sworn off men.

Earlier today, when Noah had told her the only way Cami was staying with him and Riley was if she did too, she hadn't protested. There'd been benefits, not the friends-with-benefits kind—at least, that wasn't what she'd been thinking at the time. She'd been thinking of all the opportunities she'd have to change his mind about closing the station.

She hadn't been surprised he'd insisted. He was doing her a huge favor, and it wasn't fair to expect him to look after her aunt. But he'd been hinting that Willow should stay at the beach house when it was just him and Riley. It had been obvious the siblings hadn't spent much time together, and Noah was at a loss as to what he was supposed to do with his baby sister.

"Fine, they can both stay with you," Noah said.

She gritted her teeth and turned to Riley. "Why don't you listen to your audiobook, honey? It'll distract you." She glanced at her aunt, who was watching Willow with an eyebrow raised, looking every one of her experienced forty-seven years or at least thirty-two years. She was remarkably well preserved.

"I'm not tired," Cami said with a cheeky grin on her gorgeous face. "And your conversation is too interesting to miss."

Willow didn't know her aunt but sensed, whether she was seventeen or forty-seven, that no one won an argument with her, and since they were only five minutes from her place, Willow didn't have time to test her theory.

She faced forward and lowered her voice. "Riley doesn't want to stay with me, Noah. She wants to stay with you, her brother. She needs this time with you. And you know why my aunt can't stay with me."

"I don't," Cami said into Willow's ear.

Willow swore, swiveling her head to her aunt, who was right in her face. "What are you doing? Put your seat belt back on and sit back."

"Not until you tell me why I can't stay with you," her aunt said, looking every inch the mutinous teenager.

"I told you. We don't want anyone to tell the family that you're in town before they get back from their vacation. It'll ruin the surprise," Willow said with what she felt was incredible patience. She couldn't tell her aunt the truth. Seventeen-year-old Cami adored her family, and the last thing Willow wanted was to hurt her.

"I can't believe they went on vacation and left me home on my own," Cami grumbled, struggling with her seat belt. Riley leaned over to help her.

Willow covered her face with her palm. There was no way she'd survive a week of this. Through her fingers, her street came into view. It couldn't be. She spread her fingers to get a better look. It was!

She swallowed a panicked yelp at the sight of the people carrying boxes out of her house before demanding, "Noah, do not stop at my place. Drive past it and drive fast."

"Faster than twenty-five miles an hour?"

Okay, that was kind of funny. But right now, she could do without a teasing Noah. He obviously hadn't noticed that her mother, her grandmother, and Bruno were moving her out of her house.

"Fifty. A hundred. I don't care, just make sure we're a blur," she said, twisting in her seat as she undid her seat belt. She dove into the back seat to hide her aunt from her family's view.

"Willow, what the hell are you...?" Noah growled, and then he must've seen what she had and hit the gas.

She wanted to kiss him—again—but she was too busy fending off her aunt's slaps.

"Are you nuts?" Cami cried. "You could've given Riley a concussion and me another one."

"Stop slapping me or you're going to give me a concussion. I was just trying to help you do up your seat belt and then Noah hit a bump."

A big hand landed on her butt, and she shivered when strong, warm fingers grazed the bare skin of her back.

Noah hauled her over the seat and into the front. "Next time, give me some warning," he muttered.

She opened her mouth to tell him she could use a warning next time he planned on touching her but was afraid her face was flushed and she'd sound as turned on as she felt.

She cleared her throat. "Stop at the next corner and I'll get out. I don't know how long this will take but I'll meet you at the beach house."

"You can't ride your scooter to the beach house carrying bags for you and Cami. I'll drop them off and come back and give you a hand," Noah said as he pulled alongside the curb at the corner of the next street over from hers.

"Okay, but don't rush. It might take a while to get rid of my . . . movers." She looked back at her aunt. "Do what Noah tells you, and no leaving the beach house." She smiled at Riley. "I'll see you soon, honey."

As Willow opened the door to get out of the car, Cami said, "I'll need a bathing suit and some shorts and T-shirts, and don't forget, my boobs are bigger than yours so nothing too low cut or Ma will have a conniption."

" 'Cause your boobs are fake and mine aren't," Willow said under her breath as she got out of the car.

"I heard you," Cami said. "And they're not fake. They're just . . . swollen."

Noah rubbed his hand over his mouth, his broad shoulders shaking with silent laughter.

"It's not funny," Willow grumbled. Then she looked at her aunt. "Is there anything else you need?"

"Underwear, but not the kind you wear. I don't want to walk around with a string up my butt, thank you very much."

"Good, because I wasn't going to share my underwear with you. You can wear your granny panties." Willow slammed the door on her aunt defending her underwear and Noah laughing out loud. She didn't slam the door because he was laughing but because of how her body responded to him laughing.

The worrisome warm fuzzies disappeared as soon as she rounded the corner onto her street. "Mom, Nonna, Bruno, put those boxes back in my house!" she shouted, waving her arms to get their attention.

"Where have you been?" Her mother dropped the box she'd been carrying onto the front lawn and put her hands on her hips. "I've been calling you all morning."

Willow had sent her mom a text before turning off her phone when they'd arrived at the hospital that morning. She'd turned it back on when she called the station.

"I told you I was busy and wouldn't be answering my phone." Her gaze moved over the three of them. "What's going on?"

"Unless you've found a place to live, we're moving you into your zia's apartment," her mom said, looking decidedly unhappy with Willow.

"I have two weeks before I have to move out," she said, taking a box from her grandmother.

"You *had* two weeks. Mr. Lowell's son got back to town late yesterday afternoon, and Mr. Lowell wanted to measure for his furniture." Her grandmother gave her a sour look while stabbing a finger at the open door. "And he walked into that mess."

Her face hot with embarrassment, Willow carried the box into the house. "He had no right to do that."

"*Bella*, you didn't sign a lease. He can do what he wants," Bruno said, following her inside with two boxes, his voice gentle.

Willow turned away from his kind, familiar face. She didn't want him to see her cry. Her grandmother was right. The house was a mess. She was a mess. And they'd never forgive her when they found out what she'd done.

She pulled herself together and forced a smile. "You don't have to worry about me. I've got this." There was no help for it now. She had to stay at the beach house. "I have a place until the end of August. I'll just..." She looked around her living room. "I'll put everything in storage." She set the box on the floor and walked to her mom and gave her a hug. "Sorry I worried you. You too, Nonna and Bruno." She hugged them both. "Now go. I know you're busy."

"You can't do this on your own," Bruno said. "You have to be out by tonight."

"I won't be doing it on my own but I'm also not letting Mr. Lowell change the agreement just because it suits him."

"Good for you. I always thought he was a *culo*," her grandmother said.

"Ma, don't encourage her." Her mother raised an eyebrow at Willow. "I don't like to say I told you so, but I did."

"I know. But honestly, Mom. I've got this."

"Are you sure? I don't want Mr. Lowell to make trouble for you. It might be better if one of us plays intermediary."

"I have a lawyer friend who can be pretty persuasive. I'll have him call Mr. Lowell. I just need a few extra days."

"Does this lawyer friend have a name?" her mom asked.

"Noah," Willow mumbled. Then, plastering a wide smile on her face, she shooed them out the door. "Now off you go. I'll see you at six."

Her mother shook her head. "No. You have enough on your plate. You're off the schedule until you settle into your new place."

Willow opened her mouth to argue. She couldn't afford to lose the money. Her mom patted her cheek. "Don't argue with your mother. And don't think you can keep this lawyer friend of yours a secret."

No secret was safe around her mom, grandmother, and aunt, unless it was one of their own. "I'm not. He's just a friend," she said as she ushered them onto the walkway. "I love you guys, and I really do appreciate your rushing over here to help me out."

"We love you too, even though you can be a pain in our *culi*, *bella*," her grandmother said.

"Don't listen to her. You've never been a pain in our *culi*. You're our darling girl," Bruno said.

Willow flung her arms around him and gave him a kiss on the cheek. "I love you best."

Her grandmother rolled her eyes. "This one," she said, jerking a thumb at Willow. "She's been wrapping men around her baby finger since she could talk. And you," her grandmother lifted her chin at Bruno. "Are you forgetting the time she snuck half the teenagers of Sunshine Bay into the restaurant after we were closed and had a party, or the time she packed up all the boxed and canned goods we had in the kitchen and gave it to the food pantry without telling us, or the time she took in two stray dogs and hid . . ."

Willow took a page out of Cami's book and covered her ears, humming loudly as she closed the front door. Then she leaned her back against it, dropped her hands to her sides, and looked around the house. Overwhelmed, she slid down the door and sat on the floor while the tears she could no longer hold back rolled down her cheeks.

She didn't know how long she'd been sitting there when the door began opening, sliding her butt across the floor. "Willow?"

"Hey, I told you not to rush." She kept her back to Noah as she got up off the floor, scrubbing her hands over her face to get rid of the evidence that she'd been crying. She turned with what she hoped looked like a bright and happy smile on her face.

His eyes narrowed on her while he carried two boxes inside. "I didn't rush. I dropped you off over an hour ago."

She briefly closed her eyes at the knowledge that she'd been sitting there feeling sorry for herself for that long. "Time flies when you're having fun, I guess." She glanced around, pointing to a clear space near the couch. "You can just drop them there, thanks. I'll organize them later."

"Are you going to tell me why your family was moving you out and why you've been crying?"

"I haven't been crying. It's just dusty in here."

He put down the boxes and then came back to her, took her by the hand, moved the boxes over with his foot, and led her to the couch. "Sit."

She didn't have the bandwidth to argue and did as he said. He sat beside her, resting his arm along the back of the couch. "Now tell me what's going on."

Chapter Ten

Y ou were right," Willow admitted to Noah. "I don't have a lease. I had a verbal agreement with my landlord. He dropped by yesterday after we'd left." She waved her arm around the room. "Saw that it was a disaster and decided he wants me out by tonight, not two weeks from now. Instead of calling me, he called my family, and because I'm going behind their back, I'd turned off my phone so I didn't have to outright lie about where I was if they called, and my mom couldn't reach me. So they did what they always do. Clean up my mess." She blew out a soggy breath and then realized what she'd done.

The last thing she needed was Noah thinking he couldn't depend on her. How would he ever trust her ideas for Channel 5 if he thought she was a flake?

"Okay, that didn't come out right. It's not like I make a mess of my life every other week. I'm honestly very dependable. You can ask Don and my coworkers at Channel 5," she said. "Today was the first full day I've taken off since I started working there. I never call in sick. Last winter, I did the weather, outside I might add, with a temperature of a hundred and two. I'd never let my coworkers down. Ever."

"You don't have to convince me, Willow. I believe you. But I don't like to think of you going to work when you're sick."

"I didn't have a choice." She made a face. "I probably shouldn't tell you this because it makes me look irresponsible, but I'm in debt and live paycheck to paycheck. I can't afford to lose a shift at either Channel 5 or the restaurant. But no lie, it's not my fault." She tilted her head from side to side. "It's partially my fault. I like to have fun and party, or at least I used to, so I didn't have much of a rainy-day fund when things went sideways with the house flip."

"Your business with Megan?"

Willow nodded. "There's good money to be made in house flipping. I'd bought my first home the year before and wanted to have extra money set aside in case . . . Well, I wasn't a fan of appearing on air in a bikini, and Don and I had a few arguments about it so I was worried—"

She knew she should've kept her mouth shut when Noah got that stone-cold expression on his face but she didn't want him to think she'd thought about quitting her job and needed the extra money in case she did. She'd actually thought Don might fire her, and then she'd need the money. But she didn't want to tell Noah *that*.

"Excuse me. Don made you wear a *bikini* to do the weather?"

"Yes. But it's not what you think. He wasn't exploiting me."

"What do you call it if not exploitation?"

"I didn't know it then, but he was trying to save the station by increasing revenue, and Beach Babe, a local swimwear shop, would only advertise if I wore their suits on air." She pulled her phone from the back pocket of her jeans, went to her photos, and scrolled to one from the previous July. She showed him. "See, it wasn't that bad."

She pointed to the yellow rubber duck she wore around her waist. "My cameraman at the time didn't shoot me below Super Duck. And just to clear up something Megan said, I'm not a heartbreaker. I used to date my previous cameraman, and we remained good friends after we broke up. I'm friends with all my ex-boyfriends." At least the ones who weren't jerks.

She glanced at Noah and sighed. His face was no longer stone-cold but the muscle jumping in his clenched jaw suggested he was still ticked. She nudged him with her elbow, and his eyes came to her. Oh boy. There wasn't a hint of indigo in his irises, they were entirely black.

She needed to change the subject. "So...my house flipping business with Megan. You've probably guessed that it didn't work out as we'd hoped. Definitely not how I hoped anyway. Megan put up the money, at least in the beginning she did, and I was the working partner. And let me tell you, all I did was work. But there were some issues with the house, which by the way we got for a steal, something Megan took credit for, but I later found out it was because she'd waived the inspection. Hence the problems we ran into."

She pulled up some before photos of the house on her phone and showed Noah. "Along with the interior needing to be completely updated, the house needed new wiring, plumbing, and a roof."

She showed him a photo of herself and her ex-boyfriend tossing the old, moldy tiles off the roof. "That's my ex. I couldn't have done it without him. I retiled the kitchen with help from another ex-boyfriend, same with the cabinetry and countertops. But even with my exes helping, and me working what sometimes felt like twenty-four-seven, we were delayed."

Willow brought up interior and exterior photos of the house from when it had gone up for sale. No matter that the house flip had turned Willow's life upside down, she was proud of what she'd accomplished with a lot of help from her friends.

"Megan had anticipated putting the house on the market within three months. It took us nine. Even though I was the working partner, Megan insisted I contribute, which I understood. We weren't only delayed. We were way over budget. But the only way I could come up with the money was to sell my house and use the little equity I had in it."

Scrolling through her photos, Willow found one of her house. It was a cute two-bedroom Cape Cod with pink window boxes and pink shutters. She'd loved her house, and she got a little emotional looking at the picture. She turned it to Noah.

"Megan sold my house for me and waived her commission, but she wanted to sell it fast, so she dropped the price within two days of putting it on the market. I didn't get what I'd expected, and of course, I'd promised Megan the expected amount so I had to take out a loan." Willow gestured to the room at large. "She found me a place to rent, though. It was a little over my budget, but the rental market was tight. Luckily, Mr. Lowell's her uncle, and she was able to convince him to rent to me."

Noah stared at her, opened his mouth, and then closed it.

"What were you going to say?"

He raised a finger. "I need a minute." He bowed his head, gave it a slow shake, and then raised his gaze to her. "Have you heard the saying *With friends like that, who needs enemies?*"

"She's not that bad."

He made a disbelieving sound in his throat.

"Okay, you're right. But she hasn't always been like this. Her husband cheated on her, and they had a messy divorce."

"What time did Mr. Lowell call your mother?"

She frowned. "What does that have to do with Megan?"

He tapped his finger on her phone. "Check if Megan called you earlier today and the time of the first call your mother made to you after hearing from Megan's uncle."

She went to the recent calls and scrolled through them. "Megan called at nine thirty this morning."

"Which is thirty minutes after Robyn informed her that I was pausing the sale of the beach house."

"Okay, but—"

"What was the time of your mother's first call to you?"

"Ten." She lifted her gaze from the screen to Noah. "Do you really think that because Megan believed I'm the reason you paused the sale that she'd tell her uncle to kick me out?"

He raised an eyebrow.

She bowed her head. "You do."

"It doesn't matter what I think, Willow. What do you think?"

"That I'm an idiot."

"You're not an idiot. What you are is a woman who sees the best in people, is loyal, perhaps to a fault, and trusts that the people she cares about are as good and kind as she is."

"Ugh, you make me sound like a cross between someone who walks around wearing rose-colored glasses and a doormat. I'm not a pushover, you know."

"You weren't a pushover when you were fifteen, and within the past twenty-four hours, you've demonstrated you haven't changed. Several times, as a matter of fact." He once again tapped her phone. "So what are you going to do about your landlord?"

She wrinkled her nose. "I thought maybe you could call him and go all lawyerly on his *culo*?"

His lips twitched. "*Culo?*"

"Ass."

He smiled. "I have a better idea. You call him and go all Willow Rosetti on his *culo*."

With some coaching from Noah, that's exactly what she did. And Noah had been right. Megan had called her uncle and told him to kick her out. Total mean girl move, and Willow planned to have it out with her, just not today.

She disconnected the call, wishing that she had a landline. Stabbing her finger on the End button wasn't nearly as satisfying as slamming the phone in Mr. Lowell's ear would've been.

Noah leaned against the boxes he'd begun piling in a corner of the living room when she'd started her call with her landlord. In the time she'd been on the phone, he'd cleared the floor of boxes. She felt as if she could finally breathe again.

His arms crossed over his broad chest, he grinned. "You didn't just kick his *culo*. You stomped on it."

"I so did," she said, grinning back at him as she got up off the couch.

"No celebratory dance?"

"Only if you join me," she teased, walking toward him.

He shook his head. "I don't dance."

"Oh, come on. You can't not dance. Everyone dances. And I know you can because I spent an entire day teaching you that summer," she said, bringing up the song they'd danced to on her phone. It was Celine Dion's "Because You Loved Me."

She turned up the volume and set the phone on the nearest box, holding out her hand as the lyrics filled the room. "Remember?"

He nodded, surprising her by taking her hand and drawing her into his arms. "Of course I remember. You changed *loved* to *liked*."

She smiled at the memory. "I thought you were going to run off when the song started playing."

"I nearly did. But I wasn't about to waste an opportunity to get you in my arms, even if I was terrified I'd mess up and step on your toes."

She leaned back. "You wanted to get me in your arms?"

"I was fifteen, you were beautiful, and I had a crush on you, Willow. Of course I wanted to get you in my arms."

She stared at him. "You did not have a crush on me. I would've known if you did. We were friends, best friends, and I was far from beautiful. I had clown hair."

His lips lifted at the corners. "You did, but I still thought you were the most beautiful girl in the world." He angled his head. "You must've known how I felt. I kissed you, and it was definitely not a forgettable kiss."

Despite being shocked that Noah had had feelings for her back then, Willow laughed. "It was a memorable kiss." His braces had gotten caught on her bottom lip. "No one I kissed before or after you has left such a lasting impression."

"I should hope not. I made you bleed. But in my defense, you weren't just the first girl I had a crush on or I had danced with. You were the first girl I kissed."

He lifted his hand from her waist and brought it to her mouth, gently rubbing his thumb back and forth over her bottom lip. "I'm glad I didn't leave a scar."

"Is that why you didn't come back to Hidden Cove on your last day?"

"I was embarrassed. Mortified, actually. But no, my grandfather had a heart attack a few hours after I got back. We left the beach house right away and never came back. At least I didn't. Life changed after my grandfather died, and not for the better."

"I'm so sorry, Noah. I wish I had known. I wish we'd found a way to keep in touch. I missed you."

"I missed you too," he murmured as his head lowered, and her heart skipped an excited beat, maybe two or three or four.

Her lips parted on a sigh, and it felt as if she were floating on air. She went up on her toes, meeting him halfway. His lips touched hers, and she was about to close her eyes and allow herself to bask in the moment. They'd been back together for a little more than forty-eight hours, yet it felt as if she'd been waiting forever for him to kiss her.

He brushed his lips softly over hers and then raised his head. "We can't do this, Willow. I wish we could, but we can't."

"Trust me, we can," she said, looping her arms around his neck.

He smoothed his hands up her arms, took her hands in his, and stepped back. "We can't. Technically, I'm your boss."

"Yes, but I want you to kiss me."

"It doesn't matter if it's consensual."

"I get the whole power imbalance thing, Noah. And if it was anyone other than you, I'd agree with you. But—" His ringing phone interrupted her.

She didn't miss his murmured, "Saved by the ring." Or the smile playing on his lips.

Lips that would be on hers if she had her way. "I hate your phone," she said, at the same time noting that he was no longer smiling. His face was stone cold, and his jaw was clenched. "Who is it?"

"Billy," he said as he brought the phone to his ear. Her worry must've shown on her face because he reassured her. "She's staying with us this summer, Willow. No matter what he tries to pull."

She nodded, unable to keep from smiling and smiling hugely. She was relieved Noah wouldn't give in to Billy, but even better, he'd referred to them as an *us*.

As though he knew what she was thinking, he raised his eyebrows and shook his head before saying, "Billy" into the phone in his low, cold voice. Willow shivered, glad she wasn't on the receiving end of that voice.

Then her phone rang, and she glanced at the screen. She wouldn't be on the receiving end of Noah's scary voice but she'd be on the receiving end of her sister's. "Hey, Sage."

"What have you done?"

"Why are you assuming I've done something?"

"Your voicemail. You used your chirpy voice."

"I don't have a chirpy voice."

"You have three minutes to tell me what you've done, after which I will lecture you for seven minutes, and then I will hang up because I have a ton of work before court in the morning."

"I'm invoking the Cousins Pact, so no lectures allowed. That's the rule. You have to support me no matter what."

Willow, her sister, and their cousin had made up the Cousins Pact when they were young. If any of them had upsetting news to share with their mothers, aunts, or grandmother, they had each other's backs no matter what. This was the first time anyone other than their cousin had invoked the pact.

"I'm your sister, and I always have your back."

"You do, but this is bigger than you and me, babe. We need Lila in on this too."

"It's after midnight in England so you've got me, *babe*. Now spill."

Willow spilled, her shoulders inching up around her ears every time her sister yelled either "What were you thinking?" or a swear word, of which there were several. And unlike Willow, her sister rarely swore. After Willow finished, she waited for Sage to say something. All she heard was heavy breathing.

A warm hand settled around the back of Willow's neck, and she looked up. "You okay?" Noah asked.

"Who's that?" her sister snapped.

"I told you. Noah's here helping me pack up my place, and he's hiding Cami at his beach house."

"Leave it to you to rope your boss into helping you hide your aunt."

"She's your aunt too. And he's not my boss." Noah gave her a neck a light squeeze. She rolled her eyes at him. "Okay, so he's sort of my boss. But he's also my Summer Noah. I told you about him, remember?"

"The guy you mooned over for months when you were fifteen?"

"I didn't moon over him. And this conversation isn't getting us anywhere." What it was was embarrassing. "We need to come up with a plan. When can you get here?"

"Friday night at the earliest. But in the meantime, we can

arrange a time to talk to Lila and figure out how to break the news that you brought home the woman whose name isn't allowed to be uttered in our family's presence."

"It would help if we knew why they're estranged. You should hear her, Sage. She adores Mom, Nonna, and Zia. At least she did when she was seventeen." Willow chewed on her thumbnail and then admitted, "I feel sorry for her. I want to help her reunite with the family."

"This never would've happened if it was Lila or me. You're a soft touch. You can't resist a stray or a sob story."

"She's not a dog. She's family. And I'm not a soft touch. I'm—"

"A soft touch," Noah said, his warm breath caressing her ear.

"I think I like your Summer Noah," her sister said.

"Because he agrees with you."

"That and he has a great voice. Let me talk to him."

"I'm not letting you talk to him."

"It's fine. I'll talk to your sister," Noah offered.

"You are not talking to my sister." She didn't trust Sage not to embarrass her further. She had a habit of cross-examining Willow's boyfriends as if they were the cheating, slimeball exes of the clients her sister represented. Not that Noah was her boyfriend. "She has to go."

"Actually, I do. Tell Noah I'm looking forward to meeting him this weekend. I'll coordinate a time for our chat with Lila, little sister. Don't do anything I wouldn't...Scratch that. He's your boss so do not even go there."

"He's not my boss." She sighed when Noah gave her another neck squeeze. "Good luck in court tomorrow. Love you."

"Love you too, even though you're ruining my weekend."

"All you do on your weekends is work. How am I...Oh, is there something we should talk about, big sister?"

"Goodbye, Will," her sister said, and disconnected.

Willow was definitely following up on that. Sage sounded nervous, and she was never nervous. About anything.

"So...my Summer Noah?"

"It's nothing. It's just how I differentiate between you and the other Noahs."

"You have other Noahs?"

"No. Just you. But you're m...Summer Noah, Mercedes Man Noah, Bennett CEO Noah, and Now Noah."

He threw back his head and laughed.

"I'm adding another Noah. Annoying Noah. Although Mercedes Man Noah and Bennett CEO Noah are annoying too."

"What about Now Noah?"

"Does Now Noah still think he's my boss or is he going to finish what he started?" She sighed at the look in his eyes. "He's annoying too."

Chapter Eleven

Willow stomped into the TV station the next afternoon. She'd been summoned by the Big Boss, as Veronica and apparently everyone at the station now referred to Noah. Willow had gotten the call while she was helping with the pet rescue event that was being held that weekend. As part of her job at Channel 5, she was the face of the station at community events. She did everything from appearing in parades—in costume—to helping organize the events and lending an extra pair of hands as herself.

Her involvement with the events was her favorite part of her job and took up most of her time. During the summer, though, she was routinely run off her feet. At any other time, she wouldn't mind. She liked being busy and loved helping out her community. But with everything going on in her life at the moment, she could use three of herself.

After filming this morning—a disaster, but what else was new—she'd changed and headed straight to the farm where the pet rescue event was being held. In an hour, she had a meeting with the organizing committee for the silent auction. No matter what the Big Boss wanted, she had no intention of missing the committee meeting. It had taken her months to convince her mother to donate three of her paintings. Willow couldn't wait for everyone to see how talented her mother was, including her mother.

So yes, she was ticked Noah was demanding she meet with him with no thought whatsoever for *her* schedule. And if he was using this meeting as a way to show Willow he was her actual boss, not her sort-of boss, to strengthen the case he'd made against them indulging in a summer fling, then she'd be unhappier than she already was.

As she walked through the lobby and took note of the hum of activity at the station, she thought she might have to give Noah a pass. At least when it came to pulling her away from helping set up the pet rescue event. It was possible no one at the station had had time to inform him that she was busy too.

She would've informed him herself if she'd seen him. But no, after they'd gotten back to the beach house from her place the day before, he'd stuck around long enough to eat five slices of pizza and then headed to the station to work. She had no idea when he had gotten back. She only knew that he'd been gone by the time she'd gotten out of bed that morning. Something else that had contributed to her bad mood, and she was rarely in a bad mood.

She'd been right. Noah was annoying.

"Who peed in your cornflakes this morning?" Naomi greeted Willow as she approached the reception desk.

She raised an eyebrow. "Was that your body double behind the camera this morning?"

"They didn't pee on—" Naomi began before being interrupted by Veronica.

"The Big Boss is waiting, Will. You need to get in there right away," Veronica said, her smile blinding.

Willow stared at her friend, who'd barely been able to crack a smile this past week, now wearing one so wide that it had to be hurting her cheeks while passing on Noah's edict. There was only one reason Willow could think of for Veronica's blinding smile, and she felt as if she'd been punched in the chest. In the past week, the one time Veronica had been as happy as she appeared to be right now was when Willow asked her to fill in for her. Noah was giving Veronica her job, and Willow knew why.

"Veronica's right. Get your butt in there, babe," Naomi said, smiling.

Willow blinked at her friend and cameraperson, whispering, "You're smiling."

Naomi shared a glance with Veronica and then shook her head. "I'm not smiling," she said, turning her smile upside down.

Willow looked around the station. Several of the crew and newscasters gave her big waves with big smiles on their faces. She wanted to yell at them. To remind them that they loved her weather reports. They thought they were hysterical. They were the bright spot in their mornings and afternoons. They'd told her so themselves.

"Willow, get in there. The Big Boss is waiting," Don said with a wide smile as he walked up to the reception desk, three boxes of doughnuts from O Holey Glazed piled in his arms.

Don didn't smile, and he didn't bring in doughnuts. Willow brought in doughnuts. She couldn't believe it. They were celebrating her being fired!

Her throat got tight, and the backs of her eyes burned. *Do not let them see you cry*, she ordered herself. And without looking at her friends and colleagues, she stomped to Don's former office. She didn't knock or wait for Noah to wave her in. She swung open the door and stomped to one of the two chairs in front of the desk.

He was on the phone and smiled, and then, obviously sensing she was not in a happy place, his smile faded. He pointed at the chair she stood behind, indicating that she should take a seat while waiting for him to finish his call.

She stayed where she was. Her fingers curved around the back of the chair, her knuckles whitening with the strength of her grip.

His brow furrowed as he returned his attention to whomever he was speaking to. "Thank you. I appreciate you thinking of me but I'm not interested in the position at this time."

Willow shook her head. Here she was trying to hang on to a part-time job, and he had job opportunities he wasn't interested in falling into his lap. He probably didn't even have to work.

He smiled at whatever the person said next. She wanted to tell him they couldn't see him, but then he laughed. Not his deep, rumbly laugh that she loved, or that she used to love, she reminded herself, lowering her gaze from his gorgeous face. It was a polite laugh.

She looked up from her hands gripping the chair to see his gaze moving over her, and she shifted from one foot to the other. She'd wiped her sneakers on the sidewalk a few times to ensure she hadn't brought anything from the barn in with her. She'd picked hay off her frayed denim shorts that were almost but not quite short-shorts, and off the sleeveless white cotton shirt she wore tied at her waist. She tugged it down to cover the strip of bare skin there, but it rode up as soon as she put her hand back on the chair.

Noah's gaze moved to her hair, which she wore in a ponytail, her sunglasses holding back the tendrils that had escaped when she was helping wrangle the dogs. She imagined Noah was horrified that she hadn't changed before meeting with him.

He, it had to be said, looked every inch the successful CEO in a shirt that matched the color of his eyes and fit his broad shoulders and his wide chest to perfection. His shirt sleeves were rolled up, showing off his powerful forearms. Distractedly, she wondered when he found time to work out.

"I will. And again, thank you for the offer," he said before disconnecting. He put his phone on his desk, leaned back in the chair, and opened his mouth.

She didn't give him a chance to get a word out. "If you think by firing me that will leave us free and clear to have a summer fling, you had better think again. Because it doesn't matter that I was all for us having one. If I'm honest, and I always am, unlike some people I know," she said, keeping her gaze focused on his chin, "I might've been the one to suggest a fling or at least strongly hint at it, but you're gorgeous and you can be considerate and kind, and even when you're in annoying, demanding CEO Noah mode, it's all kinds of sexy, so it's understandable why I'd want to make out with you. But now?"

She shook her head. "That's totally off the table so you should reconsider firing me if that's the reason you were going to, and I can't think of any other reason..." Her shoulders drooped, and the fight went out of her. "I guess I can. I suck as a weatherperson, but you're closing the station so can't you just leave me with my dignity and a paycheck until you do?"

She blew out a breath. "Veronica's my friend, and I know she wants to work on camera, and she did a great job replacing me. But I need my paycheck, Noah. You know I do."

"Willow, sit down. Please."

Her head snapped up at what sounded like amusement in his voice. He was rubbing a hand across his mouth, and his eyes were warm and crinkled at the corners.

"Are you laughing at me?"

"No. I'm smiling." He lowered his hand from his mouth and gestured at the chair. "And if you would've stopped staring at my chest at any point during your—"

"I wasn't staring at your chest. I was staring at your chin."

His lips twitched, and she growled low in her throat, rounding the chair and throwing herself onto the seat. "You have a warped sense of humor if you found anything I said funny. In fact, it's rude...no, it's just plain mean that you'd sit there laughing at me while I poured out my heart to you."

"I didn't say I was laughing. I said I was smiling. And Willow"—he didn't continue until she raised her gaze to his— "I was smiling because while you were telling me you wouldn't have a fling with me, you told me I was gorgeous, considerate, kind, and even when I annoy you, you find me sexy."

"That was before you were going to fire me!"

"You're not fired. I had no intention of firing you and have no idea how you came to that ridiculous conclusion. And frankly, I find it insulting that you believe I would do something like that."

Willow straightened in the chair. "You're not firing me?"

"No. I'm not. Now would you be so kind as to enlighten me as to why you believed that I was?"

She flung her arm behind her. "Because no one's acting like themselves." She explained about Veronica, Naomi, and Don. "And the rest of the crew were giving me big waves and smiles."

"All right. I'll admit I don't have a clue how a woman's mind works, but how a woman who is adored by her colleagues could come to the conclusion they were happy because she'd been fired is beyond me. As—"

She groaned. "I know. I'm an idiot. But you have to see it from my—"

"You are far from an idiot, and I'd appreciate it if you would stop calling yourself one. You also didn't let me finish. I was going to say, as beyond me as that same woman believing she *sucks*"—he made air quotes—"at her job when her five-minute weather reports have drawn the highest ratings on Channel 5 for the past year."

"It's the over-seventy crowd. They're obsessed with the weather, and even though I get it wrong thirty, maybe forty percent of the time, they're loyal. I also helped raise twenty thousand dollars for the senior center, so there's that. But Noah, if you'd watched my weather reports, you'd understand why I say I suck."

He pointed at the screen behind him. "I watched this morning," he said, and then pressed his lips together as his shoulders started shaking.

"It's not funny."

"No. It was hilarious."

"Trust me, having a poodle and a Yorkshire terrier peeing on you is not funny. This kind of thing happens to me all the time. All the dogs in the park were leashed, like they're supposed to be, except those two, and they made a beeline straight for me. And really, do I look like a fire hydrant?"

She sighed when his warm, deep laugh washed over her, and then she continued talking to distract herself from the way his eyes lit up when he laughed. "The owner was nice, though. When he finally caught up with us, he apologized and offered to have my costume dry-cleaned." After he'd gotten *his* laughter under control.

"Exactly how far did the dogs chase you?" he asked, sputtering a laugh as soon as the question was out of his mouth.

"According to Naomi, a mile. She said I should consider signing up for the five-mile charity run in August. She's positive I beat last year's winning time, and I was running in a costume."

He'd stopped laughing, his indigo gaze darkening as it moved over her face. "There's a reason people tune in to watch you, Willow."

She nodded. "I know. I already told you what it was. The seniors are seriously obsessed with the weather. I'm sure they tuned in to watch Veronica too."

"You're right about Veronica. She should be on camera. But her numbers won't compare with yours. And that's because you have the indefinable *it* factor. Everyone sees it but you. It's like your mother's painting. The heart of you shines through when you're on air, and it's absolutely captivating. Your talent is wasted delivering a five-minute weather report, Willow. Your concept for *Good Morning, Sunshine!* would've been the perfect vehicle for you."

He had no idea how much his words meant to her. He didn't think she was a joke like everyone else. Noah Elliot, the CEO of Bennett Broadcasting, thought she was good at her job, and that ... well, that meant the world to her.

She swallowed hard against the emotion tightening her throat. "Thank you," she murmured.

"You have no reason to thank me. I'm just stating a fact." His cell phone beeped, and he glanced at the screen. "I have a conference call that I can't put off so we—"

She got up from the chair. "Of course. I can come back when you're finished."

"Willow, would you please sit down," he said, sounding frustrated. "What I meant was that I don't have time to get to the bottom of why you seem oblivious to your talent and why you were willing to settle for a five-minute weather spot. But before I get tied up with this call, you need to know what I wanted to speak to you about, otherwise everyone in Sunshine Bay will know but you."

"It's Megan, isn't it?" She nodded and held up her phone. "She got to the Beaches first, and they've been sending me texts on her behalf." She shook her head, as frustrated with her squad now as she had been when they began sending her texts all in caps with angry-face emoji. "I can't believe—"

He held up his hand, cutting her off. "This has nothing to do with Megan and the...Beaches. Whatever they are."

She opened her mouth to tell him.

"I wasn't asking. I don't want to know. What I want is to tell you what I asked Don to keep to himself until I had spoken to you, which he's obviously been unable to do. I'd planned to tell you when I saw you tonight, since you didn't have a free moment in your schedule today, seeing as you spend your entire day when you're not on air volunteering for community events. Which, by the way, is something we'll be discussing tonight."

Her spine stiffened at the way he spoke about her schedule, as if he didn't appreciate her not being at his beck and call. "Oh, so you were actually planning on coming home tonight? Color me shocked since I haven't heard from you or seen you since you left the beach house at seven last night." Realizing she sounded like a petulant girlfriend, she said, "I meant

Riley hasn't seen or heard from you since you left the beach house at seven last night."

"I got back from the station at two in the morning, Willow. I didn't think you'd appreciate me waking you but I won't make that mistake again," he said with a promise in his voice that had her imagining how he would wake her. "My reasoning for not waking you when I left for the station at five this morning was the same."

"That's insane, Noah. You can't function on that little sleep."

He shrugged. "I won't have to for much longer. We have two sale agreements left to finalize. There were issues with one of them, but they've since been resolved. And this morning I wanted to look over Channel 5's financials before talking to Don." He studied her for a moment and then straightened in his chair to type something into his computer. "I'm giving you, and Don obviously, three weeks to find an interested buyer for the station."

She froze in the chair. "I don't understand. Why would you do that?"

He angled his head. "That wasn't the reaction I expected."

"I guess I'm in shock." She glanced over her shoulder at her coworkers, who sprang into action as if they hadn't been watching what was going on in Don's office. Then she returned her gaze to Noah. "I'd convinced everyone, including myself, that we could change your mind. But I guess I didn't believe it because I..." She lifted a shoulder, stuck for words.

"It's the responsibility," he murmured.

"Pardon?"

"I should've anticipated how you'd react. I might've given

you the opportunity you wanted, Willow, but I've also placed a heavy burden on your shoulders. The hopes and dreams of your colleagues. And that's because Don's not the heart of the station, you are."

Even though she had a feeling Noah was right about her reaction—she felt more like throwing up than like dancing for joy—Don wanted to save the station as much as she did, She opened her mouth to come to his defense.

"Whether you believe it or not, that's how your coworkers see you, Willow. I had an opportunity to speak with several of them last night between conference calls. I learned a lot about your colleagues and the inner workings of the station. That's the problem with being a corporation as big as Bennett Broadcasting, we look at numbers, not people."

"Is that why you changed your mind?"

He nodded. "I just emailed you the contact information for potential buyers. Don has a copy too. Robyn will be sending both of you the feedback we received when we initially put up the offering for Channel 5. It isn't fun reading, but it's best you go in prepared."

"You still don't believe we can find a buyer, do you?"

"I'm sorry, but no, I don't." He smiled. "Then again, you convinced me to stay with Riley at the beach house for the summer and to let your aunt hide out there, so when you're involved, anything is possible."

Noah was right, she thought, reminded of Audrey Hepburn's quote "Nothing is impossible. The word itself says 'I'm possible.'" And the panic that had kept her from fully appreciating Noah's news was replaced with hope and the urge to celebrate. She wanted to leap from the chair and do a happy dance.

As though he sensed the change that had come over her, Noah's smile widened, and she no longer wanted to dance. She wanted to throw herself across his desk and kiss him all over his gorgeous face.

Instead, she said, "I appreciate your faith in me, but finding a buyer in three weeks won't be easy. Is there any chance we could get an extra week? Maybe two?"

"I'm afraid not. We set a target of September thirteenth for the dissolution of the corporation, and the paperwork is underway. Seventy-five percent of our head office staff are moving on to other jobs or have opted to retire at the end of this month. I'm pushing it by giving you three weeks, but we'll make it happen if you find an interested buyer."

His phone rang, and he glanced at the screen. "I have to take this."

As Willow got up from the chair and walked to the door, she turned. "Mr. Elliot"—he looked at her with his brow furrowed, no doubt at her formal address—"you should probably know that I have a crush on you."

A slow smile curved his lips. "The feeling is mutual, Ms. Rosetti," he said, lifting his chin at the door as he brought the phone to his ear. "You should join your coworkers. They've been waiting to celebrate with you."

She danced out of his office, yelling, "Whoo-hoo!" to the cheers of her coworkers, but it was Noah's deep laugh following her out the door that made her smile, and she smiled hugely.

Chapter Twelve

Riley sat in the sand reading *A Game of Thrones*, the first book in the Song of Ice and Fire series. It was Noah's book. He'd written his name inside the front cover. She liked fantasy, and judging from the books lining the shelves in the living room at the beach house, her brother did too. At least he had when he was her age.

But this book was different from what she usually read, and she was having a hard time getting into it. Although maybe it wasn't the book's fault, she thought, when Cami yelled, "Get your nose out of the book and come bodysurf with me."

"Later. The water's cold," Riley said, keeping her eyes glued to the page. Willow's aunt was wearing a yellow polka-dot bikini that left little to the imagination.

Cami threw herself down beside Riley, spraying her with water and sand.

"Don't do that. You have a broken arm and a concussion. You're supposed to take it easy." She didn't know what Willow and her brother had been thinking, leaving her to babysit Cami. Then again, they might've thought Cami would be looking after her since Willow's aunt was the adult and Riley was the kid. If so, it had been a big miscalculation on their part.

"You're such a worrywart. Look." Cami sat up and waved her cast in front of Riley's face.

Right, she was a worrywart because she wanted to protect Cami's cast from getting wet and had covered it in plastic wrap and tape when every excuse she'd tried to dissuade Cami from going swimming had failed.

"Stop waving your arm in my face. You're getting the pages wet." Riley tightened her grip on the book in case Cami tried ripping it out of her hands again, but she'd already lost Cami's attention. As she'd discovered, Cami had the attention span of a gnat.

"Hey! Over here," Cami cried, leaping to her feet, jumping up and down, and waving her arm.

Riley looked to where Cami was waving, and her eyes got big. "Cami, stop waving at them. You're supposed to be in hiding, remember?"

It was one of the reasons Riley had tried to dissuade Cami from going swimming. The beach house was surrounded by trees and sat in a sheltered part of the bay with its own private beach, but there were plenty of boats on the water and a sandbar three hundred yards from shore. Cami was trying get the attention of three teenage boys who'd jumped off an idling speedboat onto the sandbar.

Riley opened her mouth to tell Cami to stop being creepy. She was old enough to be their mother. But she didn't want to freak Cami out by reminding her she was forty-seven, not seventeen.

"I'm starving. Let's go eat," Riley said as she stood up, brushing sand off her shorts.

Cami stopped waving to frown at her. "We had breakfast three hours ago."

"It's not my fault you slept in, and it's two in the afternoon. If we don't eat now, we'll ruin our dinner." To think she'd been glad when Cami finally woke up, Riley thought with a sigh.

Cami laughed. "You act like you're fifteen going on thirty." She grabbed Riley's hand. "I have a better idea. Let's swim to the sandbar and say hi."

"I told you. I don't know how to swim." Riley pulled her hand free. "Besides, you're not supposed to be talking to anyone."

"Oh, he's really cute, isn't he?" Cami said, pointing at the sandbar, acting as if Riley hadn't said anything. "The tall one wearing the fluorescent-green board shorts."

Riley sighed. "Yeah. Sure. Whatever."

Cami glanced at her. "Do you like boys? It's fine if you like girls or even if you don't like boys or girls."

"I like boys." They didn't seem to like her, though. At least not in a boyfriend-girlfriend way. In New York, she had two friends who were boys. They'd all lived on the same street.

Cami cocked her head. "You don't have a boyfriend, do you?"

"No! I'm fifteen." She'd considered putting "Get a boyfriend" on her wish list, but what she really wanted was a friend.

"What's your age have to do with it? Flynn and I, that's my boyfriend, we started dating when I was fifteen." Cami's eyes lit up and she grabbed Riley's hand. "I know how to get their attention. Come on, get in the water."

"How many times do I have to tell you? I don't swim."

"That's the point. Flynn was a lifeguard. A hot lifeguard, so you know what that means."

"I really don't."

Cami arched an eyebrow. "I think I know why you've never had a boyfriend. Anyway, Flynn being hot meant that all the girls were trying to get his attention." Cami pranced in front of her, tossing her hair and making flirty faces.

Riley laughed, and Cami grinned, taking her flirty-girl routine to a whole other level. The harder Riley laughed, the more outrageous Cami became.

Tears of laughter had blurred her vision, so it took a moment for Riley to notice that Cami's boobs were in danger of falling out of her bikini. "Stop. You're going to . . . lose your top."

"I bet that'll get their attention." Cami's hands moved to the ties at her back. "Stupid cast," she muttered, turning her back to Riley.

She held up her hands. "Uh, no way. I'm not helping you flash those guys."

"Fine. We'll go with my first plan," Cami said, reaching for Riley's hand. "It worked on Flynn so I'm sure it'll work on them."

"What plan?" Riley asked as Cami tugged on her hand.

"We'll pretend you're drowning."

"We can't do that!" Riley cried, digging in her heels, but it was useless against Cami's freakish strength. She obviously worked out, a lot.

"Yes we can. How do you think I got Flynn's attention?" Cami fluttered her lashes and grinned, and then she pushed Riley into the water.

Riley landed flat on her back, sputtering as a wave washed over her head. She sat up, pushing her hair from her face.

"That's not funny." She scowled at Cami but she wasn't paying attention to her. She was frowning at the sandbar.

"Oh sure, I tell you I can't swim. You throw me in the water, and you don't even check if I'm okay," Riley muttered, twisting the water from her T-shirt as she walked to shore.

"It's not even a foot deep," Cami said, waving her hand at another boat pulling up to the sandbar with four girls inside. "I told you we should've swam over and said hi."

Riley threw up her hands. "I can't swim!"

"Someone's hangry." Cami laughed, and then her eyes lit up with a look that made Riley nervous. "I know. Let's go to the food truck! They make the best lobster rolls. Have you had a lobster roll? You have to try one. They're to die for."

Here we go again, Riley thought. "We can't leave the beach house. You don't want to ruin your family's surprise, remember?"

"I knew you were going to say that so I've come up with a plan."

"I don't like your plans," Riley muttered, picking up her book, the beach towels, Cami's suntan lotion that smelled like coconut and didn't have any SPF, Cami's water bottle, and her sunglasses.

Cami grinned. "You'll like this one. Trust me," she said as she ran across the sand, up the retaining wall steps, and across the grass to the beach house without looking back or offering to help carry the stuff.

Riley thought maybe she'd misjudged her when Cami turned and walked onto the grass, her eyes scanning the beach. "I forgot my flip-flops." She pointed at the yellow flip-flops sticking out of the sand. "Can you grab them?"

Riley looked down at her arms and then sent a pointed

stare in Cami's direction, which had no effect on Cami whatsoever because she was already in the house and closing the door behind her.

After a return trip to the beach and back to the house, Riley went straight to the laundry room on the main floor and dumped everything on top of the washing machine. She heard the shower running upstairs and decided to sort it later. She didn't want to risk leaving Cami alone for more than five minutes, and Riley needed to take a shower too.

She grabbed her book and raced up the curved wooden staircase. There were four bedrooms on the second level. Cami had complained that Riley and Willow's rooms had balconies and hers didn't. Riley had a feeling her brother had given Cami a room without a balcony for a reason. Except that after spending half a day with Cami, Riley didn't think anyone would be able to stop her if she decided to escape.

Riley paused outside her bedroom. The shower was still on in Cami's room, and she was singing ... "Macarena." Riley snorted a laugh and shook her head. Cami had weird taste in music, she thought as she rushed into her bedroom and stripped off her clothes.

She was on alert the entire time she showered, listening for any sign that Cami might be pulling off the great escape on Riley's watch. She was congratulating herself on setting a record for fastest time showering and washing her hair when she heard someone knocking on the front door.

"I've got it," she yelled, panicked that Cami would beat her to the door. Riley hopped into her shorts and grabbed a T-shirt. Shoving her head through the opening, she was attempting to get her arms through the holes as she opened her bedroom door and Cami ran past.

"Wait!" Riley called, hurrying after her. "You can't answer the door."

"Yes I can. Look," Cami said from where she now stood at the bottom of the stairs, wearing a daisy-printed sundress with a yellow straw sun hat in her hand. She put it on her head, stuck a pair of oversize white-flower sunglasses on her face, and struck a pose. "Ta-da. I look like one of those old ladies who lunch. Now we can go to the food truck. Woo-hoo!" She took off like a shot for the door.

Riley ran down the stairs, reaching Cami a second before she threw open the front door. A woman wearing white heels, a white sundress, and a white sun hat stood on the other side of the door with a bouquet of blood-red roses in one hand and a bottle of red wine in the other.

She looked from Cami to Riley and smiled. "Hi. I'm looking for Noah Elliot? Would he be home?"

Cami crossed her arms. "Who are you?"

Riley wanted to know the same thing, but jeez, did Cami have to be so rude? She nudged her with an elbow. Cami glanced at Riley and shrugged.

"Hi. I'm Noah's sister Riley, and this is my, ah, friend."

"Noah's not home, and neither is Willow."

The woman gaped at Cami. "Excuse me. *Willow Rosetti* is living here?"

Beside her, Cami stiffened, and Riley decided she had to get rid of this woman and fast. She didn't like the way she'd said Willow's name, as if it left a bad taste in her mouth, and she had a feeling, even if Cami didn't remember or know Willow, that she wouldn't let anyone get away with disparaging her family. How she'd go about that was what worried Riley.

Riley nodded in response to the woman's question and started closing the door. "They'll be home around six."

Cami placed a hand on the door above Riley's head, holding it open. "You haven't told us your name."

"Megan. I'm Noah's real estate agent."

"Is that right," Cami said, in a tone as disparaging as Megan's had been when she'd said Willow's name. Only Cami was way better at it. "Well, unless you didn't get the memo from your boss, you are no longer Noah's real estate agent. He fired your ass over the way you spoke to Willow."

Uh-oh, Riley thought, sucking in a breath when Cami leaned toward Megan. "And that was before he found out you had Willow kicked out of her rental. Bad move, really, really bad move, Meggie. You should know better than to mess with a Rosetti."

Megan's eyes narrowed "Who are you?"

"Queen of the mean girls, and if—"

Riley moved in front of Cami, cutting her off. "We have to go now. We'll tell my brother you dropped by." She stepped back, pushing into Cami so she had no choice but to do the same, and began closing the door. But before she did, she felt the need to stand up for Willow too. "You should apologize to Willow. You weren't very nice to her, and she's a really good person."

Before Megan had a chance to respond, Cami slammed the door in her face. Then Cami leaned her back against it and started laughing while mimicking Riley: " 'You weren't very nice to her, and she's a really good person.' "

"It's true," Riley said, heat rising to her cheeks.

Cami lowered her sunglasses, her gaze moving over Riley's face. "I'm sorry. I didn't mean to embarrass you." Then she grinned. "Don't worry, though, a few weeks with me, and we'll up your mean girl game. No one will mess with you then."

"Right, because you're queen of the mean girls."

There were mean girls in every school, including Riley's old one. She wasn't looking forward to dealing with them at her new school, so she could probably use a few tips. She just didn't know if she'd survive a few more weeks with Cami. Riley's nerves were already shot, and it had only been twenty-four hours, and Cami had slept through more than half of them.

"That was great, wasn't it? Did you see her face?"

"Yeah, and I saw the way she was looking at you too."

"She has no idea I'm a Rosetti."

"Maybe not, but..." She trailed off. She'd been going to say it wasn't only the fact that Cami was a Rosetti they had to hide. They also had to keep actress Camilla Monroe under wraps.

Riley covered the lapse by saying, "You're right."

Cami walked over to the window and peeked through the blinds. "Okay, she's gone. Let's go." She opened the door and stepped onto the deck. "Do me a favor and get the old-lady bag that PA Gail tried to pass off as mine. I'll meet you in the car."

Riley lunged for Cami, grabbing her arm. "We don't have a car, and you can't drive."

"I can so. I've been driving for a year, and I've been driving my mom's station wagon. It looks exactly like the one Noah pulled out of the garage last night to make room for Willow's stuff."

Think, Riley, think. "We can't. I don't have keys for the car."

Cami shrugged. "That's fine. I can hot-wire it."

"No, you can't!"

"Can so." She rubbed her fingers between her eyes, looking as if she was in pain. "Someone taught me how. I just don't remember who."

If she couldn't remember the person, Riley decided she wouldn't remember how to start the car so she could go along with the plan instead of risking Cami throwing a tantrum. "Okay. I'll get your purse."

She ran back up the stairs and headed straight for Cami's room. She opened the door and stood there with her mouth hanging open. The bed was unmade, and there were clothes everywhere. Cami's suitcases—all three of them—were open and empty on the floor, and so was the suitcase Willow had brought for her.

At the sound of Cami walking around downstairs, Riley shook off her shock at the mess and hurried into the room. It took her five minutes to find Cami's purse under the sheets at the foot of the bed. She opened the purse, feeling bad for invading Cami's privacy, but she wanted to make sure there was nothing inside that would set her off. Yesterday, when Noah had gone back for Willow, Cami had found her phone. It was just Riley's luck the phone had face ID, and it opened right away because Cami was looking at herself in the screen.

Luckily, because the Wi-Fi sucked at the beach house, Cami hadn't seen much but messages from Hugh and Jeff. Cami didn't know who the men were but Riley did. She lived in LA and watched entertainment news. Hugh was a big-time movie director, and Jeff was Cami's cheating ex. She didn't share this with Cami. Getting a glimpse of their messages on the home screen had upset her enough.

Riley figured it was because at seventeen, Cami had dreamed of becoming an actress, and Hugh had been informing her she hadn't gotten the part she'd auditioned for. He had been really nice about it and promised he'd keep Cami in mind for another project and hoped to talk to her soon.

Cami's cheating ex hadn't been nice at all. His girlfriend had gotten the part, and he'd rubbed it in Cami's face. He'd ended the text by recommending a real estate agent for Cami's house. After that, Riley had hidden the phone.

Riley pulled out Cami's wallet and considered hiding it too, afraid the driver's license photo would upset her. Riley hadn't missed the towel covering the bathroom mirror or the mirror face down on the dresser. But if Cami actually thought she was driving them to the food truck, it would be the first thing she looked for. Riley put the wallet back and then, with one last look around the room, she shut the door. Maybe once Cami got over her disappointment at not going to the food truck, they could clean her room, Riley thought as she ran down the stairs.

Noah wouldn't be happy if he saw the mess, and Riley didn't want him upset. The last thing she wanted was him having an excuse to kick out Cami and Willow. Riley liked having Willow around, and Cami might drive her crazy, but she liked having her there too.

Riley closed the front door behind her and froze at the sound of an engine revving.

Chapter Thirteen

Riley sprinted around the beach house to the garage. Cami sat behind the wheel of an ancient powder-blue station wagon in the middle of the crushed-shell driveway.

Leaning on the horn, she waved her casted arm out the open window. "Hurry up. I'm starving."

Riley dragged her feet, trying to come up with a reason for them not to go. The car door creaked as she opened it. "We won't be able to stop at the food truck, you know."

Cami frowned. "Why not?"

"Because you'll have to shut off the car when you park, and you can't hot-wire it in front of everyone." Riley didn't know how to hot-wire a car so she was guessing you had to play with the wires under the hood. But just in case she was wrong, she added, "That's if you can get it started a second time. The car's old, and so are the wires. You might even set it on fire."

Cami waved her off. "I didn't hot-wire it. I couldn't remember how. But I found the keys in the kitchen." She pointed at the key in the ignition.

Riley groaned. That explained why she'd heard Cami walking around downstairs. Riley got into the passenger seat and put Cami's purse on the floor, her brain racing for some way out of this as she reached for the handle to close the door. "Are you sure you should be driving with a broken arm? I don't think it's legal."

"Don't be such a worrywart," Cami said, and without any warning, she reversed out of the driveway at an alarming speed.

Riley yelped. "My door isn't closed!"

Cami yanked the wheel hard to the left, and the door slammed shut. "It is now." She laughed, speeding along the dirt road.

"Stop laughing. I could've fallen out." Riley choked on the dust billowing through the open windows. "And slow down. You don't want to get stopped for speeding."

"Relax. I'm not speeding." Cami nodded at the radio. "Put on some music."

Riley turned on the radio, praying it announced some freak weather event, like a hurricane approaching Sunshine Bay, and that everyone should stay inside. There was a faint sound of tinny music beneath the crackles. Every station was the same. "If you want music, you'll have to sing," Riley said, and turned off the radio.

"Good idea. We'll have a sing-off. I'll sing my favorite song, and then you'll sing yours." She glanced at Riley. "Trust me. It's fun. My mom, sisters, and I do it on our Sunday drives. You should hear my sister Eva sing. She's da bomb. She's in Europe now touring with her band. Just small venues, but you wait, one day she'll be a star." She slapped her hand on the wheel. "I bet that's where my mom and Gia are." Cami's shoulders slumped, and her bottom lip quivered. "I can't believe they left me behind."

"I'll go first," Riley blurted, feeling bad for Cami and hoping to distract her. "I'm not very good, though."

"Who cares?" Cami waved her hand. "Sing."

"Okay. Let me see if I can pull up my playlist on my phone," Riley said, thinking she'd get a signal now that they'd hit a paved road, indicating they were closer to town. She found her playlist and tapped on Billie Eilish's "When the Party's Over." It worked. She turned up the volume, hoping it would drown her out, and began singing.

When the song was over, Cami cried, "I love that!"

Riley smiled. "Me too. It's one of my favorites. What are you going to sing? I can bring up the music."

"Hmm." Cami tapped a forefinger on her lips and then she smiled. "I know. 'Alone' by Heart."

Riley scrolled through her phone. "Got it," she said, and pressed Play.

It wasn't a slow, quiet song like the one Riley had chosen, and Cami sang it like a rock star, throwing her head from side to side and tapping her cast on the steering wheel as if it were a drum, which made Riley nervous. But she ended up getting caught up in the song and moving in her seat to the beat.

"That's a great song, and you have a great voice, Cami," Riley said when it was over.

"Told you this was fun." Cami grinned. "Find one we can sing together."

In the end, it was Cami who decided what they'd sing. They were old songs Riley hadn't heard before, like "Sittin' on the Dock of the Bay," "Summer Breeze," and "California Girls," but by the second song, Riley was singing as loud and as proud as Cami.

She turned to smile at Cami as the last song ended, about

to share that this was the most fun she'd had in more than a year, when she noticed where they were, and the words backed up in her throat.

"Look!" Cami cried, and slammed on the brakes, almost sending Riley face-forward into the dashboard.

Her seat belt snapped back, holding her in place. "I know!" Riley cried. "We're on Main Street. We have to get out of here, Cami."

"I know where we are," Cami said, sticking her arm out the window and pointing at a bench on the sidewalk. "I wanted you to look at *that*."

"I don't know what you want me to...Oh." Megan's face covered the back of the bench. It was an advertisement for the real estate business where she worked with the words "Top Seller!" above her head.

"Hand me Gail's bag." Cami motioned for her purse.

Riley unsnapped her seat belt and grabbed the bag, holding it to her chest. "Why do you want it?"

"Why do you think I want it?"

"I asked you first."

Cami rolled her eyes, grabbing the bag from Riley's hands. "I need a marker. Nail polish or lipstick would work too."

Riley's eyes went wide. "No. No way." She shook her head. "You can't deface her sign. Someone will see you." And they would. The sidewalks on both sides of Main Street were crowded with people. Sunshine Bay might be a small beach town but it was popular with tourists.

"Got it!" Cami cried triumphantly, holding up a red marker. "Don't worry. I'm good at this sort of thing. No one will know what I'm up to. Trust me," she said, and opened her car door, stepping onto the sidewalk.

Riley's stomach knotted with nerves as Cami got out of the car and strode toward the bench. Riley didn't do this sort of thing. She was a rule follower. At least she had been. But this wasn't the same as orchestrating her escape from LA. She'd been desperate then.

Sliding down in the seat, she peeked over the dashboard to see what Cami was up to. She was sitting on the bench, trying to get the cap off the marker with her teeth. A man was watching her with his head cocked. All Riley could think was, *She's going to get caught*, and, looking both ways, she opened the car door.

Slamming it shut, she rounded the hood of the car and got between Cami and the guy checking her out. Riley turned her head and mimicked her brother's raised-eyebrow look. It worked! The guy shrugged and walked away.

"Trade places," Riley told Cami, nudging her off the bench. She held out her hand for the marker. "I've seen you try and write with your left hand. You take forever."

"I'm not writing anything," she said, but handed Riley the marker and got up from the bench.

"What are you . . . I mean, what am I doing, then?"

"Devil horns and a mustache. Add a goatee if you have time."

"Seriously?"

"If you don't want to do it, give me back my marker."

"I'll do it. Just keep your back to the crowd and keep an eye out for anyone you know. If you see someone, get back in the car and duck down."

"You're not the boss of me, you know?"

"What are you, six? Now don't distract me. We gotta get out of here ASAP." Riley glanced around and then got to work on the devil horns. She leaned back to look at her handiwork. "I think they'd look better filled in, don't you?" she asked Cami, but she was no longer standing there. Riley looked around and spotted her a few feet away, staring at a store's window.

"Cami!" she whisper-shouted.

She walked back to Riley, looking freaked out. "There's something wrong. I was just here the other day, and I bought a top at Surf to Shore. It's a hardware store now." She rubbed her thumb and forefinger up and down the bridge of her nose.

A familiar voice called Riley's name, and she and Cami looked across the road. Cars started beeping, and several drivers shouted out their open windows, shaking their fingers at Willow, who was weaving her way through traffic on a pink electric scooter. "Sorry! Sorry!" she yelled, waving an apologetic hand.

When Willow reached the sidewalk, she shut off the motor, stepped off the scooter, and parked it in front of the station wagon. "What are you two doing...?" She trailed off, and her eyes went wide. "Riley, what—"

Cami snagged the marker from Riley. "Don't blame her. It was my idea."

"Cami, how could you do that to her?"

"It's okay. I wanted to, Willow. I heard what Megan said to you. When you were talking in Noah's car."

Willow frowned. "But you were listening to your audiobook."

"I'd paused it to listen," she admitted sheepishly.

Cami laughed. "I knew you were listening."

"Because I knew you were faking that you were asleep and wanted to find out why." She shrugged. "Anyway, Cami and I heard how Megan spoke to you, and it wasn't nice." She glanced at Cami. "I mean, she was a total bitch."

Willow blinked at her and then turned on her aunt. "Really? You were looking after her for six hours, and she's already swearing?"

"Oh, so you're going to tell us Megan isn't a b—" Cami began.

"Of course she is, or at least she's been acting like one for a while now, even if I didn't always see it. But it doesn't mean I want you calling her names or defacing her face."

"So you don't care that she dropped by the beach house looking for Noah and introducing herself as his real estate agent?" Cami asked.

"She what?"

Cami nodded. "I didn't think you'd be happy about that. And let me tell you, she was not happy to hear you were staying at the beach house."

"Sh—crap," Willow said, looking panicked. "She didn't recognize you, did she?"

"Why would she? It's not like she knows me," Cami said.

Riley caught Willow's eye and shook her head.

"Okay, good." Willow leaned over and attempted to rub out the devil horns. When that didn't work, she snagged the marker from Cami's hand. "That's just great. It's permanent marker." She glanced around. "We have to get out of here. Come on."

Cami hung back. "What happened to Surf to Shore? They were right there just the other day," she said, pointing at the hardware store.

"Uh, they went out of business, I think," Willow said, and then hustled her aunt and Riley to the station wagon, grabbing her scooter on the way by. "Pop the trunk for me."

"I think it's too old to pop," Riley said as she and Cami got into the car. She leaned across Cami to hand the keys out the window to Willow.

After loading her scooter and closing the trunk, Willow opened the driver-side door. "I'll drive. You get in the back."

"You're no fun," Cami grumbled, but did as Willow said.

"I think you've had enough fun for one day," Willow said, eyeing her aunt in the rearview mirror.

"We were having fun," Cami muttered, and then leaned forward, resting her arms on the backs of the seats. "Can we get lobster rolls at the food truck? We're starved."

"Um, which food truck are you talking about?"

"You know. The one at the turnoff to Grady's pond."

Willow made a face at the windshield, and Riley guessed that there was no longer a food truck at the turnoff to the pond.

Riley glanced at Cami, remembering how panicked she'd looked when the store she'd shopped at was no longer there. She felt bad for her and vowed to be more patient when Cami pulled crazy stuff. She was probably just acting out because she was scared. Although she didn't look scared now. But she was a really good actress so maybe she was faking it.

"Right. I think they're closed today," Willow said. "But I was planning on making something special for dinner anyway."

"Last night you said you couldn't cook," Cami reminded Willow.

"I can cook. I'm just not great at it but I don't have to be. I eat at . . . Anyway, I thought it would be fun for all of us to cook together. What do you say?"

Riley nodded. "I'd like to."

Cami shrugged. "I guess if Riley wants to, I do too."

Riley smiled. She liked that Cami seemed to think of her as a friend now. Even if she was old enough to be Riley's mother.

"Great. I'll just have to stop at the market and pick up a couple things. We're going to film my 5 o'clock weather report at the beach house so I don't have to rush off but I thought we'd make something simple. Any ideas?"

"I'm good with whatever." Riley was more excited about watching Willow film her weather report than cooking, if she was being honest.

"Well, I'm not," Cami said. "I vote for bucatini carbonara. Eva and I make it all the time, and it's easy."

"Perfect." Willow leaned over and grabbed Cami's bag off the floor, tossing it to her in the back seat. "See if you can find some paper and a pen, and you can make me a list of what I need," she said as she eased the car into traffic.

"It's like four ingredients," Cami huffed.

Riley figured Willow was trying to distract her aunt from seeing all the changes on Main Street. "Yeah, but maybe we can pick up some snacks too," she said, listing some ideas. "Write those down."

Cami sighed as she dug around in the bag. "Fine."

By the time Willow turned into the market's parking lot, Cami had finished the list. She looked up and didn't even blink so Riley assumed the market was the same as Cami remembered.

"This thing is the size of a boat," Willow said. "I was hoping to find a spot at the back of the lot but I'll have to park here." She pulled in beside the sidewalk and unbuckled her seat belt. "Riley, it'll be quicker if you come in and help me." She glanced at her aunt as she opened the driver-side door.

"Cami, scrunch down so no one can see you, and whatever you do, don't talk to anyone or get out of the car. We'll be ten minutes at most."

Riley looked at Willow, thinking she didn't know her aunt very well if she was going to leave her alone and expect her to do what she said. "Here." Riley handed her iPad to Cami. "You can listen to my playlist."

"Okay." She took the iPad, and her brow furrowed. "How do I do that?"

It took Riley five minutes to teach Cami how to use her iPad. When they left to go into the grocery store, she was listening to the Rolling Stones and dancing in the back seat.

Willow smiled at Riley. "Thank you for being so awesome. You're wonderful with my aunt and I really appreciate it."

Riley's cheeks got warm, and she ducked her head. "It's not a big deal. Cami's nice and fun to be around."

"I'm not sure Noah will approve of my aunt's idea of fun, but I'm glad you two had a good time." Willow pointed at the dairy section. "If you can grab a pound of butter, a dozen eggs, and some cream, I'll get the rest." She picked up a basket and handed it to Riley. "Get yourself some ice cream or popsicles. Yogurt too."

"Thanks," Riley said, and hurried down the aisle. It took her about three minutes to get everything Willow had asked for, plus a carton of ice cream and some yogurt. It took her longer to find Willow. She caught a glimpse of her in the snack food aisle, surrounded by people. She seemed to know everyone in the store, and they all wanted to talk to her.

Riley didn't want to be rude, but she was worried about Cami and interrupted Willow's conversation with an older man named Amos, who was arguing with Willow about that morning's weather report. "Sorry to interrupt. But if it's okay, I'll go wait with...my friend in the car." She handed Willow the basket.

Willow glanced at her phone. "Sh—crap. Sorry, guys. I've gotta go," Willow said, and dashed to the cash register. "You go, Riley. I'll be right there."

Riley didn't want to draw attention by sprinting for the door so she fast-walked instead, telling herself as she did that she was overreacting. As soon as she exited the store, she discovered she wasn't. Cami wasn't in the car, and she'd left in a hurry. The back passenger-side door was open. Riley walked around the parking lot but there was no sign of her. She wondered if Cami had gotten tired of waiting and gone looking for them in the store. It was something Riley would do.

As she ran back to the store, Willow walked out the door with two bags of groceries in her arms. She took one look at Riley and her gaze shot to the car.

"Maybe she's in the..." Riley trailed off when across the road she spotted a familiar yellow sun hat weaving among the crowd on the sidewalk and heard a familiar voice yelling, "Flynn! Wait up. It's me. It's Cami."

Chapter Fourteen

Is it safe to come out? You're not going to strangle me or tell me you're kicking me and Cami out of the beach house?" Willow asked as she walked across the lawn to where a broody Noah sat by the fire.

For the first time in weeks, she hadn't been hit, chased, peed on, or pooped on (by a flock of seagulls) while filming her weather report. It was the aftermath that had led to this moment.

They'd planned on filming from the dock, but when they were setting up, a group of teenage boys offered to take them out in their speedboat. They were so excited about the idea of appearing in her broadcast that neither Willow nor Naomi had the heart to say no. They should've said no. The filming went smoothly but things went sideways as soon as they returned to the dock and Cami got a look at the boys.

It was the first time she'd come out of her bedroom since the Flynn debacle at the grocery store. The second Willow had pulled into the driveway, Cami had bolted from the car. Heartbroken that the teenager she'd thought was Flynn wasn't. Willow hadn't had a choice. She'd had to remind her aunt that she was forty-seven and not seventeen and Flynn was no longer a part of her life. To say it hadn't gone well would be an understatement.

So of course Willow had been thrilled when Cami ventured out of her room, smiling at the boys with an excited gleam in her eyes. Okay, so the excited gleam had worried her, and she'd learned soon enough that it should.

When Cami tried to drag Riley over to meet the boys, literally drag her, a fight had broken out between them, and everyone had learned just how much *fun* they'd had earlier in the day.

And because if Willow had any luck at all, it was bad luck, Noah had arrived in time to hear about Cami's near flashing and Riley's near drowning, which was bad enough. But they didn't stop there. Oh no, they had to share what had happened on Main Street.

"What are my other options?" Noah asked, tracking her approach as a lion tracks its prey.

"An angry kiss?" She blamed the way the firelight danced on the hard angles of his gorgeous face for the suggestion.

"As tempted as I am to find out what an angry kiss feels like, I don't think it would be conducive to the conversation we're about to have."

"Just to say, my vote would be for the angry kiss instead of the conversation," she shared as she took a seat on the Adirondack chair beside him.

"Noted. But you've piqued my curiosity. Just how good is an angry kiss?"

"I wouldn't know. I've never had one." She tilted her head, thinking back to her last boyfriend. "Unless you count someone kissing me to shut me up as an angry kiss."

His lips twitched. "I admit I've been tempted to kiss you for the same reason."

"Maybe we should stick to the conversation you wanted to have," she said, smiling when he laughed. "But teasing aside, Noah, I'd understand if you want Cami and me to leave."

"I don't want *you* to leave. Your aunt is another story, but for reasons unfathomable to me, Riley informed me that she wouldn't speak to me for a month if I asked Cami to leave. I didn't tell her that wasn't her best negotiating tactic."

After Cami and Riley stopped arguing, Noah had taken his sister down to the beach to talk, and Willow had brought her aunt inside to do the same. She had a feeling Noah's conversation with Riley had been more productive than hers with her aunt.

"You didn't have to. She'd figured it out by the time she came in to help us with dinner. She said, I quote, 'My brother is the only person I know who would be happy living on his own on a deserted island.'"

"She's not entirely wrong. I do like quiet and my own space."

"I think you'd be bored in a week."

"I'm looking forward to finding out."

"What do you mean?"

"An hour after the company is dissolved on the thirteenth, I leave for a polar expedition in the Canadian High Arctic, and then every six weeks after that, I'll be joining expeditions in remote locations around the world." He couldn't hide his excitement. There was a light in his eyes that she hadn't seen in the past few days.

But she had seen it over the course of their three weeks together during the summer of 2011. "I remember you talking about this. Not this exactly, but how you wanted to travel the world. The places you wanted to see." He'd had an insatiable curiosity she'd admired. She had been a little in awe of him, even back then.

"I hadn't thought about it before, but now that you mention it, I guess I did begin planning my itinerary then. I've refined it over the years but it hasn't deviated much from the original plan." His gaze followed the sparks from the fire shooting up into the night sky. "I didn't think I'd have the opportunity for another ten years, at least. My mother's death, sadly, expedited things."

"Your mother had planned to dissolve the company in ten years?"

He nodded. "She was tired. I should've pushed the issue for her sake, not mine, but she had other people in her ear. Over the past three years, I acted in the capacity of her co-CEO to take some of the burden off her and to give her more time with my sister."

"Riley mentioned you were head of the legal department. Did you continue in both roles?"

"I did. My mother didn't like to delegate or give up control, unless it was to a member of the family, and I was the only one. It was the same when my grandfather ran the company. My mother had been the head of public relations, and she'd stepped into his shoes hours after he died. I don't think she ever felt comfortable in the role."

"Since you're dissolving the corporation, I'm guessing you didn't either."

"I didn't want any part of it, to be honest. But I wasn't given a choice. Like my uncle, I'd been groomed for the role since birth. Unlike me, from what I've been told, he couldn't wait to take over the reins of the family business. My mother used to joke if Will, that was her brother, had had his way, he would've staged a coup and thrown my grandfather over."

"I didn't know you had an uncle."

"He died the summer of '94. Totaled his car just outside of Sunshine Bay. He was only eighteen." He glanced at the beach house. "My grandparents closed up the beach house and rarely came back. It was my mother who convinced them not to sell. She loved it here, and so did my father."

"I've never heard you mention your father."

"My parents divorced when I was ten. My father didn't appreciate how much time my mother gave to the company. He blamed my grandfather for their divorce."

"Do you have a relationship with him?"

"A phone call now and then. He remarried six months after the divorce was finalized and started a new family. And before you ask, no, I don't have a relationship with them. My father didn't encourage it."

"That's horrible. It's all horrible," she said, getting emotional. "I hate that your father made you feel unwanted and that you weren't allowed to choose what you wanted to do with your life. No one should do that to a child." She crossed her arms. "Your family sucked. Not your mother or Riley, obviously. Or your uncle. It's really sad he died so young. But everyone else sucked."

His lips twitched. "My grandfather and grandmother Bennett were very nice, if somewhat demanding."

"Are you laughing at me?"

"No. Maybe a little." He grinned and reached for her hand, giving it a light squeeze. "I appreciate your anger on my behalf. I really do. But it's unwarranted."

"How can you say that?"

"Easily. I've led a privileged life. I might not have wanted it or asked for it, but because of who my family is, at twenty-four, I walked into a role at the company that I hadn't earned. But as much as I didn't want to be involved in the company, I enjoyed the work, and more, the people I worked with. I also was, and am, extremely well compensated."

"I've seen how hard you work, Noah. And I know how smart you are so don't try and tell me you didn't deserve your position. You're just being modest."

"And you're being sweet."

"Don't try and distract me. Riley told me a little about your relationship with your stepfather, so I know things didn't get better for you. Was Billy the reason you hung out with me instead of with your family?"

"I don't know any fifteen-year-old boy who'd prefer spending their summer vacation with their family when they could spend it with a gorgeous fifteen-year-old girl who made them laugh."

"Now look who's being sweet." She smiled. "And be honest, I didn't always make you laugh."

"You're right, and I was reminded of the many times you drove me crazy when I heard what Cami got up to today."

"You can't compare me to my aunt. I was not that wild. I didn't nearly flash my boobs at a bunch of boys or ask you to pretend you're drowning to get someone's attention."

"You didn't flash your boobs at a bunch of boys, you flashed them at me."

"It's not the same. It was an accidental flashing. I didn't lose my bikini top on purpose. A rogue wave took me out."

He lifted his hands. "You didn't hear me complaining, did you?"

"No." She laughed. "You turned bright red, stammered

something unintelligible while pointing at my boobs, and then dove under the water and didn't resurface for what felt like ten minutes."

"I was smooth, wasn't I?" He laughed. "But to my credit, I found your bikini top."

"You did, and you gallantly kept your back to me when you handed it over. I could've done without the knot-tying lecture that followed, though, and the demonstration."

"You never know when you'll be called upon to tie a good knot."

"This is true, but what isn't true is you insinuating I'm just like my aunt. I didn't make you do anything you didn't want to."

He held up his hand and began ticking off his fingers. "Snorkeling, which is when I had my near-drowning experience."

"Okay, but just to point out, you could swim, and I rescued you."

He raised an eyebrow and continued. "Surfing, skateboarding, biking ten miles on the hottest day of the year, and off-roading on that guy's ATV that you *borrowed*." He held up his other hand.

She leaned over and pulled his hands down. "I get it. I pushed you out of your comfort zone, but you have to admit you had fun. And just think, if I hadn't, you wouldn't have realized you were an adventurer at heart and started planning your trip around the world."

"I'm not sure I'd go that far, but I did have an incredible amount of fun with you." He glanced at the beach house. "That said, I would prefer if my baby sister didn't have the same kind of fun with your aunt as I did with you."

"I don't think you have to worry about that. The teenage

version of my aunt is all about boys, and I was all about having fun, even if that fun made you uncomfortable at times."

He stared at her. "You can't possibly believe that makes me feel better."

"I did, but obviously I was wrong. I'll talk to Cami and set some boundaries."

"I'm not sure Cami knows the meaning of boundaries. At least the seventeen-year-old version of your aunt. I'm going to have nightmares for a week just thinking about them driving around in that car. I never should've listened to the rental agent and kept it for renters to use."

He had a point, and she imagined, with what had happened to Noah's uncle Will, his reaction to his baby sister driving around with Cami would have been even more visceral than hers. "I don't have anything going on tomorrow other than my weather reports and a meeting first thing in the morning with Don and the rest of the team to go over the package we're sending to prospective buyers, so I can spend the day with Cami and Riley."

"I have a couple of calls I can't put off, and I'd like to sit in on the meeting with you, Don, and the team, but other than that, I've cleared my schedule so I can hang around here if you need to pack."

"Thank you, but I've had so many offers of help, it'll probably take me less than three hours to finish up packing and move everything here. I've scheduled the move for Saturday during dinner service at La Dolce Vita so my family can't help. Is that okay with you?"

"I'm good with whatever works for you." He lowered his voice. "After what happened downtown today, do you really think you can keep your aunt under wraps for much longer?"

"I just have to keep her hidden for a few more days. The restaurant only opens for dinner service on Mondays, and it's usually slow, so my sister and I figure that's the best day to break the news to our family. We just want to confirm with my cousin. We're going to talk tomorrow." She glanced at the beach house. "It would help if Cami got her memory back between now and Monday. If I knew what caused the estrangement, maybe we could avoid some of the drama."

"I'm sure it'll be fine."

"You don't know my family. Drama is all but guaranteed. A lot of yelling, swearing, and guilting me, and at some point, we'll probably have to call 911 or Father Patrick because my nonna will think she's having a heart attack." She winced at the thought that it might not be an act this time. "Bruno, her fiancé, is really good at calming her down so fingers crossed"—she crossed hers and held them up—"it won't come to that. And my sister and cousin will have my back, so I should be good. For Cami's sake, I just hope that they can get past whatever tore them apart. Knowing how the family feels about her, it hurts my heart when Cami talks about them. She loves them so much."

He reached over and tucked her hair behind her ear. "Just don't let them hurt *your* heart."

A flock of butterflies took flight in her stomach at his words. They felt meaningful, important somehow, as if the flirty thing they'd been doing for the past couple of days had shifted into something deeper. She wondered if that's why they sat staring into each other's eyes, as if holding their breath. Waiting for one of them to break the silence and say what they were thinking. Then again, maybe she'd read more into his words and gentle touch than he'd meant and he was simply waiting for her to respond.

But before she had a chance to say something, Noah cleared his throat, gave her a half smile, and came to his feet. "They're too quiet in there. I'm getting worried."

"I'm sure they're fine. They were doing makeovers, and I asked them to come up with a menu for the week. Cami's cooking, in case you're wondering, not me."

"Her carbonara was amazing so you'll get no complaints from me. I could've done without the water fight, though." He gave her a pointed look.

She held up her hands. "It wasn't me who started it. They ganged up on me. I had to defend myself. But if you thought that was bad, you should've seen the water fights my sister, cousin, and I had." She shrugged. "Besides, they helped clean up, they had fun, and there were no boys involved."

"Not for lack of your aunt trying. But Cami does make Riley laugh. If you close your eyes and listen to them, it's as if they've known each other for weeks and are the best of friends. When they're not fighting, that is. It's when you open your eyes and see your sister's new best friend is a forty-seven-year-old woman that it gets weird."

"It's not that weird. I have friends who are decades older than me."

"Yes, but you're twenty-eight, not fifteen."

"Riley's mature for her age. It's as if she's fifteen going on thirty. You were the same."

"A lot of good it did me keeping you out of trouble."

"We're not back to that, are we?"

"No, we're back to me checking on what kind of trouble

your aunt might be getting my baby sister into. While I'm doing that, would you like me to get you a glass of wine?"

"That would be nice, thanks." She smiled, relaxing in the chair and looking out over the water. She'd grown up with a similar view. It was one of the things she'd missed when she'd moved out on her own. She couldn't afford the homes or rentals on the water. Even the homes a few blocks away had been out of her price range. She had no reason to complain, though. In Sunshine Bay, you were never more than a ten-minute walk to the ocean. That said, she was going to enjoy every minute of her time here.

"Willow!"

She startled at Noah's bellow, cursed her aunt for whatever she'd done now, and ran to the beach house. She threw open the screen door. Noah stood in the living room with his back to her. "What's going on?"

He turned, walked toward her, handed her an empty bottle of wine, and said, "You deal with her, or I will."

At the same time he did this, Willow got a look at Cami and Riley sitting on the couch, and her jaw dropped.

"It's not a trick of the lighting. My sister's hair is pink."

"I'm sure it'll wash out."

"I don't care about her hair, Willow. What I do care about is that my fifteen-year-old sister is drunk."

"I'm not drunk! She is." Riley jerked her thumb at Cami, who apparently thought that was hysterical and collapsed on the couch giggling. Riley smiled, showing off her purple teeth.

Noah looked at them, shook his head, and then stalked to the door, letting it slam shut behind him.

An hour later, Willow rejoined Noah by the fire. "Riley's okay. She had half a glass of wine, and I washed her hair. It was food dye so most of it came out. She's sleeping, and so is my aunt, who will be hungover in the morning. On a positive note, she probably won't want to do anything other than lie around all day tomorrow."

He turned his head to look at her.

"I know, I know, and I'm not trying to make excuses for Cami but Riley said she was still upset about Flynn."

"So my sister tried to cheer her up by drinking with her?" he said in a familiar sardonic tone that a few days ago would've made her grit her teeth, but she didn't blame him for being angry.

"No. Cami tried to cheer herself up by drinking, which I'm sure her forty-seven-year-old self knows only makes things worse, but her seventeen-year-old self doesn't. If it's any consolation, Cami didn't push Riley to drink. My aunt apparently didn't feel like sharing, but Riley was curious. At least she tried it when she was in a safe environment, right?"

He raised an eyebrow.

"Exactly how angry are you right now? Angry enough to kick my aunt out or could we compromise and you could pretend to strangle her?" She searched his face. "No? How about an angry kiss? With me, not my aunt."

"I'm not angry at you. I'm angry at—"

She gasped. "You can't kiss my aunt. First of all, she's drunk, and she's sleeping. Secondly, I don't want you to kiss my aunt. I want you to kiss—"

He cut her off before she told him the truth and said "me," and he did this by leaning in and kissing her. It was nothing like the lip-lock they'd shared at fifteen, which had been a literal lip-lock. Noah Elliot had learned to kiss, and like everything else he did, he did it exceptionally well.

"You've clearly been practicing," she said when they came up for air. "And just for the record, that wasn't an angry kiss, was it?"

"Did you really stop kissing me to talk about what type of kiss it was?"

"No. Of course not. I just thought we were taking a breather, and I was complimenting your technique. You're a very good kisser." She leaned in. "I promise not to interrupt you again."

He smiled. "Glad to hear it. And just for the record, that was not an angry kiss. That was also not me trying to shut you up with a kiss, although it did cross my mind. That was me not being able to resist the temptation that is you for a second longer, even when I know I should."

"You really, really shouldn't," she murmured, and then she kissed him.

Riley's voice coming through the screen door interrupted them. "Um, Willow, Cami's throwing up."

Chapter Fifteen

Cami woke up, squinting against the sunlight flooding her bedroom at the beach house. What had she been thinking, drinking a bottle of wine the previous night? She groaned, pressing a hand to her pounding head. You'd think she would've learned her lesson after what happened the last time. It was how she'd ended up with a broken arm...and ruined her relationship with Flynn.

She raised her arm, studying her cast. Her friends' names, written in colored markers and accompanied by stick-figure drawings to cheer her up, were missing. Just like three decades of her memories. Tears trickled down her cheeks as she stared at the plain, white cast. She felt as if she was losing her mind.

Yesterday had been the worst. She hadn't recognized half the stores on Main Street, and then she'd seen that boy. He looked just like Flynn. The boy she'd loved. The boy who'd broken her heart. A boy who was now a man, and she was still seventeen, stuck in the body of a forty-seven-year-old woman.

It was easier being seventeen, easier not to open the door to her memories. She'd tried. She really had. Even when the pain in her head nearly brought her to her knees, she'd tried to remember. But it wasn't pain that kept her from opening the door to her memories, it was fear. It was like when she was a little girl and had been afraid to open her closet door at night, positive there was a monster inside. Something warned her that there was a monster lurking behind the door where her memories were stored, and she wasn't about to let it out.

She shot out of bed, ignoring the pounding in her head as she ran for the bedroom door and pulled it open. "Riley! Where are you?"

"In my bedroom!"

Her panic subsided at the reassuring sound of Riley's voice. Riley poked her head out of her room and frowned. "What's wrong?"

"Nothing." Cami smiled with a shrug. "Just looking for you." She joined Riley in her room and looked around. It was spotless. The only thing out of place was the box on Riley's bed. "What are you doing?"

"Remember I told you I wanted to find some of my mom's stuff?" Riley asked while walking back to her bed. "I found this box of photos from when my mom was young." She held one up. "Come see."

Cami's vision blurred around the edges, and she took a step back, and then another and another until she was standing in the hall. "No." She shook her head. "No."

"Cami, what is it? What's wrong?"

She pressed a hand against her stomach. "I don't know. I'm not feeling so good."

Riley sighed. "That's what you get for drinking almost an entire bottle of wine." She returned the photo to the box. "I'll make you some toast."

Cami gave Riley a shaky smile when she reached her side, and pulled her in for a hug. "You're the best friend I've ever had."

"Really?"

Cami nodded. "Really."

Riley gave her a shy smile. "You're the best friend I've ever had too."

"You're sure you're not mad at me for dyeing your hair pink or getting you in trouble with Noah?" Cami asked, following her down the stairs.

"A whole head of pink hair was a bit much, but I like the streaks," Riley said, holding out the pink-streaked curly locks that framed her face before letting them go and walking to the kitchen. "And it's not like you made me drink the wine."

"Yeah, but I don't think Noah cares whether I made you drink it or not. I'm pretty sure he hates me." She looked around the kitchen. "Where are they, anyway?"

"At the station for a meeting. Willow said they'll be home around noon. And my brother doesn't hate you, Cami. He's just not used to having anyone living with him, especially, uh, teenage girls. He likes everything nice and orderly, and he likes his quiet." Riley grinned. "And you're like having a tornado in the house."

"It's not just that. He thinks I'm a bad influence. He's your brother, and he's protective. I'm pretty sure if it wasn't for you and Willow, he would've kicked me out of the beach house last night. But I get it. If I were him, I'd want to kick me out too. I'll apologize when he gets home. I won't do anything else to get us in trouble, Riley. Promise."

Riley turned from putting four slices of bread into the toaster. "You don't seem like yourself. Are you sure you're okay? Other than being hungover, I mean."

She lifted a shoulder. "I don't like people being mad at me."

"I know what would make Noah happy."

"What?"

"After we have some toast, we'll go up and clean your room. Then I'll take a pic and send it to Noah. I guarantee that'll put him in a good mood before he comes home."

"I guess. If you think it'll work."

"I know it will. And I bet you'll feel better too."

An hour and a half later, they stood in the middle of Cami's spotlessly clean bedroom. Not a thing was out of place. They'd even vacuumed and dusted.

"Noah had better appreciate this. I'm exhausted." Cami sniffed herself and made a face. "I think I sweated out the wine. I'm going to take a shower."

"How are you exhausted? You sat on the bed and bossed me around."

"My arm's in a cast, Riley. It's not like I could pick up anything too heavy."

"Clothes aren't heavy, and they're not that difficult to hold, even one-handed."

Cami grinned as she walked to the bathroom, feeling a lot better than she had earlier that morning. Maybe Riley was right: having a clean room worked wonders. "I'll make it up to you."

"How are you going to do that?" Riley grumbled from where she sat on the edge of the bed, waiting for a response from Noah to her email. She'd sent him a pic of Cami pretending to vacuum her room.

"I'll think about it when I'm in the shower."

"Well, it better be good." Riley grinned, holding up her iPad. "Noah's so happy that *you* cleaned your room, he's picking up lobster rolls for lunch."

"Woo-hoo!" Cami cried. "This is going to be the best day!"

Forty minutes later, Cami watched as Riley stood at the foot of the dock, worrying her bottom lip between her teeth. "This is a really bad idea."

"No," Cami said. "It's a great idea. You're spending your summer at the beach, and you don't know how to swim. I bet Noah will be even happier with me than he is now if I teach you." Cami raised herself out of the water and rested her arms on the end of the dock. "I'm a really good swimmer, Riley. You're safe with me. I promise."

"You won't throw me in or do anything crazy?" Riley asked, taking tentative steps along the dock toward her.

"Cross my heart." She drew an *x* on her chest. "You can hold on to the ladder. You don't have to let go unless you want to."

"Okay. I guess I can do that." Riley slipped off her denim shorts to reveal a navy one-piece bathing suit, dropping her beach towel on top of them.

Once she'd taught her to swim, Cami decided she was going to take Riley bathing suit shopping. "All we're going to do is practice kicking for now," she told Riley, who climbed down the ladder as if she were going to her execution.

As the water lapped at her calves, Riley shrieked, "It's freezing!"

"Go fast and get it over with. You'll get used to it," Cami said, treading water beside the ladder.

Riley shot her a dirty look but did as she said.

"Now hang on to the bottom rungs and let your legs float out behind you and then start kicking."

After about ten minutes of kicking, Riley glanced at her. "Is this all I'm going to do?"

"Would you be okay letting go of the ladder? Just try one hand for now if you're not."

"Okay." Riley nodded and took her left hand off the bottom rung. "Now what?"

"Just keep kicking, and once you're comfortable, we'll tread water. Like this." She showed Riley how. "Trust me, you'll be fine. You've got a strong kick. But if you get nervous, you can just grab the ladder."

Riley nodded. "I'm going to let go now."

"Just keep kicking and move your arms," Cami instructed, keeping a close eye on her.

Riley's eyes got big. "Look, Cami. I'm doing it."

"You are, and you're doing great."

"Can you teach me to swim now?"

"Let's practice treading water for a while longer. It's one of the most important things to learn. We'll try floating next, and then we'll go closer to shore, and I'll teach you how to do the dog paddle."

"The dog paddle?" Riley groaned, making a face.

"Hey, that's the first stroke I learned."

In the end, Riley didn't care that she was doing the dog paddle. All she cared about was that she was able to swim six feet to where Cami stood in four feet of water. "You did it!" Cami cheered.

"I did it! I can swim!" Riley threw herself at Cami and hugged her. "Can you teach me how to swim like you now?"

"We'll practice what you've learned for the next couple of days, and then you can try the front crawl. Okay?"

Riley sighed. "Okay." Then her face lit up at the sounds of car doors shutting, and seconds later, Noah and Willow rounded the side of the beach house. Riley waved her arms. "Noah, Willow, come here! Come watch me swim."

Cami felt like a proud mother watching Riley show Noah

and Willow what she'd learned, but nothing compared to the feeling she got when they hugged and praised her for teaching Riley to swim. She didn't think the day could get much better, but it did.

They had a picnic on the beach, and the lobster rolls were as amazing as Cami remembered. After they ate, they played beach volleyball. Noah had found a net in the garage. He'd found horseshoes too, and they played that later. Mostly because Cami and Riley got tired of Noah and Willow beating them at beach volleyball. They were so competitive!

The way they kept smiling at each other was annoying too. Cami didn't know why, but she had the weirdest urge to pull Willow away from Noah every time they hugged after winning a game. Maybe she was just jealous that Willow had a boyfriend and she didn't.

Cami watched Willow bend over to throw her horseshoe, and she wasn't the only one watching. She narrowed her eyes at Noah. "Dude, stop checking out her butt."

"I wasn't checking out her butt. I was checking out her, uh, form." Noah cleared his throat. "Her throwing form. Stance. Whatever."

"Why? It's not like you need any pointers, and Willow hasn't come close to the stake with any of her throws," Cami said, nodding to where Willow's horseshoe had landed, almost a foot from the stake.

"Which is why I was checking out her form. To give her pointers."

Willow grinned at Noah as she walked toward him. "You can give me pointers anytime," she said, and then she went up on her toes and whispered something in his ear.

Cami rolled her eyes at the expression on Noah's face. He

looked as if he wanted to throw Willow over his shoulder and run into the house. "You two are so annoying," she said, walking away to collect the horseshoes.

"Why are they annoying?" Riley asked, joining them with a can of soda for herself and one for Cami.

"They're flirting again." She didn't expect any support from Riley. She practically beamed every time she caught Noah and Willow giving each other goo-goo eyes.

Totally called it, Cami thought when Riley's face split in an ear-to-ear grin.

At a chiming sound coming from the back pocket of her denim shorts, Willow pulled out her phone and made a face. "I hate to bail on you, guys, but I have a Zoom call. Wish me luck," she said to Noah.

He tucked Willow's hair behind her ear. "It'll be fine," he said, and then he pulled his phone from the pocket of his board shorts and held it up. "Text me if you need backup."

"What's a Zoom call, and why would you need backup?" Cami asked, looking from Willow to Noah. She didn't miss their shared glance.

I shouldn't have asked, she thought when Willow explained that she'd be talking to people on her laptop and how it worked. It made Cami's head hurt.

"It's just a meeting about Channel 5 stuff," Willow added before sharing another glance with Noah.

He nodded and smiled at Cami and Riley. "Come on, you two. Best three out of five. The loser does the dishes tonight."

"No way," Cami said as Willow jogged up the steps to the beach house. "Cooks don't clean. It's a rule."

"It's between you and Riley, then. I'm cooking tonight."

Riley snorted. "You don't cook. Mrs. D does."

"Yeah, but this is different. I'm grilling. Prepare to be amazed, Tink."

"It sounds like I'd better prepare a backup dinner," Cami quipped, and she and Riley discussed what she was going to make in between throwing horseshoes and trying to distract Noah. It didn't work. He still beat them, and Cami and Riley were tied for cleanup duty.

Noah glanced at his phone and then at the beach house. "How about another game of beach volleyball? I'll take on the two of you."

"I'm in. Cami?" Riley asked.

"Sure. I just have to go to the bathroom."

"Are you sure you can't wait?" Noah asked, looking uncomfortable. "Willow should be off her call in a few minutes."

"Uh, no, I can't." She shook her head and walked away, wondering what the big deal was.

"Be quiet and be quick, Cami. Don't disturb Willow," Noah called after her.

"Yeah, yeah," she said as she ran up the stairs and hurried across the deck, opening the door and closing it quietly behind her. She heard Willow's voice as soon as she walked into the house and stopped in her tracks.

"Of course I want her to get her memory back, Sage. The last thing I want is for Cami to face Nonna, Zia, and Mom with no idea that she's been estranged from the family for twenty-five years."

Cami pressed a hand to her mouth, muffling her cry. Her knees went weak, and she leaned against the door. It couldn't be true. There had to be some mistake. She eased away from the door, tiptoeing closer to the kitchen, where Willow sat at the table with her back to her. Cami stayed out of view behind the wall separating the kitchen and living room.

"Maybe you should've thought about that before you contacted Cami behind the family's back," a woman said.

Cami didn't like the way the woman spoke to Willow, and she peeked around the edge of the wall. She could see two women on the laptop's screen. The one on the left had auburn hair and looked as if she was sitting in an office. Cami could see her sister Gia in the woman's features. The woman on the right, despite her blond hair, looked enough like Cami's sister Eva that there was no denying they were related. Cami drew her head back, leaning against the wall for support. They really were her nieces.

"I know, Sage. We've gone over this already, and I've apologized."

"Willow's right, Sage. Let it go. Cami's here, and now we just have to figure out a way to reunite her with the family without making things worse," the other woman said.

"Easy for you to say, Lila. You and Zia Eva won't be here."

Cami decided Sage was a pain in the ass. She'd inherited that particular gene from her grandmother, not her mother, that was for sure. Her grandmother and mother who, from the sounds of it, no longer loved Cami. She squeezed her eyes closed to keep the tears at bay, wondering what she could've done that was so bad they'd cut her off from the family. It had to be her mother and sisters who'd cut her out of their lives because Cami loved her family too much to be separated from them for weeks, let alone decades.

"Really, Sage? You're not being helpful at all. Did you have a bad day in court or what?" Willow asked.

Cami wondered if Sage was a lawyer. It wouldn't surprise her if she was. She had a tough, know-it-all voice. But maybe she was a judge. She sounded judge-y.

"Sorry, Lila. It's been a stressful week."

Cami peeked around the wall. Sage was pushing her fingers through her hair. She looked stressed, and Cami felt a little bad for judging her. She knew only too well what it felt like to have a tough week.

Well, she felt bad until Sage continued talking. "Look, I know that you don't want to hear this, Will, but if we don't want to have World War Three on our hands, and you don't want Cami to get hurt, you have to help her regain her memory. Stop tiptoeing around. Give it to her straight. Ask the hard questions."

"The doctor said not to pressure her, Sage. I don't want to upset her. I did that yesterday when I had to explain to her that the boy she was chasing down Main Street wasn't Flynn, and she wasn't seventeen."

Cami winced at the memory.

"Poor kid. She must have terrified him," Sage said.

Seriously? Cami knew who had inherited her sister Gia's compassionate nature, and it sure as heck wasn't Sage.

"But Will, if we're going to break the news to the family on Monday, you're going to have to toughen up. I reached out to a former client. She specializes in traumatic brain injuries and amnesia, and she thinks it's possible Cami has a painful memory that she's blocking. So start asking her questions about what was going on that summer. There's a reason she's stuck at seventeen."

"I think it's because she broke her arm that summer too," Willow said. "And broke up with Flynn."

"Or maybe she's stuck at seventeen because those are some of her happiest memories," Lila suggested.

Okay, Lila sounded nice, but if Cami breaking her arm and breaking up with her boyfriend were her happiest memories, her life must really suck.

"You might be right. She has every reason to want to forget this past year, what with her husband cheating on her and then ending up having to pay him alimony, not to mention her career has tanked," Willow said.

Cami covered her ears, chanting, *Yadda, yadda, yadda* in her head. She had to get out of there. Why had she listened, anyway? She lowered her hands from her ears, slowly backing away from the wall before turning and tiptoeing to the powder room. She had her hand on the knob when the door to the beach house opened and Noah and Riley walked inside.

Noah glanced her way and frowned. She had to pretend she was coming out of the bathroom, not going in. She walked over to them with a smile and whispered, "I thought we were playing beach volleyball."

"Okay. That sounds like a plan," they heard Willow say. "Send pics of the wedding, Lila. Give our love to everyone. And Sage, I'll see you tomorrow, right?"

Oh no, they'd made a plan. Cami didn't like the sound of that, especially if Sage was involved with said plan.

"We were worried about you," Riley said to Cami. "Are you okay?"

"Better now, thanks." She nodded, thinking that was as good an excuse as any for why she'd been MIA.

Willow walked out of the kitchen, and her eyes shot to Cami. "Uh, is everything okay?"

"Yeah." Cami nodded. She didn't want Willow to guess

she'd overheard her. "Come on, we're going to play beach volleyball. Let's go." She sounded manic. Like she had something to hide. And the way Noah's narrowed eyes moved over her face, she worried he'd figured it out.

"It's almost four. I should probably get organized for my broadcast," Willow said.

"Okay, but first come upstairs. I want to show you guys something. I found a box of pictures. Wait until you see Uncle Will."

Cami's heart began to race. Will. Will...Bennett. She knew that name.

"You won't believe how much he looks like Noah, Willow. Well, except he has fair hair, not dark," Riley said as she ran upstairs.

She expected them to follow but Cami couldn't move. She didn't only recognize his name, she remembered him. Will was the boy she'd flirted with at the dunes. The boy who... She staggered, clutching her head, moaning as the door to her memories opened.

"I can't, Will. I have to go home. It's late."

"I got us a hotel room, Cami. I'm beat. We'll leave first thing in the morning. I promise. Your mom won't even know you've been gone."

"You don't know my mother." She put the blame on her mother but it was more than that. Cami didn't want to stay in a hotel room with Will. She liked him a lot, but she didn't love him. She loved Flynn, and she felt guilty enough.

Last week, she'd had sex with Will. She hadn't meant for it to happen, but he was hot, and he was sweet, and he made her feel beautiful, and she'd missed Flynn. She'd been angry at him too.

"She'll ground me for the rest of the summer, Will. We'll drive home with the windows open, we'll get some coffee, and I'll talk to

you the entire way back to Sunshine Bay. I won't let you fall asleep. I promise I won't. It's an hour drive. It'll be fine."

"Whatever," he said, taking his car keys out of his pocket. His strides were long and angry as he led the way to his red Corvette.

She hurried to catch up with him. "Don't be mad at me, Will." She felt like crying, and from the way Will's expression softened, she had a feeling that he'd read the emotion on her face.

"As if I could stay mad at you for long." He opened the car door for her and smirked. "Guess what we're listening to all the way home."

"No, not Smashing Pumpkins!"

"Yep. That's your payback for ruining the night I had planned. You're missing out, babe. Big-time."

She was about to promise she'd make it up to him but didn't want to lie to him. She wanted to stay friends, just not friends who had sex. "You're a great guy, Will Bennett."

He frowned as he got behind the wheel. "This isn't you giving me the brush-off, is it?"

"No, of course not."

"So we're still on for kitesurfing tomorrow?"

"As long as my mother doesn't discover I snuck out, we are."

"Then we'd better get you home."

"Cami?"

Willow's voice jerked Cami from the memory, and she lifted her gaze to where Willow stood with Noah, looking concerned. Cami remembered. She remembered everything. Drawing on her acting abilities, she forced a smile. She couldn't tell them she'd gotten her memory back. Not yet. Not until she made amends for everything she'd done.

Chapter Sixteen

Willow's sister hadn't been at the beach house for more than twenty minutes before she was dragging her onto the deck. "I have to talk to my baby sis for a minute," Sage said, smiling at Noah, Riley, and Cami before sliding the door closed.

"Sage! We're going to be late. I promised I'd be at the farm half an hour before the event started."

Something urgent had come up at work, and her sister hadn't been able to make it until today. Willow had just been grateful that Riley could come to the pet rescue event with her and Noah. The past two days had been mostly drama-free when it came to Cami, but after the episode with her headache the other day, Willow didn't feel comfortable leaving her aunt on her own. She wasn't acting like the woman—teenager—Willow had come to know. She was pale, subdued, and a little needy.

Sage took Willow by the hand, moving her out of view of their audience on the other side of the glass doors. Then she crossed her arms and gave Willow what she thought of as her sister's lawyerly look, which usually meant Willow had done something Sage disapproved of. Since her sister already knew about their aunt, Willow couldn't think of anything that warranted the narrowing of Sage's stunning green eyes or her downturned pouty lips.

"If you think staring at me is going to make me cop to whatever you think I've done, you're wrong." Sage routinely used her intimidating stare and drawn-out silences to get confessions from her clients and their exes. It had to be said that her sister was very good at her job. "You're wasting both our time because I have no idea what your problem is."

"Really? So you didn't kiss Mr. Tall, Dark, and Devastatingly Handsome?"

Willow grinned. "If you think he's devastatingly handsome now, wait until you see him when he's all broody and ticked off."

"You did kiss him!"

She'd given herself away so there was no sense in denying it. "I did, and his kisses are as devastating as his face."

"Kisses? You kissed him more than once?"

"Well, yeah. I basically told you he kissed like a dream so why wouldn't I kiss him again? Besides, Cami interrupted us the other night." She frowned. "Now that I think about it, she interrupted us yesterday afternoon and last night too. I wonder if she's doing it on purpose?"

The day before, on the drive home from picking up pizzas for her friends who were helping her move, Willow had been bouncing ideas off Noah. He'd been so supportive of them that by the time they'd pulled into the driveway, she was more confident than ever that they'd find a buyer for the station, and she'd thrown her arms around his neck and kissed him. They would've kept kissing if Cami hadn't opened the back door of the Mercedes and started unloading the pizzas.

Then, the previous night, after they'd gotten the last of Willow's boxes stored in the garage at the beach house and her friends had left, she'd been so happy she'd checked moving off her list that her thank-you kiss got downright steamy. It might've gotten steamier if her aunt hadn't appeared to tell them she and Riley had set up the Monopoly board and were waiting for them to play.

Willow noted her sister's expression and waved her hand. "I know what you're going to say, and it's not a problem. Noah's helping us sell the station, so we're more like colleagues now."

"I don't have a good feeling about this, Will."

"Why? We're consenting adults who enjoy spending time together." She glanced at the door and lowered her voice. "I really like him, Sage."

"I know you do, and that's what I'm worried about. I don't want you to get your heart broken."

"I won't. This, whatever this is between us, has an end date so it's not like it can be anything more than a summer fling. He's leaving in September to travel around the world for a year."

"What if he asked you to go with him?"

Her laugh was a little forced, not because her sister's question was ridiculous, which it was, but because her time with Noah had an expiration date. "You do know me, don't you? The thought of traveling and long-term relationships gives me hives. Besides, I'll be living my dream right here in Sunshine Bay. It's going to happen, Sage. We're going to sell the station. I can feel it, right here." She placed a hand over her heart.

The patio door slid open, and Noah stuck his head out. "Sorry, Sage, but if your sister doesn't leave now, she's going to be late, and we all know if Willow Rosetti isn't there running the show, the event is doomed to fail."

She rolled her eyes at him. "I never said that. I don't think I'm indispensable. Noah's just trying to make a point. He thinks I volunteer for too many community events," she explained to her sister as they walked into the kitchen.

"No. What I think, and what I told you, is that Don should've found room in the budget to pay for the forty hours a week you spend promoting Channel 5."

"See, I'm not the only one who thinks Don's been exploiting you," her sister said, looking at Noah with a new level of respect.

"I told you. Don . . . Never mind. We've got to get going." Willow grabbed her purse off the counter and turned to Cami, who was looking at Willow with a mutinous expression on her face. She hadn't been happy to learn she was spending the day with Sage. For some reason, Cami had taken almost an instant dislike to Willow's sister. Sage hadn't helped her case, peppering Cami with questions about her memory almost the second she'd walked into the beach house.

"You two have fun," Willow said with a smile.

Cami crossed her arms. "Why can't we go with you guys?"

"Because Sage wants to spend time with you, and she's taking you shopping." Two towns over. "How awesome is that?"

Cami gave Sage an up-and-down look. "I don't want to shop where she shops."

Sage's brow furrowed. "What's wrong with where I shop?"

"Uh, you dress like a librarian."

Her aunt kind of had a point. "That's not nice, Cami," Willow said.

"What do you mean 'That's not nice, Cami'? How about 'That's not true, Cami'?" her sister said.

Noah saved her from having to respond. "It's just for one more day, Cami. Your family will be back tomorrow, and then the four of us can do things together without worrying about ruining the surprise."

Cami was dressed in what she thought of as her old-lady disguise—heels, a designer sundress, floppy straw hat, and oversize sunglasses. Only this time she also wore a red wig from the time Willow had gone to a Halloween party dressed as the Little Mermaid.

"Fine," Cami said, looking as if it was anything but fine.

Willow gave her sister a hug and whispered in her ear, "I know she can be annoying, but talk to her about Mom, Zia, and Nonna, and you'll see what I mean. Just don't mention Flynn. And check out those links I sent you about Jeff, her ex," she added.

If anything would earn their aunt Sage's sympathy, it would be how big a jerk Cami's ex was and how badly Cami's lawyer had messed up her divorce.

Willow pulled out her phone as soon as they got into Noah's car and sent a quick text to the coordinator of the pet rescue event, letting her know she'd be a little late. As she did, social media alerts began pinging on her phone. She was thinking that it was a good sign the event would be a success until she got a look at the alerts.

"Oh no!" Willow cried.

"What's wrong?" Noah asked, glancing at her as he pulled out of the driveway and onto the road.

"The Beaches! They're harassing Megan on social media.

It's awful, and I have no idea why they're doing it." She'd been a little surprised when they'd shown up to help her move. She'd sensed they still weren't over what they considered her betrayal of Megan, and it wasn't as if she'd set them straight. "Last night, it was obvious they were still on Team Megan, wasn't it?"

"Willow, there were at least thirty people helping you move. I have no idea who you're talking about," Noah said.

Not only had the Beaches shown up to help, so had Willow's exes and half the station.

"I know who they are," Riley piped up from the back seat. "Cami and I, um, heard them talking when they were carrying the boxes to your bedroom."

She could tell by the way Riley hesitated that her friends had had a few things to say about the way Willow had treated Megan, none of it good, apparently. "Don't worry about it. They're just being protective of Megan. They don't know the whole story."

"And the reason they don't is because you're protecting Megan for some unknown reason," Noah said, sounding unhappy about it.

Willow held up her phone. "Because I was afraid something like this would happen."

"Um, well, they kind of know everything now," Riley mumbled.

Willow turned in her seat to look at Riley. "What do you mean they know everything?"

"We didn't like how they were talking about you, and I might've said we needed to tell them what really happened, but I chickened out. Cami didn't, and she marched into your room and told them what Megan had said and done to you.

And then she told them what she thought of them talking about you behind your back and called them a bunch of beaches. Only she didn't use the word *beaches*, if you know what I mean." Riley couldn't hide her smile. "Cami must've really been the queen of the mean girls in high school. It was awesome."

Scrolling through the comments on social while listening to Riley, Willow groaned. She had to do something.

Noah reached over, curving his warm hand around the back of her neck and giving it a squeeze. "Megan had to know there would be consequences to her actions. This is on her, not you."

"And your friends," Riley said. "It wasn't nice what Megan said and did to you, but they're not being very nice either. They should know better than to bully someone on social media."

Willow smiled at Riley. "I told you, Noah. You don't have to worry about your sister. She's the smartest kid I know."

"Of course she is. She takes after her big brother," Noah said, smiling at Riley in the rearview mirror.

The smile Riley gave her big brother in return made Willow's heart squeeze. It took so little of Noah's attention to make Riley happy, and Willow felt bad about how much of his time and attention she'd taken in the past few days. She knew Riley liked having her and Cami around, but Willow vowed to put more of an effort into thinking of ways for Noah and Riley to do things on their own and develop the close brother-and-sister relationship Riley so badly wanted.

No time like the present, she thought, and held up her phone. "I have to shut this down so why don't you two play 'get to know you'?" Noah and Riley stared at her. "You know the car game, don't you?"

"No, and we're less than seven minutes from the farm," Noah said.

She looked out the windows at the passing scenery. "That's okay."

"I'll play," Riley said.

Since neither of them knew how to play, Willow had to come up with a work-around. She smiled when an idea came to her. "I've got it. What's your favorite book?"

Riley groaned. "I can't pick one favorite."

"You sound like your brother. He said the same thing when I asked him to name his favorite book. Yours was *Harry Potter and the Chamber of Horrors*, wasn't it?" she teased.

He shook his head. "You never did get the titles right. But the Harry Potter series wasn't one of my favorites, which I know you know, since you teased me relentlessly about it."

"The Harry Potter series is the best," Riley objected.

Willow hid her smile, and while Noah and Riley argued the merits of their favorite books, she texted the Beaches in their group chat, which she noticed no longer included Megan. Willow let them know she wasn't happy about their posts on social. Told them to grow up and take them down or else she was done with them.

By the time they reached the farm, the posts were gone, and the parking lot was almost full. "Yay!" Willow cheered. "We're going to raise so much money for the shelter today. Come on."

She hip-checked Noah as they walked through the gate. "I promise, you'll have fun."

He lowered his sunglasses. "Remind me how you talked me into this."

"It was too far for me to ride my scooter, and you wouldn't let me drive your car or the station wagon."

He stopped, looked around at the crowd of people congregating around the different events, and said, "I have a few calls to make. I'll wait for you and Riley in the car."

"The event is three hours long. You're not sitting in the car, and you're not going home."

He raised an eyebrow. "And why is that?"

She smiled. "Because I want you here and so does Riley."

He blew out a breath. "Fine."

She gave him a relieved hug. "You're the best."

"What I am is a sucker for your smile."

She groaned. "Noah, you can't say things like that to me, not when I can't kiss you."

His lips twitched. "We could go back to the car and make out."

Willow was giving serious consideration to his suggestion—she was obviously a sucker for his kisses—when she heard a familiar voice calling her name. "That's the event organizer. I'd better see what she wants." She looked around for Riley and spotted her standing at the ring where several dogs were jumping hurdles. She pointed her out to Noah. "I'll meet you there in a few minutes."

She joined them five minutes later. "So, we have a little problem, and I need you guys to help me out." She explained that three of their volunteers had bailed at the last minute. "I have to help the photographer, and I need you guys to help out over there."

Noah followed her finger and then swung his head to face her. "No. Absolutely not. You can babysit two picnic tables full of children. Riley and I will help the photographer."

Willow smiled. That's what she'd thought he'd say. "Just so you know, you wouldn't be babysitting the children. You'd be helping them build doghouses out of craft sticks and empty shoeboxes for their stuffed animals. But I'm happy to do it, and you guys can help dress people's pets for the photo shoots." She pointed at the long line of proud pet owners and their fur babies wending its way around the red barn. "You're up to date on your hepatitis B and tetanus shots, right? If not, I could get the volunteers at the face painting to help out at the craft table, and you and Riley could take their places. I bet you'd both be great at face painting." Willow pressed her lips together to keep from laughing at Noah's horrified expression.

"I could do the face painting," Riley said.

"We're building doghouses," Noah said to his sister, and leaned into Willow until they were nose-to-nose. "You owe me more than a smile for this."

"I definitely do," she agreed with a straight face. She walked with them to the picnic tables and introduced them to the other volunteer. The woman was so relieved that they were there to help that she looked as if she might kiss them.

Three hours later, as Noah and Riley walked around the barn, looking none the worse for wear, Willow decided they'd gotten off easy. She knew the same couldn't be said for her when Noah froze five feet from where she sat on the ground and Riley gaped at her.

"What happened to your hair?" Riley asked.

"What's wrong with it?"

"Remember how you used to say you had clown hair?" Noah asked, attempting not to laugh and failing.

"Amos's cat climbed me like a tree, and he liked my head so much, it took three of us to pull him off." She pushed herself off the ground and then winced. "He scratched me." She held up her arm. "I was also bitten twice." She pointed at her hand and thigh. "So don't even think of complaining about building doghouses with the rug rats."

"Wouldn't dream of it. We had a great time, didn't we, Tink?"

Riley, with her lips still pressed together in an obvious effort not to laugh, nodded.

Willow sighed. That had been the whole point of getting them to work the build-a-doghouse station together. "I'm glad." She motioned for them to follow her to the barn. "I want to find out how much we raised, and then we can go."

One of the veterinarians who volunteered at the shelter ran over as soon as they entered the barn and gave her a big hug. "We surpassed our goal, and it's all thanks to you, Willow. Can you forgive us for doubting you?"

The committee had pushed back—and pushed back hard—on her ideas for pet photo shoots, the build-a-doghouse station, and the dog relay. They hadn't thought the work involved would be worth the return.

"I'm just happy it all worked out and that so many people came out to help." She introduced Noah and Riley. Catching the speculative gleam in the veterinarian's eyes, Willow distracted her by asking, "Were all the rescues rehomed?"

"Almost eighty percent, and we have a few people still on the fence."

"Lucky?" she asked hopefully about the eight-month-old black Lab/golden retriever mix.

"I'm afraid not." The woman gestured to one of several carriers on the ground. "It's a shame because, once he gets past the adolescent stage, he'll make a wonderful family pet."

"Can I give him a quick cuddle before you take him back to the shelter?"

"Of course." She walked over to the carrier and let the dog out. Willow knelt on a bed of hay, and the puppy ran to her, nipping and licking her as he jumped up and down.

Noah crouched beside her and picked up the dog. "No biting." Lucky cocked his head and then settled almost immediately in Noah's arms. "Good boy," he said, stroking the dog's silky black coat.

Riley sat beside Noah. "Can I hold him, please?" She squealed with delight when Noah handed him over. "He's so cute," she cried, laughing when Lucky started eating her hair.

Noah scooped him out of Riley's arms and once again told Lucky not to bite, waiting for him to settle in his arms before stroking him.

"What?" he asked when Willow and Riley looked at him and crossed their arms.

"You're hogging him," Willow said.

"I'm not hogging him. I'm calming him down. You've been bitten enough for one day, don't you think?"

"He's got baby teeth. They don't hurt."

"He didn't bite me." Riley knotted her hair at the nape of her neck and then held out her arms. When Noah handed him over, she cuddled him to her chest.

The event organizer walked over. "Willow Rosetti, when will I ever stop doubting you? You told us you'd find Lucky a home, and it looks like you did."

Willow shot a panicked glance at Noah, afraid he'd think she'd set him up. She would never do that, not to him or to Riley, and not to Lucky. "I did. I did say that but I didn't mean Riley and Noah. We're just giving Lucky a cuddle before we leave. But I promise, I'll keep trying to find him a home."

"Can we keep him, Noah, please? We can't let him go back to the shelter. He doesn't have a mom. He needs a family. Everyone needs a family." She held Lucky up to her cheek, giving her brother pleading eyes. But Noah missed them because he was glaring at Willow.

I'm sorry, she mouthed, feeling horrible for the position she'd unintentionally put Noah in. She stood up, moving away to give Noah and Riley some privacy.

The event organizer whispered an apology before walking to the other end of the barn with the veterinarian.

"Noah, please? I'll take care of him. You won't have to take him for walks or feed him. I'll train him."

He put his arm around his sister. "I'm sorry, Tink, but you know you can't have a dog. Billy—"

"If you tell him it's part of the deal, he'll say yes. You know he will. All he cares about is the money. You can talk to the managers of my trust fund and make it a stipulation for me going back to LA."

Noah looked gutted by what his sister had just revealed and he bowed his head.

"Please, Noah," Riley pleaded again.

He kissed the top of his sister's head. "Sure, Tink. Whatever you want."

Riley jumped to her feet with Lucky in her arms and ran to Willow. "You really are my fairy godmother. I told you I had a dog on my wish list, and you made it happen. You're the best, Willow."

Chapter Seventeen

Willow sat on the Adirondack chair beside her sister watching the sun rise over the bay. It was a beautiful morning, peaceful and quiet. The only sound breaking the silence was the lulling *shush* of the waves rolling onto the shore.

Willow took a sip of her coffee and glanced at Sage. "You're supposed to be helping me figure out why Mom called at the butt crack of dawn, not sleeping."

"I'm trying to figure out why I agreed to a sleepover in the first place. I'm renaming it a wakeover, and I'm renaming the dog Demon Spawn."

"He's a puppy, and it was his first night in his new home. And you agreed to stay over to spend time with your aunt and so you didn't have to lie to Mom and Nonna. You don't think they somehow found out about Cami, do you?"

"What did Mom say again? I must've fallen asleep while you were telling me."

"Seriously? You were looking right at me."

"I didn't have my morning coffee yet." Sage lifted her mug to her lips and took a sip. "You can tell me now."

"It wasn't so much what she said, it was how she said it.

She sounded...I don't know, nervous. Upset. I heard Nonna yelling in the background. In Italian so I don't know what she said, but she sounded upset too."

"Nonna's upset and yelling about something eighty percent of the time so you can't go by that. But Mom rarely gets upset or nervous, unless it has to do with her art."

"That must be it. She's anxious about the auction." Willow relaxed on the chair. "I feel better now. Thank you."

"That's it? You woke me up fifteen minutes after I'd finally fallen asleep, dragged me downstairs, handed me a cup of coffee, and then made me come out here...for that?"

"You should be thanking me. If I hadn't, you wouldn't have gotten to enjoy the spectacular sunrise or this gorgeous morning."

"What's gorgeous about it? The grass is wet, gnats are swarming my head, and I'm sitting on a hard chair and not sleeping in a bed." Her sister stiffened. "Tell me that's not what I think it is?"

Willow pretended she didn't hear Lucky barking and took a sip of her coffee to keep from laughing at her sister's expression. Just as she got her amusement under control, the door opened and Noah walked out with Lucky on a leash.

"I take it back," Sage whispered. "That's worth waking up for."

Her sister wasn't wrong, and Willow had been right about Noah working out. And she knew this because his tanned muscular chest and rock-hard abs were on display. He was bare chested, his navy sleep pants riding low on his hips as he walked Lucky to a tree a hundred yards from where they sat. He had seriously sexy bedhead and looked half-asleep.

"Are you drooling?"

Willow wiped a hand over her mouth. "My jaw must've dropped, and coffee dribbled out."

"You've been living with him for almost a week, and you haven't seen him half-naked before?"

"He's not half-naked. He's wearing sleep pants. And the last time I saw him without a shirt was thirteen years ago. He's changed, a lot."

"Yeah, I bet he has. Not many fifteen-year-old have abs like that. We can count them when he turns around. I'm guessing eight." Sage tilted her head to the side. "Although the view from the back is pretty spectacular too. Look at his shoulders...and his butt," Sage murmured, saying exactly what Willow was thinking.

"I can hear you, you know," Noah said, his sleep-laden voice rough and deep.

"Oops. We thought you were sleepwalking." Her sister grinned, turning to Willow when Noah walked toward them. "You were right about his broody face."

Noah scowled at Sage. "You'd have a broody face too if you had less than an hour's sleep."

"You weren't the only one not sleeping. Your house isn't soundproof, you know," Sage said.

"Blame your sister." He took Willow's mug from her hand, downing what looked like the rest of her coffee.

"It's not my fault," she pointed out instead of suggesting he get his own cup of coffee. She'd have had to string more than four words together, and with a bare-chested Noah standing in front of her, that was most definitely beyond her.

Sage snorted and stood up. "I'll let you two *fight* it out." She waggled her eyebrows at Willow from behind Noah's back. It was annoying having a sister who knew her so well. "I need at least five hours of sleep before we break the news about the teenager from hell to Mom and Nonna."

"Sage, she's not that bad."

"Will, she and demon dog are a match made in hell."

Noah laughed, taking a seat in the chair Sage had vacated and stretching out his long legs.

Willow shook her head. Even his feet were beautiful. "Don't encourage her," she said, leaning down to pick up Lucky, who was snuffling the grass.

"What are you two doing up, anyway?"

"Ask my sister. I'm going to bed, and Will, after you two *chat*, you should grab a few hours' sleep before we have our showdown with the fam."

"I can't. I told you, Sage. Mom wants me to meet her at the beach at seven."

Her sister frowned. "Are you sure you got the time right? She has her early-morning yoga class."

"She canceled it. That's why I told you I was worried they'd somehow heard about Cami. But I'm sure you're right, and it's about the silent auction." She prayed her sister didn't decide she'd been wrong and send Willow's nerves into overdrive.

"This isn't good. Mom never cancels her yoga classes, and what's with meeting you at the beach? Not her apartment or the restaurant?"

Her sister really had been sleeping when she was talking to her. "She wants to go for a walk."

"Babe, you buried the lede." Sage lowered herself onto the front step. "This isn't good."

"I'm sorry, but what's wrong with your mom wanting to go for a walk on the beach with you?" Noah asked, reaching over and removing strands of Willow's hair from Lucky's mouth before he took the dog from her.

"It's our mom's thing," Willow said, stealing Lucky back. She needed something to calm her nerves, and she didn't think cuddling up to a half-naked Noah was a good idea. "If ever she had bad news to share, like when our *bisnonna*, great-grandmother, died or when our cousin was going to spend her summers in England, she took us for a walk on the beach."

"So much for sleeping," Sage grumbled. "We have about an hour to prepare and get ready."

"You can't come."

"Of course I can. I'm not letting you do this on your own."

"Mom doesn't want you there. She told me she wanted to talk to me on my own."

"She actually said she doesn't want me there? Because that intimates that she knows I'm here and means they know about Cami. Or it's possible that she wants to talk to you about me. I wonder—"

"She knows you're here. I had to tell her. She must've heard that I was with Noah and Riley at the pet rescue event yesterday, and when I admitted I've been staying here, she got weirdly upset. She made me feel like I was seventeen, and she'd caught me sleeping over at my boyfriend's, and his parents weren't home."

"Or at your boss's vacation home. The same boss who is closing your beloved Channel 5."

"That's it! With everything going on, I totally forgot to tell her Noah's not closing the station."

Noah scratched his head. "Uh, Willow, that's not what I said."

"I know, I know, and I'll explain it all to my mom when

I see her. But you have no idea how relieved I am. I've been worrying myself sick over nothing."

"Not exactly nothing," Sage said, getting up from the step. "We still have to break the news about the teenager from hell." Her sister nodded at Lucky. "I bet Demon Spawn would love to go for a walk with you and Mom."

"Don't listen to her. You're the best doggy," Willow said, cuddling and kissing Lucky as her sister walked into the house, closing the door behind her.

"Is this how it's going to be from now on? You're going to give your kisses to the dog instead of me?"

"You didn't act like you wanted me to kiss you last night. You acted like you wanted to strangle me."

"I admit I was tempted to when I thought you'd orchestrated the whole thing with Lucky." He raised his hand when she opened her mouth to defend herself. "I knew within a couple minutes that you had nothing to do with it. I was angry at myself and spent the rest of the night kicking my ass for not being there for Riley when she needed me."

"But in your own way, you were, Noah. For three years, you worked your job and your mother's so she had more time to spend with Riley."

"She still put in fifty hours a week, Willow. I should've forced the issue. I should've given her an ultimatum. If I had, Riley wouldn't have lost her mother and been forced to live with Billy."

Willow put Lucky down and moved to sit on Noah's lap. His arms went around her, and she cupped the side of his face with her hand, stroking his beard-stubbled cheek with her thumb. "Riley wasn't the only one who lost their mother. Have you even taken time to grieve?"

"I'm not fifteen. I didn't have to move away from the only home I've ever known." He held her gaze. "She truly believes Billy wants her because of her trust fund. When she said that . . ." He shook his head.

"Do you think that's the only reason he wants her?"

"I did threaten to get the trustees to freeze her trust fund and to do an investigation of all expenditures if he didn't let her stay the summer with me . . . but no, I don't believe it. I'd like to think I would've fought him for custody if I did. Billy might've been a lousy husband and stepfather, but he adored Riley. For the first four years of her life, he raised her. He was a stay-at-home dad, which I admit, in my mind, at the time, validated my opinion that the only reason he was with my mother was for a free ride."

Willow winced, and he nodded. "Yeah, I know. I could, and can, be an ass."

"Maybe an overprotective son and big brother."

"If I was an overprotective brother, I would've called Riley at least once a week and checked up on her." He speared his fingers through his hair. "I don't know why I didn't. I meant to, and then between selling off my mother's personal estate and dissolving the corporation, there never seemed to be enough time in the day."

"You need to cut yourself some slack. It's in the past. You have a second chance. You and Riley can make up for the time you lost. And maybe you need to give Billy one too. At least don't threaten him before you have a conversation about Riley."

"What did I do to get so lucky to have you—" He sighed when Lucky jumped onto Willow's lap. "I wasn't calling you—" Lucky cut him off by excitedly licking his face.

Willow laughed, picked up Lucky, stood, and then returned the puppy to Noah's lap. "I'd better get going." She kissed the top of Lucky's head. "You should bring him to bed with you instead of putting him in the crate. He's probably as tired as you are, and you'll all get some sleep."

"I'd rather bring you to bed with me, but I'll settle for a kiss."

She leaned in, placing a hand on his chest while fighting the urge to tell him her choice would be option one. She kissed him on the top of his head instead.

"That wasn't exactly the kiss I was hoping for."

"After what you just said, I don't trust myself with Half-Naked Noah. We have two *teenagers* and my sister in the house, and I have a meeting with my mom in"—she looked at her phone—"an hour, and I have to convince her you are a great guy or I'm afraid she'll lock me away in her apartment."

"No lock could keep me out," he said, then he grabbed her hand and brought it to his lips, kissing her palm. "Thanks for what you said about Riley. It helped."

"She loves you, Noah. Never doubt that she does." Willow walked to the house, afraid that she might be falling a little in love with Noah herself.

Chapter Eighteen

An hour later, as Willow walked to where her mother stood on the beach in front of La Dolce Vita, all thoughts about her feelings for Noah disappeared. Her mother looked as if she'd been crying for a week.

Willow ran across the sand and wrapped her arms around her. "Mom, what's wrong?"

"Oh, baby, I'm so sorry," she said, holding Willow tight. "I'd hoped and prayed that I'd never have to do this to you. But I don't have a choice."

Willow stepped back. "You're scaring me."

"I know." She nodded and then lifted her chin at the almost deserted stretch of sand to the left of the restaurant. "Let's walk."

The other side of the beach was starting to fill with people saving their spots with chairs and umbrellas.

"Mom, if this is about Noah, you don't have anything to worry about. He's . . ." She trailed off and lifted a shoulder. "I think I'm falling in love with him," she admitted.

Her mom stopped walking to stare at her, and then her face crumpled. She covered it with her hands, silently sobbing into them.

"Mom, stop," Willow pleaded. She couldn't remember ever seeing her mother this upset, and the muscles in her chest tightened with panic. "I can't make it better if you don't tell me what's wrong. And if you're worried about the Rosetti curse, you're worrying for nothing. Zia and Lila broke it. We're no more cursed in love than anyone else. We can fall in love and marry whomever we want."

Her mom lowered her hands, revealing her pale, tear-streaked face and bloodshot eyes. "You can't, baby. You can't fall in love with Noah," she whispered.

"Why? I don't understand what you have against him. You haven't even met him. If you had, you'd know there's no better man than him. He's beautiful and brilliant, and more than that, he's kind, and caring, and thoughtful, and he makes me laugh. He believes in me, Mom. He makes me believe in myself."

Her mother gave an angry shake of her head, shocking Willow by swearing. They heard a gasp and turned to see a family walking toward them, a woman carrying a toddler on her hip shooting an offended glare their way.

Her mother mouthed an apology at the woman before saying to Willow, "I think it's best if we continue this in the restaurant."

"No. Just say whatever it is you have to say."

"I'm sorry, honey. I didn't think this through." She reached for Willow's hand and squeezed. "But trust me, this isn't something you'll want to hear with an audience."

Whatever her mother needed to tell her was sounding worse than Willow could've imagined, and she had to order her legs to start moving. She followed her up the stairs and onto the deck, barely able to resist the urge to tug her hand free of her mother's when she opened the door. As she walked into the restaurant, Willow instinctively knew her life was about to change, and not for the better.

After closing the door behind her, Willow followed her mother to the family table and pulled out a chair, expecting her mother to do the same. But as Willow lowered herself onto the seat, her mother knelt in front of her, taking both of her hands in hers.

"I love you, Willow. I loved you from the moment I held you in my arms. You have been nothing but a blessing to me, to our family, and I would cut off my arms, my legs, I would do anything not to hurt you, but I can't protect you from this."

"I love you too, Mom. There's nothing you could tell me that will change how I feel about you."

Her mother's bottom lip trembled, and a tear rolled down her cheek. "I pray that's true because I don't know what I'd do if I lost you."

"Mom, please, just tell me."

"Your father was Will Bennett. You and Noah are related, honey. You're first cousins."

Willow felt as if she was going to be sick and surged to her feet, nearly knocking her mother over. "No, no, it can't be true." She paced in front of the table. She couldn't think straight. She couldn't comprehend what her mother was telling her.

"You're in shock, honey. Please sit down and let me explain."

"Explain what, Mom? That you cheated on our father? That much I understand." She couldn't remember ever being this angry at her mother, and there was nothing she could do to temper the emotion that came out in her voice. "Why you wouldn't tell me before now, before I was falling in love with...with my...Noah, is what I don't understand, and I don't think I ever will."

"I didn't know. I had no idea you even knew Noah, let alone that you've been living with him for almost a week!" Her mother shook her head. "I'm sorry. I'm not angry at you, and you have every right to be angry at me, to hate me," she said on a broken sob. "But please, honey, please sit and let me try and explain."

"I don't hate you, Mom. I'm just...The way I feel about Noah..." She shook her head, unable to go on, and lowered herself onto the chair, feeling numb.

Her mother sat on the chair beside Willow, turning to face her. "I didn't cheat on my husband with Will Bennett."

"I don't understand."

"My sister, Camilla, isn't your zia, honey. She's your biological mother."

Willow's body went warm and then cold and then back to warm. Not from shock this time but from relief. "Mom, Cami was in love with Flynn, not Noah's uncle. All she talks about is Flynn. She chased a teenager down Main Street..." She trailed off at her mother's wide-eyed expression and realized what she'd just revealed.

Willow winced. "I'm sorry," she said, and then she told her mother everything that had transpired in the last week and why she had done what she'd done.

"I can't really get mad at you after keeping the secret of your paternity for all this time, and I understand why you did what you did. Though your zia and nonna might not be as understanding, but we'll deal with that later."

"Why, Mom? What did Cami do that was so horrible that

you guys cut her out of your lives for decades? She's family, and she loves you. She gave me to you to raise as your own."

"It's not as simple as that. But that can wait for another time. What I want to know is why you're accepting this so well. I was worried you wouldn't be able to forgive me, that you'd hate me for lying to you for all these years. But you're more upset that Noah is your cousin."

"We don't know that he is. Not for sure. Flynn could just as easily be my father." She prayed with all her heart that he was. "Cami hasn't mentioned Will once. All she's talked about is Flynn."

"My sister believed Will was your father, honey. It's why she named you Willow. In his honor. She was devastated by his death."

"She was just as devastated when Flynn left her to go back to college that summer."

"She was, and she did love him. And, according to Camilla, they'd been intimate just days before Flynn announced he was leaving."

"So you agree, there is a chance Flynn's my father?"

"Yes, there's a chance. But it's a very small chance. You and Noah can take a DNA test. We'll talk to Sage about it. Right now, though, I'd like you to tell me why you're not more upset about my sister being your mother."

"She's not my mother, you are. And nothing will ever change that. I might not entirely understand why you kept it from me, but there's nothing for me to forgive. I'm grateful that you kept me and raised me and loved me like your own."

"We're the ones who are grateful for the gift that you are. And I didn't love you *like* my own. You are mine, and you were from the moment Camilla left you with—"

A knock on the glass interrupted her mother, and they looked to see Carmen opening the door and poking her head inside, her worried gaze moving from her daughter to Willow.

"Your mother, she told you, *si*? You're okay? You're not angry with us?"

"No, I'm not angry, Nonna. I love you, all of you, and that will never change," Willow said. "But I have something to tell you, and I hope you'll be as forgiving as me." She pushed out a chair with her foot. "Come sit."

Once her grandmother was seated, Willow cleared her throat. "So, Cami is here in Sunshine Bay. She's been staying at the beach house with me, Noah, and his sister Riley. And before you start yelling at me, just remember how long you've been keeping me in the dark, and it wasn't completely my fault that Cami's here. She was in an accident and has amnesia. She thinks she's seventeen, and she loves you, Nonna, so much. You too, Mom. You and Zia."

Her grandmother bowed her head, and Willow's mother reached over and rubbed Carmen's arm.

"What happened? I think I deserve to know, don't you?"

"She's right, Gia. She deserves the truth," her grandmother said, then looked at Willow. "You girls, you don't think the Rosetti curse is real, but just ask your mother, she knows that it is. She didn't listen to me and married that man, a photographer. Bah, he was a *culo*."

"Ma."

"What? Did he not leave you on your own with no money and two *bambine* to raise, while he followed your sister to Hollywood?"

Willow's jaw dropped. "Cami had an affair with your husband?"

"No. He thought he was in love with her, but Camilla did nothing to encourage him." Her mother rubbed her finger along an initial carved into the table. "She came to live with us in New York when she was five months pregnant. Camilla was in a bad way. She was angry and depressed. I tried to get her help but she refused. A month after she had you, my husband encouraged her to consider modeling. He helped put together a portfolio for her, and he'd accompany her on go-sees in hopes of landing himself a job in the industry."

Carmen nodded. "He used both my daughters."

"He used Camilla, but he didn't use me. He didn't, Ma," she said when Carmen opened her mouth to argue.

"He saw what you didn't, Gia. He knew one day your talent, your art, would bring you fame and fortune, and he'd ride on your coattails, just like he did your sister's."

"Oh, Ma, please. I wasn't that good. I'm a mediocre artist at best."

"Mom! Your paintings are incredible."

Gia rolled her eyes. "You're biased, just like your nonna. But we're not here to talk about me. We're here to talk about Camilla. And as beautiful as she is now, she was absolutely stunning as a teenager, and the camera loved her. It didn't surprise me when she landed a lucrative modeling contract in LA, and I encouraged her to take it. I didn't encourage my husband to follow her to LA, and neither did Camilla, but he did."

"It sounds like Nonna's right, and he was a *culo*. Although I can think of a few other expletives that fit the bill." Willow smiled at Carmen when she snorted and then said to her mom, "I'm guessing Cami asked you to keep me when she went to LA?"

"I offered before she could ask. The plan was for you to stay with me until she got on her feet. But then a year went by and Camilla rarely checked in anymore, let alone visited, so I asked her for legal custody of you." She placed her hand over Willow's. "In my heart, you were mine, and I couldn't think of giving you up. Sage would've been as devastated as I would've been."

It wasn't until that moment that the fact Sage wasn't her sister, but her cousin, sank in. Willow briefly closed her eyes, fighting back tears. It didn't matter, she told herself, just as it didn't matter that Gia wasn't her biological mother. They were the mother and sister of her heart, and nothing changed that.

Willow cleared the emotion from her throat. "What did Cami say when you asked for custody of me?"

"She asked for more time. She wasn't ready to give you up." Her mother smiled at Carmen. "So I called my mother and asked to come home, and she and Eva arrived at my door seven hours later, helped pack up the house and you girls, and moved us home."

"You see, this is exactly why I don't understand how you could cut Cami out of your lives. You guys are always there for one another no matter what." Willow, Sage, and Lila were the same.

Her mother and grandmother shared a look. Willow was about to call them on it when her phone pinged. She glanced at the text and grimaced. "So, uh, Sage wants to know what's going on. She's planning on bringing Cami to the restaurant. We told her you were coming home today."

Her mother's lips flattened, and she crossed her arms. "I don't want to see her."

"Mom!" Willow looked to her grandmother for help. "Nonna?"

Her grandmother bit her bottom lip, casting a tentative glance at her daughter.

Sensing she might have an ally in Carmen, Willow pushed on, "Whatever happened between you guys was a long time ago. Isn't it about time you let it go? Don't you think Cami's been punished long enough? She doesn't have anyone, and she loves you. All of you."

"If Willow can forgive Camilla, maybe it's time we did too, Gia."

"She doesn't kn—" Willow's mother clamped her mouth shut.

"Mom, Cami has no memories past seventeen. She's lost and lonely, and she needs her family. All of her family. Please, for me, can't you just try and remember the sister you once loved?"

"Tell your sister to bring Camilla," her grandmother said, raising a hand when Gia sputtered a protest. "If you don't want to be here, that's fine. But I want to see my daughter."

"As if I'm going to let you deal with her on your own. Just don't expect me to fawn all over her. She always got away with everything, and I don't plan on letting her waltz in here thinking everything is forgiven."

Chapter Nineteen

Camilla winced as she lifted the queen-size mattress with both hands and then swallowed a celebratory cheer. After her memory had returned three days ago, whenever the opportunity arose—which was rarely—she'd searched every room in the beach house for her phone, positive Riley would have hidden it anywhere but in Camilla's room. She supposed she had Lucky to thank for finally finding it. He'd barked almost the entire night, covering the sounds of her searching her bedroom.

Lifting her leg, Camilla slid it between the mattress and box spring, reaching for the phone with the tips of her toes. It took several attempts before she managed to pull it to the edge of the mattress. She let the mattress drop back onto the bed and then stuck in her hand and retrieved her phone.

She sat on the bed and made the call she'd been desperate to make for the past three days.

It was early but she knew Gail would want to hear from her. She was the one person who knew Willow was Camilla's daughter. She didn't know about Will, though. Camilla had never been able to talk about the accident to anyone, even her many therapists. It was her deep, dark secret, and she intended to keep it that way.

As the phone rang, she shook her head, remembering how her seventeen-year-old self had referred to Gail.

Gail picked up on the first ring. "Cami, is everything okay?"

"It's so good to hear your voice." Camilla practically groaned in relief. This was the longest she'd gone without talking to Gail since she hired her. "I have my memory back."

"Thank God. I've been dying to know how everything is going. Now tell me, are you okay?"

"I'm . . . honestly, I don't know how I am. On the one hand, having amnesia ended up being a blessing in disguise. I've gotten to know Willow in a way that I don't think I would have had I known she was my daughter." She picked at a loose thread on the comforter. "She's everything a mother could want in a daughter, Gail. She's sweet, and kind, and compassionate, and funny, and . . . I want to have a relationship with her, but I'm afraid, once she finds out that I'm her mother, she won't want anything to do with me."

"I understand why you're afraid, Cami, but I don't think that's something you have to worry about. The woman I met, and the woman you're describing, doesn't seem like the type of person who would intentionally hurt anyone."

"You're right, at least about Willow. But once my mother and sisters know I'm in town, the gloves will come off. They won't let me have a relationship with her, Gail. I know they won't."

"I can't believe they don't know you're in town yet. How's that even possible?"

Camilla told her about Noah and Riley and hiding out at the beach house. And then she told Gail about everything that seventeen-year-old Cami had gotten up to, and she and

Gail laughed so hard that Camilla had to bury her face in the comforter to muffle the sound.

"It's funny now, but trust me, it wasn't funny then. I was positive I was losing my mind," Camilla admitted after she'd gotten her laughter under control. "And my reunion with my mother and sisters will be far from funny." She felt sick to her stomach thinking about it.

"When are you meeting with them?"

"Today, I think. I overheard Willow talking to her cousins about it on Zoom."

"You need to tell Willow before your mother and sisters do, Cami. That way you can control the narrative."

She knew exactly what narrative Gail was talking about. "I can't tell her. Not yet. I have to pretend I have amnesia for at least another week."

"A week? Why on earth do—"

"I need to remind my family that they once loved me, Gail. And while they might hate forty-seven-year-old Camilla, they loved seventeen-year-old Cami. So that's who I'll be. And it'll give me more time with Willow. If this doesn't go the way that I hope, I need more time with my daughter. Even if she doesn't know I'm her mother."

"I understand. I wish I didn't, but I do. But now that you have your memory back, it'll be harder for you to pull off."

"I know. And to make matters worse, Willow is falling in love with Noah, who just happens to be her cousin. So I have to figure out a way to either break them up or keep them apart." Other than annoying Willow and Noah, she wasn't having much luck at either.

"Cami!"

"I know, I know. And it would make it easier if Noah was

a jerk, but he isn't. He's perfect for Willow, and he adores her." She bowed her head. "She's going to be devastated, Gail, and it's all my fault."

"It's not. You've just gotten your memory back. There was nothing you could do. It's as much your sisters' and your mother's fault. They know who Willow's father was."

"Yes, but I have a feeling they don't know Willow's involved with his nephew." She leaned back against the pillows. "Now tell me how you've been. You obviously were able to keep the accident and my hospital stay under wraps, and the reporters haven't gotten wind of me being in Sunshine Bay, so thank you very much for that."

"It's why you pay me the big bucks."

There was something in Gail's voice that made Camilla frown. "Are you okay? You sound off."

"We'll talk about it another—"

"No, we won't. I've just spent the last twenty minutes talking about myself and the mess I've made of my life. I'd much rather talk about you. Please tell me you've screwed something up and you need my advice for a change."

At the long, drawn-out silence, Camilla's pulse kicked into overdrive. "Gail?"

"Lilianna Rose's family approached me. They've offered me a job as her PA. She's young, and they're inexperienced and overwhelmed. They want someone who knows the ins and the outs of the business to guide her."

Camilla briefly closed her eyes. Lilianna's star was rising, and hers was fading. Who was she kidding? Her star had crashed and burned. "Not so inexperienced if they approached you. There's no one better for the job. Lilianna Rose would be lucky to have you."

"I can't believe I'm even considering taking it."

Gail wasn't only her PA. They'd been together for twenty years, and she considered her a friend. Her one true friend. And now she had to be that for her. "Take it. The kid needs you, the same as I did. She's going to be big, Gail, and she seems sweet. You and I both know what this business can do to sweet young things. She needs you to protect her."

"You know I wouldn't even consider it if I thought you needed me. I—"

"You realize who you're talking to, right? The woman who's screwed up her life."

"You haven't, but you will if you don't take the time to rebuild the relationships with your daughter and your family. I know how much you've missed them. And it's not like I'm going anywhere. We're friends. I'll always be there for you."

"I know you will, and I know you're right. I need to take some time away from the business."

"Have you given any more thought to selling the house?"

It wasn't a house. It was a forty-thousand-square-foot mansion on three acres and, as hard as she'd tried to make it a home, it had never felt like one. The beach house felt more like a home than hers ever had. "I'm going to sell."

"Are you moving back to Sunshine Bay?"

"I'm not sure. I'll probably end up—"

There was a knock on her bedroom door.

"Crap, I have to go." She ended the call and shoved the phone under her pillow as her door opened and Riley poked her head inside with a wide smile.

"I've got great news. You're going to La Dolce Vita to see your family."

Chapter Twenty

Camilla wanted to howl, she wanted to crawl under the covers and sleep for a week. She wanted a bloody cigarette and a bottle of wine. Her seventeen-year-old self might've wanted nothing more than to be reunited with the family she adored, but Camilla didn't.

Three days before, she'd been reeling, her mind ripped apart by the memories of Will and of this past week with Willow, Riley, and Noah, and the only thing she had been able to think about was making things right between herself and her family. But now, faced with the reality of the situation, she was terrified. She had no idea how to repair the damage she'd done.

How had she gotten herself into this mess? And that was the problem. She hadn't, not really. It was her seventeen-year-old self's fault. She'd taken over Camilla's body and her brain for a week and orchestrated the reunion with her family, who hated her.

Camilla gave Riley a wan smile. "I don't think I can go. I feel queasy." Would Cami say "queasy"? Probably not. "Woozy, I mean."

Camilla rolled her eyes at herself. She was an actress, a

damn good one, no matter what her ex and some of the critics said. She just had to get into character. "I'll go see my mom and sisters tomorrow."

"But it's all you talked about this week," Riley said. "I'm sure you'll feel better once you see them."

Camilla pressed a hand to her stomach. She felt as nervous as she had at her first major audition. But Riley was right. All she'd do was sit there worrying about it anyway. She had to rip the Band-Aid off. "Are you coming with me?"

"Um, I guess. If you want me to." Riley tucked her hair behind her ear.

The food dye still hadn't completely washed out. Camilla must've subconsciously been thinking of Hugh's PA, Pinky, when she dyed Riley's hair. Surprisingly, the pink streaks looked cute on Riley. She was a sweet kid who had no idea how pretty she was. One day, she'd be a knockout.

Camilla nodded. "I do."

It was true. Riley was an old soul and had a calming presence. She was also the one person Camilla felt bad lying to. Well, she didn't feel great lying to anyone, but Riley had been a good friend to Cami. And she'd put up with a crapload from her too. But even more than that, she'd confided in Cami. Riley was lonely, or she had been before coming to Sunshine Bay. Camilla had been too, even if she hadn't realized it until she'd lost her memory.

"Okay. I'll tell Noah and Sage you'll be down in five minutes." Riley smiled. "You can dress however you want. You don't have to wear a disguise anymore."

"Yay!" Camilla said instead of "Damn it." Riley would expect her to dress like a teenager, which meant Camilla had to wear one of the outfits Willow had brought her.

As soon as the door closed, she rummaged through the suitcases on the floor, looking for something of her daughter's to wear. At the bottom of a pile, she found a pair of baggy linen capris with a drawstring and a white, three-quarter-sleeve T-shirt and put them on.

She glanced at the flip-flops and sneakers she'd been wearing all week and looked longingly at her Jimmy Choos. Her daughter dressed as if she were seventeen.

"Cami!" Sage shouted from downstairs.

"I'm coming!" she yelled at her niece, sticking her feet into the flip-flops and running down the hall. Sage, Noah, and Riley were waiting for her at the bottom of the stairs. She glanced at the wooden railing and sighed, throwing her leg over it and sliding down like when she'd believed she was seventeen and had wanted to make Riley laugh. It hurt her crotch. Weirdly, it hadn't last week. Unlike then, she also struggled to get off the railing at the bottom of the stairs. She wondered if her body had remembered it was forty-seven, not seventeen.

"Quick recovery," Sage said dryly, an eyebrow raised.

"The painkillers kicked in. Woo-hoo!" She pumped her fist, inwardly rolling her eyes and wondering, not for the first time, if she'd had ADHD growing up, but she didn't think you grew out of it. One of her many therapists over the years had told her she suspected she had undiagnosed PTSD. Camilla had dumped her and moved on to the next. She'd been afraid she was getting too close to the truth.

"Noah's taking his car so you can come with me," Sage said.

Camilla shook her head. "I'm going with Riley." No way was she getting stuck on her own in the car with her niece.

Sage had questioned her nonstop during their shopping trip the other day.

Noah shared a glance with Sage, who shrugged. He tossed the keys to Riley, and Camilla snagged them, shocking the hell out of herself. She went with it. "I'll drive."

"Good try," Noah said. "You're sitting in the back seat with Riley. I just have to put Lucky in the crate."

Camilla and Riley helped him corral Lucky. Riley kissed and cuddled the dog that Sage had named Demon Spawn— it was the one thing Camilla and her niece agreed upon— before putting him in the crate. Then they headed for Noah's Mercedes. They were arguing over what music to play when Noah slid behind the wheel, ending their argument by putting on the radio.

Camilla had enjoyed the distraction while it lasted. The closer they got to her family's restaurant the more nervous she became.

"Are you excited?" Riley asked.

"Yeah. But I'm a little nervous too." She was a good actress but she'd have to be an extraordinary one to cover her nerves, so she went with the partial truth.

She caught Noah glancing at her in the rearview mirror, adding for his benefit, "I don't know why my mom and sister left me behind. I must've done something really bad. I just can't remember what I did." She knew exactly what she had done and wished she didn't.

"It doesn't matter," Riley said. "They've been gone for a while so they'll be really happy to see you."

Camilla smiled and gave Riley's hand a squeeze. She was an awesome kid, sweet and empathetic. She reminded her a little of Will. She had his eyes. Camilla got choked up thinking about him and looked out the window. Noah and Riley had lost their uncle because of her. She didn't know how she'd make it up to them, but she vowed she would. For some reason, the vow eased the ball of emotion stuck in her throat. Maybe because she'd never thought she'd have the opportunity to make it up to Will's family in some way, and now she did.

Her muscles tensed when Noah drove down the familiar road and the weathered gray siding of the restaurant came into view. By the time he pulled into the parking lot, Camilla felt lightheaded, her breathing short and choppy. She couldn't do this. She couldn't face her family. Too much time had passed. She should've made the effort years before. But failed marriages, failed romances, and now a failing career had gotten in the way, and the thought of facing them when her life wasn't perfect hadn't been acceptable to her. She'd needed the armor of success to withstand their enmity.

"It'll be okay. You'll see, Cami. Willow's there. She'll smooth things over if your family's mad at you." Riley grinned. "And don't forget, you're queen of the mean girls. You don't take shit from any—"

"Riley," Noah warned, and then he looked back at Camilla. "My sister's right. Whatever happens, Willow is there for you, and so are we." His lips twitched. "Sage too."

"She calls me the teenager from hell."

"People give people they care about nicknames," Riley said confidently, and then leaned over and opened Camilla's door.

"Easy for you to say. Your brother calls you Tink, not the teenager from hell," she grumbled, and got out of the car. She did some deep-breathing exercises. They were second nature to her, and her body responded almost immediately. "Chin up, tits out," she said under her breath.

She hadn't realized Riley was standing right behind her until she burst out laughing.

"What's so funny?" Noah asked, coming around the car to join them.

"Cami," Riley said without elaborating.

Sage pulled in beside them and got out of the car. "Do me a favor," she said to Camilla when she reached them. "Don't tell Carmen she's old."

"Why would I do that?" Camilla asked, at the same time inwardly cringing. She'd been doing it for the past week, or her alter ego had. She'd even called Willow and Noah old. How ridiculous was that?

"Because you... Just promise me you won't. It's going to be bad enough without you ticking off Carmen, and she's sensitive about her age."

"She's not sensitive about her age," she said, even though she wanted to kiss Sage for giving her an out. She would've had to do the *You're old* thing or Willow, Noah, and Riley would've suspected something was off.

Camilla shrugged. "Whatever. I won't say anything. But like I said, I don't know what you're worried about. My mother always looks great."

She did, and so did Camilla's sisters. She might not have seen them in person in twenty-five years, but she'd been following their videos on La Dolce Vita's Instagram and TikTok for the past ten months. She'd take a break every once in a while. Their mother-daughters-sisters bonds were plain to see. It had been hard watching them together and knowing what she'd missed for all these years, and why. She had no one to blame but herself.

Her mouth went dry when Noah opened the restaurant

door, holding it open for them. His phone rang, and he took it out of his pocket, glancing at the screen. "Sorry. I have to take this. Go ahead. I'll probably be a few minutes."

Camilla cast a nervous glance at Noah. He gave her shoulder a squeeze. "It'll be fine, Cami."

She nodded and followed Sage inside. Riley gave Camilla a little push from behind. She stutter-stepped, not from the push but because she didn't recognize the restaurant. Everything had changed. This had been as much her home as the apartment where their mother raised them, maybe more so. She hadn't been prepared for this.

"What's wrong?" Riley asked, and Sage stopped, turning to face them.

"Nothing's the same. It's all wrong," Camilla whispered, her nose tickling and her eyes burning.

"I'm sorry, Cami. I should've warned you," Sage said.

"Is this why they went on vacation? They renovated?" Camilla asked, getting back into character.

"Yeah. It is," Sage said. "Come on. Everyone's at the family table."

Camilla looked around as she followed, squealing when she saw the fountain. Every time their mother or nonna caught them making wishes at the fountain, they'd remind them that you made your own wishes come true. But Camilla couldn't help herself. She was thrilled to see something that hadn't changed. She ran to the fountain and hugged Venus.

She let go of the statue and searched her pockets. "Does anyone have a quarter?"

Sage handed her one.

"Thanks. Do you have one for Riley? We have to do it together."

Sage took another quarter from her wallet, handing it to Riley.

"Okay, are you ready?" Camilla asked Riley. She nodded. "All right, hold tight to your quarter, then make your wish, and toss it into the fountain. Then you have to thank Venus for making it come true."

"No wonder my wishes never came true. No one told me you had to thank Venus," Sage said.

"Of course you do." Camilla clutched the quarter in her fist and wished for a way to right the wrongs of her past and to win back the love of her family. Blinking away tears, she tossed the coin in the fountain and whispered, "Thank you."

Riley did the same, hesitating a minute before hugging Venus and thanking her.

Camilla caught the glint of tears in Riley's eyes and took her hand. "Your wish is going to come true. I just know it is."

Riley nodded. "Yours too."

Camilla couldn't put it off any longer and went to take a step forward but her body locked in place. Riley nudged her and mouthed, *Chin up, tits out.*

Camilla burst out laughing.

Her mother, who was standing near the family table, put her hands on her hips. "What's so funny?"

It took a moment for Camilla to respond as she drank in the sight of her mother. Then, with the laughter still in her voice, Camilla told her in Italian what Riley had said to her.

Carmen nodded, the hint of a smile playing on her lips, and then, because they believed Camilla was seventeen-year-old Cami, she did what she'd wanted to do for the past twenty-five years. She ran to her mother, threw her arms around her, and cried, "I missed you so much," and then she burst into tears.

Chapter Twenty-One

Willow half rose from her chair, prepared to intervene in case her grandmother pushed Cami away. While she knew from their earlier conversation that her mother had no intention of forgiving Cami, her aunt, who'd joined them via Zoom fifteen minutes before, seemed willing to put the past behind them, and so had Carmen. But now Willow wasn't so sure. Her grandmother wasn't embracing Cami, her arms hung limply at her sides, but her mouth was working and her eyes were shiny.

Sage pulled out the chair beside Willow and took a seat. "Stop worrying and sit down," she whispered. "It'll be fine. Look at Nonna's face."

Willow wasn't looking at her grandmother now. She was listening to Cami.

"I don't know what I did to make you guys leave me behind," she sobbed, "but whatever it was, I'm sorry. I'm so sorry. Please say you forgive me. Please."

Carmen lifted her hands, framing Cami's tear-streaked face between them. "It's done, *cara*. It's been too long. You're forgiven." She kissed Cami on both cheeks, and then she stepped back and took her daughter by the hand. "Come, we'll get the food. We'll celebrate." Carmen smiled at Riley.

"You come too. You can tell me what trouble my daughter got you into this week."

Sitting across from Willow, her mom threw up her hands, her expression stony. "That's it?" she muttered. "We just welcome her back to the family like she didn't—"

"Gia, enough. It's done," Willow heard her aunt Eva whisper fiercely.

"Ma. I wasn't that bad!" Cami laughed, oblivious to her sisters quarreling behind her. But then she spun around. "Wait. I haven't said hi to Gia yet." She flashed her sister a movie-star smile and ran over, giving her a hug.

"This won't be good," Sage murmured.

Their mother sat stiffly while her sister embraced her. Cami obviously hadn't noticed Gia's less-than-welcoming expression or the fact that she didn't hug her back. "I missed you so much! Don't leave me here by myself again." She looked around. "Where's Eva? Didn't she come home with you?"

Willow's aunt leaned forward, bringing her nose to the screen. "I'm here, Cami. I'm, uh, in London."

Cami moved to the laptop on the table. "When are you coming home?"

"Soon. We'll be home soon."

"Good." Cami gave her sister a teary-eyed smile. "I've missed you."

"I've missed you too," Eva said on a hoarse whisper, leaning against Lila, who put her arm around her mother.

Carmen called to Cami, saying something in Italian. Cami grinned, waving. "I've gotta go. Don't want to piss off Mussolini."

Eva laughed. "You haven't changed. Only you could get away with saying that to Ma."

Cami grinned and ran to Carmen, who was shaking her head with a smile. Hooking her arms through her mother's and Riley's, Cami skipped to the kitchen.

Her tanned face darkening, her green eyes narrowing at her sister on the screen, Gia began yelling at Eva in Italian. Eva fired back in Italian, and then the two of them went at it.

"We have to learn to speak Italian. We're missing all the good stuff," Sage said, and then got up, rounding the table to calm their mother down. She put an arm around Gia's shoulders. "Take a breath."

Willow's uncle appeared behind her aunt, wrapped an arm around her neck, and then lowered his mouth to her ear. He was talking to her in Italian, and whatever he said had her aunt nodding and smiling up at him.

Willow glanced from her aunt, uncle, and cousin to her mom and her sister, and for some reason, she felt very much alone sitting by herself on the other side of the table. A warm hand curved around the back of her neck, and she looked up to see Noah looking down at her, concern darkening his indigo eyes. "Are you okay?"

She shook her head, and he raised his gaze, looking from her mother to her aunt on the screen. Her aunt's eyes went wide, no doubt at the stone-cold expression on Noah's face.

"It's not what you think," Willow told him, realizing how it must look to him, especially with her obviously trying not to cry.

"Maybe you should tell me what's going on, then."

"I will." She pushed back from the table and stood.

Sage got up and came around the table. Taking Willow by the shoulders, she searched her face. "You told me you were okay. You said you were good."

"I am. It's just..." She glanced at Noah and then returned her gaze to her sister.

Sage nodded. "Right. Go talk to him."

"I'm Gia. Willow's mother. I apologize for what you walked into. We're not usually like this. It's been an emotional day."

"Your daughter and I are taking a walk, and I'd appreciate it if you don't upset Cami while we're gone. She's had a rough day." His voice was as cold as the winter winds off the bay. "Sage?"

"I've got her covered, Noah. You don't have to worry about Cami or Riley. I promise."

He nodded, his gaze moving around the table as if daring anyone to say a word. They didn't. Her mother, aunt, and cousin stared at him in stunned silence. She thought her uncle might've laughed. Probably because the Rosetti women were rarely stunned speechless. He might not have found it funny if he'd heard the part of their conversation where her family learned Willow was falling for a man who was quite possibly her first cousin. Her grandmother hadn't been fazed by the news. According to her, half the marriages in Southern Italy were between first cousins. Lila had quipped, "In what century?"

But it wasn't as if that were something Willow, or Noah, she was sure, would even consider. They'd have to settle for being friends. She supposed that was why, when he guided her onto the back deck and then down the stairs, she was holding back tears.

"You should've called me, Willow. Or at the very least waited until Sage was here to tell your family about Cami." He stood in the sand at the bottom of the stairs, scowling at the window as if he was contemplating strangling her entire family. Then he looked at her, and his expression softened, and he put his arms around her, drawing her close.

"That's not why I'm crying. My mom wasn't happy about Cami, but my zia, nonna, and cousin were okay with it. I think they might actually be happy she's here. At least seventeen-year-old Cami."

He leaned back and looked down at her. "So what's with the tears?"

She pressed her palm on his chest and then moved it, waving her hand between them. "It's about you and me . . . about us. There can't be an us. I mean, I don't know if there's an us—"

"There's an us. We've been an us since we were fifteen."

"We were a different kind of an us than the us I'm talking about."

"We were fifteen. We couldn't be the us we are now or the us that I'm very much hoping we'll be."

"I wanted that too. I wanted it so much," she said, stepping back and swiping a finger under her lashes. "And now we can't be anything more than Summer Noah and Willow. Even that might be too close."

"I think I'm missing something."

"You are. I'm sorry. It's just been a lot." She looked around and then took him by the hand, leading him away from the restaurant to the water's edge. "My mother's my mother, but she's not my biological mother. Cami is." She squeezed his hand. "And Noah, my mom says that your uncle is my father."

He let go of her hand and stared at her, looking stunned.

"I'm sorry. I shouldn't have blurted it out like that. But Noah, I'm almost certain we're not cousins. At least fifty percent certain."

"Willow, you have nothing to apologize for." He took her hand. "Why don't we sit down?"

"I'm not sure I want to. That's what my mother said before she dropped her bomb, bombs on me."

"You really have had a hell of day, haven't you?" he said, drawing her into his arms and resting his chin on the top of her head. "Don't worry. I'd hug you even if you are my cousin."

She buried her face in his chest. "I don't want you to be my cousin."

"Trust me, sweetheart. I don't want to be your cousin any more than you want to be mine." He gave her a light squeeze. "Talk to me. Tell me how you're feeling, really feeling. I'm assuming when you told Sage you're good, you were referring to learning Cami was your biological mom. But I can't believe it would be that easy for you to bounce back after that kind of news."

She nodded. "I haven't had a chance to completely process it. I don't know what it says about me, but I couldn't get past the cousin thing."

He stepped away from her, placing a hand on the small of her back. "Come on. Let's sit over here." He guided her several feet from the shore, and they sat side by side on the sand.

She leaned against him. "Do you think there's something wrong with me that all I could focus on was you and me?"

"No, but I'm biased. I like that your biggest concern was how it impacted us. And, like you said, it's a lot to process."

"It's not just that. My mom was torn up. You saw her. She looks like she's been crying for a week, and she feels guilty, so guilty. I couldn't make her feel worse by asking questions or letting her see that I was angry that they've kept it from me for all this time." She shook her head. "Not angry, disappointed, I guess."

"You can be honest with me, Willow. I'm not going to judge you. I want to be here for you. I want you to be able to say whatever it is you're feeling."

"Ugh." She flopped onto her back in the sand. "Stop being Mr. Perfect. Stop saying exactly what I need to hear."

He lay on his back beside her, turned his head, and winked at her. "Perfect Noah, I think I like it."

She nudged him with her elbow. "I'm being serious."

"So was I. Talk to me."

She blew out a breath. "I can't be mad at Cami. Maybe because I've gotten to know her this past week, and she was just a year older than she is now—a year older than she thinks she is, I mean—when she had me. Can you imagine?"

"No. In fact, the idea of the Cami we know having a baby is slightly terrifying. She's lucky she had your mother to turn to, and you're lucky that it was Gia who raised you. I don't mean to sound judgmental. I know plenty of young women who raise children on their own without the help of their family and do a fantastic job, Robyn for one. But think about what Cami must've been dealing with at the time. Not only was she a pregnant seventeen-year-old, the father of her baby had recently died in a tragic car accident."

"I can't imagine." She picked up a handful of sand, watching as it seeped through her fingers. "So you think it's true. I am your cousin."

"There's a possibility Flynn is your father. We'll take a DNA test. Riley will too. We'll have an answer by the end of the week." He took her hand, gently shaking it to get her to look at him. "If my uncle was your father, Willow, you're entitled to a third of the sale of the corporation."

She pulled her hand from his and shook her head. "No, I'm not. It's yours and Riley's, and I want no part of it. I mean it, Noah."

"It's what my uncle would have wanted. My grandparents and my mother too. But more important, it's what I'd want, and so would Riley."

"No. The subject is closed. I won't take money that belongs to you and Riley."

"At the risk of sounding like a self-entitled ass, Riley and I have more money than we could spend in three lifetimes, and that was before the sale of Bennett Broadcasting. Both my grandparents' families were wealthy and invested well. They left everything to my mother, and she had extensive portfolios apart from the Bennett Broadcasting Group. I've established a foundation, and with Riley's consent, the funds from the sale of the corporation will go directly into it. Once the company is dissolved, I'll be moving key staff, including Robyn, to the foundation." He rubbed his head. "Totally sounded like an ass."

"You don't. You couldn't. And I think it's wonderful you're establishing a charitable foundation." She smiled. "And I'm really glad Robyn will still be working for you."

"I thought you would be. But I don't think you realize what this would mean for you. The other sales have been finalized, and while, technically, legally, you could contest the sale, I'd ask that you don't. It would put too many jobs at risk as well as organizations that are depending on the money we've earmarked for charitable donations. But I'd personally give you what you were entitled to." He held up his hand when she opened her mouth to protest. "Let me finish, please. A third of Channel 5 would be yours, as well as a third of the beach house."

Okay, so she hadn't thought about that.

"You would have the means to buy Riley and me out."

"That's your home. Yours and Riley's. I'm not taking it. I'm not family. Even if we found out that I am, technically, I'm not."

"Sweetheart, I'm selling the beach house and closing Channel 5."

"Unless we can find a buyer," she reminded him, and that's when what he was saying truly sank in. "I could buy it?"

His lips twitched. "You could. In fact, you could probably buy a thousand Channel 5's."

"I don't want a thousand Channel 5's. I just want one."

"I know, and that's why I"—he cleared his throat—"admire you so much."

Her chest got tight and the backs of her eyes burned. She was almost positive he'd been going to tell her he loved her. "You know how much the station means to me," she said, struggling to get the words past the lump of emotion clogging her throat. "How much I've wanted to save it. How I'd do anything to save it. But now that there's a chance my dream of saving the station might come true, I don't want to pay the price. It's too high. I'd have to give up the dream of me and you."

Chapter Twenty-Two

Riley sat on the couch with Lucky on her lap, listening to the rain splatter against the windows. He'd kept them up half the night barking. She supposed it was better than when he'd kept them up the entire night. Her brother was frustrated that none of the tricks in the dog training manual were working. But Riley didn't think Noah's bad mood had anything to do with frustration or a lack of sleep. He was upset Willow might be their cousin. Willow wasn't her normal, cheerful self either.

It had been hard watching them moping around the beach house the past two days, especially when Riley felt partially to blame. The first thing that had come to mind when Cami told her to make a wish the other day at La Dolce Vita was that she wanted them to be a family—Noah, Willow, Cami, and her. Later that night, she'd learned her wish might come true.

She should've been more specific. If it were just her, she'd love having Willow as a cousin. But she wanted her brother to be happy, Willow too. And neither of them would be if the DNA test they had taken yesterday confirmed they were cousins. Her brother and Willow were already trying to keep their distance. They weren't mad at each other or anything like that. It was just the opposite. Anyone could see they were falling in love, or they had been before they'd found out Cami was Willow's mother and that she'd had sex with Riley's uncle the summer he died.

Her brother had been uncomfortable talking about the sex part. He probably would've skipped right over it if Willow hadn't been there. He got way more uncomfortable when Willow seemed to think it was a good time to talk about sex, specifically teenage girls feeling pressured and having sex before they were ready, and about consent and all that stuff. The way Noah and Willow had argued about it had been kind of funny. Or it would've been if they hadn't been talking about *her* having sex. As if.

A Game of Thrones had disappeared the next morning. So had half the books on the living room bookshelves. Riley had already guessed Noah was responsible. He'd confirmed it when he handed her a stack of Sweet Valley High books. They were her mom's. She'd written her name and the date on the inside covers the way Noah did. She'd read them the summer she'd turned fifteen. It made Riley feel close to her, and she got a little emotional when she thanked her brother for the books.

Seeing the tears in her eyes, Noah probably would've escaped to his study if it hadn't been for Willow. As with the sex talk, she'd seemed to think it would be a good time for Noah and Riley to talk about their mom. There was nothing Riley wanted more than to talk about her, but she knew from experience that her brother didn't like to. He'd changed the subject any time Riley had brought her up in the past.

Willow didn't let him get away with it, though. She asked

about his summers with their mom, drawing out memories that Noah appeared to have forgotten. Riley hoped Willow got her dream job hosting a morning show. She'd make a really great interviewer. Although her brother probably wouldn't have agreed, being on the receiving end of her questions.

Noah had a lot of memories of his summers at the beach house when their mom was married to his dad. He even had some stories about the summers their mom had spent at the beach house when she was young. Riley had soaked them in, storing them up, wishing she were recording Noah while he was sharing them. Without Willow there to pester and prod him, Riley had a feeling she wouldn't hear any more stories. And that was her biggest worry if Willow turned out to be their cousin. It would be too hard for Noah and Willow to be around each other, and they'd go their separate ways.

Lucky jumped off Riley's lap and scampered to the door, barking. There was no one there but he did the same thing when either Willow or Noah came home. She glanced at the time on her iPad. They had a meeting at the station about the sale, and she didn't expect them home for another hour.

Willow and Noah weren't sharing about the possibility they were cousins so they were still trying to find a buyer for the station. From what Riley had overheard, there were just two potential buyers left on their list, and it wasn't looking hopeful.

"Come here, Lucky. No one's there." He ignored her and kept barking, loudly.

She was surprised Cami wasn't yelling or threatening him from her bedroom. She was holed up in there again. Riley didn't know what she was doing but she did know her reunion with her sister Gia wasn't going well.

Cami had come home early from helping out at the restaurant and retreated to her bedroom. Riley figured that was why Cami and Willow were still staying at the beach house. At least one of the reasons. Riley was pretty sure she was the other one. She'd had a mini-meltdown when Carmen insisted that Cami and Willow move into one of the family's empty apartments. Gia hadn't seemed impressed with the idea either. At least when it came to Cami.

Whatever the reason, Riley was glad they were there. It'd be boring if it were just Noah and her. A little lonely too. "Treat. Do you want a treat?" she called to Lucky.

He swung his head from her to the door and went back to barking.

She was about to go to the kitchen and get him a treat when there was on a knock on the door and the knob began turning.

"Don't open the door!" Riley cried, sprinting across the living room. It was too late. Willow's sister walked in carrying boxes of pizza. Lucky shot through Sage's legs, knocking her off balance, and the pizza boxes went flying.

Lucky stopped to sniff one, and Riley lunged. He slipped through her hands and scampered down the stairs.

"Sorry!" Riley shouted over her shoulder as she ran after Lucky, calling his name.

He didn't stop. He rounded the garage and tore down the driveway. "Treat, Lucky, treat!" Riley yelled, her heart racing as he took off down the road, terrified he'd get hit by a car.

This wasn't the first time he'd made a great escape, but her brother, Willow, and Cami had been with her the last time. Even with the four of them, it had taken thirty minutes to find and capture him.

Riley guessed she'd been chasing him for fifteen minutes down the dirt road that had turned muddy from the rain and wasn't any closer to catching him. It was just her luck that the rain hadn't let up. Definitely not the sunny afternoon Willow had predicted in this morning's forecast. She'd be hearing from Amos, that was for sure.

Willow's friend Veronica, the receptionist at the station, had gotten so tired of fielding his complaints that she'd given Willow's cell phone number to Amos. He called her twice a day. Willow routinely put him on speaker when Riley was there. Willow always let him know he was on speaker, and that Riley was there, so she felt as if she knew him too. He'd even ask her opinion after giving Willow the what for, as he called it.

It was all kinds of hilarious. Willow thought it was hilarious too. She also thought Amos was a much better weather forecaster than she was. Not that Riley would say anything to Willow, but she was kind of right.

Thunder rumbled in the distance. *Please be afraid of the thunder*, Riley thought. If he was, Lucky might run back to her, seeking comfort. She could swear there was a quarter of a mile between them now. He was a black dot on the middle of the road.

"Crap!" she cried when, instead of running back to her, the black dot veered to the right and disappeared into some bushes.

She pumped her arms in an effort to pick up her pace while praying she'd find him shivering in the bushes instead of making a beeline for the water. But she was relieved she didn't have to worry about him getting hit by a car. For now.

As she closed in on the bushes he'd disappeared into, she

heard a dog barking. It was a much lower, fiercer bark than Lucky's. She spotted a thick tree branch on the side of the road and picked it up. Then she moved toward the bush. "Lucky," she whispered, hoping to avoid alerting the other dog to her presence. It was growling now.

"August, you're going to miss the best part! He'll be fine. It's probably just a squirrel," a girl called out.

"Come here, boy," a guy said, probably the August person the girl had called to.

"August!" the girl cried, sounding all kinds of whiny.

"Go watch the movie, Zoe. Killer's got something cornered in the bush."

The dog's name was Killer? Riley shoved her way into the bushes, wincing as the branches clawed at her arms and neck. She burst out the other side, waving her stick like a sword.

A guy wearing board shorts and a T-shirt stared at her. "What the hell?" Then he frowned. "I've seen you before."

Oh no, not him! She knew Sunshine Bay was a small town, but really? She had to run into the guy Cami had chased down Main Street. Could her day get any worse? Apparently, it could.

"What's going on, Aug?" A guy sauntered over. It was Green Board Shorts Guy from the sandbar. He looked around August, and his eyes lit up with recognition. "I know you. You were with the crazy blond woman who was trying to pick us up. She did the same thing to you, didn't she, Aug?"

"She's not crazy," Riley muttered. "She has a head injury. Now if you don't mind getting your killer dog out of here, I'd like to get my *puppy* and go home." She pointed her stick at the huge black dog digging under a bush a few feet away.

"You might want to drop the stick," August advised at the same time the big, black dog spotted her.

"Killer, no!" August yelled, moving toward her, but his giant dog was faster, and he took a flying leap, pushing her onto the ground. Then he licked her face, stole her stick, and took off.

August was trying not to laugh but Green Board Shorts Guy was busting a gut. August offered his hand. "Sorry about that. He's playful." His gaze moved to the bush the dog had been digging under. "Is that your dog?" he asked, just as Lucky darted out of the bush and took off after Killer.

"I don't believe this!" She threw up her hands and ran after both Lucky and Killer, only she hadn't factored in that the grass was wet and slippery, and she slid down the slope in the lawn. Both dogs sat and watched her grass-surfing action.

"What do you think, Aug? Ten-pointer?" Green Board Shorts Guy asked, grinning at Riley.

August didn't get the chance to tell his friend what he thought, not that Riley cared. Two teenage girls in short-shorts and tight tank tops were standing in the window, banging on the glass. When they got the boys' attention, they simultaneously cocked their heads and pointed at her. They must've raised their voices because Riley heard their "Who's *that*?" loud and clear.

Definitely mean girls. She rolled her eyes, making sure they saw her do it. *Total Cami move*, she thought with a small smile. August must've seen her roll her eyes at them because he laughed. She tossed her wet hair in another move that would make Cami proud and carefully picked her way to the dogs.

"I'm warning you, Lucky, if you move, I'm going..." She swore in Italian when Lucky ran for the dock, this time with Killer chasing after him. Riley hoped her brother never learned Italian.

She did her slip-and-slide thing to the dock, giving Giant Killer Dog—he came up to her waist—a wide berth as she moved around him, and made her way to Lucky. There was only one way for Lucky to escape, and she was almost positive he wouldn't jump in the water. They'd tried to get him to go in the day before, and he'd refused.

"All right, you be a good boy and don't move, and I'll give you a treat when we get home," she said, slowly bending over in order to scoop him up without startling him, ignoring August, who yelled above the sound of pounding feet, "Be careful. Killer—"

Whatever else he was about to say was cut off by her screaming when Killer headbutted her, sending her into the water. It was a good thing she'd been almost at the edge of the dock or she could've been seriously injured. Lucky, who'd obviously been well named, sat looking down at her with his tongue lolling and his tail wagging.

August and Green Board Shorts Guy weren't laughing when they hauled her out of the water. They both looked concerned. "Are you okay?" August asked.

"Yeah," she said, feeling like a drowned rat. Her jeans were waterlogged and her top was...plastered to her chest. She didn't think she could pull off Cami's *chin up, tits out*—she didn't have much of a chest to speak of—definitely a lot less than the girls in the window. She hunched over, scooted past August and his friend, and scooped up Lucky, holding him to her chest.

"Thanks for pulling me out of the water. I've gotta go now. Bye," she said, and hotfooted it down the dock.

"Hey, uh, Rainbow Girl," August called out.

She turned and frowned.

He shrugged. "I don't know your name. You've got a rainbow on your T-shirt."

"Riley. My name's Riley."

"August, and Ty." He jerked a thumb at his friend and then looped his fingers under Killer's collar. "If you give me a minute, I'll put Kill inside and give you a ride home."

"Thanks, but I can walk."

"Aren't you staying at the Bennett place?" Ty asked.

"Yeah, but it's not that far, and I can't get much wetter than I already am. Thanks for the offer, though."

"Riley, it's at least a two-mile walk. Just give me a couple minutes," August said, loping off without waiting for her response.

"He'll just come after you so you might as well give in," Ty said, then grimaced. "About the blond lady. I'm sorry I called her crazy. It's just that it was a little weird. She's like what . . . thirty? And she was flirting with a bunch of teenagers."

"She has amnesia. She thinks she's seventeen."

"Seriously? Does she not see herself?" He held up his hand. "I mean, she's hot. I just don't understand how she can't see that she's a lot older than seventeen." He ran his hand over his wet hair. "I'll just shut up now."

Riley smiled. He seemed like a nice guy, plus, Cami was right. He was super cute. Although Riley thought August was cuter. "It's okay. I think Cami sees what she wants to see." She grinned. "And she covers all the mirrors."

"Yeah?" He laughed, glancing at the window when the

dark-haired girl banged on the glass. "I'm being summoned. It was nice meeting you, Riley. You're welcome to hang out with us at the sandbar whenever we're there. You can bring your friend too."

"Thanks." She had a feeling the mean girls would make sure the invitation was rescinded if they found out about it.

August rounded the cottage. He had a blue blanket and held it out to her, lifting his chin at Lucky asleep in her arms. "Is it okay if I wrap the blanket around you?"

She nodded, her cheeks getting warm. "Thanks."

"No problem. The red truck." He pointed at the truck in the driveway. "I'll be back in five," he told his friend.

Ty nodded and walked around the side of the cottage with them. "When's everyone else supposed to get here?"

"Around six," August said, opening the truck's passenger-side door for her. "You need a hand?"

"I'm okay, thanks." It wasn't easy but she managed to get into the seat without dropping Lucky or losing the blanket.

August closed the door, rounded the hood, and then got in and slid behind the wheel. "Did Ty apologize about calling your . . . She's not your mother, is she?"

She shook her head. She knew he hadn't meant to, but it felt a little as if he'd punched her in the stomach. She wondered if that was how her brother felt every time he walked into the beach house and remembered their mom. Maybe that was why he wanted to sell it.

"No." Her voice came out husky, and she cleared her throat. "I mean, he did apologize. But Cami's not my mother. She's my friend." She explained about the accident and how Cami thought she was seventeen.

"So she knew my dad then?"

"Your dad's name is Flynn?" she asked, excitement bubbling up inside her. Maybe she could get the answers her brother and Willow needed.

"Yeah. Flynn Monroe."

Whoa, Cami must've really loved the guy if she'd stolen his last name. "Did he go to high school in Sunshine Bay?"

He nodded. "He grew up here. We move around a lot because of his job. I'm staying with his father, my grandfather, for the summer."

"Did he ever mention dating someone named Cami?"

"That's the lady's name?"

She nodded.

"Not that I know of. But hang on." He pressed a button, and the sound of a phone ringing came through the speaker.

"You're calling your dad?" she whispered.

"Yeah. You've got me curious now." The phone connected.

"Hey, bud, what's up?" A man's deep voice came through the speaker.

"Weird question for you, but did you ever date someone named Cami?"

"I did, but it was a long time ago, bud. Why do you want to know?"

Riley made big eyes and shook her head.

"One of Gramp's friends mentioned it. He said you dated her when you were my age."

"Yeah, we dated for a couple years in high school. And then I went to college and met your mom. I haven't seen Cami in . . . it must be thirty years."

"Dad, I didn't think you cheated on Mom."

His father chuckled. "Good to know. I'm heading into a meeting, but I'll give you a call tonight."

August glanced at Riley. "I've got a thing tonight. I'll be home late."

"Okay. But let your grandfather know when you'll be home. I don't want him worrying about you. You know what he's like."

"I know, Dad. I'm the one living with him."

"Is he behaving himself?"

"Yeah." He grinned. "But the lady who does the weather probably doesn't think so. He calls her all the time. You should hear him on the phone with her, Dad. It's like he's obsessed with her weather reports."

His father laughed. "Yeah, I've been around a couple times when he was watching her on TV. He yells through her entire weather report. But I wouldn't worry about it, bud. She's a nice woman. I know the family. She's Cami's niece."

"Seriously?" He looked at Riley and raised his eyebrows.

She nodded, still reeling from the fact she'd found the love of Cami's life, was actually listening to him on the phone, and August was Amos's grandson. How wild was that? She couldn't wait to get home and tell Cami, Noah, and Willow the news. Well, maybe not Cami. She didn't know she was Willow's mother. Willow didn't want to upset her and thought it best if they keep it a secret for now.

"Seriously. I gotta go, bud. Love you. I'll see you in a few weeks."

"'Kay, Dad. Love you too."

Riley liked that August didn't seem embarrassed to tell his dad he loved him with her in the truck.

"Wow. I wasn't expecting that. Were you?"

"More like I was hoping Cami's Flynn was your dad." She made a face. "Sorry. I didn't mean it the way it sounded."

He glanced at her. "My mom died seven years ago."

"I'm so sorry, August." She held Lucky tighter. "My mom died fifteen months ago."

He nodded slowly. "That explains your reaction when I asked if Cami was your mom. I'm sorry. I know how tough it is. Do you have siblings?"

"Just my brother, but he's thirteen years older than me." She winced. "I forgot. I have twin brothers too. They're one."

He laughed. "You forgot you have two other brothers?"

"Long story." She shrugged. "It's been a lot. But what about you, do you have siblings?"

"Two older sisters, and they make sure I don't forget about them. They're twenty-six and twenty-four, and they act like they're my mothers." He smiled. "Most of the time, I don't mind."

"That's nice." August was nice too. Really nice. So she was hoping he wouldn't get weirded out by what she was about to ask. "You know how I mentioned Cami has amnesia?"

"It's not exactly something you forget."

"Right. It's just I was wondering if you have a picture of you, your dad, and your sisters that I could show her. I know it sounds weird, but it might help jog her memory. We don't want her to stay stuck at seventeen forever."

"Sure, happy to help," he said, turning into the driveway of the beach house. He parked the car and grabbed his phone off the console, put in his password, and then scrolled through his photos. "Do you have a phone or an email address?"

She didn't share that her mother wouldn't let her have a phone until she was sixteen. Her birthday was in two weeks, and she was totally asking her brother for one. She gave August her email address.

"I, um, know your grandfather," she said. "If Willow's at home when he calls, she puts him on speaker. It's my favorite part of the day. He's hilarious. And you don't have to worry. Willow doesn't mind. Your dad's right. She's super nice."

He slapped his forehead. "You're the Riley he keeps talking about. He thinks you're sweet and super smart."

She smiled. "I like him too." Lucky poked his head out of the blanket and licked her chin. "I guess I'd better go. Thanks for everything, August. You have no idea how helpful you've been."

"The least I could do after my dog knocked you down and then pushed you off the dock."

"What kind of dog is he?"

"Bernese mountain dog. We got him when we were living in Switzerland." His lips lifted at the corner. "We used to get our groceries in France and Italy. I learned to swear in several languages, including Italian."

"Okay, just as long as you don't tell my brother what I'm really saying. He thinks I'm saying 'achoo.'"

He laughed and helped her out of the blanket.

Her stomach got all squishy inside. She wanted to pump her fist that she'd made him laugh. She wondered if that was how Willow felt when she made Noah laugh. Riley couldn't remember her brother laughing as much as he did in Sunshine Bay.

"Thanks again, August. It was really nice meeting you," she said as she got out of the truck.

"Nice meeting you, Rainbow Girl. Maybe I'll see you around."

She waved goodbye as he pulled out of the driveway and thought about adding another item to her wish list.

Chapter Twenty-Three

Camilla sat cross-legged on her bed, waiting for her call to Gail to connect. They'd both been busy the past couple of days, Gail with contract negotiations with Lilianna Rose's parents and Camilla with her family. Admittedly, Camilla had been spending quite a bit of time in her bedroom, catching up on sleep. Staying in character 24-7 was exhausting. She'd been tempted to confess that she'd regained her memory several times, but she couldn't do it. Not with her sister Gia making it clear that she wanted her gone.

She didn't blame her. Camilla knew she had a lot to make up for, not only with Gia but also with her daughter. Noah and Riley too. But her sister, who'd once been easygoing and the peacemaker of the family, had turned into an unforgiving hard-ass. Their relationship wasn't showing any sign of improving. If anything, it was getting worse.

"Hey, sorry I missed your call earlier," Camilla said as soon as Gail picked up.

"You haven't been online, have you?"

"No. What's going on?" She held her breath, praying that photos of her in Sunshine Bay hadn't surfaced.

"About two hours ago, TMZ broke the news that Hugh's

PA Emily and your ex's girlfriend, Giselle, aren't BFFs like you suspected. They're lovers. There's a video online of them making out last night at the Polo Bar in NYC. It's already gone viral."

She let out the breath she'd been holding. The news wasn't as bad as she'd feared, but it wasn't good either. "As much as I want to say, 'Karma is a bitch' and laugh my ass off that Jeff got exactly what he deserves, I can't help worrying that somehow this will blow back on me. You know as well as I do that an unhappy Jeff doesn't bode well for me."

"I do, and knowing Jeff as well as you do—"

"You probably know him better than me. You saw through him from the beginning."

"I'll refrain from saying I told you so."

"Oh please, you've been saying it for the past year."

"I have, haven't I?" Gail laughed. "Well, let's hope I'm wrong this time because you don't need something else to deal with, but my guess is you'll be hearing from him within the next seventy-two hours."

"I've already heard from him, remember? He wanted to crow about Giselle getting the part of Rachel West. Honestly, I don't know what Hugh was thinking."

"He won't be crowing the next time you hear from him. He'll be declaring his undying love for you, putting the entire blame for your breakup on Giselle. He's going to crucify her in the press."

"You're probably right. He's such a snake. I feel sorry for Giselle, and Pinky, as surprising as that may be."

"It isn't surprising, not to me. You're one of the most compassionate and forgiving women I know."

"I'm sure I can find a hundred people who would disagree

with you," she said, cocking her head at the sound of voices wending their way upstairs. "Sounds like the gang is all home. I'd better go. I've spent the past three hours in my bedroom. They're going to start wondering what I'm doing up here." She'd planned on going down when the demon dog woke her up with his incessant barking, but then she'd heard Sage swearing and hadn't wanted to face her niece without backup. She wasn't up for another round of twenty questions.

"Do me a favor and call Hugh. He texted again this morning, checking up on you," Gail said.

She knew he was worried about her. He'd sent her a couple of texts. The first one had been to let her know Giselle had gotten the part. He'd been sweet and apologetic and told her to give him a call.

"He still has no idea about the accident? Nothing has leaked in the press?" Camilla asked.

"He has no idea. No one does. But I have received several requests for a comment from you about Giselle and Pinky, so you'll need to be careful. And if Jeff frames this the way I think he will, the paparazzi will be hunting you down."

"He's the gift that keeps on giving, isn't he?"

After they'd said their goodbyes and disconnected, a thought came to Camilla. She grinned and texted Gail. "What do you think of me hiring Pinky as my new PA?" she typed, adding several laughing emoji.

"Brilliant!!! And I'm being serious. But we both know Hugh. He'll stand by Pinky and Giselle. Call him!!"

"Texting him now, Mom."

She responded to his last text. "Sorry it's taken so long for me to respond! A few things came up that I had to deal with. I'm sure you're snowed under with the breaking

Giselle-and-Pinky news. I hope it doesn't prove too much of a distraction. Thanks for checking up on me. You can take me out for a drink when you get your Oscar nom."

As she got off the bed, her phone rang. She frowned at the screen. It was Hugh. She connected the call, and his deep voice came over the line. "Pinky?"

She laughed. "Emily of the pink hair."

"Ah, it's purple now." She heard the smile in his voice. "So are you going to tell me what's really been going on? And don't give me the 'things came up' line, Cami. You're the ultimate professional, and you missed the read-through with Clive."

For some reason, it hit her just then that the only people in her world who didn't call her Camilla were Hugh and Gail. And if the other people who mattered most to her called her Cami, maybe it was time that she did too. Maybe it would reconnect her to the girl she used to be. The girl who'd had big dreams and who'd lived life to the fullest, enjoying every moment as if it were a precious gift. She wanted to be that Cami again.

She crawled back onto her bed and leaned against the pillows. Maybe it was that warm, sexy voice of his and the fact that she'd considered him a friend for more than fifteen years, or maybe it was because her life was such a mess and she was feeling a little lost, but whatever the reason, she decided to confide in Hugh. She trusted him, and the people she trusted were few and far between.

"How much time do you have?" she asked.

"For you, all the time in the world."

"How did you and I never hook up?"

"You were either married or getting married."

"I'm an idiot."

"You might not have the best taste in men, but you're far from an idiot. Now stop trying to distract me and tell me what's going on."

She did. She told him everything from how she'd gotten pregnant at seventeen to where she was now, trying to make things right. The one thing she didn't tell him about was Will and the part she'd played in his death.

Other than offering a murmured word of comfort when she got a little emotional, Hugh mostly stayed quiet.

"So there you have it. The messy, complicated story of my life."

"I get first option on the movie rights."

She laughed. "I'm not writing my life story, Hugh."

"I'm begging you. Please, write this story."

"You're serious?"

"I've never been more serious in my life."

"First off, I'm not a writer. Second, I couldn't open myself up like that. People would crucify me."

"You've been in the business long enough to know that some will, but people need stories like yours, Cami. They need someone like you, a gorgeous woman who seems to have it all, to show them that no one's perfect, that you've been knocked down and got back up, that your mistakes don't define you, and that there's always light at the end of the tunnel. We can talk about the actual writing of the book. I think you can do it, and I'd like to see you give it a try. I'm happy to read your first few chapters. But I know several authors who've worked on celebrity biographies."

"I can't believe that not only do you want me to do this, but you think I can."

"The Cami Monroe I know can do anything she sets her mind to."

"There's more to the story, Hugh. I've never told anyone. It's ugly, and it's... it's unforgivable. If anyone found out, I could be in serious trouble."

"Hang on a sec." She heard him talking to someone in the background. "As you know, I have a situation to deal with here, but as soon as everything calms down, I'm coming to you."

"Hugh, no. You're busy. You don't have to drop everything to come hold my hand. I'm fine, honestly."

"I'm not coming to hold your hand, Cami. I'm coming to convince you that you need to write your story, and to hear the part of it that you haven't shared with anyone."

"I can't, Hugh. I can't tell anyone, not even you," she said, the panic coming out in her voice.

"You don't have to tell me, but I'm still coming."

"You're busy!"

"Cami, for the first time since I've known you, you're not in a relationship. Do you really think I'm going to risk you meeting someone before I can convince you to give me a chance?"

She grabbed a pillow and hugged it to her chest, tears rolling down her cheeks. She didn't deserve a man like Hugh in her life. He was beautiful inside and out. So she did the only thing she knew that would convince him she wasn't worth it. She told him about the night she'd killed Will Bennett.

When she was finished, she buried her face in the pillow. Over her muffled sobs, she heard him swear and waited for the sound of him disconnecting.

Instead, his voice came over the line, deep and pissed off. "Baby, your sense of timing sucks."

"I . . . What?" She sat up and wiped her eyes.

"You know what I'm dealing with, Cami. It's not like I can charter a plane and come to you. My phone is blowing up, I have producers losing their minds, and—"

"After everything I just told you, you still want to see me?"

He blew out a breath. "Someone's just walked in so I can't say what I want to. But nothing you could tell me would change my mind about you or what I want with you. I'll call you tonight."

She heard someone yelling in the background seconds before Hugh disconnected, and she stared at the phone, stunned that what she'd told him hadn't changed his mind about her. And then, under the shock and disbelief, a tiny flicker of hope rose inside her. It had been a long time since she'd felt hopeful about anything, and it scared the hell out of her.

Her fingers trembling, she texted the person she turned to in moments like this. "I talked to Hugh. Gail, he likes me. He really, really likes me. Me!" She pressed Send and then closed her eyes after rereading what she'd sent. She sounded seventeen. She was about to text Gail to just ignore her when her phone rang.

As soon as she connected the call, Gail said, "On a scale of one to ten, how scared are you?"

"Twenty."

"That's what I figured. Now, for once in your life, you're going to listen to me, Cami. If you blow this because you don't think you deserve that man, I am coming to kick your ass, and I'll kick it all the way around Sunshine Bay."

"Are you going to wear your pointy shoes?" Cami asked, half laughing, half sobbing. "I told him everything, Gail.

Things I've never told anyone, not even you, and he didn't care."

"Of course you did. You're the queen of self-sabotage."

"No, I'm not. I'm queen of the mean girls."

"You like to pretend you're queen of the mean girls. Although I have to admit, you have gotten much better at putting the trolls in their place over the past ten years. You can't see me, but I'm rubbing my knuckles on my chest. I've taught you well."

"You have. I couldn't have become queen of mean without you." She wiped her eyes. "I couldn't have done any of this without you, Gail. I love you, you know. You're my best friend."

"Cami! Damn it, you've made me cry, and I don't cry! I knew this would happen. I never should've told you about the job offer."

"Don't you even think of backing out. I'll call Lilianna Rose's family myself. You are taking that job or I'll come kick your ass all around New York City, and my shoes are way pointer than yours." After the two of them stopped laugh-crying, Cami said, "You need to know what I told Hugh. I should've told you years ago, but I didn't want to lose you. I didn't want you to hate me."

"Cami, there's nothing you could tell me, absolutely nothing, that would make me love you any less than I do."

After Cami finished telling Gail about that night, she heard her sniff before clearing her throat. "I always knew there had to be a reason why you kept dating, and marry-ing, men who didn't deserve you. And it wasn't just about the men you gravitated toward. You've been punishing yourself for thirty years, and it stops now. What happened to Will was horrible, but it wasn't your fault. It was a tragic accident."

"I don't know how you can say that, Gail. I told him I'd stay awake. He wouldn't have been on the road that night if it wasn't for me. If I—"

"Enough. I'm serious, Cami. Enough. You can't change what happened. But somehow, someway, you have to come to terms with this. We'll figure it out. We'll get you into therapy with the therapist who diagnosed you with PTSD. She couldn't help you before because you didn't tell her about the accident. She'll be able to help you now."

"I have to make amends for what I did. I have to—" A knock on her door cut her off, and Cami whispered into the phone, "I've gotta go."

Chapter Twenty-Four

The door to Cami's bedroom opened, and Willow poked her head inside. "I'm going out, and I just wanted to make sure you're okay."

"I'm good." She smiled, knowing she looked far from good when Willow's eyes narrowed and she walked into the room, standing with her hands fisted on her hips. "Sage said you didn't go help Nonna at the restaurant today. Did something happen with my mother? Did she say something to hurt your feelings? And don't try and tell me everything's fine because you've obviously been crying, and Riley said you've locked yourself in the room for most of the day."

"I didn't want to get in the way, and I knew Gia didn't want me there. I don't really blame her." She raised her casted arm. "I knocked a couple things over in the kitchen. Gia thought I did it on purpose. I think she's mad at me for whatever I did that made them leave me behind. I just wish they'd tell me what I did so I could make it up to them." Other than the part about not knowing why her sister hated her, everything she'd said was true.

"I'll talk to my mom." Willow worried her bottom lip

between her teeth as she studied Cami. "Maybe I shouldn't go out tonight."

"That's what I've been telling you for the last twenty minutes," Noah said, coming into Cami's room.

Something had been up with Willow and Noah for the past couple of days. When they weren't avoiding each other, they were sniping at each other. Cami figured it was sexual tension making them act that way. When they were within ten feet of each other, the room practically sizzled with it. If it were anyone else, she'd tell them to do it already. But they couldn't, and it was her fault that they couldn't. And as much as she didn't like to see either of them unhappy, it made her job of keeping them apart easier.

"I don't believe you," Willow said to Noah. "You actually followed me up here to continue a conversation that I told you was over. O-V-E-R."

"I came to check on Cami. You just happened to be here," Noah said, crossing his arms. He had that broody look on his face that she knew Willow loved, but she didn't look as if she loved it at the moment.

"What are you guys fighting about?" Cami asked.

"We're not fighting," Noah said. "We have a difference of opinion, that's all."

"We're fighting," Willow told Cami. "He ordered me not to go out for a drink with Megan."

"I didn't order you," Noah defended himself. "I simply said I didn't think it was a good idea."

"I agree with Noah," Cami said. She was not a fan of Megan or of her daughter putting herself in a position to get hurt again.

"I do too," Riley said, coming into the room.

"What is wrong with you people? Have none of you ever made a mistake?" Willow shook her head. "You don't know Megan like I do. Did she mess up? Of course she did. But everyone deserves a second chance. You don't throw away a twenty-year friendship, or any relationship for that matter, just because someone did or said something that hurt you." She walked to the door. "Now I'm going to get ready to go out, and the three of you are just going to have to suck it up."

Cami stared after Willow, and that flicker of hope that had been there since she'd talked to Hugh got a little bit bigger. Her daughter didn't throw away friendships or relationships because someone screwed up. She believed in second chances, and that gave Cami hope that Willow would give her one too when she found out she was her mother.

"I'm going with you," Noah said as he followed Willow out of Cami's bedroom.

Riley sat on the side of Cami's bed as the argument continued in the hall.

"You're not going with me!"

"Fine. I'm driving you, and don't even think about arguing with me."

"Fine!"

"I have work to do at the station so I'll pick you up when you finish your drink."

"You'll be waiting all night. After the past couple of days I've had, I need more than one drink."

Riley made an *eek* face at Cami, and they both winced when a door slammed and Noah swore and another door slammed.

"We can't let Willow go alone, Cami. You know what Megan's like."

"You . . . we can't go to a bar, Riley. You're underage." She chewed on her thumbnail. "But you're right. Willow might need backup." She sounded as if she was ready to party, and when a Rosetti partied, she partied hard. "I'll go, and you can stay here."

Riley shook her head. "Are you crazy? I'm not staying here all by myself. We're in the middle of nowhere."

"Noah will kill me if he finds out I took you to a bar, Riley."

"He'll never know, and it's not like I'll be drinking."

"Okay, fine." Cami got off the bed and walked to the door, closing it. "And if we're really doing this, you need to look twenty-one."

Cami and her sisters had started sneaking into bars when they were sixteen. She had fond memories of those times, but unlike Cami and her sisters, Riley had led a sheltered life. She was sweetly innocent.

"Maybe we should just stay home. I'm sure Willow will be fine."

Riley frowned. "What's wrong with you? You're acting weird."

Dammit. "Easy for you to say. You're not the one who Noah will strangle if we get caught."

"He won't find out. Besides, Willow needs our protection. You know she does. She's too nice, and she lets people walk all over her. I bet Megan is plotting to embarrass her somehow, and that won't look good for Willow, not with them trying to sell Channel 5."

Riley made a strong case for them going, and Cami folded like an accordion.

Twenty minutes later, she was wearing a pair of Willow's

loose dusty-rose pants that had uneven painted black lines and a wide, gathered elastic waistband, paired with a black, scoop-neck tank top. She added a black ball cap over her blond hair to complete her disguise of a seventeen-year-old going on twenty-one.

She'd found a cute off-the-shoulder white ruffled Swiss-dot top for Riley and paired it with a flirty powder-blue skirt decorated in tiny white flowers. Cami had curled Riley's hair in long, loose waves that framed her face and done her makeup.

She cast an experienced eye over Riley. "If I didn't know you were fifteen, I'd think you were at least twenty-one. You look gorgeous, Riley." It was the truth. The kid was stunning.

"It's the makeup. You're really good at it, Cami."

"It's not. I hardly used any. I just used enough to enhance your incredible bone structure and amazing eyes." She looked down at Riley's feet. "But the sneakers have to go."

Cami walked over to the piles of her clothes and footwear and found what she was looking for. She held up a pair of delicate white heels. "Try them on."

"I can't wear heels," Riley protested.

It took almost thirty minutes of Riley practicing walking in the shoes for her to get the hang of it. Then they had to cordon off Lucky in the living room. Riley didn't want to leave him in his crate. So by the time they'd gotten in the station wagon and were headed for the bar, Willow had at least an hour's head start.

"Are you sure she'll still be at this bar?" Riley asked, tottering in her heels on the sand.

Cami hooked her arm through Riley's. Last Call had been one of her family's favorite bars. The locals considered it their bar, and it tended to get rowdy. It was on the beach just down from the pier. Christmas lights were strung along the wooden roofline, and the front of the bar was completely open to the outside when the weather was good, and it was a beautiful night, warm with a light breeze. The bar was packed with people spilling out onto the sand, drinking and dancing to the music that drifted down the beach.

"If she isn't at Last Call, we'll try Surfside on Main Street."

"Um, that might not be a good idea, Cami. The station is on Main Street, and Noah's there, remember?"

"Right," she said as they made their way through the crowd. "Play it cool. You look twenty-one. You are twenty-one."

Riley nodded, her gaze moving around the bar. "I see her." She raised her hand.

"Don't point her out. Just tell me where she is, and we'll get close enough that we can intervene if Megan gets nasty." Or if she looked as if she was about to cause a scene or if Willow did.

"She's sitting at the bar with Megan. Left side, four stools from the end."

"Got her." The two women had their heads bent together. Willow had on a cute sleeveless A-line shift dress trimmed with gold ribbon. Thankfully, instead of sneakers, she wore gold sandals. No heels, of course. The lights of the bar shimmered like sunshine on her golden hair.

Cami searched for a table and found one in the perfect location. She caught Riley by the hand. "We've gotta move fast. The table right behind Willow and Megan is free."

"There are three guys headed for it, and they're big."

Riley was right. They were. "Leave it to me." Cami wove her way through the bar, dragging Riley behind her, reaching the table half a second before the bodybuilders. Grabbing a chair, she pushed Riley into it and lowered herself onto the one beside her.

"Hi, boys." Cami tipped her head back. "Is one of those for me?"

"If I say yes, what do I get for it?" the tallest guy asked.

"A thank-you?"

He put the beer in front of her. "We're giving you our table, and I'm giving you my beer. I think that deserves more than a thank-you, don't you?"

She picked up the beer, took a sip, and said with a flirty smile, "A thank you, and a dance . . . with the three of you."

The other two men put their beers in front of her, and she laughed. "You haven't seen me dance yet."

"We don't have to to know that you'll be good," the first guy said. "We're picking the song, though." He winked. "Drink up." Then he looked at Riley. "What are you drinking, beautiful?"

Riley stared at him with her mouth hanging open.

Cami dropped the flirty smile and gave the guy a look that had him backing off with his hands up. "Okay, mama. I won't go there." He lifted his chin at his friends, and they sauntered back to the bar.

"He called me beautiful," Riley whispered. "And they gave you their beers and didn't fight over the table just because you said you'd dance with them."

"You are beautiful, and this is a do-what-I-say-and-not-what-I-do moment. Don't do what I just did."

"Don't worry, I wouldn't have been able to even if I wanted to, and I really don't want to."

Their backs were to Megan and Willow, and Cami glanced over her shoulder. "We need to move the table closer. I can't hear what they're saying." Although from what she could see, Willow looked a little tipsy. Her hand movements were exaggerated.

Cami and Riley couldn't move their chairs back more than a few inches without getting in the way of anyone going up to the bar. Cami leaned back anyway. She still couldn't hear them. "I'll get you a soda."

She tugged the brim of the ball cap lower and got up from the chair, moving the beers to the far side of the table. "Don't talk to anyone and don't look around or make eye contact with anyone." She grabbed the drinks menu and handed it to Riley. "Pretend you're studying this."

She picked up her wallet and made her way to the corner of the bar, four stools away from Megan and Willow. She angled her back to them, keeping an eye on Riley while she waited to be served.

"I'll need to see ID," the bearded man behind the bar said.

Cami wanted to cheer. She was being carded! She couldn't wait to tell Gail. She looked up to smile at the bartender while coming up with an excuse not to show him her ID. And that's when she realized he was talking to the girl beside her, who looked twelve.

"I'd kiss you if I wasn't married," the girl said, pulling out her ID. "I'm thirty-two."

Bully for you, Cami thought, rolling her eyes. The bearded bartender didn't ask for Cami's ID, but he did cock his head when he handed her the soda. "Do I know you?"

"I don't think so," she said, changing her voice to low and sexy. "It's my first time here. Great place." She should've gone with high-pitched and annoying, she thought, when he studied her with interest. She gave a little wave and turned her head to the right as she slowly walked behind Megan and Willow.

"I knew she looked familiar!" Megan said.

"Keep your voice down," Willow whisper-shouted. "No one can know Cami's my mother or that she's in town."

"Okay. But Will, one look at you two together, and everyone will know she's your mother."

Cami tripped over her feet, reaching for the back of a chair to keep herself from falling on her face. Willow knew she was her mother, and she didn't hate her. She still talked to her even though she knew the truth. She still smiled and laughed with her. She liked her. She really, really liked her. And the little flicker of hope inside her grew bigger.

"My mother is having a hard enough time dealing with everything," Willow said. "She doesn't need it playing out in the tabloids."

The flicker of hope sputtered and went out, and Cami moved away before Willow or Megan saw her. She hadn't understood why her relationship with her sister was getting worse, not better. Now she did. Gia didn't want her around now that Willow knew she was Cami's biological daughter. She didn't want Cami to have a relationship with her daughter.

Gia was afraid she'd come between her and Willow, and Cami had backed herself into a corner. Until she told her family she had her memory back, she couldn't tell her sister that she would never, not in a million years, do anything to come between her and Willow. She just wanted to be a part of her daughter's life. She didn't think that was too much to ask, but maybe it was.

Riley frowned when Cami pulled out her chair and sat down. "What's wrong?"

"Nothing." She smiled, handing Riley her soda. "Megan's being nice to Willow." She picked up a beer and took a long swallow.

"That's good," Riley said, taking a sip of her soda as she took in the crowded bar. Her eyes got big, and her head whipped around to Cami.

"What is it?"

"I see someone I know," Riley said, her cheeks flushed.

"Really?" Cami looked around. "I didn't think you knew anyone in Sunshine Bay."

"I just met him today. I mean, I met both of them." She held her finger behind her glass, pointing at the entrance to the bar.

"The two guys with the group of teenagers trying to sneak in?"

Riley nodded. "It's the guy you thought was Flynn, and the other one is Green Board Shorts Guy from the sandbar."

Well, that was embarrassing. But she had to act as if it weren't. "Cool! Should we call them over? They're super cute. I call dibs on the guy who looks like Flynn."

"Are you crazy?" Riley cried. "We're not calling them over!"

Aware of how close they were sitting to Willow, Cami whispered, "Keep your voice down." And she slowly turned her head to catch a glimpse of her daughter at the same time that Willow and Megan glanced their way. Cami whipped her head around. "They're looking at us. Stare straight ahead."

Beside her, Riley froze.

Cami let out the breath she'd been holding when Willow didn't march over or call out their names. "That was close. We have to be careful."

"Maybe we should go."

"You're probably right. Megan seems to be trying to make amends, and Willow—"

"Will, Megs!" a group of women shrieked, arms in the air as they ran to their friends at the bar. "Time to par-tay, Beaches!"

Riley sighed. "I guess we're staying."

"It'll be okay. We'll keep a low profile, and if Megan gets out of hand, we'll call . . . Sage."

"There's one problem. I don't have a phone or Sage's number."

"Me neither." Cami tapped her pointer finger on her lips, trying to come up with an idea. "I've got it. We'll yell fire, everyone will run out of the bar, and then we'll grab her."

Three minutes later, Cami's hope of keeping a low profile ended. She'd forgotten about the bodybuilders. A microphone screeched, and she glanced toward the stage to the left of the bar. Last Call was famous for its karaoke. She couldn't see through the crowd, but she recognized the deep voice booming, "Hey, Pretty Badass, your daddies are waiting. Get up here and shake your booty for us."

"Is he frigging shitting me?"

Riley tugged on Cami's arm. "Shh. Everyone's looking over here."

She hadn't realized she was standing. But seriously. "*Pretty* Badass. I'm a straight-on badass."

"Your hat says *Pretty Badass*," Riley pointed out.

Cami took it off and turned it around. "Okay, but my daddies? Shake my booty? What are we, in the eighties?"

"We're waiting, mama-licious!" the three of them yelled into the mic, and then Donna Summer's "Love to Love You Baby" came through the speakers.

"I love that song!" a woman behind her yelled.

Cami turned her head. "Good. You go dance with him." Just then she realized how loudly she'd spoken, and swore under her breath in Italian. Riley said the same thing, only not under her breath, when Willow marched over to their table.

"Cami! What are you doing here?" Willow picked up the half-empty beer mug. "You shouldn't be drinking with a head injury!"

"Told you," Riley muttered.

Which drew Willow's wide-eyed gaze to her. "Riley?" She swatted Cami's shoulder. "What were you thinking? She's under..."—she glanced at the bartender and lowered her voice—"age."

"So am I." Cami inwardly rolled her eyes at herself. This was getting exhausting. "And don't try and tell me you didn't sneak into the bars when you were our ages," Cami said, with all the teenage attitude she could muster. She never should've brought Riley to the bar.

"We so did." Megan giggled, beaming at Cami in drunken glee. She must've started drinking before Willow got there. "I just love your mov—"

Willow elbowed her. "Outfit. She loves your outfit. Right, Megan?"

"Oh, yeah, right." Megan frowned. "Don't you have a top and pants like that?"

"They're mine." Willow glanced toward the stage, where the bodybuilders were now dancing with the Beaches. "What's up with those guys?"

"We stole their table, and they gave Cami their beer. She promised to dance with them," Riley said.

"Thanks a lot, pal," Cami said, looking up when the bartender arrived at their table with a tray of shots.

"Courtesy of the guys at the bar, the three at that table." He hitched his thumb behind him, then he lifted his chin at a group of women three tables over from theirs. "And the ladies at that table." As he set the shots down, he glanced at Cami. "Are you sure I don't know you?"

"Of course you know her. Everyone knows—ouch." Megan glared at Willow. "Why did you kick...Ohhh." Her "oh" went on for at least a minute.

Cami pressed her lips together to keep from laughing. Then she smiled up at the bartender. "They say we all have a twin. Maybe you know mine."

"She looks exactly like Camilla Monroe. The actress."

Willow stared at Megan. "I should've cut you off four drinks ago."

Seventeen-year-old Cami wouldn't know who Camilla Monroe was, so she stayed quiet.

"No idea who you're talking about," the bartender said as his gaze moved from Cami to Willow. He nodded. "Now I know why you look familiar. You two could be twins. You're not related to the Rosettis, are you?"

"It's our song," Willow cried, pumping her fists, undoubtedly in an effort to distract the bartender, which it did. But probably not in the way her daughter had intended.

"Stop the music," he bellowed. "We've got a Heartbreaker in the house, and this is her song." He grinned at Willow. "No dancing on the table. Take the stage, ladies."

"Yay!" the Beaches yelled from the dance floor, and Megan jumped to her feet, scooting past Willow to pull both Riley and Cami off their chairs. "Come on!" she cried, rushing for the stage, bouncing off chairs as she went.

"I don't think this is a good idea," Cami said.

"Neither do I," Riley said.

"Ditto," Willow agreed, looking around as people began chanting, "Sing, sing, sing." She made a face when the Beaches ran toward them. "But trust me, if we try to escape now, the Beaches will tackle us, and we'll make a bigger scene." Then she smiled at Riley. "Didn't you have 'Do something you've never done before' on your wish list?"

"I can think of way more fun things to do that I've never done before, and way less embarrassing."

"You've never sung karaoke with me. It's all kinds of fun," Willow said.

"Or with me," Cami added. "My sister Eva can sing, but I'm the dancer in the family." Karaoke had been one of her favorite things to do at the bar with her sisters. And the thought that she was going to get the chance to do it with her daughter made her happy. So happy that she thought she might cry.

"We'll just see about that," Willow said with a grin. "Come on."

The Beaches and Megan ran onto the stage with them, cheering when Beyoncé's "Single Ladies (Put a Ring on It)" came over the speakers. Cami had danced to the song with Beyoncé herself, so she knew all the moves but her daughter did too, and so did Riley. They were laughing and singing, and her daughter was right beside her, and Cami thought it might just be the most fun night of her life. And because it was, when the song ended, she cried, "Let's do another one!"

Riley tugged on her hand. "We've gotta go."

Cami followed the direction of her panicked gaze. The teenager who looked like Flynn and the cute boy from the sandbar were pushing their way through the crowd to get to them, and that's when Cami noticed how many people were holding up their phones and taking pictures, and then she heard the whispers: "It's Camilla Monroe. I'm sure it is. Here in Sunshine Bay? No way."

Willow must've heard them too. "We've gotta get out of here," she said, just before a large group of people surged toward the stage.

"Camilla! My mom loves you! I love your movies! Take a picture with us, please!"

"I'm not an actress! I'm not who you think I am!" Cami shouted, not only for the crowd's benefit but for her daughter's and Riley's. But their audience couldn't be convinced, and she searched the bar for an escape route. "It's okay," she told Riley, tightening her grip on her hand. "I've got you."

"We've got you," Willow corrected, taking Riley's other hand.

"This way, mama-licious," one of the bodybuilders said as he and his friends waded through the crowd.

The Beaches, who'd been staring in shocked silence, came alive. "We've got you too," they said, closing ranks behind them.

The bodybuilders and the Beaches formed a tight circle around Cami, Willow, and Riley, hustling them out of the bar and onto the beach, and that's when they heard the sirens.

"Rainbow Girl," someone yelled, and then Flynn's look-alike was there, reaching for Riley's hand. "I'm her friend," he told the bodybuilder who'd grabbed him by the arm.

"He is," Riley said, and the bodybuilder lifted his arm, letting him into their protective circle.

"The cops will be here any minute. I'll get Riley out of here and back to the beach house. I haven't been drinking," he said, glancing from Cami to Willow.

Cami looked at Willow, who nodded.

"Riley?" Cami asked before giving the okay.

She took the boy's hand. "Noah can't know I was here. I want to go with August."

"Okay. You take good care of her," Cami told August. "She's precious cargo."

Riley and August got away in the nick of time. A shrill whistle rent the air, silencing the rowdy crowd trailing behind them.

"No one move. Let us through," said a commanding voice and two cops made their way through the crowd. They weren't alone.

"I swear, if I have any luck at all, it's bad luck," Willow muttered, and that's when Cami knew she'd seen Noah too.

Chapter Twenty-Five

Willow sat in the passenger seat of Noah's car two days later. She was meeting with one of the heads of Boston's top-rated news stations, the only one left on their prospective-buyers list who hadn't said no.

"I appreciate you driving me, Noah. I know you have a lot on your plate."

He glanced at her. "It's not a big deal, Willow. I can work from the car while you're in your meeting."

"It kind of is a big deal. We haven't exactly been on the best of terms the past two days."

"We've been through this. I don't blame you for Riley being at Last Call. I know exactly who encouraged her to go."

Of course he'd figured out that Riley had been there. If he hadn't, the videos that had gone viral this morning would've clued him in.

"And we've been over that too." She sighed. "I know you were mad that I took Cami's side, but she felt bad enough, and so did Riley. You yelling at them instead of giving them a chance to explain wasn't helping."

"I didn't yell at them. You were yelling at me, and I had no choice but to raise my voice to be heard."

"That's not the way I remember it."

"You have a selective memory."

"And you see everything in black and white, Noah. Once you make up your mind about a situation, you won't even consider there's another side to it. You're right and that's all that matters."

"When it comes to my sister's well-being I am. I don't care that Cami and Riley were at Last Call because they got it into their heads you needed protection from Megan. As far as I'm concerned, Riley needs protection from whatever other hare-brained scheme Cami comes up with."

"Don't talk about her like that. She's going through a difficult time, and you know that. You could be a little more compassionate."

"My fifteen-year-old sister could've been arrested, and now that the video is out there for all the world to see, I have to get ahead of it and convince her father to let Riley stay with me."

"I'm sorry. You're right. I didn't even think about what would happen if Billy found out. I can talk to him if you want."

"It's fine." He glanced at her. "I'm sorry too. I don't want you worrying about this before your meeting."

"All we seem to do these days is argue, and I hate it."

"I don't like it any more than you do." He lifted his hand off the steering wheel, and she thought he was going to reach for hers, but instead he rubbed it up and down the side of his face. "We're both on edge, and we both know why."

"The paternity test." She nodded. "It's almost as if we're trying to put distance between us by fighting."

"We don't have much longer to wait."

She'd been hopeful after seeing the photo Riley had shown

them of Flynn and his family. Willow shared more than a passing resemblance to his daughters. And she thought Cami taking his surname was as relevant as Cami naming her after Will.

Noah wasn't as positive. He dealt in facts and figures, not fantasies, and he wanted to wait until the DNA results came in. They'd fought about that too. That fight had been all on her. She knew Noah was right, but she'd begun worrying that with everything going on, he was questioning his feelings for her. It didn't help that they'd argued about her paternity right before Megan had asked to meet her at Last Call.

Willow rested her head against the seat, briefly closing her eyes to the traffic on either side of them. She needed a distraction from everything going on with Noah and from her nerves about the upcoming presentation. The pressure of this meeting weighed heavy on her shoulders. The future of Channel 5 would be decided today.

She turned her head, her gaze moving over Noah's handsome profile. He must've felt her studying him, and his eyes met hers, holding her gaze. She felt the familiar zing of attraction and straightened in her seat. This wasn't helping.

"Would you mind if I go over the presentation with you?" she asked.

"Of course not."

By the time Noah pulled into the parking lot beside the office tower, Willow had gone over the presentation so many times she had a feeling she'd be reciting it in her sleep.

"You've got this, Willow. There's nothing they could ask you that you don't know the answer to," he reassured her as he opened her door.

She got out of the car and smoothed her skirt instead of

kissing him like she wanted to. "Thank you." She looked around the packed parking lot, the sun beating down on the Mercedes. "Are you sure you want to wait here? There's a restaurant across the road. A couple coffee shops too."

"I'm good. We'll go out and celebrate after your meeting."

She held up two fingers and crossed them while glancing up at the imposing glass-and-steel building.

"Don't be nervous. They wouldn't have scheduled a face-to-face if they weren't interested."

An hour and a half later, she learned they were interested, just not in buying Channel 5. Noah was leaning against the car when she walked across the lot toward him.

"Ted called you, didn't he?" For the first ten minutes of the meeting, Ted, the head honcho at the station, had talked about Noah and how much he respected and admired him.

"He did, and before you ask, I had nothing to do with you getting a face-to-face with them, or with their offer. Ted wanted me to put in a good word for them, that's all. They want you for you, Willow. They'd be stupid not to. And Ted is not a stupid man." His gaze roamed her face. "Why don't we go and get something to eat? You can tell me what you think about the offer. But you should know that they're willing to negotiate."

"Negotiate? Noah, I can't believe the compensation package they offered me," she said as he guided her across the parking lot with his hand at the small of her back.

"Whatever they offered you, you're worth ten times more."

She sputtered a laugh. "You're biased."

"Personally, I am. But not professionally. You're the only one who doesn't recognize how talented you are, Willow," he said as they stood waiting for the traffic light to change.

"You're great for my ego, you know. But Noah, this isn't just about me. How can I even think about entertaining their offer when Naomi, Victoria, and everyone else at Channel 5 will be out of a job?"

Noah held open the door to the crowded upscale restaurant. "Is that the only thing holding you back from accepting?"

A couple of weeks before, she probably wouldn't have even entertained the offer. She would've been overcome with anxiety at the thought of leaving her family and Sunshine Bay and would've refused almost immediately. But she'd begun to wonder if some of her anxiety had more to do with her not believing in herself and her broadcasting chops than it had to do with leaving Sunshine Bay. Lately, thanks to Noah's unwavering support and faith in her, she'd started seeing herself as he did.

"Willow?"

She glanced at Noah. He and the hostess were looking at her as if expecting a response to something one of them had said.

"They don't have any tables available inside." Noah clued her in. "Are you okay on the rooftop patio?"

"Of course. Sorry about that," she murmured to Noah as they followed the hostess up the stairs. "My mind was elsewhere."

He reached for her hand and gave it a comforting squeeze. "Understandable."

When they were seated at a glass table under a black umbrella, a waitress came over to take their order. Willow ordered a lavender lemonade and Noah ordered a citrus spritzer. They settled on a platter of seafood appetizers to share.

Noah leaned back in his chair. "Would it make it easier for

you to accept the offer if I told you that I'll do whatever I can to ensure everyone at Channel 5 finds a job?"

She looked away, blinking the gathering moisture from her eyes. He really was perfect. The kindest, most considerate man she'd ever known. The smile she offered him wobbled. "It would."

"I'm sensing a *but*."

The waiter approached with their order. Willow waited until he walked away to tell Noah how she was feeling. "When Ted and his management team were talking about their plans for me, I realized how different it would be from working with everyone at Channel 5. They're a major network, so I knew it wouldn't be the same, and this will probably sound naive to you, but our vision for a new, improved Channel 5 didn't just come from Don, Victoria, Naomi, and me, everyone gave their input. It was a group decision. We're a team." She took a sip of her lemonade. "But I'm not sure everyone else feels the same as me."

"Maybe I'm missing something, but unless you have another buyer interested in the station, it's a moot point."

"And here I had been thinking you were the kindest, most considerate man I've ever known," she grumbled.

His lips twitched. "That's an improvement over how you've been thinking about me lately."

"Did you miss the part where I said I *had been*?"

He held her gaze. "I've missed a lot about you these past few days."

"Ditto," she murmured.

He glanced at the couples at the surrounding tables, who were clearly enjoying a romantic lunch.

"This might not have been the best idea." Now that she'd

noticed the couples, she couldn't seem to look away. That could've been Noah and her just a few days ago, before they'd learned the truth. *It still could be*, a hopeful voice whispered in her head. She wondered if Noah was thinking the same thing.

Obviously not, she decided, when the next words out of his mouth were, "So if you're not going to accept the job, what are you going to do?"

She didn't relish the idea of bringing up Last Call or Megan, but there was no way around it if she was going to tell him the idea Megan had shared with her the other night. "Megan didn't only invite me to Last Call to offer an apology and an explanation for her behavior. She—"

"What could Megan possibly say that would explain how she acted, not to mention earn your forgiveness?" He looked at her. "Please tell me you didn't accept her apology."

"It was a heartfelt apology, Noah. She cried."

He snorted and picked up a shrimp.

"Okay, so she sniffled, but she was on the verge of tears. And her apology was genuine."

He raised an eyebrow and bit into the shrimp, baring his straight, white teeth.

"You weren't there so you can't judge, and just to say, you're being pretty judgy. She was having a really bad day when she found out you were pausing the sale. One of her coworkers had just told her she was dating Megan's ex, and not only was she dating him, she'd gotten the listing of his friend's vacation home, which puts her in the running for Real Estate Agent of the Year."

"So that somehow makes it okay for Megan to say what she did to you?" He picked up a crab cake, dipping it rather forcefully into the spicy rémoulade.

"You know, we did a story about how your body doesn't absorb nutrients if you're angry or upset when you're eating."

"Obviously that's not a problem for you. You don't get angry." He paused with the crab cake halfway to his mouth. "Except you do with me. I wonder why that is?"

"Despite what you seem to think, you're not the only one I get upset with. But life's too short to hold a grudge. And like I said, Megan apologized, profusely."

"Did she also apologize for forcing you to sell your home and putting you in debt?"

"She didn't force me to sell. It was the only way for me to get the money. But yes, she did apologize for that too, and before you ask, she also apologized for her uncle asking me to leave two weeks earlier than I expected." Even she had to admit she sounded like a doormat if all it had taken for her to forgive Megan was a heartfelt apology.

The thing was that Megan had offered her more than an apology. She'd come up with an idea for saving Channel 5 if their efforts to sell the station failed. She'd broached the idea of an employee buyout, and she'd spent a lot of time researching the ins and outs. She had the facts and figures to back it up. She'd also offered to loan Willow the money for the buyout to make up for the losses Willow had sustained from the house flip. An offer Willow appreciated but wouldn't accept, and given how Noah felt about Megan, she wasn't comfortable mentioning the employee buyout to him, at least not yet.

"What does Megan have to do with your plans for the future?" he asked after swallowing his crab cake. His eyes narrowed. "Please tell me you're not flipping houses with her again."

"No, but she gave me an idea, and before you ask, I'm not

telling you what it is. Not until I talk to everyone at Channel 5."

"So you really aren't going to accept Ted's offer?"

"I have forty-eight hours to give them my decision. If I can't get everyone at Channel 5 on board, I'll accept the offer."

She chewed on her bottom lip. She had to organize a meeting with her coworkers today and present Megan's idea. And then they'd have to present the offer to Noah. "Would you be available to meet with us around two tomorrow?"

It would mean pulling an all-nighter, but they had no time to waste. They had to meet Noah's deadline for the sale.

"I have a conference call at two. Would three work?"

The silent auction was the next night, and she had to help with the setup, but she could make it work.

"Absolutely. Thank you." She picked up a crab cake. "Now let's talk about what you're going to say to Billy."

Chapter Twenty-Six

The next afternoon, Willow stood at the receptionist desk at Channel 5 with Veronica and Naomi, trying to get a look at what was going on in Noah's office while pretending she wasn't.

"Stop picking apart the flowers," Naomi said. "You're making a mess of Veronica's desk."

"I'm not picking . . ." She looked down at the vase of daisies. Half of them were petal-less. It looked as if it had snowed on Veronica's desk.

"Sorry." She swept the petals into her palm and dumped them into the wastepaper basket. "I'm just nervous. I can't believe you guys aren't."

"Oh," Veronica said, "I thought it was a 'He loves me, he loves me not' kind of deal, not that you were nervous."

If she were plucking daisy petals about Noah, it wouldn't be about his feelings for her, it would be "He's my cousin, he's not my cousin."

Naomi frowned. "Why are you nervous? I might not be Megan's biggest fan, but she did a great job on the offer."

"I know she did, but it's less than Noah's asking price, and we only have guarantees for half the amount we're offering."

"But once everyone we talked to comes through, we're two-thirds of the way there," Veronica said.

After Megan had presented her research for the buyout to everyone at Channel 5 the night before, they'd voted. Ninety-five percent of Willow's coworkers were on board while the other five percent opted to take Noah up on his offer to help them find jobs, which Willow had shared before they'd voted. She'd also shared that she'd received a job offer from Ted. She wanted to be fully transparent. As an added benefit, it showed how much she believed in their ability to make a go of this.

While Don and Megan went over the details of the offer and the presentation, Willow and her coworkers had worked the phones, offering members of the community the opportunity to invest.

"Don has the list of potential stakeholders, but he can't include them until their agreements have been signed and verified," Willow said.

"I can't believe we're having to convince Ms. Positivity that the deal will go through," Naomi said to Veronica while raising an eyebrow at Willow. "We expected you to arrive this morning in your cheerleader's uniform, pom-poms waving, entertaining us with backflips and side splits. The guys are disappointed in you."

"They would've been more disappointed if I attempted a backflip and broke my neck."

Naomi laughed. "I forgot. You never did manage to nail one, did you?"

"No. I didn't. And you're right. We can do this. The committee members for the silent auction are all on board, so we'll make one last pitch to the community tonight."

"Was that supposed to be a pep talk?" Naomi asked,

frowning. "What's up with you? You haven't been yourself in days."

"Naomi's right, Will. What's going on with you?" Veronica asked.

"It's my mom," she admitted. "She's not coming tonight, and she withdrew her paintings from the auction."

"I'm sorry. I know how excited you were to showcase her talent." Naomi hugged her. "There'll be other opportunities, Will."

"Naomi's right. We can feature her on *Good Morning, Sunshine!*" Veronica said. "But I kind of get it, Will. It can't be easy for her with all the coverage about Cami and your family's estrangement. If I were Gia, I wouldn't want to come with the amount of press in town."

"How's Cami holding up?" Naomi asked.

Willow had told Naomi and Veronica that Cami was her biological mother. She trusted them to keep it to themselves. Although she thought it was only a matter of time before some ambitious reporter ferreted out the truth.

"She's oblivious. It's the one good thing about her not having her memory back. Seventeen-year-old Cami doesn't know social media exists, and she's convinced herself that the crowd at Last Call mistook her for Camilla Monroe. Riley's been keeping her busy at the beach house. Obviously, she won't be coming tonight either."

Willow didn't share that Cami wasn't acting like herself. At first, Willow had thought it was because Noah had been angry about her taking Riley to Last Call. But she'd begun to suspect there was more going on. Cami was spending an inordinate amount of time in her bedroom, and she hadn't asked to go to La Dolce Vita, which obviously they wouldn't have allowed because the press had camped out in front of the restaurant. Well, they had until her grandmother had run the reporters off.

"Don's coming out of Noah's office," Veronica whispered.

Willow was afraid to look. "Does he look happy? What does Noah look like?"

"Hot, but then he always does." Naomi laughed. "Here comes Don."

Don walked over. "The Big Boss wants to see you, Willow."

"Oh, okay," she said, and started to walk away. "Wait a sec. You didn't tell us how it went."

"I think Noah wants to tell you himself."

As she walked toward his office, Naomi yelled, "Yes!" and Veronica yelled, "Woo-hoo!" and then cheers broke out in the station. She should've known Noah would agree to the offer.

He raised an eyebrow when she walked into his office. "No happy dance?"

She did a little dance instead of running across his office and throwing herself into his arms like she wanted to.

"And before you tell me you told me so, I'll admit you were right to give Megan a second chance. She put a lot of time and effort into the offer without expecting anything for herself." He looked down at his desk before raising his gaze to hers. "I'm listing the beach house with her, Willow. I considered keeping it but I think it's time for a fresh start, for Riley and for me. We have to move on. It's not easy living with the memories. And if you and I are . . ." He trailed off.

"I know." She nodded, looking at her hands twisting on her lap. Then she raised her gaze to his. "You haven't gotten back the test results?"

"Trust me, either way, you'll find out when I do. I won't open the portal with our results until you're with me. I called the lab this morning. We should receive the results later today or first thing tomorrow morning."

"It'll be good to know," she said, her voice thick with emotion.

"Or it won't." He got up from behind his desk and came around to sit in the chair beside her. "We haven't talked about it. But if the results come back, and we're related, I can't be a part of your life, Willow. The last thing I want is to lose you, even as a friend. But I can't do it. I thought I could, but I can't." He held her gaze. "I'm sorry."

"No. I feel the same way. But I don't want to lose Riley too."

"You won't. Riley's already talked to me about it. When and if the time comes, I'll talk to Billy about Riley visiting you, and vice versa. On the other hand, if we get the results we're hoping for..." He reached for her hand and gave it a gentle squeeze before immediately releasing it. "Probably best to keep those plans to myself until we know for sure."

"That sounds promising."

"Let's just say I think you'll be happy about it." He stood up. "And since I can't be this close to you without wanting to take you in my arms and kiss you, I'll get back behind my desk."

"Just so you know, that's not far enough away."

"Thank you for that, Ms. Rosetti. Now we should get down to business." He held up the offer. "It helped that Megan knew we're awaiting the DNA results and how that may impact the offer. She mentioned that in the event you receive the money you're entitled to, the offer will remain unchanged."

"I can tell by your expression that you don't agree with my decision, but if we put off the offer until I receive the money—which I'll reiterate that I'll be taking under duress—it'll push out the sale past the deadline."

"It won't have any impact on the sale whatsoever. Within seventy-two hours of us receiving the results that you're my uncle's daughter, the money will be transferred into your account. I've been working with our legal and accounting departments since we learned there was a possibility you were a Bennett to ensure I'd have everything ready for you to sign off on. I hired an outside team of attorneys and accountants to act on your behalf—your sister vetted them, by the way—and they've been receiving the reports as soon as they're generated."

"I . . ." She shook her head, stunned at what he'd done. "You didn't have to do that. I trust you, Noah. I trust you with all my heart."

He bowed his head and nodded. His voice was gruff when he said, "Thank you. But I wouldn't have felt right otherwise." He lifted his head, a grin that looked a little forced on his face. "And you know your sister. She probably would've sued me if I had done it any other way."

"She can be overprotective." Not any more than Noah, as he'd just proved. Her throat clogged and her eyes filled when she thought about everything he'd done to ensure she received what he believed she was entitled to.

She had to get out of there before she started crying ugly tears. "I should get going. I have to make sure everything's ready for tonight. And Riley and Cami are giving me a make-over." She did a fake shudder. "Wish me luck."

"Just one, two more things, actually. Why would you leave

the offer as is if you receive the money? Why wouldn't you buy the station yourself? You could own it outright."

"I like the thought of us all owning it together. We've always been like a family. As it is, I'm the only one who doesn't have the money to invest, but they're giving me shares anyway."

"They're not giving them to you, Willow. You agreed to work for free for a year, which is the other thing I want to talk to you about."

"I can tell exactly how you feel about this, Noah. So thanks but no thanks. I don't want to talk about this with you."

"Because you know I'm right."

"No! Because we'll have another fight if we do. It's not like I'll be destitute. I'll be working more hours at La Dolce Vita and living in my zia's apartment."

"I'll give you the money for the buy-in. We can set it up as an interest-free loan if it makes you feel better."

"I can't accept it, Noah. I need to do this on my own. You, out of anyone, should be able to understand that. My family has been helping me out for as long as I can remember. I need to prove to myself that I can do this."

He nodded, his gaze moving over her face. "In case we get the results neither of us wants, there's something I need to say to you, something I'll never be able to say to you again." He bowed his head, blew out a breath, and then raised his gaze to hers. "I love you, Willow Rosetti."

She covered her mouth, a sob escaping between her fingers as tears rolled down her cheeks. "I love you too," she whispered, the words muffled behind her hand as she unsteadily came to her feet, and then she turned and ran from his office.

She didn't stop to talk to her celebrating coworkers. She headed straight for the exit doors, ignoring Naomi and Veronica calling her name. The only way she kept it together through the rest of the afternoon and into the evening was by clinging to the hope that it wasn't the last time she would hear Noah say those words. He hadn't come back to the beach house before she'd left for the auction, but she'd seen him arrive with Riley just before the dinner was served. They'd sat at a table with Don and his wife while Willow had sat with the committee members. She'd avoided looking at Noah throughout her entire presentation and the auction. She'd been afraid she wouldn't be able to keep it together.

But now that her duties were over, she'd searched Windemere's ballroom for him and couldn't see him. She spotted Riley sitting at a table with August and Amos and walked over. She owed Amos a big thank-you anyway. He'd stood up during her presentation, declared that everyone in Sunshine Bay should do what they could to keep Channel 5 on the air, and then walked up to the stage and handed her a check for five thousand dollars with the stipulation that he have some say over her weather reports.

She introduced herself to August and then turned to his grandfather. "Thanks for becoming a stakeholder in Channel 5, Amos. I promise you won't regret it."

"You might," August said, earning him a scowl from his grandfather and a giggle from Riley.

Willow laughed. "I'm getting another lobster costume in his size."

"That'll be the day you'll catch me in a lobster costume," Amos said gruffly, but she caught the twinkle in his eyes.

Blue eyes that she couldn't help but notice were the same shade as hers and his grandson's.

August looked up from his phone with a grin. "Dad says he's going to become a stakeholder in Channel 5 too. Only he's buying more shares so he can override any decisions you make, Gramps."

"Give me that thing," he said, taking his grandson's phone. The three of them bit back smiles as Amos tried typing out a response to his son, cursing at the small keys.

Willow smiled at Riley. "Are you having fun?"

Riley nodded, casting a sidelong glance at August before returning her gaze to Willow. "Your speech was great, and I won the date with you. Noah bid for it."

"Awesome. We'll have to plan what we're going to do. And speaking of your brother, I haven't seen him since the auction ended."

"He said he had something to do but he'd be back . . . There he is." Riley pointed at the dance floor, and then she frowned. "Sage is with him. She looks kind of frazzled."

Willow turned to see Noah and Sage skirting the couples on the dance floor. Her sister looked beyond frazzled. Her black suit was wrinkled, and she had a serious case of bed-head, while Noah in his black suit looked as if he'd stepped off the cover of a magazine. Willow might've spent a few minutes enjoying the view if it weren't for the fierce expression on his face. Her first thought was, *What has Cami done now?*

She figured she was about to find out when Noah grabbed her by the hand, nodded a polite hello to the Monroe family, and then said to Riley, "Willow and I have to leave. Sage is your chaperone. She'll be taking you home at ten."

"Is everything okay?" Willow asked, her gaze moving from Noah to her sister.

Sage opened her mouth, but before she had a chance to respond, Noah said, "We have to go," and half dragged Willow across the dance floor. She smiled apologies at the people whose dancing they interrupted and the people whose chairs they bumped against as they wove their way past the tables and the bar and out the inn's entrance doors.

"Noah, what's going on?" she asked as he opened the passenger-side door of the Mercedes for her.

Her mouth fell open when he closed it without answering. What the . . . He jogged around the hood of the car with that same fierce expression on his face, opened the door, slid behind the wheel, slammed the door shut, and pulled onto Main Street.

Her heart in her throat, she managed to whisper, "Did Cami do something?"

He glanced at her with a frown. "No."

"Did something happen to my mom? My nonna?"

"No. Your family is fine. There's nothing to worry about."

"There is so. You're driving over forty miles an hour in a twenty-five-mile-an-hour zone."

His lips twitched. "Not until September first it isn't."

"Where are we going?"

"You'll see in approximately ten minutes. Six if you stop talking and don't give me grief for going over the speed limit."

"I won't be the one giving you grief. It'll be the cops when they pull you over." Her phone pinged, and she took it out of her purse. "Great. The committee members are mad at me for leaving without helping with the cleanup."

"They should be kissing the ground you walk on. Without you, the event wouldn't have been the success it was. You raised a phenomenal amount of money for the fine arts center. Not to mention, by my calculations, if everyone who expressed an interest in becoming stakeholders in Channel 5 is any indication, you'll have guarantees for the full amount of the offer, which means you'll have no issues with the bank when you approach them for a loan to cover operating costs for your first year."

"Don didn't mention anything about a loan."

"Don didn't actually think it was going to happen." He smiled. "But you proved him wrong, Willow."

"Not just me. Everyone at..." She trailed off as a familiar car drove by them. "I'm almost positive that was my mom and my nonna."

He turned down the road without responding, and then he parked in the empty lot.

"Why are we at Hidden Cove?"

Instead of answering the question, he got out of the car and walked around to the passenger side.

"Noah!" she cried as he opened the door. "I'm not going anywhere until you tell me what's going on."

"I lied to you."

"You did?"

"I did. I got the results of the DNA test when your brother walked over to ask my baby sister to dance."

"I don't... August is... You read the results without me?"

"I did." He helped her out of the car and then crouched in front of her, reaching for her foot. "As much as I love looking at you in those heels, you need to take them off. You'll sink in the sand."

"This is not how I saw this playing out when we finally found out we weren't related," she said, leaning against the car as he took off one of Cami's Jimmy Choos and then the other.

He tossed them in the car and then stood and closed the door. "If I kissed you now, I wouldn't want to stop, so if you can be patient a little longer, I promise to make it worth the wait."

"I think I can do that, mainly because I'm mad at you for looking at the results without me," she told him.

"Sweetheart, if we'd gotten the results when we were at the beach house, I would've opened them with you." He turned on his phone's flashlight and then handed it to her before sweeping her into his arms. "Shine it on the path."

The dark sky was littered with stars and a half moon shone on the bay but they didn't provide enough light to illuminate their way.

"There was also another reason I didn't think you'd want to read the results at the auction," he said.

"We could've gone onto the patio at Windemere and read them there."

"We could have," he said as they reached the cove where they'd spent three wonderful weeks together that long-ago summer. "But this is better, don't you think?"

She took in the small, flickering lanterns casting a warm, romantic glow over a blanket spread in the sand. There were a picnic basket, a bottle of wine, and two glasses.

"It is." She wrapped her arms around his neck, pressing a light kiss on his throat. "I'm sorry if I was cranky. It's just that I'd wanted us to be together when we read the results."

He set her on her feet in the sand. "And what if the results weren't the ones we got?" he asked as he took off his shoes and then reached for her hand, drawing her onto the blanket with him.

"You're right, and this is the perfect place to celebrate." She rested her head on his shoulder as he put in his phone's password.

He turned the screen to her.

"I don't know what I'm looking at. Whose results are those?"

"Your father's. Sage and I reached out to Flynn, and he agreed to do a swab and send it to the lab we used."

"I don't understand why you'd reach out to him. We'd know he's my father if Will wasn't."

"Technology has improved to a degree that DNA testing between cousins is fairly accurate but I didn't want us to have even the slightest doubt. I didn't think you would either. And your sister agreed."

"Have you shared the results with Flynn?"

"He would've received them when I did." Noah tucked her hair behind her ear. "When he learned Cami was your mother and not your aunt, he began questioning if he was your father. He saw the resemblance between you and his daughters." He smiled. "I gather Amos did too."

She half laughed, half sobbed, burying her face in Noah's chest. "I can't believe Amos is my grandfather."

"Are you happy about this?"

She leaned back, framing his face with her hands. "Happy? I'm ecstatic. I'm over the moon." She kissed him, and then they did everything she'd dreamed they'd do if they got the results they were hoping for.

They made love, and they laughed, and they talked, and they drank wine, and they ate the picnic her mother and grandmother had packed for them. It was after they'd made love a second time that Noah showed her the house on the bay that he wanted to buy for them, and Willow fell asleep under the stars wrapped in his arms, dreaming of a bright, happy future with the man she adored.

Chapter Twenty-Seven

Don't mind us. We're just leaving," Cami said to the couple on the hammock under the elm trees. Noah was reading a book with an arm around Willow, who was snuggled up against him reading something on her iPhone.

It was the happiest and most relaxed Cami had seen them in almost a week. If Cami hadn't overheard them talking to Riley earlier that morning when they'd gotten home, she would've flipped the hammock over. But she'd learned Flynn was Willow's father, not Will, and that had sent her tiptoeing back to her room. She didn't want them to know she'd overheard them or to catch her crying her eyes out because she'd deprived Willow of her father and Flynn of his daughter.

Neither Flynn nor Willow deserved what she'd done to them, even if it had been unintentional on her part. She had a feeling they'd be hard-pressed to believe her after the lies she'd told. Especially if they found out about the heinous act she'd committed.

That was one truth she was desperate to keep to herself, despite Gail and Hugh pressing her to confess the part she'd played in Will's death. They both believed she couldn't heal without unburdening her soul. But as much as she trusted that they had her best interests at heart, she couldn't do it. She'd lose her family all over again. She'd lose Noah and Riley too.

It was going to be bad enough when she revealed she no longer had amnesia. No one would pull any punches then. Despite that, she had to do it. She couldn't pretend she was seventeen forever, and she couldn't try to assuage Gia's fears or make amends to her family until she came out as herself.

She just wanted one more happy day, pretending to be a family with Willow, Riley, and Noah. She'd miraculously recover her memory tomorrow. Gail had bought her a reprieve from the press, releasing last year's photos of her in Italy. She'd hidden out there after Jeff's affair. Someone would eventually put it together. But for now, it was working. There were just a few die-hard paparazzi remaining in Sunshine Bay.

Noah and Willow turned their heads. "Where are you going again?" Willow asked.

Riley closed the door, giving goodbye kisses to Lucky through the screen. The kid seriously loved that dog.

"To La Dolce Vita. We told you like three times already," Riley said. "We're making you a special dinner to celebrate"— she glanced under her lashes at Cami—"uh, the good news that Channel 5 isn't closing."

It was wonderful news, and Cami couldn't be happier for her daughter. But she knew that wasn't what Riley wanted to celebrate. She wanted to celebrate Noah and Willow's good news that they were free to be in a relationship. Cami knew Riley hoped that the couple would marry one day soon.

The Rosettis didn't have a great track record when it came to love and marriage, but if anyone could beat the Rosetti curse, it was her daughter and Noah. Although Cami's sister

Eva and her niece Lila appeared to have beaten it too. Maybe it was just Cami who was cursed, her and Gia.

"Oh right," Willow said, then worried her bottom lip between her teeth.

Cami knew exactly what she was worried about but she couldn't tell her daughter they'd be careful of the paparazzi or not to worry because Cami was tracking their whereabouts online.

A few of them were hanging out at the airport while the rest were keeping an eye on Eva's house, where her sisters and mother regularly filmed their Instagram and TikTok videos. Cami didn't put it past them to be covertly staking out La Dolce Vita, although her mother had done a great job scaring them away.

Cami would've just as soon made a special dinner for Willow and Noah at the beach house, but she figured the couple wanted time alone, and Cami had missed spending time with her mother. If she got lucky, and she figured she deserved some good luck for a change, Gia would make herself scarce.

"It's okay, Willow," Riley said. "I know about the video from Last Call going viral and that there are photographers trying to get pics of me to sell to the tabloids."

Cami wanted to kiss her. No one had connected Riley in the video to heiress Riley Bennett. The kid was so damn smart. But seventeen-year-old Cami... "They do?" she asked, making big eyes. "That's da bomb!"

"It's not da bomb," Riley said. "They're calling the video *Poor Little Rich Girl Goes Wild!*"

Cami pressed her lips together while casting a covert glance at Noah and Willow, whose shoulders were shaking in an effort to contain their laughter. Willow clapped a hand over her mouth, which Cami also pretended not to see. She put her hands on her hips. "So? Your face will be plastered like everywhere. You'll get discovered!"

"I don't want to get discovered."

"I do!"

"Too bad. We're going in disguise." Riley held up hats, wigs, and sunglasses. "And if you don't promise to wear them and promise not to do anything stupid to draw the photographers' attention, we're not going to La Dolce Vita. Got it?"

"You sound just like my mother!"

"Thank you," Riley said primly.

"It wasn't a compliment," Cami muttered, while inside she was killing herself laughing.

"Well, um, it sounds like you've..." Willow burst out laughing, burying her face in Noah's chest.

"What's wrong with her?" Cami asked, fighting back a smile.

"She's punchy. She didn't get much sleep last night," Noah said.

"Well, maybe she should go back to bed," Cami said in a snotty voice.

"Great idea," Willow said, her voice muffled in Noah's chest.

"Okay. Drive careful, Cami. We'll see you at five," Noah said, not doing a very good job of disguising the fact that he couldn't wait for them to leave. "Keep an eye on Cami, Tink."

"I'm seventeen!"

"Going on twelve," Riley muttered, sending her brother and Willow into fits of laughter. "I'm not kidding about the disguise, Cami," Riley said as they walked to the station wagon. "We have to be careful. Billy saw the video online, and he lost his mind. I was across the room from Noah, and I could hear him yelling."

Okay, Cami hadn't known Riley had been outted. She must've missed that on social. "Oh no! Why didn't you tell me?"

"You already felt bad enough. And you had to put up with Noah giving you the silent treatment. Besides, it was my idea to go to Last Call, and you never told Noah or Willow."

"Of course I wouldn't tell them. You're my bestie." She slung her arm around Riley's shoulders. "Don't worry. I'm not going to do anything to get you into any more trouble. We're going to have so much fun cooking with my mother."

They were having fun with her mother until her sister walked into the kitchen, leaned over, and sniffed the pot on the stove. "The sauce is missing something," she said to their mother, ignoring Cami completely.

Cami wanted to tell her to get over herself but Gia had every right to be upset with her. But she wasn't about to let her ruin Riley's day.

"Nothing's missing. *Riley* made the sauce exactly how we always do," Cami said. Her sister was great with kids—great with everyone, really. She'd never intentionally hurt someone's feelings. Other than Cami's, obviously.

Standing at the far counter kneading the pizza dough, Riley turned. She had flour in her hair and on her nose and cheeks. She'd looked adorably flustered when they were trying to figure out how she'd managed to ruin her first two batches.

"Did I do something wrong to the sauce?" Riley asked, and Cami wanted to whack her sister with her casted arm.

Gia got an *oh crap* look on her face.

"I'm sure it's perfect. I'll just give it a taste," Gia said, smiling at Riley as she picked up a wooden spoon. "Cami never puts in enough salt."

"Don't listen to her, Riley. My mother, Eva, and I make the best sauce. Gia, not so much. Isn't that right, Ma?" she said when Carmen walked into the kitchen.

The wooden spoon stalled halfway to Gia's lips, and she turned her head, pinning Cami with a pissed-off stare.

There were a lot of reasons Cami should be sucking up to her sister right now, but fighting with her desire to make things right with Gia, there was something else. Cami was jealous of her sister's relationship with Willow, even if she had no right to be. So instead of kissing her sister's *culo*, Cami wiggled her shoulders, making the snotty duck face she used to make when she was trying to get a rise out of Gia. Her sister had hated it.

Still does, Cami thought with a grin when Gia shoved the wooden spoon in her mouth instead of telling her to go F herself like she used to.

"What are you talking about?" Carmen asked, walking over to Riley.

"Gia thinks I made a mistake with the sauce," Riley confided.

Carmen gave Gia a *what's wrong with you?* look before waving off her daughter's remark. "You didn't make a mistake. You made the sauce exactly like my Cami does, and she makes it almost as good as me." She pinched off a piece of dough, testing the elasticity. She nodded. "Better, much better. But maybe one more try, eh?" Carmen said, smiling at Riley.

Riley groaned. "I'm never going to get the hang of it. Maybe you should do it," she said hopefully to Carmen. "Willow and Noah are going to be here in an hour."

"Willow and Noah are coming?" Gia asked.

The green-eyed monster raised its head. "Yeah. Who did you think we were cooking for? Riley, Willow, Noah, and I are having a special family dinner to celebrate Willow's big news."

She'd taken it too far. She could tell by the look in her sister's eyes. Cami resisted the urge to smack herself with her casted arm and walked over to Riley. "I know what you're missing!" she crowed like a teenager hopped up on a high instead of filled with shame. "The secret ingredient. Love!"

Behind her, she heard what sounded like her sister slamming the wooden spoon on the stove and braced herself for what was to come. She deserved whatever her sister dished out. She just hoped she said it in Italian so Riley wouldn't understand.

Carmen got to Gia first, removing her from the kitchen before all hell broke loose. It wasn't the first time her mother had had to intervene with her daughters. The Rosettis fought as hard as they loved.

She heard her mother and sister yelling at each other in Italian. Carmen was defending Cami, and her sister wasn't happy. She shared just how unhappy she was by reminding their mother what a piece of work Cami was. Gia didn't want her spending time with Willow, and when Cami got her memory back, her sister intended to share that with her daughter. There was no room in their lives for Cami now, no matter how much Carmen wanted it. Cami clenched her teeth. Her sister might be able to keep her from her daughter, but no way in hell was she keeping Cami from her mother.

"I think Gia's mad. You shouldn't have said it like that, Cami. You made it sound like it was just us."

"I want it just to be us." One night, that was all she wanted. "Maybe we should bring dinner home."

"There's not going to be a dinner if I don't get this right," Riley said, and Cami reminded herself that today was about the girl she'd come to care about having fun.

She tested the dough. "My mother is the pizza queen and won't settle for anything but perfection. But nothing in life is perfect. This dough is pretty damn close, though. And way better than Gia ever made," she added with a grin.

"You really don't like your sister, do you?"

"I love her." She cleared her throat. "We're just different, that's all." She patted the dough. "Okay, you'll have to do the work and shape the pies," she said, holding up her casted arm. "We'll do the fun part together."

"You mean like putting the toppings on them?"

"No, the best part, throwing the pies!"

"You're a pro," Cami said fifteen minutes later when Riley's pie did a perfect spin in the air on her first try. "Where's your phone?" Noah had caved and bought her one the day before.

"Over there." Riley pointed at the opposite counter.

"Go get it, and put on 'That's Amore' by Dean Martin."

"Dean who?"

"Never mind who, just put it on," she said, awkwardly tossing her pie in the air. She couldn't wait to get her cast removed.

Riley laughed when the pie landed on Cami's head. "We can't use that one now," she said.

"Why? My hair's clean, and it was on there like for two seconds. Did you find the song?"

Riley pressed Play, and Cami closed her eyes as the memories of singing the song in the kitchen with her mother and sisters washed over her. She opened them to see Riley staring at her. "Are you crying?"

"No! I got flour in my eyes." She wiped at them. "Now let's sing and throw some pies."

They were laughing and singing when another voice joined in and Carmen swiped Cami's pie in the air and showed Riley why she was the pizza queen.

"You're a show-off," Cami said to her mother after Carmen finished dressing her pie in half the time it took Cami and Riley. She hugged her. "But I love you even if you made me look bad."

Her mother leaned back and patted her cheek. "I love you too, *cara*."

Cami's eyes filled with tears, and she buried her face in her mother's shoulder. "I missed you," she whispered.

"Willow and Noah are on their way," Gia said as she walked into the kitchen. She smiled at Riley. "Let's get the pies in the oven."

Cami wondered if Willow had called her mother or if Gia had called her daughter. She wondered what they'd said about her, about the celebratory dinner Cami had planned for just the four of them. It would never be just the four of them.

While the pies were in the oven, Cami and Riley made the Caesar salad.

"Why don't you bring it out to the table?" Gia said to Riley. "You can help my mother set the family table."

Riley's gaze moved from Gia to Cami. "Okay," she said, glancing over her shoulder as she walked away.

Cami nodded and smiled, letting Riley know she wouldn't fight with her sister and ruin the dinner. She glanced at Gia, who was leaning against the counter with her arms crossed.

Cami held up her hands. "I'm not fighting with you."

"No, what you're going to do is listen to me. I'm sick and tired of everyone tiptoeing around you because you have amnesia. All you've done since you've come back here is cause problems between me and my family. *Be nice to her, be patient with her, she thinks she's seventeen.* Well, you're not! You're a forty-seven-year-old woman who nearly destroyed this family once, and I'm not letting you do it again."

"I know I'm forty-seven. I got my memory back, and do you know why I didn't tell anyone, Gia? I didn't tell them because I knew you'd do exactly what you're doing now, try to get rid of me. And the only way I thought I'd have a chance to make amends to *my* family is to be the Cami they once loved. I want that, I need that, and I..." She trailed off, unable to say she deserved it. "I won't let you stop me from repairing my relationship with Ma, Eva, my nieces, or my daughter."

Gia glanced away and then a determined look came over her face. "Your daughter," she said. "That's rich."

"I loved her. You know I did. I didn't want to leave her. But I had no choice."

"Just like you had no choice but to kidnap her? To steal her from us? She was four years old, and you stole her from the only family she knew. You traumatized her, and you traumatized us."

"All I wanted was to spend some time with her but you wouldn't let me. You treated me like a stranger. You acted as if I was going to hurt her. You wouldn't even let me take her to the beach. You had to go with me."

"Because she didn't know you! I was trying to protect her, protect you."

"You threatened me. You said you'd call the police. But she was my daughter!" Cami shook off the memories of Willow crying for her mother, refusing to eat. "I brought her back."

"Yeah, three weeks later."

"I signed the papers. I gave you custody, and did as you demanded. I stayed away from her, from you, Ma, and Eva. For twenty-five years, I stayed away."

"You make it sound like you were a doting mother, but you abandoned her when she was four months old. You wanted to be a star. Well, you got your wish, Cami. So just leave us all the hell alone."

"No. You're wrong. I left her because I couldn't look at her without being reminded of Will. Every time I closed my eyes, I saw him in that car. I still do."

"Cami—"

"It was my fault, Gia. I was with Will the night he died. The only reason he was on the road that night was because of me. He was tired. He didn't want to drive, but I begged him to."

"Cami, stop. You have to st—"

"I promised I'd stay awake and make sure he didn't fall asleep at the wheel, but I didn't keep my promise. I'm the reason he died, Gia. The boy I believed was Willow's father died because of me. And I didn't stay with him. I left him there, bleeding out on the side of—"

Someone gasped, and she turned her head. Riley stood staring at her with tears streaming down her pale face. Noah stood behind his sister, his hands resting on her shoulders, the expression on his face stone cold. Willow stood beside him sobbing into her hand.

Cami turned her horrified gaze on her sister. "You knew. You knew they were there all along."

"I just wanted them to hear and see for themselves who you really are." She shook her head. "But Cami, I didn't know. I didn't know about Will. I tried to stop you."

Chapter Twenty-Eight

Willow stood in stunned silence, shocked by what Cami had just revealed. She didn't know what to say, what to do.

"She's a liar. You're a liar!" Riley yelled. "You pretended to be my friend."

"I wasn't pretending, Riley," Cami said, her expression shattered. "I care about you. I wouldn't do anything to purposely hurt you."

"You killed my uncle! You left him to die on the side of the road. You destroyed my family. You're the reason my mother died." Her voice broke on a sob, and she turned into Noah's arms. "I want to go home. I want to leave."

"Riley, honey." Willow reached out to comfort her, but Noah moved his sister out of her reach.

"Noah?" Willow searched his face, and everything inside her froze.

His eyes were cold, his face hard and expressionless. "My sister's right," he said, turning that ice-cold gaze on Cami. "You destroyed our family. My mother was supposed to go to the concert that night with her brother. Because of you, she blamed herself for his death, and it haunted her. Because of you, my grandfather blamed himself for buying the car

Will died in, and it haunted him. Because of you, my grandmother blamed him too, and their relationship was never the same. My mother was never supposed to take over the company. Will was, but because of you, he died, and my mother had to take over. Because of you, she died of a heart attack at fifty-two."

"Noah!" Willow gasped. "You can't believe that. It was an accident, a horrible accident, but that's what it was. You can't blame Cami for—"

"You're going to defend her to me?"

He'd never spoken to her like that, even when he was Mercedes Man, and she knew, no matter how much she loved him or he loved her, they wouldn't be able to get past this. But she had to try. She couldn't lose him.

"We need to talk. Just us. You, me, and Riley. We can get—"

"No. I won't let another Rosetti destroy our lives."

"How can you say that to me after last night, after everything we've been through, after everything we've shared?"

"The day I walked into the station, what was it you said, 'No man can resist a Rosetti when they have their mind set on something'?"

Willow cringed. He had seen her pretending to reel him in on her imaginary fishing line, and he'd repeated almost verbatim what she'd said.

"Your mother reeled my uncle in, and he died because of her. You reeled me in, and I nearly gave up my dreams for you. I suppose I should be grateful to you, Cami, for opening my eyes before it was too late. And maybe I would be if you hadn't betrayed my sister's trust."

His eyes moved over them. "Riley and I are leaving Sunshine Bay, but before we do, I'll be asking the police to reopen the investigation into my uncle's *accident*."

"Please don't do this," Willow pleaded. "Don't leave like this. You're in shock. You both are."

Riley lifted her head, looking from Willow to her brother. "Noah, Willow didn't know. It's not her—"

"It doesn't matter, Tink. There's no coming back from this." Taking his sister's hand, he turned and walked away.

Willow wrapped her arms around her waist, struggling to come to terms with what had just happened. She couldn't believe Noah was leaving her without a backward glance.

Sage strode into the restaurant, looking over her shoulder and then back at them. "What the hell is wrong with Noah and Riley? They..." Her gaze moved over Willow, her mother, who'd come to wrap her arms around her, and Cami, who stood sobbing in Carmen's arms.

Sage stared at them. "Did...did someone die?"

"No. I mean, someone did. Noah's uncle, and—" her mother began, glancing at Cami.

"Don't worry, Gia. You got your wish. I'm leaving. I just..." She walked toward Willow, her gait unsteady. "I never meant for this to happen." She lifted a trembling hand to her mouth. "I'm sorry, sorrier than you'll ever know. Your mother's right. Noah's right. I destroy everyone I care about."

"Would someone tell me what the hell happened?" Sage said at the same time that Bruno walked into the restaurant, took one look at Willow's grandmother, and rushed to her side. "*Cara,*" he said, gathering her into his arms.

Willow's gaze moved over her family, and she stepped

from her mother's embrace. "The family table now. All of you, and that includes you, Cami. We're a family. We don't fall apart when bad things happen. We come together. I just watched the man I love walk out that door, with his sister, who I love too, and I'm not letting anyone else I love walk away from me."

"Okay, *bella*. Anything you want," Bruno said, guiding Carmen to the table. When he got her grandmother seated, he came to Willow and rocked her in his arms. "No one could walk away from you. They'd have to be a fool to, and that man is no fool. He'll realize his mistake, and then he'll come back to you, begging your forgiveness, but he'll have to go through us first, and he better have a good reason for making you cry."

"He does, Bruno." She told him everything Cami had said and how Noah and Riley had reacted when they'd learned the part she'd played in Will's accident.

Bruno scrubbed his hand up and down his face. Then he glanced at Cami, who was sitting by herself at the end of the table, staring at her iPhone. Willow's mother sat at the other end, comforting Carmen, while Sage paced in front of the table with her phone pressed to her ear, every so often shooting worried glances Cami's way.

"I remember the morning we heard about the accident like it was yesterday. You tend to do that when someone dies young in a small town. It hit everyone pretty hard. But Cami"—he shook his head—"she was bad off. Carmen was worried about her, we all were. She was always a wild one, a lot like Eva.

"Like you." He smiled. "She could make your nonna laugh like no one else, and dance? That girl could dance. She loved to have fun and party. Then she met Flynn, and she calmed down. Still fun, and happy, always with a smile on her face, looking for the next adventure, but Flynn settled her. Will started coming around after she broke her arm at the sand dunes. He was a nice kid, a little on the wild side, though, which concerned your nonna, but he made Cami smile, and she'd been worried about her after Flynn left, so she let it be.

"Maybe if . . ." He shook his head. "All this to say, it makes sense now how Cami acted after the accident. She must've been desperate for some way to drown her pain, the guilt."

"She drank?"

He nodded. "She was out of control. Totaled your nonna's car, skipped school, didn't show up for work, stayed out to all hours. You name it, she did it. And then one day she packed her bags and was gone."

"She found out she was pregnant with me."

"She did, and aren't we the lucky ones to have been blessed with you." He kissed her forehead. "Now I'm going to close the restaurant. And then I'm going to put food on the table, bring out the wine, and then you and me, *bella*, we'll sort this crapola out."

"I think it might take more than you and me, Bruno," Willow said.

"It looks like we have backup." He nodded at Megan, who fast-walked toward her.

"What's happened?" Megan asked, looking from Willow to her family gathered around the table.

"Cami and my mom got into it in the kitchen, and—"

"No. I mean what happened with you and Noah? He just called me and canceled his offer on the house. He told you about it, didn't he?"

She nodded, afraid she'd start blubbering if she opened her mouth.

Sage strode toward them, searched Willow's face, and then gave her a one-armed hug. "Look, I know you're upset. But it's not over between you and Noah, no matter what he said. And right now—"

"What?" Megan shrieked.

Sage breathed in through her nostrils and then briefed Megan on the situation, as only Sage could do. Bluntly, with no emotion. Just the facts in bullet points. Willow wished she could be more like her sister. She didn't care if she was technically her cousin. She'd always be her sister.

Megan fanned herself with both of her hands. "This is too much to take in. How do you deal with this?"

"By pulling on your big-girl panties. And if you're going to add to the drama, you need to leave because we have all the drama our family can deal with right now," Sage told Megan.

Willow sighed. "Sage."

Megan waved her off. "No. She's right. You and your family got me through my divorce, and I'm going to get you and your family through this. And just saying, she's right about Noah. He adores you. You just have to give him time."

"You and Sage weren't here. You didn't hear him."

"We'll sort the Noah situation out later," Sage said. "Because right now we have bigger things to deal with."

Megan's eyes widened. "There's more?"

"Yeah. Mom mentioned Noah said he was calling the police to reopen the investigation into his uncle's accident. I made a few calls, and it looks like he did. I imagine we'll be getting a visit from Sunshine Bay's finest in the next couple of hours. Now, everyone to the table. We hash things out so that when the cops arrive, we present a united front."

There was a knock on the front door of the restaurant. Bruno walked to the table with two golden-brown Margherita pizzas and put them down. "I'll send whoever it is away."

Cami looked at the pizzas and burst into tears. Willow walked over and hugged her. "Riley will forgive you. It might take time, but she will."

"I don't deserve her forgiveness, or Noah's. Everything they said was true. I don't deserve yours either."

"Why don't you deserve mine? I've had a beautiful life. You gave me to my mom. I've had a family who loves and supports me. It's you who've missed out, Cami. You've paid for your mistakes a thousand times over. Maybe it's time for you to forgive yourself." She straightened and looked her mother in the eye. "And it's time for you to forgive your sister."

"You weren't there. You don't know what we went through when she took you from us. You don't understand—" her mother began before Willow cut her off.

Actually, Willow finally understood a lot of things. She understood why she'd panicked at the thought of leaving her family and Sunshine Bay. She also could understand how traumatic it must've been for her mother, her grandmother, and her aunt when Cami had taken her. But Cami had paid a price far greater than any of them.

"Twenty-five years, Mom. Twenty-five years without her family. You were there, you heard her, you have a better understanding why she left me. You know what she was dealing with. And as awful as it must've been for you, I think, deep down, you understand why she took me when I was a little girl. You need to forgive her, and you need to forgive her now."

"Willow, it's okay. I understand how Gia feels," Cami said.

"Willow's right," Carmen said. "I won't be here forever. I want my family with me, all my girls. I want everyone to get along. I want to be a family again."

"Okay, Ma." Gia nodded and got up from her chair. She walked over to Cami and gave her a hug. "I forgive you. But just so you know, I'm Willow's mom, and I don't like sharing."

Cami laughed through a sob. "Tell me about it." She wiped away her tears and said to Willow, "Your mother was like a little squirrel. She had all these secret hiding places in her room."

"Yeah, because you and Eva stole my stuff all the time."

Cami and Gia argued back and forth, but it was the normal arguing between sisters, and Willow's heart lightened just a bit. She glanced at her grandmother, who was chuckling. She caught Willow looking at her and mouthed, *It'll be okay.*

And then Megan said what Willow was thinking: "The Rosettis are back together again. Watch out, Sunshine Bay!"

Okay, so she could've done without the last part. Willow moved away from Cami to take a seat, turning as Bruno returned from getting rid of whoever had been knocking on the front door. Only he hadn't gotten rid of them. Naomi and Veronica followed behind him.

Naomi looked around the table, frowning. "Will, what's going on?"

"What are you guys doing here?" Willow asked.

"We thought you and Noah were having dinner here tonight, and we came to share the good news." Veronica glanced around the restaurant. "Where is he?"

Willow nodded at her sister. "You're up."

Sage gave her a *seriously?* look, but then took pity on her and gave Naomi and Veronica the lowdown, Sage style. Willow took a seat, unable to block out the memory of Noah's voice or his expression, devoid of love. Her reaction to the memory must've shown on her face. Naomi and Veronica both hugged her, and then they surprised her by hugging Cami.

Willow didn't know why she was surprised. She had the best friends. They'd understand how difficult this must be for Cami, reliving a moment she'd kept secret all this time. In the end, as hard as it was, Willow thought it was time for Cami's secret to come to light. And it wasn't as if it would remain a secret for long with the SBPD involved.

"Sit, girls. Have some pizza," Carmen said. "And tell us your good news."

Naomi and Veronica each pulled out a chair. "We have guarantees for the full amount of the buyout, and then some," Naomi said. "According to Don, if the people at the auction who said they wanted to invest come through, we won't have to take out a loan for the first year's operating costs."

"How's that possible?" Willow asked.

Naomi glanced at Cami, who cleared her throat before addressing Willow. "I wanted to invest in you and your future. I didn't get to do anything for you growing—"

"Oh, shut up, Cami." Gia scowled at her sister and then looked at Willow. "She paid for you to go to college. I didn't ask for it. I found an envelope with my name on it on the bar the morning of your high school graduation."

Willow had refused Noah's offer, but she couldn't bring herself to refuse Cami's. She didn't want her to take it as a rejection. She'd been through enough.

"And your uncle and aunt bought shares too. Quite a bit of them. And, uh, so did Carmen, your mom, your sister, your cousin and her husband, Bruno, and..." Naomi looked at Veronica. "Am I missing anyone?"

Veronica nodded. "Probably, but I can't remember who."

Naomi grinned. "If you would've had time, you could've funded the buyout on your own, Will."

A horrible thought came to Willow, and her gaze shot to Megan. She must've had the same thought because she scrolled through her phone.

"No. We're good," Megan said. "Noah just canceled his bid on the house. But honestly, no matter how mad he is right now, he wouldn't do that to you, Willow."

She nodded at the same time they heard another knock on the door. Willow didn't want to offend Megan, Naomi, and Veronica or she would've told Bruno not to get it. He walked out of the kitchen carrying two platters of calamari and two platters of zucchini sticks and put them on the table. "If this keeps up, we'll have to pull more tables over, and I'll need a hand in the kitchen."

Carmen moved to stand.

"You sit, Ma. I'll give Bruno a hand," Cami said.

"I will too. After I eat. I'm starved," Gia said.

"You always ate like a horse when you were stressed," Cami said, which set off another round of sisterly bickering, which had her grandmother grinning around a zucchini stick.

Then Willow's mother glanced toward the front of the restaurant and blinked. "Who is that? He looks exactly like Flynn."

"He's Flynn's son. August," Willow said.

"Does he know he's your brother?" her mother whispered.

"He's your what?" Naomi asked.

"You can explain this one," Sage said, and popped a calamari ring into her mouth.

Willow didn't get a chance. August looked around the table and then his gaze settled on her. "Uh, sorry to interrupt, but Riley asked me to join you guys for pizza."

"When? When did she ask you?"

"It was before, Willow," Cami said gently.

"Of course it was. I don't know what I was thinking." She turned back to August. "I'm sorry. Riley and Noah left Sunshine Bay."

"Is something wrong? Her dad didn't make her go back to LA, did he?"

"No. I—"

Sage interrupted her, giving August the Sage Notes version of events, which Willow hadn't asked or wanted her to do, and she kicked her under the table. "What was that for?" her sister groused.

Before Willow could respond, Cami said, "If you talk to Riley, will you tell her how sorry I am, August? I can't get her on her phone."

Willow imagined she'd blocked her. She was tempted to try texting Noah, but she wanted to wait until morning. She didn't want to text him if they were on the road. She had a feeling they'd left Sunshine Bay almost right away.

August glanced at Willow. "Are you okay?"

"Not great, but it can't get worse, right?" Why had she said that? Of course it could get worse.

August looked around the table and then back at her. "I talked to my dad. I know, you know."

Willow had talked to Flynn earlier that afternoon. She

couldn't believe it had been mere hours ago. It felt like a life-time. She and Noah had just gotten out of the shower when her phone rang. Noah had laughed at her reaction. She'd felt as if she'd been caught in the act by her father. It wasn't the easiest conversation she'd ever had, but she was looking forward to getting to know Flynn. Even though she'd only spoken to him for an hour, she could understand how he'd been a calming presence in Cami's life.

Willow returned her attention to August. "It must've come as a shock to you. Are you okay with it? Sorry. I'm sure you don't want to have this conversation in front of a bunch of strangers."

"It's okay. I'm good with it," he said, and grinned. "I figure now that you're part of the family, you'll have to take turns with me looking after Gramps."

Willow laughed. "I have a feeling Amos plans on hanging out at the station twenty-four-seven, so I'll have paid my dues in full and then some."

"I should probably get going." He glanced at Cami. "I'm sorry for what happened to you. If I talk to Riley, I'll tell her you're sorry. But she probably already knows that. It'll just take her some time to admit it to herself."

Carmen wagged a zucchini stick at him. "You're a smart boy, a good boy, just like your father. Come, sit and eat."

"Sure. I just have to make a call first." He turned and walked to the other side of the restaurant.

"I love him!" Megan said. "Does he have an older brother?" Willow threw a zucchini stick at her. "What?"

"You promised you were going to do you for a year."

"That's what you said last fall, and look how that..." She stuffed a zucchini stick in her mouth.

August walked back to the table and held out his phone. "My dad wants to talk to you, Cami."

When Cami hesitated, Carmen said, "Talk to him, *cara*."

Cami nodded and took the phone from August. "Thank you," she said, and got up from her chair, walking to the back door. She opened it and stepped onto the deck.

Carmen got up from her chair and patted August's cheek. "Come make pizza with me."

"I want to make pizza too," Megan cried, and that's how they all ended up in the kitchen, making pizza and singing, "That's Amore."

Cami joined them twenty minutes later. She seemed better after talking to Flynn, smiling and laughing a little, which was a good thing since the next knock on the door was the police.

"I'll get it," Sage said, and strode to the door, sighing when she realized they'd followed her. She opened the door, ushering the officer inside. "Everyone but Cami back to the table. We'll take a seat over here." Sage gestured at a table for four at the front of the restaurant and the officer followed her and Cami.

Everyone else walked back to the table. No one felt like eating as they listened to the low murmur of voices at the front of the restaurant. Carmen wrung her hands, and Bruno placed one of his over hers. "It was an accident. She'll be fine," he quietly assured her.

"This is a good thing, Nonna. It doesn't matter what we tell Cami. She needs someone in a position of authority to tell her she's not responsible."

"Willow's right," her mother and Bruno agreed.

They talked among themselves in an attempt to distract

Carmen. Thirty minutes later, they all went quiet at the sound of chairs moving, craning their necks to get a look at Cami.

Instead, they heard Sage say, "Seriously? He just grilled you for a half an hour, and you're inviting him to eat with us?"

"He didn't grill me, Sage. He was very kind. Please join us, Officer."

"I appreciate the offer, ma'am, but I'm on duty," he said as he walked to the door, and then he turned, his gaze moving over them. "I'll be sending a copy of my report to Mr. Elliot. The investigation is officially closed. Nothing I've heard impacts the initial investigation's findings. In fact, Ms. Monroe's account confirms what we already knew. The crash involving William Bennett was an accident. Ms. Monroe didn't cause his death, nor did she flee the scene of an accident or fail to give aid. She called 911 from the nearest pay phone, and Mr. Bennett died on impact." He looked at Cami. "I hope that allows you to put this to rest."

She nodded. "Thank you."

"Have a good evening, folks."

They didn't celebrate. It didn't feel right. Time would tell if Cami would be able to move on from the accident but Willow thought maybe it had helped. Now to see if an official report that exonerated Cami would change Noah's mind.

An hour later, everyone got up to leave. Willow hugged and kissed her family goodbye and then headed to the door with her sister. Sage drove her to the beach house. There was a light on in the living room, and for a second, she felt hope rising inside her that Noah hadn't left. But it quickly deflated when she noticed his car was gone. It got worse when she walked into the beach house. Not only were Noah and Riley gone, so was Lucky. She didn't know why that hit her so hard, but it did.

Sage patted her shoulder. "I'll make you a cup of tea." Moments later, she returned with a piece of paper. "Noah left you a note." She handed it to her.

In his bold, masculine scrawl, he'd written, *Willow, you can live at the beach house until you've found a place to stay or until the beach house is sold. I'm sure Megan will keep you informed when she receives an offer.*

"I don't want any tea, thanks," Willow said to Sage.

She walked up the stairs and down the hall to Noah's bedroom. She crawled into the bed and hugged the pillow to her chest, inhaling his scent.

Her sister crawled in behind her, wrapping her arms around her. "It'll work out, Will."

"And if it doesn't?"

"Then we'll be there to help you pick up the pieces."

Chapter Twenty-Nine

Riley ran to the entryway of Noah's New York City apartment with Lucky chasing after her. "Mrs. D," she cried when the housekeeper opened the door and stepped inside, smiling at Riley and scowling at Lucky.

Mrs. D had left for her vacation three days after Noah and Riley had returned from Sunshine Bay. She hadn't been a fan of Lucky's. She'd called him a demon dog just like Willow's sister Sage. He'd kind of lived up to his nickname before Mrs. D left, chewing on the furniture and peeing on the carpet.

Riley hugged her. "I'm so glad you're back, and you don't have to worry about Lucky anymore. Noah and I trained him. He's an angel dog now."

"I'll believe it when I see it with my own eyes, lovey," Mrs. D. said, hugging her back.

"Did you and Mr. D enjoy your trip?" she asked as they walked into the living room, Mrs. D making a beeline for the kitchen.

"We did, but I was ready to come home." She put her bags on the kitchen's island. "I was worried about you two. Where's your brother?"

"In his study."

"Don't tell me he's been shut in there the entire time I've been gone, leaving you on your own."

"Oh no, Mrs. D, we've had a great time. We've done something together nearly every day."

They had, and it had been the best three weeks of her life. Well, it would've been if the thing with Cami and Willow hadn't happened, and they were with them. Still, she'd ticked off the one item on her list that she'd thought she never would. She and Noah were as close as a brother and sister could be, and it was awesome.

It was awful how it had come about, though. She'd tried blocking the memory of that afternoon at La Dolce Vita from her mind, mostly because she felt horrible about what she'd said to Cami and because Willow and Noah had broken up because of it. But she didn't think she and Noah would've become as close as they were now if things hadn't happened the way they had.

When they were in Sunshine Bay, Noah had had Willow, and she'd had Cami. The four of them had had fun together, but she hadn't really had time with her brother on her own. She supposed it was like Willow said: *After every storm, there is a rainbow*, and Riley's improved relationship with Noah was hers.

"I could've done without going to all the museums," she told Mrs. D. "But Noah *loves* them, and he did take me shopping or out to lunch or out for dinner after he'd dragged me around them for *hours*, so I can't complain."

Mrs. D chuckled. "Your brother has always loved museums. Although I don't recall him going for years. He used to go all the time with your mother and his father. They were planning to travel to every museum in the world. They spent hours together, the three of them, huddled over maps, pamphlets strewn all over the kitchen table, planning their itinerary. It was beyond me how they could be as excited about it as they were, but to each their own."

"Did they have fun?" Riley asked, thinking her brother hadn't changed. He was obsessed with the trip he was planning to explore the most remote locations in the world. She tried to be happy for him, and she was for the most part, but she'd miss him a lot.

"Oh, they didn't go, lovey. Your mother and Noah's father separated two months before they were to leave on their trip. Poor Noah was devastated. My heart broke for him."

"That's so sad."

"It was, and your mother felt horrible. She encouraged him to plan another trip to take his mind off it. And he's been planning it ever since. Although it's much more adventurous now than it was when he was ten." Mrs. D shuddered. "I swear, I'll spend the next year worrying about that man."

"Me too. But Mrs. D, what will you do when Noah's away? Are you getting another job?"

"No. There's no one else I'd work for other than your family, and I'm getting on in years. But there's no need for me to find another job. Nothing will change while Noah's away, other than I won't have anything to do. I'll be a lady of leisure, eating bonbons and watching my TV shows. And Noah wants me here in case you want to escape LA again." Mrs. D winked.

"I won't do that again, but I could come and visit you."

"I'd love that." She patted her hand. "So things with your father have improved?"

Riley nodded. "Noah and I went to LA last weekend. He had some business he had to take care of, and he brought me with him. We went to see Billy, I mean my father, and we talked. A lot. We're going to family therapy when I get back."

She made an *eek* face, and Mrs. D chuckled while unloading containers from her bags.

"I'm glad things with your father are working out for you, lovey," she said, turning to open the fridge and placing the containers on the shelves. She opened the freezer and made a squeak of dismay. "Nearly all the meals I left for you two are still here." She turned to Riley. "What did you do? Order in the entire time I was away?"

Riley shook her head with a grin. "We cooked!"

"You're telling me you and your brother cooked an actual meal together? In this kitchen?"

"We did. Lots of meals, and we went shopping for groceries together too."

Mrs. D gave her head a disbelieving shake. "And my kitchen survived, and so apparently did the two of you."

Riley didn't share that they had nearly burned down the kitchen making homemade French fries in a pot of boiling oil on the stove. Noah had ordered an air fryer the very next day.

"Since I don't have to prepare meals for the week, or clean the apartment, we can have a cup of tea together, and you can fill me in on where things stand with Noah and Willow." She searched Riley's face. "I'm pleased at least to see you're looking much better than the morning after you'd returned from Sunshine Bay."

Mrs. D plugged in the kettle and looked around. "Where has your dog gotten off to?"

Riley rolled her eyes. "He's more Noah's dog than mine. He follows him everywhere. He'll be in the study with Noah, bugging him to play fetch."

"And how is Noah?" Mrs. D asked, making up a plate of cookies.

"He's good. He's not broody or mopey or anything. We've had lots of fun together. But I can tell when he's thinking about Willow. He gets quiet, and I'm pretty sure he thinks about her a lot and misses her. I don't know why he's being so stubborn and won't get in touch with her. None of it was Willow's fault." She blinked tears from her eyes at the memory of that day. "You should've seen them together, Mrs. D. They really loved each other."

"Perhaps he just needs time. It was a lot for you both to hear that Willow's mother had been involved in your uncle's death. You didn't really know your grandparents, but Noah spent a lot of time with them. He witnessed how badly they'd been scarred by your uncle's death. Your mother too. She sometimes treated your brother as a confidant more than a son, so at a young age, he was well aware of how damaging the accident had been to your family."

"I get it. I felt the same, especially listening to Cami telling the story. She's the one who said she killed our uncle, and then she said she'd left him to die alone."

Mrs. D nodded. "That must've been horrifying and shocking for both you and Noah."

"It was, and we said some hurtful things, especially Noah. He was furious."

"I'm sure he was. And when Willow defended her mother, he would have felt betrayed given his state of mind at the time."

Riley nodded. "I think that's why he thought he and Willow wouldn't be able to get past it. But we got a copy of the police report, Mrs. D. It fully exonerated Cami. I mean, she probably shouldn't have made our uncle drive back to Sunshine Bay when he was tired, but it's not like she held a gun to his head. He could've said no. And it's not like she fell asleep on purpose. But she ran a mile to a corner store and called for help. It wouldn't have made a difference if she'd stayed anyway. We have a copy of the coroner's report. The police officer who reopened the case wrote us a personal note. He'd interviewed Cami, and from what he says she saw, she would've known immediately that our uncle hadn't survived."

"It must've been horrifying for her."

Riley nodded. "The police officer says she's suffering from PTSD because of the accident. And as much as it destroyed our family, Mrs. D, it destroyed hers too." She told her the parts that she had left out the morning after they'd come home.

"And now it's time for both families to heal," Mrs. D said, passing Riley a cup of tea, and they went to sit in the living room. "So where are you and Noah at with that?"

"I texted Cami after we got the report. Well, two days after because Noah wouldn't let me read it, and I had to sneak into his office and find it."

"Oh, Riley, that's not something you should've read on your own."

"I didn't. Noah caught me before I could read the report. We argued about it, and then he gave in and read it with me."

"So you apologized to Cami and now everything's good between you?"

"I did apologize, and she wanted to call me, but I said no. I was still mad that she'd lied to me and pretended to be my friend. But she didn't give up, and August—he's a friend I met in Sunshine Bay—he convinced me to talk to her and give her a chance to explain." Riley smiled. "And now we're good. She's going to be like...my big sister, I guess. She found a house a few blocks from my father's in LA, and she put an offer on it."

"Oh, lovey, I'm so happy for you."

Riley smiled. "Me too." Her smile faded as she thought of Noah and Willow. "I just wish Noah and Willow would talk."

"Did he apologize to Cami?"

"He didn't call her. He wrote her a letter. Cami said it made her cry. She blames herself for Noah and Willow breaking up, and we've been trying to figure out a way to get them back together or at least get them to talk."

"Does Noah know you're talking to Cami?"

Riley nodded. "Yeah, and he seems okay with it. But he doesn't ask about Willow, and when I try and bring her up, he changes the subject. He used to do that when I brought up Mom, but we talk about her now, so maybe he'll eventually talk about Willow, and I can figure out what Cami and I can do to get them back together."

"Have you talked to Willow?"

"Yeah, but she's as bad as Noah. Every time I mention him, she changes the subject. They're so annoying. Cami says she's not getting anywhere with Willow either."

"I wonder if Noah believes Willow wouldn't forgive him after what he said, and how he broke things off with her?"

"But that's just it, Willow is the most forgiving person I know." She told her about Megan and even Cami. "You'd love Willow, Mrs. D. She's the best." She showed Mrs. D some of the videos of Willow doing the weather and pictures Cami had sent of her.

"I printed off some of the pictures and left them out for Noah. He never said anything to me but I didn't see them again."

Mrs. D studied the photos. "I have an idea."

"Really?"

"Of course. I've known your brother longer than you have. You have to stop pussyfooting around and confront him."

"I don't know if I can do that."

"Lovey, you got him to not only take you to Sunshine Bay but to stay there with you."

"That wasn't me. It was Willow."

"I'm sure she helped, but your brother wants you to be happy as much as you want him to be. You need to tell him how you feel about his break-up with Willow, tell him you feel partially to blame and that it would make you feel better if they'd at least talk. Then remind him about all the good times you all had together and tell him what you told me about Willow's capacity for forgiveness. Because I do believe that's the problem."

"Will you come with me? I might need backup."

Mrs. D chuckled and got off the couch. "I used to be your mother's backup on occasion, and nothing would give me more pleasure than being yours."

Noah looked up from the papers on his desk that a courier had delivered ten minutes before Mrs. D had arrived. Riley's brother smiled. "Hey, Mrs. D. How was your vacation?"

"Lovely." She set the plate of cookies on his desk. "Are you in the middle of anything important? Riley and I would like a word."

He glanced at Riley and scratched the back of his head. "I'm just signing off on the purchase agreements for Channel 5 and the beach house."

"Well, isn't that a coincidence," Mrs. D said. "We want to talk to you about Sunshine Bay and the woman you're in love with."

"Mrs. D," Noah muttered.

Mrs. D. ignored him, took a seat on the chair in front of his desk, and smiled at Riley. "Go ahead, lovey. I'll chime in when needed."

Riley launched into the speech she'd been practicing for the past two weeks but hadn't had the nerve to deliver. Mrs. D. chimed in a few times, but other than that, Riley said exactly what she wanted to and ended with, "Willow loves you as much as you love her, and she'd forgive you anything. She forgave Megan and Cami. She believes in second chances, and she'll give you yours. I know she will, and deep down, so do you."

Noah slowly nodded, and then, looking from Mrs. D to Riley, he picked up the purchase agreements and ripped them in two. Riley gasped. She couldn't believe what he'd done. He'd just ripped up Willow's dream, and Cami and Riley's. Cami was buying the beach house so they could spend their summers there.

She was staring at the shredded papers on her brother's desk when he said, "What are you waiting for, Tink? You've gotta pack. We're leaving for Sunshine Bay in ten minutes."

Chapter Thirty

The balloons lay deflated on the station's floor, the corked champagne swam in the melted ice in a kiddie pool, and the food sat forlorn and forgotten on the groaning table. Five hours earlier, they'd been waiting for the call that would officially kick off the celebration. They'd gotten a call, just not the one they expected.

Megan walked to where Willow, Naomi, and Veronica were sitting on the floor with their backs against the wall and confetti in their hair. Someone had prematurely burst the confetti-filled balloons when the call came in.

Megan lowered her butt onto the concrete floor beside Willow.

"Any news?" Willow asked.

Megan shook her head. "The lawyer can't figure it out. When Noah called him to say the deal was off, he didn't give any explanation. And when the lawyer said we'd sue, he said, and I quote, 'I doubt it.'"

"Why? Because he thinks he's too smart and too rich for anyone to fight him in court and win?" Willow asked, thinking that sounded exactly like Mercedes Man.

But it didn't sound at all like the Noah she knew and

loved. Then again, she guessed she didn't really know him because she hadn't thought he'd be able to walk away from what they had. And as much as she wished she didn't, she still loved him. She had a feeling she always would.

"Um, no, because he owns both and it's his prerogative not to sell," Megan said.

Veronica blew a horn, said, "Boo," and lifted a bottle of champagne to her lips. She hadn't taken the news well. None of them had; the station was as quiet as a church at a funeral. Every once in a while, the silence was broken by people crying or sniffling.

"But we had a verbal agreement."

"They're tough to enforce, according to our lawyer. Any chance you'd call Noah?" Megan asked.

Willow had been waiting for this. "I don't want to, but we need answers, and if this is the only way to get them, I'll suck it up."

"I can't believe you haven't called him, Will," Naomi said. "That's not like you. You're always the first to make up."

"I was going to give him a week, but then he sent Cami a letter apologizing to her, and I thought he'd reach out to me. And I kept waiting. But I haven't heard anything from him, and now it just feels like the moment to reach out has passed. It's been three weeks. It's not like he's going to have a change of heart."

Veronica blew her horn again, said, "Boo," and lifted the champagne bottle to her lips, but Naomi took it from her.

"You've had enough, babe," Naomi said, which earned her another horn blow and another "Boo."

Willow took her phone from the pocket of her jeans, put in her password, and then scrolled through her recent calls to

Noah's name near the bottom. It was hard seeing his number there and remembering why he'd last called. It had been the day of the auction. After he'd told her he loved her. She'd been emotional, and he'd called to make sure she'd gotten to the venue okay.

If she was blinking back tears just from seeing his name and his number on her phone, she'd never look at their text exchanges, but she couldn't bring herself to delete them. It was the same as living at the beach house. As difficult as it was to stay there with all the memories, she couldn't bring herself to leave. She wouldn't have had to if the sale to Cami had gone through.

Megan was right. They needed answers. Noah had forgiven Cami. He'd been kind and heartbreakingly compassionate in his letter.

She pressed the Call icon. The phone rang several times before Noah's voice came over the line. That smooth-as-velvet deep voice. "I'm unavailable at the moment. Please leave a message."

At the beep, she said, "Noah, please call me. It's, uh, Willow."

"He knows who you are, Will. Your name shows up," Naomi said.

"Not if he deleted me it doesn't. I mean, I don't think it does," she said, barely resisting the urge to call him again just to hear his voice.

Maybe that's why she hadn't called him. It would prolong the inevitable, the torture, making it harder to move on. Or maybe she'd been avoiding calling him because then she'd know for sure they were over. This way she could sometimes convince herself they were on a break and Noah would realize how much he missed her. But in mere weeks, he'd be leaving for his trip around the world. He wouldn't have time to think about her or miss her then.

She never should've called him. It brought everything back.

Cami walked into the lobby carrying a large white box. Willow was glad for the distraction. Although she would've expected Cami to look as glum as the rest of them.

"Are you smiling?" Willow asked her.

"Who, me?" Cami asked, now looking as flattened as everyone in the station. "What do I have to smile about? I'm as disappointed as all of you. Has anyone figured out why Noah reneged on the sale?"

"No. Willow tried calling him but he's not picking up," Megan said, and then nodded at the box. "What have you got?"

"I don't know," Cami said, heading to the reception desk. "A courier asked me to sign for it when I was walking in to check on all of you."

Don walked out of his office, and Willow's eyes narrowed at his jaunty step. Then she could've sworn Don and Cami shared a silent exchange as he approached the reception desk.

"It came, did it?" he said to Cami. "I was worried it wouldn't get here in time."

Willow wanted to see what they were talking about and stood. Megan and Naomi stood too, and the three of them helped Veronica to her feet.

They got to the front desk just as Cami opened the box and pulled out a white sparkly ballgown with sheer sleeves and a ruffled V-neck.

Veronica gasped. "It's a Cinderella dress. I looove it. Where are the shoes?"

Cami looked in the box. "No Cinderella shoes, but we have bedazzled sneakers and a wand," she said, waving it around. "It's a fairy godmother costume."

"We so need a fairy godmother," Megan said.

"You've got one," Don said, grinning at Willow.

"No. No way. I'm not wearing that to do tonight's weather report."

"I will," Veronica said, bouncing on her toes.

"Sorry, it has to be Willow. The person sponsoring this week's weather segment wouldn't be pleased if we put in a substitute," Don said.

Two weeks before, they'd started a new initiative to encourage community spirit. They would run a contest, and the winner would get to choose what Willow wore to deliver the weather. Last week, she had been a duck.

Veronica blew her horn and yelled, "Boo!"

"What does it matter?" Willow asked, raising her voice to be heard over Veronica's now-incessant booing. "We're done. Finished."

Naomi covered Veronica's mouth with her hand. "I never thought I'd say this," she said to Willow, "but I miss your old positive self."

"Me too." Willow sighed. "But I can't seem to get her back."

"You will." Cami patted her shoulder. "Now off you go to get changed. We have to be at the pier in ten minutes."

"I'm not doing the weather at the pier. It's raining."

"Didn't you say this morning it will clear up by five?" Don asked, fighting a grin.

She rolled her eyes at him and then looked at Cami. "It's four ten. I don't have to be on the air until five."

"A fairy godmother is never late," Cami said, shooing her off with a smile.

Willow was beginning to think Cami was right. With all the layers of fabric, it took her nearly ten minutes to change into the dress. She should've asked Naomi to give her a hand.

As she walked back to the reception desk, the crew yelled, "Make our wishes come true, fairy godmother!"

"Did you guys polish off the champagne?" she asked, shaking her head as they waved at her with huge grins on their faces.

When she returned to the front desk, Megan and Naomi were acting as weird as the crew, beaming and giggling. She didn't count Veronica; she'd been acting weird since she got into the champagne.

Willow fisted her hands on her hips. "What's going on? You're not planning something that will wind up going viral on TikTok again, are you?"

Veronica pressed her hands to her chest. "I bet it will. Everyone loves—" Naomi clamped a hand over Veronica's mouth.

"Okay, fairy godmother, it's time for you to make all our wishes come true," Megan said, taking her by the hand.

"I'll meet you at the pier," Naomi said.

Willow noticed Cami and Don trailing behind her and Megan, along with several of the crew and newscasters. She stopped at the door. "All right, one of you is going to tell me what's going on."

"Not to get maudlin," Don said, "but this will probably be your last weather broadcast, and we want to see it live."

"My last . . . Are you serious? I won't be doing the weather after today?"

"Don't think about that now," Cami said. "Just enjoy every moment."

It hadn't even crossed her mind that they'd be closing down this soon. But it made sense. Cami was right. There's no way Willow could think about this maybe being her last broadcast without breaking down.

She looked through the glass doors and hiked up her dress. "You'd better pray these bedazzled sneakers have good grip or I'll be sliding all over the wharf."

She rode in Don's car with Megan and Cami to the pier. Willow got a glimpse of the wharf from the parking lot. "Is something going on today? The pier is packed."

With all the colorful umbrellas, the pier looked like a rainbow.

"I think there's an event on one of the charters," Cami said.

"Really? We didn't announce an event on our community news," Willow said as she got out of the car. Cami got out behind her and held an umbrella over her head.

The whispers started as she approached the pier, the crowd turning and smiling. But she was distracted by a group of familiar-looking people surrounding a man at the end of the pier. Her entire family was there, including Flynn, who'd arrived the week before, and August and Amos.

She turned on Cami. "What's everyone doing here? And why are they surrounding that guy like they're threatening..." She went up on her tiptoes and gasped. "It's Noah!" She looked back at the crowd behind her, searching the faces under the umbrellas. The Beaches were there? In the rain?

She was distracted from her squad by a woman scowling at her. It was her sister. She was holding Lucky.

Riley, standing beside Sage, grinned. "We didn't want you

to recognize us so we had Sage hold Lucky. You won't believe how well-behaved he is now, Willow. I can't wait to show you."

"I can't wait," she said, her smile wobbling.

The older woman beside Riley waved at Willow. "I'm Mrs. D. If you don't mind, would you rescue our Noah? It doesn't seem fair he's so badly outnumbered."

She nodded. "I'll see you both in a few minutes," she said, and then stomped up the wharf to her family.

"Don't be mad at them. They're just trying to protect you," Cami said, fast-walking beside her.

"I don't need anyone to protect me." She put her hands on her hips when she reached the outer edges of the group and raised her voice. "Anyone who is a Rosetti, a Monroe, a Sinclair, or a Hollingsworth, take ten giant steps back. Now."

They all turned to look at her. She felt Noah's gaze on her but she couldn't look at him, not yet. She had to rein in the overwhelming desire to run and throw herself into his arms.

"We're not roughing him up, *bella*," Bruno said. "We're just letting him know what will happen the next time he breaks your heart."

"And we want to know his intentions," her nonna said.

"And why he hasn't called you in *three* weeks!" her mother said. "He sent Cami a letter. It was a beautiful letter, by the way," she told Noah. "But you never—"

"All right, family." Willow cut off her mother. "I know you love me, and I know you're trying to protect me. But I'm twenty-eight-years old, and I can take care of myself." She waved her wand at her family. "Clear out. Now."

It took five minutes for them to join the crowd at her back. She got cheek pinches, shoulder squeezes, and a head pat from Amos, who was wearing his yellow raincoat and hat.

"It's still raining, and it's almost five. Maybe now you'll listen to your grandfather," he said before pointing a stern finger at Noah. "I'm keeping an eye on you."

"I wouldn't expect anything less, sir," Noah said.

As her grandfather walked away, Willow held out the layers of white fabric that made up the skirt, raising an eyebrow at Noah. "Was this your idea?"

"Riley's and Mrs. D's. They ordered the costume from a store in Boston before we left New York." He looked down at the wharf before raising his gaze to hers. "You made Riley's and Cami's wishes come true, Willow. I'm here hoping you'll do the same for me."

"I'm the woman you said reeled you in and manipulated you into nearly giving up your dreams. How can I possibly make your wish come true?"

"I said a lot of things that day. I could tell you I was in shock, which was true. I was also furious and felt betrayed, but none of that matters or excuses my behavior. It may have seemed impersonal that I apologized to Cami in a letter, but I wanted her to have tangible proof that she was forgiven, not a phone call she'd eventually forget or perhaps question her memory of what was said."

"It was a beautiful letter, and I'm sure she'll cherish it."

He nodded. "I wrote you a letter. Ten letters, actually. If I'd made a decision other than the one I've made, you would've received a letter too."

"You mean your decision to cancel the sales of Channel 5 and the beach house?"

"Yes, and I'll explain why I did. But before I do, we need to clear up one thing. I never said you manipulated me. But when I said I nearly gave up my dreams because of you, that was true, and given what I'd just learned, I was angry, more at myself than at you. That's why I haven't reached out to you. I needed time away from you to think about what I want. Because when I'm with you, you're all I want. The thought of leaving you to travel for a year became increasingly more difficult. But like hosting a morning show at Channel 5 has been your dream, that was mine."

"I never asked you to give up your dream for me, Noah." But every time he'd mentioned it, she'd gotten knots in her stomach at the thought of him leaving for a year. He was being honest with her. She had to be honest with him. "It would've been hard, and I can't say I would've liked you being gone that long, but we could've worked it out."

"It would've been unfair to you. We hadn't been together very long. But what I'm trying to tell you is nothing is more important to me than you, Willow. I don't want to go another day without you in my life. I don't want to travel the world without you by my side, and I'd never ask you to give up your dream for me." He took her hands in his. "I love you, and I'm sorry I hurt you. I'll spend the rest of my days making it up to you if you'll just give me a second chance."

"You did hurt me, but I understood what you were dealing with and that you were hurting too. I just wish you hadn't shut me out. I wish you had stayed here so we could've talked it out."

"I've messed up some of the most important relationships in my life. I've always held something back, protected myself. But I'm trying to do better. I realize now keeping my distance from you wasn't the wisest choice. But at the time, I thought it was the right one, for you and for me." He let go of her hands and gave her a sad smile. "Losing you will be the biggest regret of my life, Willow Rosetti."

She grabbed his hands, panic making her heart race. "Don't you dare walk away from me again, Noah Elliot. You are my dream, and I'm not letting you go. Now or ever."

"You still love me, after everything?" he asked, drawing her into his arms.

Cheers rippled through their audience, and several people muttered, "Finally."

"Ignore them," Willow said, rising up on her toes and murmuring against his lips, "Yes, even after you ripped up the purchase agreement for the station, effectively destroying my dream, I still love you. I'll always love you."

"You know me better than that. I would never destroy your dream. I ripped up the purchase agreement because I want to share your dream with you, and I want you to share mine with me."

"So you're not selling to us because you're going to keep the station and run it?"

"No. I want to invest in the station. If you and the others agree to have me on your team, that is." He'd raised his voice, lifting his gaze from hers to the crowd at her back.

He smiled when Don and her coworkers in the crowd yelled, "Yes!" and cheered. "What about you, Willow? You have my promise, I'll sign the purchase agreement no matter your answer."

"Turn down the offer of the CEO of one of the biggest private broadcasting groups in the country to be part of our team? I'm not an idiot, Noah. Of course I want you on our team. But what about your dream?"

"I would imagine we'll get holidays, won't we? We can travel then. Or we could do an expedition for a month, and you could report remotely. Take the citizens of Sunshine Bay with you on a tour of the world."

As she'd discovered the month before, the idea of leaving her family and Sunshine Bay no longer triggered a panic attack. And right then, it excited her. "We could do that, couldn't we? What about Italy? I've always wanted to see where Nonna grew up. Or France? We could walk in the lavender fields in Provence."

He smiled, love shining in his eyes. "Anywhere. I'll go anywhere with you. Or I'd go nowhere with you and have an adventure right here. I don't care, as long as you'll trust me with your heart again and give me a second chance."

"Is that your wish?"

He nodded. "Yes."

She raised her wand and tapped him on the head three times. "Granted."

He threw back his head and laughed, lifting her in his arms and spinning her around. She slid her arms around his neck. "Now kiss me. I have a weather report to do."

The sun came out just as she was about to do her broadcast, and as her gaze moved over the smiling faces of her family and friends and the man she loved, Willow thought about the storm they'd weathered. It wasn't wishes that had gotten them to where they were today, it was love. Love, sweet love.

About the Author

USA Today bestselling author **Debbie Mason** writes romantic fiction with humor and heart. The first book in her Christmas, Colorado, series, *The Trouble with Christmas*, was the inspiration for the Hallmark movie *Welcome to Christmas*. When Debbie isn't writing or reading, she enjoys cooking for her family, cuddling with her grandchildren and granddog, and walking in the woods with her husband.

You can learn more at:
AuthorDebbieMason.com
Twitter @AuthorDebMason
Facebook.com/DebbieMasonBooks
Instagram @AuthorDebMason